OMNIDISK

THE MISSION

Book One

A.R. Bingham

*For my Grandfather, Martin Robinson, the man
who showed me how much fun science fiction can be.
Thank you Papa.*

TABLE OF CONTENTS

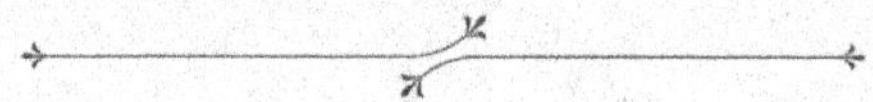

PROLOGUE

Our hero flies above the quiet city, searching for any sign of trouble. Everything seems calm until…

"Help! Somebody, help me!" a woman's voice cuts into the silence.

A purse-snatcher! With the grace of the swan and the speed of a hawk, our hero swoops in to stop the lawbreaker, his cape flapping in the wind.

"Oh no, it's Thunderfist!" the villain cries as he takes out his firearm.

Bang! Bang! Bang! Thunderfist dodges the bullets and strikes the enemy with a super powerful punch, immediately rendering him unconscious.

"Oh, thank you, sir!" the woman says as Thunderfist returns her purse.

"All in a day's work, ma'am!" our hero replies. In a flash he takes to the sky, looking for another—

"Eric! Eric Daniels, are you paying attention?"

Eric's head snapped up from his desk as he quickly wiped the drool from his mouth. Staring right into his eyes was the wrinkly face of his History teacher, Ms. Pryce.

"Um, yes, ma'am!" Eric nervously responded.

"Excellent," her large toothy grin reminded Eric of a hyena. "You can answer my question."

"S-Sure thing. The answer is… Washington?"

Ms. Pryce nodded her head and chuckled. "I'm sorry, but I'm afraid Mr. Washington didn't quite make it to World War II. The answer is President Roosevelt, whose name you may have said if you had spent any time paying attention to the lesson."

She waved her hand around for all the class to see. "This goes to show you that spending your time in la-la land instead of focusing in class serves no purpose other than to distract and rot your brain. I hope this transgression won't negatively affect Mr. Daniels' score on his next exam."

Brrrriiiiiing! Eric had never been so happy to hear the bell. He grabbed his book bag and hurried out of the classroom.

CHAPTER 1

Eric Daniels was 6'1 and sturdy looking for a seventeen-year-old. He had brown hair that he kept cut short and brown eyes to match. He didn't care much about style, jeans and a dark colored t-shirt was usually as complicated as his wardrobe got. He didn't care much for being the center of attention either, which is why he hurried down the hallway with his head bowed in embarrassment.

"Wow, she sure was hard on you today, buddy, but that's ok—I know just the thing to cheer you up!"

Eric turned around as he heard the voice of his best friend, Archibald Patterson. Eric called him Archie.

Archie was shorter than Eric and had red hair. He was slim, and his skin was pale since he would rather play video games indoors than spend time outside.

Archie usually wore shirts that had *Star Trek* or *Star Wars* or star something on it, and he could quote the exact dimensions of any fictional spaceship. Because he spent the majority of this time reading comic books or watching movies, learning all there was to know about science fiction, he had earned a reputation for just being a weird, anti-social nerd.

"Ok, Archie," Eric wasn't in the mood, but he knew better than to resist when his friend was this enthusiastic. "What do you think will cheer me up?"

"The Avengers!" Archie eyes were wide with excitement. Eric rolled his eyes and chuckled.

"Come on, you know it sounds like fun! We can head to my house and watch it right now." Archie grabbed Eric's arm and tried to pull him toward the door.

Eric nodded his head. "Archie, we're seniors now. That means I have tons of homework to do tonight. There is no way I'll have time for that. And besides, you've seen it a billion times already!"

"Seventeen times," Archie shrugged. "But who's counting? And who in their right mind would put homework before a Marvel movie? Where are your priorities?"

"My priorities?" Eric laughed in spite of himself. Archie knew how to change his mood. He'd probably be happy to know Eric was dreaming about one of their favorite comic books in class just now.

"Dude, haven't I taught you that nothing comes before superhero movies?" Archie knew he was helping his friend feel better, and he didn't plan on stopping now.

"Excuse me, professor, but I believe my priorities are right where they need to be. You, on the other hand, need to do some rearranging. You have all the same classes I do, but you're going to—"

Bam! A large, meaty hand grabbed Archie by the throat and slammed him against the lockers.

"Hey, pal, good to see ya," the offender said.

Travis Creadon, a tall boy with long brown hair who wore faded black jeans, death metal shirts and black boots every day, was staring directly into Archie's eyes with his fists clenched and ready for action. He was the nastiest bully in the school, and recently Archie had become his main focus.

"Travis." Archie gasped, the wind knocked out of his lungs. "Always a pleasure to run into you."

"Whatever. I want my money. After that, we can get on with our regularly scheduled beating."

Travis felt a hand grab him by the collar.

"Let him go, Travis!" Eric tightened his grip and narrowed his eyes. Eric hated it when people picked on someone weaker than them, especially when that person was his best friend.

Travis glared at him. "You have till the count of five to let go of me or lose your teeth. One—"

"I'm not budging until you release Archie," Eric said as he glanced around, searching the hallways for an authority figure. All he saw were a few students trying their best to avoid the conflict.

"Two—"

Eric took a deep breath. "Look, maybe we can all chill and—"

"Five!" Travis let Archie go and swung his arm, hitting Eric in the chest, and sending him sliding into the lockers across the hall. "I guess I'm gonna hafta beat you down before I get to ginger over there." He raised his arm to take another swing. "I could use a workout, anyway."

Bam! Travis dropped to the floor and clutched his leg. A familiar figure stood over Travis with her hands on her hips and a smile on her face.

Brynn looked over at Eric and Archie. "I hoped I would get to kick someone today."

Brynn was a longtime friend of Eric's. She reminded Eric of a flesh and blood version of a Barbie doll, flawless. She had long blonde hair that flowed down her back and her style of dress was impeccable. A model's height, with a fire in her eyes that said anyone who might want to mess with her was at risk of losing an arm. She had been in more fights than anyone Eric knew and never lost one.

"Wow, she's amazing," Archie whispered.

"Hey! Break it up!" Mr. Sims, the Gym teacher, shouted as he ran into the hall. "What's going on here?"

"They attacked me for no reason, sir," Travis said before anyone else could respond.

"Ok, you three, go to the principal's office, now. Travis, I suggest you go to class before I send you as well." Mr. Sims said.

"Yes, sir." Travis grinned at his would-be victims and took off down the hallway.

Eric sighed. Today was not his day.

An hour later, Eric, Brynn, and Archie walked out of the principal's office.

"Wow," said Eric. "We sure got off easy."

"What were you two doing in the principal's office?" asked a curious William Patel as he walked out of a nearby bathroom. "Let me guess; you forgot to say, 'Thank you' when someone gave you something?" William let out a loud laugh, amused by his dull joke.

Brynn rolled her eyes and looked at Eric. "I don't have time for this; I'm late enough already. I'll see you later."

Will smiled as he watched Brynn walk away. "That's Brynn, right? You two *have* to introduce me one day."

Eric chuckled. "She's not your type. She has standards."

"That's what they all say in the beginning," Will shrugged and changed the subject. "Are you two going to tell me what happened?"

Will was of Indian descent, which you could tell by his long dark brown hair, dark eyes and a slight accent. He was also confident in himself although he was shorter than most guys his age. One of Will's favorite pastimes was flirting with every attractive girl he saw. He was definitely a smart-aleck; he always had something funny or sarcastic to say. Will cared a lot about what he wore, refusing to wear anything that wasn't name brand. With his button down shirts and designer jeans, he looked like he stepped out of a fashion catalogue,

Will laughed after Eric told him of the day's events. "Fortunately for both of you, we have a principal who doesn't care. You spend an hour waiting, and all he says is: 'Don't do it again' and sends you on your merry way."

"Good, I've been through enough abuse today," Eric said as he walked down the hall. Archie and William fell into step behind him.

"By the way, thanks for the help," Archie said. "He's been hassling me for weeks."

"How does that make him different from anyone else in this school?" Will mumbled with a chuckle. He and Archie were never close. There was always friction between the two since Will was usually making fun of him.

"No thanks necessary; I'm your friend. You know I have your back," Eric replied, ignoring Will.

Will snorted. "You mean you got knocked on your back."

They all laughed. After a moment Archie said, "Didn't it feel good though? I mean, finally standing up to him?"

Will rolled his eyes. "You were saved by a chick. Not very heroic."

"She's a woman, not a chick and her name is Brynn," Archie frowned at Will. "I mean it, I'm glad we defended ourselves. Nobody steps to Travis around here."

Will stopped walking. "Because a fight with Travis means a trip to the nurse or worse. I'm glad I'm too cool for him to mess with."

Archie faced him. "If we don't defend what's right, who will? Someone has to be brave enough to take a stand and protect the weak."

Will laughed in his face. "You are the weak."

"Will's right. It's not our job to be hall monitors. Me and Brynn helped you out, but that doesn't mean we should turn this into a big statement," Eric said. "Let's try to make it to graduation day."

"I was just thinking—" Archie tried again.

"Well, don't," Will interrupted. "At least not like that. It's a good way to get yourself hurt. You're already a walking target."

Will rolled his eyes and walked off. Eric gave Archie a sympathetic look. "Look, man, I know your heart's in the right place, but it's not our job to be heroes." He patted Archie on the back. "Come on; it's time to go to class. Priorities, remember?"

As Eric walked out of his last class, he couldn't get what Archie had said earlier off of his mind. He didn't want to admit it, but what Archie said resonated with him. It felt great to stand up to Travis.

Just as he walked out the front door and headed home, a green car stopped in front of him.

"Hey, want a ride?" Brynn asked from behind the wheel. They had lived in the same neighborhood nearly all of their lives, so they often carpooled.

"Sure thing," he said. "At least I get cut one break today."

"If you're talking about Travis, all you need to do is call me if he messes with you again," she said as Eric climbed into the passenger seat. "But that's not all that's bothering you, is it?"

He hesitated. He never could keep anything from her. She knew him too well for that. "No, it isn't."

He related the conversation he had with Archie and William. "Will said what I was thinking, but Archie said what I was feeling," Eric finished. "I feel bad for not supporting him."

"I think Archie is right. People bury their heads in the sand and pretend bad things don't happen around them. Especially in high school," Brynn said.

"But who are we to decide what we should and shouldn't handle? We aren't policemen. We're teenagers. Our biggest concern should be graduating."

"Eric, have you bothered to look around our town lately? Drakeston isn't what it used to be. I heard on the news this morning that crime is at an all-time high here. Not to mention all the weird stuff that's been happening."

Eric smiled. "You don't believe all of those rumors about monster sightings and mutations, do you? Sounds like supermarket tabloid material. We live in upstate New York; nothing happens here."

Brynn turned into their subdivision. "I don't think they're just stories. My uncle told me last week he was at a restaurant and he saw some guy drop his glass and stretch his arm out to grab it before he hit the floor. He said it looked like it was made of rubber! Something is going on, but the adults are acting like the people in high school. They pretend everything is fine."

Eric laughed "Did your uncle have a few drinks that night? You sound like Archie. I can see why he likes you."

Brynn looked at Eric. "What? Archie likes me?"

Eric winced. Archie was going to kill him. "Yeah, as a person. In a friendly type way. Oh, look it's Chris!"

Eric waved at the girl raking leaves in the yard across the street from his.

Tall, gentle, shoulder-length brown hair and dark brown eyed, Christina Stephens (her friends called her "Chris" for short) stood waving at Eric. Eric couldn't help but smile back. She had a calm, peaceful presence about herself and she always seemed to be able to get along with anybody she met. She usually dressed plainly, not even putting makeup on her umber skin that all on its own made Eric think of a tree in autumn and had a prettiness that wouldn't be stifled no matter what she wore. Despite her gentle disposition, there was an intensity in her eyes that many noticed but few could place. Eric liked her from the time he first met her. Of course, he'd resolved in his mind never to confess that to anyone, not even Brynn.

"Hey, you two!" Chris said. "Eric, I heard about the fight today, are you ok?"

"Oh, it wasn't... I mean we didn't... Brynn did most of the work," Eric stammered.

"He's very modest," Brynn said with a sly smile. "Eric was so brave. He didn't hesitate to help his friend. You should find a guy like that."

Chris laughed. "Nice try, Brynn. You know I'm dating Jeff. He's a great guy. He's not off fighting bullies, but he's got a good heart. And he scored the winning touchdown for our school last week, so I guess that makes him a different kind of hero."

"I saw the game! Jeff did a great job," Eric forced a smile that disappeared as soon as he broke eye contact.

"Yeah, no feelings there at all," Brynn said as she parked the car. "All of that denial is more dangerous than any monsters, real or otherwise."

Eric chose not to comment and instead said, "I'll see you later, Brynn."

She gave him a quick wink and watched as he tried hard not to stare at Chris.

"Boys and girls," she laughed as she drove off.

Eric walked into his home. He was tired and ready to take a long nap. His eleven-year-old sister, Rebecca, met him at the door.

"Hi, Eric!" she chirped.

"Hi. Listen, I 'm tired, and I need to take a long nap, so please, Becky, try not to disturb me."

She flashed a grin. "Go, take your nap. I'm not stopping you. I'm going into the kitchen to finish my science project," she skipped off toward the kitchen, her braids swinging back and forth.

"What? Hold on a minute. It took me half the night to clean up after your last project. Please tell me you haven't already made a mess in there!"

"I didn't make a mess in there. Not a big one," she said sheepishly.

Eric walked past her and opened the kitchen doors. Inside was the biggest disaster he'd ever seen. There were globs of some awful smelling substance everywhere.

"What did you do, Rebecca?! This looks like a nuclear disaster, minus the radioactivity!"

"What's radioactive?"

"That's not the point! Why do you keep doing this?"

Eric's father came out of his room and stood at the top of the stairs.

"What's going on down there?" he yelled. Richard Daniels was a tall, broad-shouldered man. He looked like he was in peak physical condition except for the persistent bags under his eyes.

They both stepped out into the hall.

"Dad, Rebecca made a huge mess in the kitchen. It's enormous!"

"Yes, I know. Would you take care of that, please?"

Eric heard Rebecca chuckle in the background.

"Hold on! I'm not the one who made the mess, and besides, after the day I've had, I just want to—"

"Eric, please don't argue with me right now. I need to go out and handle some things so I need you to take care of matters here. So please clean it, and I'll talk to your sister about it later."

Eric sent his sister a glare that could curdle milk as he headed into the kitchen.

"Eric!" his dad screamed again.

"Yes," Eric stepped out of the kitchen once again.

"Look, before you do that, I need you to drop a package off at the post office for me. It is on the dining room table."

Happy for any excuse to leave the house again, he said, "Ok, Dad, I'll take it right now."

I need to blow off some steam after this mess, anyway, he thought to himself as he walked toward the dining room.

His father watched him. He knew he should have made Rebecca handle her mess, but that would have taken all night and would have involved so much work. He had some very important things going on and just didn't have time to address it. Things had been tough for the kids since their mother passed away from a horrible car accident a year ago. Things had been worse for him. Losing her had changed him in more ways than he thought possible. But he was determined to make things better for them.

Minutes later, Eric was on his bike heading toward the post office, thinking about what had happened at home. He wasn't happy about what his sister had done, but he felt sorry for how he reacted. His dad had been through a lot, and he relied on him. Eric was already worried enough about his dad as it was. He was so distant these days. If he wasn't working, he was sleeping. He couldn't remember the last time he'd spent a full hour with him. He needed to complain less and help out more. It's not like he had anything especially important going on in his own life.

CHAPTER 2

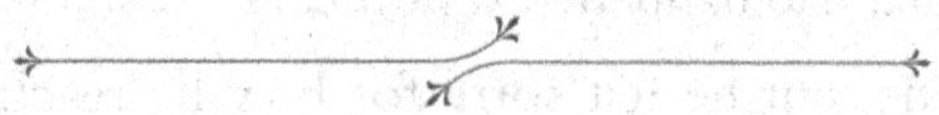

With the package safely at the post office, Eric noticed the heat of the sun beating down him. He spotted a small corner store and made his way there for a drink.

He parked his bike, walked into the store and nodded at the cashier as he went toward the area where they stored the drinks. A few seconds later, he heard the front door chime, and two men walked in. Eric could see them in the mirror that hung from the ceiling. One man was short, had a scruffy, thinning dirty brown hair and had on a pair of glasses and a brown jacket. He quickly looked around the room with a scowl on his face.

The other man was barely visible through all of his layers of clothing. All Eric could see through the mirror was that he was tall, and he had on a hat, sunglasses, a long black coat, and dark pants. One thing was evident to Eric—he was very frustrated.

"Hey, you! Where do you keep the beer around here?" the tall man's voice almost sounded like a dog growling.

"We keep the beer in the coolers along the wall, sir," the cashier's voice shook as he shared the information. Beads of sweat appeared on his forehead.

"Calm down," the short man's proper manner of speech reminded Eric of a college professor. "No need to make a fuss over some beer. You get so temperamental."

"Yeah, yeah," the taller man turned back to the cashier. "How much?"

"I.D. please?" the cashier stammered to the taller man.

"What? I don't have any stupid I.D. I want to buy my beer!"

"I'm sorry, sir. It's company poli—"

Crash! The man punched through the glass that separated them and the cashier and grabbed him by the collar.

"I said, give me the stuff, now!"

Eric dropped behind the shelf full of chips.

"Mange, drop him! We need not draw attention to ourselves!" The short man said.

Brrrrrring! The cashier reached down and activated the alarm.

"You idiot! Mange, now look at what you've done!" the short man turned around and looked out the window.

Two police officers were in their car across the street when they heard the alarm. Within seconds, they pulled in front of the store and rushed in.

A relived Eric watched events unfold. *Everything will be ok*, he said to himself.

"You two, freeze!" One of the police officers ordered as he and his partner took out their guns. "Put your hands in the air, now!"

Mange dropped the cashier and turned toward the police.

"This is exactly what I was trying to avoid! What are we going to do now?" The short man backed up with his hands in the air.

"I know what *I'm* going to do," Mange said. "Grrrrrrahhhhhh!"

What Eric witnessed seemed to happen in slow motion. Mange threw off his hat, glasses, and coat. He had a course brown beard and tan skin. There was dark brown hair that covered the back of his hands and went up his arms. He stood eight-foot-tall with no hair on his head and slightly pointy ears. Eric could see the muscles bulging from his arms and the two long feathery wings that stretched out from his back. He had sharp yellow teeth. A long furry tail hit the floor, and Eric almost jumped at its sight.

"What in the world is that?!" one of the policemen yelled.

The other officer turned towards the car. "I'm calling for back-up!"

"You're not calling anybody!" Mange's eyes glowed bright yellow.

Tzzzap! Tzzzap! Two beams of yellow light shot out of Mange's eyes and hit the gas tank of the squad car.

Boooooom! The car exploded into a huge fireball. The force of the blast threw the officers to the ground, and the front glass of the store blew out.

Eric shielded his head and face as glass littered the floor of the store.

The officers groaned and started to get back on their feet.

"Time for lights out." The shorter man smiled stuck his arms out in front of him.

Eric watched in horror as they stretched and stretched like rubber.

Bam! The two elastic fists hit the policemen in the face and knocked them back on the ground, unconscious.

What kind of freaks are these? Eric watched with a mixture of amazement and fear.

"Nice work, Slim," Mange smiled and revealed more sharp teeth.

"My name is Slymind, you idiot! And if you would learn to keep your temper, I wouldn't have to risk unnecessary exposure like this. Now, let us take our leave."

"In a minute." Mange grabbed the cashier by his shirt. "I need to tie up a loose end."

"Please, no. I have a family," the man begged.

"In that case, I am sure you will have a lovely funeral." Mange smiled, and his eyes glowed.

Eric's mind raced. I *could leave, and they would never even know I was here.*

What am I saying?! I can't leave him. He needs my help.

But it's not my responsibility. Eric hesitated.

If I don't help him, I'll never forgive myself. I know it's the right thing to do.

"Archie, I guess you win this one," Eric mumbled before he grabbed a tire iron on a nearby rack.

"Hurry, we need to leave," Slymind urged.

"I'm almost done here." Mange tightened his grip. "Just a few more—Argh!"

Eric swung the iron, and it struck the creature's head. Eric raised his arm again, and with all his might he landed another blow to Mange's head.

Finally, Mange dropped the cashier. The man crawled out the back door while Eric was the center of attention.

Mange growled and nursed his head. "I'm gonna grind you into paste!"

Eric took another swing a Mange's head. This time Mange caught the tire iron.

With no effort, he yanked it out of Eric's hands and threw it on the ground. Eric turned to run, but Mange caught him by the arm and threw him into a shelf.

"You got guts, kid; I'll give you that. I can't wait to get a closer look at them!" He slowly walked over to Eric.

Eric painfully propped himself on his shoulders. *I have to find something to fight him with before he kills me.*

His eyes darted back and forth as he looked around for a weapon. Inches away, his eyes caught sight of a can of pepper spray. He grabbed it as Mange reached down and grabbed him again.

"You won't feel a thing," Mange chuckled as his eyes glowed.

Eric clenched his jaw and lifted his hand.

SSSSSSSS! The spray hit Mange right in the eyes.

"ROOOAAAAARRR!!!" Mange released Eric and clutched at his eyes.

Eric jumped to his feet and ran for the door. Before he could register what had happened, his feet were off the floor, and he was immobilized. He couldn't move a single finger.

"I'm quite sorry, dear boy, but we must insist that you stay," The stretchy arms of Slymind had bound him so tight, he could barely breathe.

"Hold him!" Mange commanded. "I want the pleasure of finishing this myself."

His tail twitched from side to side as he walked toward Eric, savoring his moment of victory.

No, I can't die. Not now, I'm too young. Eric panicked. *Think, man, think. You can beat this. There has to be...got it!*

He watched Mange's eyes and as he expected; they started to glow.

"No stupid tricks this time, punk." Mange aimed his eyes right at Eric's head.

"Just one more 'stupid trick,'" Eric whispered.

Tzzzzzap! At nearly the exact instant the beams shot from Mange's eyes, Eric threw his body forward and twisted it around with all of his strength, putting Slymind between himself and the beam.

"Aaaaaahhhh!!!" Slymind screamed as the beams hit him in the back and propelled himself and Eric through the broken glass window and into the parking lot.

They both hit the pavement.

He's unconscious. This is my chance! Eric shook his assailant off and ran towards the street.

Thunk! A rock hit Eric in the head, and the impact brought him to his knees.

The last thing Eric saw was the ground rushing up at him before everything went dark.

"Bull's eye." Mange smiled.

"We need to finish this, fast," Slymind struggled to get to his feet. "If he gets away, he will be a huge liability, and that would not please our…employer in the least."

"Let's do it!" Mange gestured towards the unconscious Eric.

The men took a few steps towards the would-be hero.

Hssssss! Hssssss! Two small round metal balls hit the ground in front of them, and dark smoke billowed out.

"I can't see!" Mange cried.

"What is this?" Slymind fought his way through the thick smoke.

A cloaked figure leaped off the rooftop and into the smoke.

"It's him!" Mange cried.

The stranger moved with a gentle swiftness as he extracted a small bo staff from off his wrist. Within seconds, it extended itself four feet.

Mange growled and lunged at this new arrival.

He caught Mange in his midsection with a quick kick, causing him to double over and stumble. He brought his bo staff down upon Mange's head before he could react. Mange hit the ground hard and didn't move.

Slymind extended his arms in an attempt to capture their opponent. The figure leaped over the outstretched arms and brought his bo staff down on to Slymind's head. He fell to the ground, out cold.

"Grrrrrahhhhhh!" Mange ran at the figure from behind. It jumped in the air and flipped over Mange's head, landing behind him. It hit him in the head twice with the bo staff, but not hard enough to make him lose consciousness.

Tzzzzap! Mange fired his eye beams at the assailant, but it ducked under them and hit him with a roundhouse kick, finally knocking Mange out.

When the smoke cleared, the two villains were sprawled out on the ground, both unconscious.

The cloaked combatant took a few steps toward where Eric lay unconscious. The moment they reached Eric's body; a blue light surrounded the teen. The figure reached out, but it was too late. The blue light was gone, and so was Eric.

"Man, my head," Eric groaned as he opened his eyes.

White walls stared back at him.

What is this? He felt as if something were crawling on him. A thin black strip ran over the center of the bed he was lying on. It emitted a light that covered him from head to toe.

He closed his eyes and tried to catch his breath. *Okay, so now you're in some creepy room, lying on a bed with some eerie light covering you and staring at walls with some strange signs and figures on them. There has to be some logical explanation for all of this. I only wish I knew what it was right now.*

Eric slowly tried to move. *One foot on the floor. Good boy. Now let's put the other one there.* He waited for a few minutes. *Still alive. I'll try to keep it that way.*

Eric stared at the walls. As he walked over to them, he noticed that there were panels on them. He reached out, and his fingers traced the letters inscribed on them. The words weren't in any language Eric recognized.

Am I in another country? His anxiety increased. *Did terrorists or something capture me?*

His eyes searched the room for some way out. Finally, he caught sight of what appeared to be an outline of a door on the far side of the room.

"Great! No knobs. No handles. No nothing. This is crazy!" Eric said in frustration. He stood in front of the door. "Open!" He waited. Nothing.

"Abre la puerta." *What are you doing? I'm sure whoever has you locked in this place doesn't speak Spanish.*

"Think, man, think. There has to be a way to make this door open," He said aloud.

I'm sure talking to myself, isn't helping. Eric took a step closer to the door.

Swoop! The door opened immediately.

"Huh?" He stuck his head outside and looked around. To his left was a wall, to the right he saw a long, empty corridor. He took a deep breath and stepped out of the room.

Swoop! The door closed behind him, forcing him further into the corridor.

Nothing but white doors lined the hallway. No signs on any of them. Nothing that said, "this way out" or "enter here, if you want to live."

To his right, he saw two large gray double doors, to his left, a giant red door.

I always preferred red, he said to himself as he headed toward it.

When he reached the door, he found himself faced with the same problem as before: no way to open it.

"Door…open?" Eric said. Nothing. What did I do before? He took a deep breath and stepped up to the door again.

Swoop! The red door slid open. Eric started to take a step but stopped. Maybe I should have gone through the other door, who knows what—

"Please enter, Eric Daniels," said a voice. "We have much to discuss."

Outside of the store…

"I can't believe this!" Mange hit the ground with his fist. "We had him!"

"It should've been a walk in the park" Slymind agreed. "But we couldn't have known that *traitor* would show his face."

Ring! Ring!

Slymind pulled a cellular phone from his pocket and brought it to his ear. "Hello? Yes, sir, we'll get right on it." Slymind swallowed hard and hung up the phone.

"What did he say?" Mange asked.

"He needs us to head to headquarters immediately. He has an update on one of the items. And he said to grab him a…snack on the way."

Eric rubbed his eyes in disbelief. *Please tell me thig thing isn't floating.* He rubbed his eyes again. "Oh man, you *are* floating!" Standing, or more accurately, floating in front of him was a two-and-a-half-foot tall creature wearing a silky white garment that went past its ankles. Assuming they were, in fact, ankles.

Eric took a step back and tried take it all in. He stared at the creature's feet, or were those talons, like that of a bird? Eric glanced at the creature's hands—three long fingers and a stubby thumb. Eric's eyes traced its mouth. It was short, yet curved and sharp resembling a puffin's beak, with grey skin and small yet intense blue eyes that reminded Eric of a hawk.

"You…Y-You're a—" Eric couldn't form the words.

"An extraterrestrial?" finished the creature. It's voice was soft and comforting, yet it carried authority.

"What…What's going on?" Eric managed to stammer out. "Where am I?"

"You are on my vessel."

"You mean vessel as in spaceship?" Eric looked around the room. The walls were all white. There were various panels against the wall full of aqua blue buttons of diffrent sizes and shapes.

"If you would prefer to call it that, then yes, you are on my spaceship."

Eric nodded his head. "I don't believe you! This is a trick. This could be a movie set. And you're one of those animatronic things like they use at Disney World."

The alien seemed as if it was about to say something else, but it stopped. Instead it floated over to the wall and moved its hand against it. Suddenly a circle appeared out of thin air in the middle of the room. Not a solid circle, but a circle made of letters and numbers moving in a circular motion in different directions. Eric couldn't help thinking that it looked like writing was combined with art.

"As a scientist, I find that evidence is superior to any rhetoric," The alien tapped several of the characters floating around in front of him. "If you would please turn around…"

Eric spun around and felt like the air had been snatched from his lungs. One of the walls had disappeared. Eric was looking directly into space.

"No need to fear," the alien assured him. "I have merely made the wall transparent. You are not exposed to the vacuum of space."

Eric walked closer to the wall. He was looking down at earth, He could see the clouds slowly moving over what resembled a blue marble with green spots. Space was filled with stars which looked like literal bodies of living light. He could see the sun. He'd always though the sun was beautiful, but it was truly a sight to behold. It looked like a giant glowing explosion, stunning and slightly terrifying.

"I'm in space," Eric's voice was barely a whisper. Then his eyes grew wide and he spun around to face his alien host. "Why am I up here? What do you want with me? Who were those things at the store? Where do you come from? How come you know English so well? Why do you look like a bird? Are you going to eat me or try to do something weird to my body? Are you male or female or something else entirely? Do you have a name?"

"I am a male member of my species. My name can't be completely translated in your language, Mr. Daniels so, for now, you can call me Chasub," the alien replied.

"Chasub." Eric tried hard not to stare. He wanted to reach out and touch the creature. "So, what's your story? I mean why are you here?"

"I will reveal all to you…but you must first put on these." Chasub held out what looked to be a pair of metallic sunglasses.

Eric forced a laugh and took the eyewear, "Nobody told me they came out with new Ray-Bans."

"I promise they will not harm you." The alien's voice sounded earnest. "They are vital for you to understand…everything."

Although the creature was as alien a being as one could hope to see, he did seem genuine. Eric cautiously slipped the glasses over his face. In an instant, the world fell away. He was on another planet. The planet had two tangerine colored suns, blue grass and was full of small box-shaped buildings bustling with activity. They were filled with beings that looked exactly like Chasub. Some were floating in the air like Chasub and others were walking around just like humans. . They seemed content and utterly focused on their various tasks.

"Whoa!" Eric was speechless.

"My tale begins on a world far from here, the closest translation in your language I believe is, Chua. I come from a race of beings called the Zephs. We were a peaceful race with technology capable of feats beyond a human's comprehension. However, unlike you humans, we hadn't used our technology to make weapons. Our planet had no pollution. No crime. We lived in peace for hundreds of years without any interference. Until the Thyders arrived."

Like so many knives, beams of energy sliced through the peaceful scene, destroying land and property alike. Ships as black as night filled the sky, their hulls covered in blood-red symbols. The main body of the ship looked like a giant chainsaw, with the "blade" serving as the engine. There were four wings, two on the top half of the craft and two on the bottom half. Both pairs looked like menacing spikes. Eric watched in horror as energy beams shot out from the ships and dozens of members of Chasub's species were disintegrated before his eyes.

"They arrived on our planet a little more than five earth years ago. They came in large ships filled with weapons of mass destruction to strip us of our technology, our natural resources, and everything else we had. Worse yet, they wanted to make us their slaves. My people were defenseless and full of fear. Unable to fight. Unable to hide.

"Their first orbital attack caused a massive amount of damage to our world. We were completely unprepared for it. The Thyders used weapons we had forgotten even existed. Beam weapons, torpedoes, and germ weapons took the lives of thousands within hours. They stripped us of hope. Killed everything that mattered and left barely anything that resembled who we once were."

Within minutes, the peaceful scene Eric had enjoyed at the beginning of the narrative had turned into a war zone, full of burning foliage and flattened buildings. The beautiful land around him now looked like one big scar.

"Out of desperation, we sought out ways to defend what was left. It called for drastic measures. We made weapons of our own."

The scene shifted. Eric found himself in what looked like a laboratory. The same carefree Zephs he had seen earlier no longer looked so content. Their faces had a look of both sadness and hardened determination. They were all gathered around a console in the center of the room, focused on their project.

"A small group of our scientists began creating weapons that would take away peace forever. In a short time, we had airborne ships that were capable of attacking the Thyders's warships. Finally, it seemed as if we had a fighting chance.

Eric was outside again. The sky still held the threatening black ships, but this time they weren't alone. There were greenish, oval-shaped ships in the sky as well, returning fire with energy beams of their own. It was no longer a one-sided slaughter. It was a war.

"For the first time, we were able to defend ourselves and our home. In the air, we were unstoppable. During our first counterattack, we were able to destroy nearly a quarter of their ships in one day. A renewed hope surged through my people. Survival was within our grasp, so we thought. Suddenly, the taste of victory and the smell of freedom were taken as quickly as they had come."

Eric's view shifted once more. This time he saw the ships landing on the ground. He got his first look at the Thyders. They were all tall, between seven and eight feet. They were covered in light grey fur. They had cloven feet. Their entire bodies rippled with muscles. Their hands had five fingers, each one ending in a vicious looking claw. Their faces looked almost feline. They had small, triangular, upright ears, and large, penetrating eyes, but their mouths were more of an elongated snout with a flat nose like a dog. Eric gasped as he saw them charge into the homes of Zeph families, attacking those who lived there.

"The Thyders sent troops to the ground to fight us in hand to hand combat. Once again, our people were being destroyed at an alarming rate. The Thyders were large, strong and fast. We were not any of those things. We did not stand a chance. We tried making more weapons, but they found ways to defend themselves against them. We needed something new. That is why we made the Omnidisks."

Eric was in another lab. This time there were no other weapons in the room. All of the scientists had huddled around something: a small metal disk the size of a silver dollar floating in mid-air. The disk was light blue and had a gentle glow emanating from it. Every few seconds a ripple of energy would roll across its surface.

"The Omnidisks were our only means for survival. Our only way to make our bodies powerful enough to fight the Thyders. The Omnidisks were created to do one thing: enhance the physical abilities of the user. They would make the person, stronger and faster than they could ever be on their own. We produced a total of eight prototype Omnidisks, each with their own ability. We had finally done it. We had created weapons that could help us defeat the Thyders. Unfortunately, they came too late. My world was all but destroyed."

As Chasub uttered those last words Eric's view changed to a vantage point high over the ground of Chasub's homeworld. He could see nothing but charred ground and heaps of smoking rubble in every direction.

"The outpost where we created the Omnidisks was one of the last safe places on my planet, but we knew that would soon change. And we also knew that if the Thyders somehow got their hands on the Omnidisks and used their technology, their power would be unimaginable. All of the Omnidisk were powered by a Virocan energy core, each one with the power of 100 of your nuclear weapons. Merely destroying the Omnidisks was not an option in the time we had left. So, we devised a plan.

"One scientist was chosen to take our most technologically advanced ship and hide the Omnidisks on another planet. That scientist was I and the ship I used was this one. I named it *The Omega* as it is the last representation of my people's technological greatness.

"I barely made it past the Thyders's attack ships. I suffered great damage, but the Omnidisks, as well as my life, were preserved. I brought and hid them, here in Drakeston, New York."

CHAPTER 3

The last thing Eric saw was a ship shooting past several Thyder assault vessels, heading into deep space. Suddenly, he was ripped away from the view. All he could see was Chasub floating in front of him.

Silence set in as they stared at each other. Eric thought he could almost hear pain Chasub's voice.

"I'm so sorry," In the minutes since Eric had first met the alien, he had learned so much. Seeing the destruction with his own eyes made him genuinely feel for Chasub.

"As am I. I vowed to do what I could to make sure this kind of thing never happened again. That is why I need you."

"What can I do?" Eric asked, the words almost got caught in his throat. He could only think of one reason Chasub would tell him all this.

Chasub gave Eric a somber look. "Mankind, your world and all that you know and love is in grave danger."

"Because of the Thyders?" Eric asked.

"No, because of the Omnidisks."

"What? How?"

"When I hid the Omnidisks here, I was not aware of the effects their energy output could have on humans. It seems that if the Omnidisks go unused for a long period of time, they experience an energy buildup and in turn, they alter human DNA."

With the special glasses still on his face, the inside of the ship fell away from Eric once again. This time, they observed various places throughout Drakeston. A homeless man outside of a library doubled over in pain as his eyes turned yellow and tiger stripes appeared on his skin. A woman jogging through a park clutched her ears because she could suddenly hear every single noise for miles around. A businessman complained that he couldn't do it all because he was only one person. Without explanation, an exact double of himself was standing in front of him.

"The reports we've heard about these monsters." Eric's voice was almost a whisper. "It's all true. You mean to tell me that with all of your advanced technology, you didn't take that into account when you chose earth to hide the things?"

"By "things", you mean the Omnidisks."

"I mean the things that are turning humans into the creatures that tried to kill me at the store! At least now I know why I've been hearing stories of people claiming to be experiencing some strange sort of mutation," Eric sympathy turned into anger.

"If I had known, I would have taken different measures. I would have hidden the Omnidisks on a more secluded part of your planet." Chasub's voice remained even and emotionless.

"Really?"

"Yes, many humans have been affected in your area. That is the last thing I wanted."

"Why do I get the feeling that there is more you aren't telling me?" Eric crossed his arms.

Chasub hesitated for a moment. Eric watched his bird-like eyes. Waiting.

"Yes, there is more. I discovered that the energy from the Omnidisks appears to alter the minds of humans as well. It weakens the conscience of some while increasing the desire to engage in violence. The two beings you had an altercation with earlier today were examples of this. And there are many more like them. I've discovered there are two kinds."

Chasub pressed his hand against one of the buttons on the wall. Directly in front of the two of them, a translucent holographic image appeared. It was a man who seemed normal except for bright yellow eyes. "This person is an example of what I've come to call a variant. A human who has been affected by low levels of radiation from the Omnidisks. With the exception of the yellow eyes, they can pass as normal. However, they have above average strength, speed and aggression."

The alien pressed another button, and this time holographic images of Mange and Slymind appeared. "The two men you fought earlier today were more enhanced. I've called individuals like them augments. Augments have presented with a wide range of powerful abilities. I have not yet cataloged all of the mutations."

Eric groaned. "I can't believe there are guys like them all around Drakeston."

"These two augments are special. They have been stealing some very specific electronic and mechanical equipment. Based on their most likely configuration, I believe they are attempting to build a machine that can harness energy from the Omnidisks themselves."

"How is that possible?" Eric gestured at the holograms. "I met them. The stretchy one might be clever, but the one called Mange is an idiot. The two of them aren't smart enough to do this! How would they even know about the Omnidisks?"

"They're not working alone. From what my sensors have been able to detect, they are working with another augment with a very high power level. But I don't know where they are or where the machine is."

"So you basically don't know anything?"

"Well, I have been able to discover that he, the powerful augment, that is, appears to gain energy by feeding off humans."

"Huh?" Eric raised an eyebrow. "We're dealing with cannibals now too?"

"Not in the sense that you're thinking of. I have monitored your hospitals and there has been an influx of patients with minimal brain activity. I ran some simulations and concluded that by coming into physical contact with them, he feeds off of their bioelectric energy. Based on my readings, when he does this his intelligence and physical strength increase exponentially. At the same time, the people he absorbs are temporarily reduced to a vegetative state. His heightened intellect likely helped him determine why everyone is changing and he wants to find and harness that technology himself."

Eric rubbed his temples and took a deep breath. "Let me see if I understand all of this correctly. A psychotic augment is trying to find the Omnidisks so that he can use their radioactive powers to fuel his machine, which by the way, you know very little about, to accomplish some goal that you are completely unaware of."

Chasub tried to interject.

"No, let me finish," Eric stated. "And this mega-augment is capturing humans and absorbing their bioelectric energy, making himself stronger and smarter in the meantime. Is that about right?"

"Yes, that is why he must be stopped without delay."

"I agree!" Eric interrupted. "This is pretty heavy stuff, and you need help, but not mine. We have people on my planet who are in charge; why don't you go tell them?"

"I selected you for two significant reasons. The first is that in my studies of your planet, I have come to realize how volatile and warlike your governments are. They fight among themselves constantly; this is very rare on most civilized planets. If I were to present myself to them, they would be too busy assessing whether I'm a threat or not. I will never get them to listen. Worse yet, they might even try to use the Omnidisks to their own violent end. But the second and most important reason is that you are the only one with the ability to stop the augments."

Eric chuckled. "Chasub, I appreciate the compliment and all, but I didn't even make the football team. I can't take on a whole gang of super powerful bad guys."

Chasub looked right into Eric's eyes. "Not in your current state, but that is what I have been trying to tell you. The Omnidisks…" Chasub hesitated again.

Eric watched and waited. He knew whatever Chasub was nervous about was not good.

"First, let me explain something," Chasub stated. "My people put a security measure in the Omnidisks in case they ever did fall into the wrong hands. Our goal was to program the Omnidisks to only be usable by an authorized person. We succeeded; all unauthorized users were completely locked out. But the safeguards don't work the same way with humans. If an unauthorized person tried to use the Omnidisk, they are able to access its power somehow. But the energy from it would poison them and they would get very sick."

"Great. So, either we will all be mutated by the Omnidisks, killed by the mega-augment who wants our energy or poisoned by the energy of the Omnidisk if some poor fool finds one and tries to use the thing. All in all, we're doomed."

"That's what I hope to stop. Awhile after I brought the Omnidisks here, my sensors detected an amazing occurrence. The authorized user program in the Omnidisks began to scan and lock onto a human's DNA of their own accord. It is almost as if they choose someone to wield them."

"That's incredible. But that has nothing to do with me. I'd hate to meet the poor victim who got picked to—"

Chasub stared hard at Eric.

"Please tell me they have a sense of humor on your planet," Eric begged.

"I am afraid this is no laughing matter," said Chasub.

"Why can't you do it? You have all of this technology here; you can fight them on your own. You came to my town and put these things here. Fix your own mess!" Eric's hands were shaking when he finished his statement.

"Eric, if I thought I had a chance of vanquishing this threat on my own, I would do it in an instant. But these augments are a significant threat to your world, and if I die, no one will be left who could eliminate the threat they cause."

Eric bowed his head and groaned. "Now he's talking about death."

Chasub floated closer to Eric. "Yes, death is a factor here. Your life will be at risk at times but think of the countless lives you can save. Even if there wasn't a danger of the augments finding the Omnidisks, you saw firsthand how ruthless they could be. Innocent people need your help, and this is your chance to save them. To make a difference. The Omnidisks selected you. You, Eric, are the one chosen to wield the power of the Omnidisks."

"Why me?"

"The algorithm was complicated. They were designed to look for both physiological and psychological factors. Maybe it was because they saw something in your DNA. Perhaps they mapped your brain and sensed a desire to help. In all candor, it could have been a random choice. Whatever the case, I know what you are capable of. You have the potential to be a leader, Eric. You are an example of all that is right and just according to your planet and mine. You proved it in that store. You risked your life for one man. You're a hero."

"Do you really think I can do it?" he asked.

"You may be the only one who can," Chasub said.

Eric thought about all he had learned. In the past hour, his whole world had changed. He couldn't see how he could fix all of it. He began to refuse but was almost surprised to hear himself say… "Ok. Show me what to do."

An unconscious homeless man was helplessly draped over the shoulders of Mange as he and Slymind entered into an abandoned power plant. Neither of them spoke while they made their way toward the basement.

The air was damp and stale as Mange walked over to a familiar cement brick that had a hidden keypad behind it.

"Hurry up!" an impatient Slymind exclaimed. "I thought you could see better in the dark."

"If you're in such a rush, why don't you carry this guy," Mange squinted as he typed in the combination

Before Slymind could reply, a massive black hole opened in the floor underneath them. The transparent plastic they were standing on lowered them through the opening. The speed of their descent caused Slymind's coat to billow up around him.

"I hate that thing," Mange shifted the man on his shoulders.

"I designed it myself; its perfectly safe," Slymind reminded his partner as they found their way to a single locked door.

As they walked through the door, they both took note of the gigantic machine that stood in the center of the room.

"I can't believe we're almost done," Slymind said to nobody in particular.

"Welcome home, gentleman." Mange and Slymind jumped as a spoke to them from the shadows.

"Sorry, we didn't see you there-" Mange began to reply.

"Don't!" The figure bellowed. "Do not say my name. You know the rules. My anonymity, is key. You know how to address me."

"Sorry…Command," Mange bowed his head.

Slymind stepped forward. "We brought you something."

On cue, Mange dropped the homeless man onto the floor.

The homeless man groaned and opened his eyes. "Where am I?" he asked.

When his gaze settled on Mange and Slymind, he gasped and began crawling across the floor.

Slymind and Mange watched him as he tried to make his way toward Command.

"Please help me! They're monsters!"

Command extended his hand. "Of course, I'll help you. All you need to do is give me your hand."

"Oh thank you. Wait, what's happening?! No! Please let me go!"

The augment's hand began to glow. The glow spread from his hand to the homeless man's whole body. A moment later, the homeless man was lying on the floor, unmoving, with closed eyes and shallow breathing.

Command took a deep breath, a broad grin spreading over his face as he momentarily looked at the ceiling. "Thank you, gentlemen; that was quite satisfying. I'm ready for your report now."

Mange and Slymind stared at each other.

"Well?"

Slymind spoke first. "Well, sir, there was an incident today at a store—"

"Why was that?" Command asked calmly, already anticipating the response.

"The stupid clerk wouldn't listen!" Mange said. "I got mad…sir."

Command stared at Mange but didn't stay a word. Mange swallowed hard and took a few steps backward.

"Haven't I told you a million times to control yourself in public? We can't afford to have our cover blown, especially now." Command had the unique ability to sound angry yet appear completely calm.

"I know. You've told me lots of times. I'm sorry," Mange stared at the ground. Command was the only person on earth who scared him.

"Were there any witnesses?"

The duo stared at each other again.

"It's one thing for Mange here to lose his temper, but it's another for me to lose mine" Command took a step forward and lowered his voice. It was almost a whisper. "Again, I ask. Were there any witnesses?"

"There was a boy—" Slymind started to say,

"A boy?" Command crossed his arms and stepped closer. "You two super powerful beings dare to come to me and say the whole operation is at risk because of a boy? Is this boy alive?"

"Yes, but only because he had help," Slymind said

"Help? From who?"

"The *traitor.*" Mange bared his teeth.

"Ah. Him." Command nodded as the pieces came together in his head. "He's still tracking us. That is very unfortunate."

"Let me have a go at him; I'll tear him to shreds!" Mange swiped at the air.

"Hah! Like you did today?" Slymind chuckled.

Mange glared at him, his eyes starting to glow.

"He is not our priority right now," Command said. "I have something much more important for you to take care of."

Command walked over to a table and grabbed a small black box with several buttons and a screen. It looked like a Mp3 player. "This device is a scanner. It's taken me months, but I've finally programmed it to find the source of the energy that changed us."

"How does it work?" Mange asked, frowning with confusion.

The leader nodded. "I doubt you would understand if I told you. The last component it needs is an emerald. This scanner will burn through a small piece of emerald in a few weeks so I will need a large emerald I can chip away at as needed."

"You mean like the emerald that is going to be on display at the museum tomorrow?" Slymind asked with a smile on his face.

Command returned the smile, "Yes. That is exactly the emerald that I need. Tomorrow, both of you will go and steal it for me. And this time, if anyone gets in your way…make sure they regret it."

A nervous Eric stood at the side of a confident Chasub as they each stared at a wall that contained a single blue button.

Chasub pressed the blue button, and a panel slid out of the wall. "Even before I found you, I prepared this as an offensive tool for whoever found the Omnidisks."

Eric rested his eyes on a large red watch.

"Take it," Chasub instructed.

"Nice," Eric said. "I won't be late to class anymore. But how is this going to help me fight the augments?"

"If you look carefully, you will observe four separate buttons, two on the left side of the watch and two on the right side."

"I see them. I assume they aren't there to set the day and month," Eric said, half joking.

"No, they are not. The one button on the upper left side of the watch will instantly put you in direct communication with the ship and with me."

"Good, because I'm sure my cell phone doesn't get that type of reception."

"Let me know when you are ready to be serious." Chasub's voice had a hint of annoyance.

Eric's face grew warm with embarrassment. "I'm sorry. Just nervous and trying to take all this in."

"I understand, but we have much work to do."

"I hear you." Eric took a deep breath. "Okay, tell me more about how this thing works."

"The button on the lower left side of the watch will activate a scan for the nearest Omnidisk. It will alert us both when one is found."

"That shouldn't take too long, should it?" Eric examined the screen. "I mean, you were the one who hid them here on earth, right? So, you should know where to find them."

"I don't," Chasub looked directly at Eric.

Eric took a few steps back. "How is that possible? You're the only one on the ship."

"I couldn't take the risk of the Thyders getting to them if they captured me. So, I used our Molecular Flinger to randomize the coordinates, and I sent the Omnidisks to different places in Drakeston."

"Wait, the Molecular Flinger? What in the world is that?"

"That is the name of the instant transportation device my people invented. It uses energy to transport people or things to another place instantaneously. I used it to save you from the augments. The closest translation I have for it in your language is Molecular Flinger. So, in English, I flung them to your planet."

"That doesn't sound too scientific," Eric said with a chuckle.

"That is beside the point," Chasub sounded slightly offended,

"Relax, I was only kidding around. But was making it so you didn't know where the Omnidisks went a smart move?"

"It was necessary." Chasub's voice was calm again. "I needed to be sure that if I were captured or tracked, there would be no record of the Omnidisks' whereabouts."

"Couldn't you have designed something so that at least you could find them later?"

Chasub gestured to Eric's arm. "Hence the watch. I thought this was the safest way to protect everyone."

"I guess you thought wrong," Eric grumbled.

"Please, pay special attention to the button in the upper right corner," Chasub ignored Eric's remark.

"What does that one do?" Eric asked.

"That feature is best left to a demonstration. Press it."

"This should be interesting," Eric gave Chasub a weak smile and pressed the button.

A bright red light engulfed Eric's entire body. His clothes started to shift. He felt a tightness that ran from his feet to his shoulders. Right as he thought his heart was about to burst from sheer panic, it all stopped.

Eric could see Chasub looking at him with what appeared to be satisfaction.

"What, what happened?" Everything had happened in seconds, but Eric was still breathless.

"See for yourself." Chasub tapped the wall, and a reflective mirror-like surface appeared.

"Wow!" Eric exclaimed as he caught a good glimpse of himself. "This is cool!" His entire body was now in a red and black uniform. The uniform had black stripes going along the sides, shoulders, hands, and in the center of the chest. The suit had crimson red legs, lines on the waist as well as red forearms and red covering his chest with the exception of the black circle. He also had a black belt with a circular buckle.

His mask covered only his eyes and the area around them. It was made of the same material as the rest of the suit. "Wow!" was all Eric could say.

"It pleases you?" Chasub asked.

"I love it! It makes me look all muscular and stuff. Red is definitely my color."

"I believe the color is crimson."

"Whatever, man, this thing is way cool. What is this stuff made out of?"

"It is made out of material from my planet. It is nearly indestructible. We plannéd to use it for our ground troops."

Eric barely heard him as he kept staring at himself in the mirror.

Chasub was satisfied to see Eric's confidence growing as he looked at the suit. "I need to explain your uniform's abilities."

"I'm all ears," Eric turned to the alien.

"First, the suit is designed to increase your level of resistance from physical attacks as well as slightly increasing your strength and agility. The mask has an audio and visual link to *The Omega,* so when you're on earth, I can see what you see and hear what you hear. And it is bulletproof. However, I must warn you that the augments you will be fighting don't typically use guns. The mask also contains an awareness transmitter. It doesn't conceal much of your face physically, but it does send out a very subtle signal that tricks the brain into thinking you look different than you do."

"Cool! Can it make me look like Denzel Washington?" Eric grinned.

"Do I need to increase the temperature? And who is that? Is he any relation to the first President, George Washington?" Chasub asked.

Eric struggled to respond through his laughter. "You know what? Just keep going."

"The suit also has a built-in antigravity generator, similar to what I use to stay afloat." Chasub drew attention to the metal belt around his waist.

That stopped Eric's laughter "Wait… are you telling me that I can fly with this thing? I thought floating was just something your people did."

"Yes, you have a maximum speed of Mach 2. But while the suit will help, but it's not going to be enough to protect you against those augments. You also need to know how to fight, so while you were unconscious, I embedded something into your brain."

"What?" Eric started feeling his head, looking for a surgical scar.

"Relax, Eric, there was no surgery involved. I downloaded various self-defense techniques from across your world into your mind: Karate, Dambe, Capoeira, even Boxing.

"So I'm some kind of kung-fu master now?" Eric asked as he feebly tried to kick. "It doesn't seem to be working."

"It is implanted in your subconscious. You won't be able to access it until you are in an actual combat situation."

"You mean I won't know what to do unless I'm in the middle of a fight?"

"Yes. Anytime you are in a dangerous situation, your desire for self-preservation will give you access to these skills. As you gain more experience, you will be able to call on these skills at will. I have another tool for you."

Chasub opened a smaller panel and pulled out what appeared to be a silver set of brass knuckles

"Isn't this a little low-tech or you?" Eric laughed.

"By now you should know things are rarely what they seem. Slip it on."

Eric put his fingers through the holes, and instantly the silver metal expanded until it covered the top half of his hand. "Very cool."

"I offered to make the ship warmer," Chasub reminded him before gesturing to several buttons on the device. "In any case, this is called an Illuminator. Its advanced scanning capabilities allow you to project a holographic map of any area you may be in and show you anything that may be of interest, including the Omnidisks.

This device can also serve as a weapon. The controls for this weapon are simple. I have used your number system to represent power levels. I have the numbers one through ten displayed here. One is the lowest setting. Three should be strong enough to render a person unconscious. Seven can kill an average person. Ten can vaporize nearly anything. Be careful with that level. Use it wisely."

"Amazing," Eric turned toward Chasub. I know I was a little anxious at first, but now I feel like it's possible for me to do this."

"You were more than a little apprehensive," Chasub stated as he smiled at Eric. "Your concern is normal and quite understandable. You are taking on a great responsibility, which is why I will give you one last thing. Follow me."

Eric followed Chasub to another panel on the wall. "This is the most important item I will give you. I only sent seven Omnidisks to Earth. There was one I kept on the ship." Chasub tapped several buttons on the panel, waited a few seconds and tapped several more before the panel opened and he flew to the side.

Eric's eyes widened as he beheld a small silver circle the size of a silver dollar glowing before him.

"This is the Eternity Omnidisk. It contains the power of limited invulnerability," Chasub stated as he reached inside the panel and pulled the Omnidisk out.

"So I can't die while I have this? Nice."

Chasub made a clicking sound with his mouth Eric thought might be laughter. "Nothing can completely protect you from death. It simply gives you the ability to tolerate high levels of physical harm. It will prevent you from getting any mortal wounds except in the most extreme circumstances. Take it. It is yours."

Eric reached out and touched the Omnidisk with his index finger. A surge of energy sprinted through his body, reaching every cell from his head to his feet. His body felt as if it was about to explode. He snatched back his finger.

"What a rush."

"It goes on your belt."

"Where?" Eric looked down in confusion.

"Move it closer to your body; it will go where it needs to."

Eric hesitated as he moved the Omnidisk close to himself. Within seconds, a circular slot opened on his buckle and Eric put the Omnidisk in it.

As Eric glanced at himself again, a sudden chill ran through him.

"Don't worry, Eric, you can do this."

"Can I? I mean, we are talking about saving the world."

Chasub's alien voice became full of determination. "Eric, you're not alone. I'm here with you. We can do this together."

"Right. Together," Eric began to pace back and forth. "Look for Omnidisks, stop the augments, save the world. Are you sure they picked me? Maybe they got it wrong. Maybe when you flung them to earth using your Molecular Flicker thing, they got damaged somehow."

"I'm sure. Now I think you need to return home before anyone notices you're missing." Chasub floated over to a machine and began to press buttons on its console.

"I'm sure my dad is already wondering where I am," Eric checked the time on his new watch.

"You will be fine. Tell him anything, except what actually happened, and before I send you to Earth, I think you might want to change into your civilian clothes."

Eric stared at this watch, unsure which button to select.

"Press the same button you used to transform."

"Of course, I knew that." Eric stared at this watch again. "Hey, what is this fourth button on the lower right for?"

"It's for emergencies only. It transports you here on the ship if you need to make a quick exit to a safe place. Try not to use it unless absolutely necessary."

"Why, what will happen?"

"It draws a lot of power from the ship's main power core, and it causes damage to the Molecular Flinger. It is best if I'm the one to bring you here," Chasub pointed at Eric. "Now, we've got to get you home so, please go ahead and transform into your regular clothes."

Eric pointed to the button.

Chasub nodded as he watched Eric transform.

"Wait for me to contact you."

"I will," said Eric. "Assuming I'm not grounded forever."

A blue light surrounded Eric for the second time that day, and in an instant, he was sent to Earth.

CHAPTER 4

"Man, that last starship battle, that was more than fantastic! The way Picard…Hey, earth to Eric. Anybody home?" Archie waved his hand in front of Eric's face.

Eric blinked and looked blankly at Archie. "Sorry. I've been through some stuff, and I need to think."

"Yeah, I noticed. I've been talking to myself for the last ten minutes. I saw you in class earlier today and you looked as if the Death Star could have appeared and you wouldn't have seen a thing. Why don't—"

"Move, Ginger!" A passing football player shoved Archie into the lockers as he passed.

"Jerk." Eric glared down the hall before checking on his friend. "You're getting it from both sides of the social structure."

"Unfortunately, our bullies are equal opportunity." Archie bit his tongue for a moment and looked his friend directly in the eye. "Look, man, I've tried to wait and be supportive, but you still haven't told me anything. What's going on?"

Eric placed a hand on his shoulder. "I'm sorry and know that it's not that I don't trust you. It's just that this thing that I'm going through is big. Huge. I need to think it through, alone."

"You haven't kept a secret from me since kindergarten. Remember when you broke that toy fire truck? I never told the teacher. I never tell. Right?"

All Eric could do was nod his head in agreement.

"We've been friends forever! You tell me about *everything*. Well, everything except for your crush on Chris—"

"I do *not*—" Eric started.

"Whatever," Archie cut off his denial. "You usually trust me, and I have never betrayed that trust. So why change your mind now?"

Eric thought about it. He realized that he was right; if he could trust anyone with his secret, it was Archie. And he could use a friend to talk to.

Eric smiled at Archie. "Ok, you asked for it. I don't know if you're going to believe this, but here's the deal..."

A half hour later, Eric had covered nearly everything that had happened to him the day before.

"And so, when I got home, I had to tell my dad that the reason I was out so long was because the police took forever questioning me about the attack. I'm not too sure he even believed me, but he didn't argue it, so I left it alone. His mind is always so preoccupied these days, I'm not surprised."

Archie stared with his mouth wide open for a full minute.

"That is so awesome! You saw an alien, an actual alien. I knew they were real! I KNEW it! You were in a spaceship...In space! You got awesome never-before-seen technology. And now you get to fight augments! You're a freaking kung-fu master! Man, it's like a movie or something. But better, because it's you. You're our only hope. I can't believe this; I'm best friends with a superhero. Wait until we tell everyone!"

"No way, Archie. You can't mention any of this to anyone. Not a thing. Ok?" Eric looked closely at Archie.

Archie saluted. "Aye aye, sir!"

Eric chuckled. "Maybe it won't be so bad having someone to share my secret with."

"I told you that you needed to tell me. I bet you feel better now. Dude, you're going to save the world! Okay, now that I know, let's train or something. I'm going to help you to become the best hero ever!"

Beep! Beep! Eric's watch began to sound before he could respond to Archie. He pressed a button.

"Eric? Are you there?" Chasub's face appeared on the front of the watch.

"Yes, I'm here," Eric responded. "Is there—"

"Greetings, advanced alien being!" Archie grabbed Eric's wrist and began talking into the watch. "My name is Archibald Patterson. I come in peace!"

"You'll leave in pieces if you don't stop acting stupid." Eric snatched his arm back. "Sorry about that."

"Eric, I thought we agreed that no one was to know about this," Chasub's tone was a little stiffer than usual, causing Eric to believe he was irritated at Archie's knowledge of their plan.

"I know. Look, he's cool. Trust me. No matter how…odd he may seem." Eric glared at Archie. "I know I can trust him."

"It is not wise for you to—"

"Chasub, if this is going to work, you have to learn to trust my judgment. Archie won't let us down," Eric assured him.

"I suppose nothing can be done about it now," Chasub conceded. "Something important has occurred."

"An Omnidisk?" Eric asked.

"Not yet. I have been trying to think of some way for you to gain experience in combat. I don't want you facing the augments for the first time without having some combat experience."

"I faced them before," Eric reminded him.

Archie snickered in the background, remembering what Eric had told him about the encounter. "You sure did."

Eric shot him a quick look. "What? I did fine…kind of."

"You need real experience using all the tools that I gave you. I've been monitoring the transmissions of the police officers in your area, along with the alarm systems of large establishments. A silent alarm at a bank has been activated. It is less than a mile from your current position. My scans tell me that some variants are the ones behind the crime. You'll need to get there before the police do and try to take care of the situation without being spotted."

"What do you mean, try?" Eric asked sarcastically. "I know the bank you're talking about. I'll head there right away."

"Excellent. Keep me posted," Chasub stated as he ended the connection.

"We're going to stop a bank robbery? Excellent!" Archie cried. "Let's go."

Archie started running towards the bank. Eric rolled his eyes and ran after him.

A few minutes later, Eric and Archie reached the bank on their bikes and hid behind a few bushes.

"No cops yet," Archie said as he looked out at the street.

"Then it's my time to shine," Eric said as he smiled at Archie.

Eric activated his watch. A red light surrounded him, and he once again felt his clothes shifting. Seconds later he was in full uniform.

Archie's eyes seemed to triple in size. "You really do look like a superhero! I love the costume. I'm sure you have a name to match right?"

"Name?" Eric asked.

"Yeah, a superhero name. You can't go by 'Eric.'"

Eric patted him on the back. "Ok buddy, you can pick my name while I go in here and stop some bad guys."

Archie looked shocked. "I'm not going in with you?"

"Too dangerous. Besides, you don't have a way of disguising yourself and the last time I checked, you don't know how to fight."

Archie thought about it for a moment and sighed in defeat. "You're right."

"Good. Now stay here and keep a lookout for the police. I'm going in."

Eric walked over toward the building, found a side door and snuck in.

"Eric?"

"Whoa!" Eric turned around and began looking for the source of the voice.

"Eric, it's me, Chasub. I told you I would have audio and visual contact. The audio goes both ways, I can talk to you and hear what you hear and you can talk to me."

"Well, thank you for giving me a heart attack," Eric said. "It wouldn't kill you to give me some warning next time."

"Focus. Try to find the robbers."

Eric made his way to the lobby of the bank and noticed that all of the tellers' booths were empty and not one customer was around. He could feel his heart beginning to pound. He ducked behind a counter and saw that the visible security cameras looked as if they had been knocked out.

"Definitely a bank robbery," Eric whispered.

"Be careful but try to see if you can determine the robbers' exact location."

Eric moved quietly through the area, ducking behind counters as much as possible.

"I don't see anything. What could've possibly—Aah!" Eric almost tripped over the security guard lying on the floor. He had a large bump on his head."

"He is not dead, merely unconscious," Chasub said.

"How do you know?" Eric asked.

"I installed sensors into the area of the mask where your eyes are. Faint life signs are coming from him. On the other hand, I am sensing a stronger life sign very close to you. I believe there is coming from behind you."

A gruff voice spoke just as Chasub finished his statement. "Don't move." Eric felt a gun press against the back of his head.

Thanks for the warning, Eric thought bitterly.

"A little early for Halloween, isn't it, kid?" the voice asked.

"What's happening?" Chasub asked.

"There is a gun pointed at my head, so I'm a little busy right now," Eric whispered.

"You're darn right you are, so I suggest you shut up and get moving." Eric was shoved through a door on the other side of the room and into the vault. "Get in there!"

Eric's heart was racing as he scanned the scene. The bank tellers and customers were on their knees with their hands behind their head. He could see the fear in their eyes as they slowly looked over at him. The silence in the air was thick. Hovering over them was a man dressed in all black. He had a ski mask covering his face. Eric took note of another man emptying lockboxes filled with money into big bags. Both of their eyes briefly flashed yellow.

Definitely variants. Eric thought to himself.

"Who's the freak in the mask?" Asked the man guarding the hostages.

"It doesn't matter, as soon as we are done here we'll take care of all of them," The man behind Eric stated as he gave him a hard shove to the floor.

"If you were going to mount a rescue, now would be a good time," Chasub whispered.

Fear and anticipation filled every breath that Eric had. He knew what he needed to do, but he wasn't sure if he had the courage to do it. *I'm the only one who can do this.*

Eric counted to three in his head.

"Aaaaaaah!" Eric ducked his head, grabbed the man's wrist and pointed it at the ceiling before kicking him in the chest and knocking him to the ground.

Bang! The gun went off, and the bullet hit the ceiling. People scrambled to the other side of the room.

Eric narrowed his eyes at his opponent. *Bullets are flying. Time to focus.*

Archie's head shot up from his hiding place from behind the bushes. *That was a gunshot!*

Eric might be hurt!

Archie knew Eric telling him to stay hidden made perfect sense. He was happy for his friend. He had powers and a great new super suit! Archie. He had no problem playing a supporting role while Eric handled the heavy work. But now they were shooting. Eric had been discovered and he couldn't stand by and let his best friend in the world get hurt.

Archie glanced over at the dumpster behind the building and noticed an old pipe on the ground next to it.

Hold on, buddy, Arche ran for the dumpster. *The cavalry is on the way.*

Eric balanced on his back foot and kicked the gun out of his opponent's hand. The variant tried to get on his feet, but Eric hit him in the chest. When the man hit the floor, he pointed at Eric and cried out, "Get him!"

One of the other robbers charged at Eric with a lockbox. He took a swing. Eric ducked and kicked at his attacker. The robber stumbled dodged and came at Eric again. This time his strike connected. Eric felt the lockbox slam into the side of his face. The robber, sensing he had the upper hand, swung again.

Eric fell into the wall, his face throbbing. Eric looked over and saw the robber charging at him a third time.

Eric ducked again, and he felt his legs move out from his body as they swept the feet from under the robber. The lockbox hit the floor. His arm extended and his fist connected with the left side of the robber's face. The robber hit the floor hard. This time he stayed there.

The first robber tried to charge Eric. This time he merely sidestepped the man until he rushed past and kicked him between the shoulder blades. He slammed against the wall, fell on the floor and didn't move.

Bam! Someone hit him from behind with a gun. This time it was Eric who hit the floor.

"You're a good fighter for a freak in a mask. I'll have them carve that on your tombstone." The criminal cocked his gun.

"Let him go!" Archie ran behind the variant and swung a pipe at him.

The robber's eyes flashed yellow before he dodged, grabbed Archie by the front of his shirt and threw him into a wall.

Archie groaned in pain before his gaze settled on attacker aiming at him. *This is why Robin doesn't try to save Batman.*

"Hey!" The robber spun around to see Eric back on his feet. "We're not done yet."

Bang! Bang! The variant shot Eric twice in the chest.

"No!" Archie cried from the floor.

"It's ok," Eric said with a smile. "There's not a scratch on me. Chasub, this uniform is as good as advertised."

"How?" The thief looked at his gun and back at Eric.

"I dress to impress," Eric stepped forward and punched him hard in the face. He was out cold.

"All right!" The captives climbed to their feet and started clapping and cheering. "Who are you? What's your name?"

Before Eric could speak, he heard police sirens in the distance. He grabbed Archie's arm and pulled him out the door. They took cover in some bushes before anybody saw them.

"That was so awesome! I've never felt a rush like that! Aren't you going to thank me?" Archie was grinning ear to ear.

"Thank you?!" Eric fumed. "I can't believe you did something so stupid!"

Archie looked shocked. "I saved your life! He was going to shoot!"

Eric scoffed. "No, that's what I have the suit for; it's bulletproof!"

"Oh. Well, I helped distract him. And I didn't get hurt," Archie rubbed his back. "Not badly anyway. Everything went fine."

"Wrong again! I wear this mask for a reason. You went in there with your face exposed. If someone figures out who you are, they could connect you to me and blow my whole cover!"

"I was trying to help!" Archie argued.

"I didn't need your help! I have equipment and fighting skills. *That* is my help You can't take on one school bully without me!" Eric regretted the words as soon as they left his lips.

Archie frowned. "You aren't the boss of me. I thought it was cool, you being a superhero and all, but now you're acting like a jerk. I liked you better without the costume."

Archie grabbed his bike and took off down the street.

Eric dropped his head and sighed.

"You were right," Chasub said.

"Whatever," Eric said, watching Archie.

"You did the right thing." The alien insisted. "He needs to understand the dangers, or he could die."

"Then why do I feel so crummy?" Eric said. "I can't just let him go away mad like that. I'll talk to you later."

Eric reverted to his regular clothing, picked up his bike and rode after Archie.

"Archie!" Eric could still see him in the distance. Right as he opened his mouth to scream Archie's name again, his watch started making a steady beeping noise.

Eric activated the communicator on his watch. "I told you we can talk later. I have to fix things with Archie."

"Something more important is happening," Chasub said. "I have detected Mange and Slymind. I am sending you their coordinates.

"I need to get to Archie; I can't leave things like this."

"You'll have to deal with that situation another time. This is the mission. Right now, we need to find out what those two are planning. They might lead you to their superior or the machine. Either way, following them is more important."

Eric looked for Archie, but he didn't see him anywhere. *Tomorrow*, he promised himself as he rode toward the coordinates Chasub gave him. *I'll talk to him tomorrow.*

CHAPTER 5

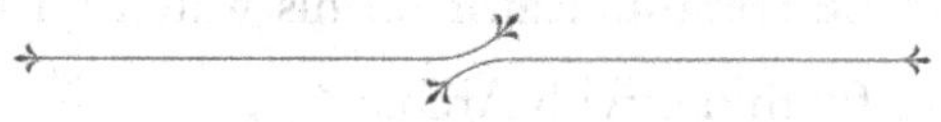

When he got close, Eric followed Mange and Slymind, watching them from a distance as they entered into the Drakeston Museum.

What could they possibly want in there? he wondered.

After waiting a few minutes, Eric climbed the stairs and walked inside. He hid behind one of the museum sculptures. He stuck his head out from behind the statue and his eyes darted back and forth, looking for his quarry. Seconds later, he saw them staring at a huge emerald display, but from a distance.

Obviously, they are trying to not bring attention to themselves from the security guards. What's the deal with the emerald? Why are they so interested in it? I need to get a little closer so I can hear what they're saying.

"There it is," said Slymind. "We have to take it to Command now."

"How are we going to do that without being noticed?" Mange asked. "The security guards have guns."

Slymind rolled his eyes. "That is why I am the one with the brains. We're augments, remember? We'll do what we do best. You will scare the crap out of them and, while they are focusing on you, I will swipe the emerald."

"What about the people here?"

"Once you take off your disguise, anyone would be scared of you. They'll run!"

"I hate when you're right." Mange growled.

"Whatever, just get ready."

Eric reopened his connection with Chasub. "They plan on taking the emerald in the museum. Why would they care about that?"

"I do not know. They may merely be interested in obtaining currency. Unless…" Chasub was silent for a few seconds. "The molecular composition of the emeralds of your world are very similar to one of the crystals on my world. They are useful in tracking the Omnidisks' energy."

"So, that means that they must be trying to make a scanner, right?"

"You must stop them! If they can track the Omnidisks, it will make things much more difficult for us," Chasub said.

"I thought you said that if they tried to track the Omnidisks, the signal would get scrambled? Wasn't that one of their safeguards?

Eric could hear Chasub entering information into his computer. "The molecular composition of the emeralds changes all of that. It simply tracks the energy from the Omnidisks without setting off their internal scrambler. Clever, but horrible for us."

"Tell me about it."

Mange and Slymind walked over to the emerald.

"They're making their move," Eric said.

"Then make yours," Chasub ordered.

Eric looked around to be sure nobody could see him. He activated his watch and changed into his uniform.

Roooooooaaaarrr!!!

Mange threw off his disguise and began terrorizing the museum residents and security guards.

"It's a monster! Shoot it!" one of the guards yelled.

Slymind super-stretched his arms and punched out two of the guards.

Tzzzzzap! Mange shot two more with his eye beams, propelling them into the wall.

The last one fainted from fright.

"Grab the emerald!" Slymind yelled at Mange.

Time for a little target practice. Eric took out the Illuminator and slid it onto his hand.

"Freeze!" Eric stepped out and pointed the weapon at Slymind.

Slymind laughed. "What is this? Look at this, Mange! A hero, complete with costume!"

"Too bad I have to mess it up," Mange said.

"I'm the one with the weapon," Eric said.

"That? It looks like you got it out of a vending machine," Slymind scoffed.

Tseeew! Eric shot a green beam of energy at the wall behind Mange. The Illuminator was set on level five, so it left a smoking black mark.

"I doubt you would find something that could do *that* in a vending machine," Eric tried to make his voice deeper than usual.

Mange's eyes started to glow. "I'm gonna—"

"No, I'll take care of him. Secure the emerald," Slymind ordered.

All of Slymind's appendages began to stretch. His arms, legs, and midsection extended to unbelievable lengths.

Tseeew! Tseeew! Tseeew! Eric fired three shots at Slymind. He dodged all of them.

Tseeew! Tseeew! He missed two more times.

"You must fire with better accuracy!" Chasub exclaimed through the suit's communicator.

"I'm trying! He moves like a cobra!" Eric responded as he fired more shots.

Faster than the eye could see, Slymind threw a punch and Eric flew through the air and hit a wall.

"Eric, where is your weapon?" Chasub asked.

Eric looked around as he climbed to his feet. His Illuminator was on the floor a few feet away. Slymind tried to punch Eric again. He jumped out of the way just in time and ran for the illuminator.

"I don't think so!" Mange jumped between Eric and his weapon.

Eric high kicked him in the chest. Mange stumbled back. Eric kicked again; this time Mange caught Eric's leg and threw him into a display case.

The glass shattered instantly upon impact with Eric's body. He groaned with pain as his body hit the floor.

"For a punk in a bad costume, you came pretty well prepared," said Slymind as he and Mange stood over Eric. "I'm almost sorry that I'm going to have to mess up your pretty little suit."

Eric lifted the front half of his body. "I'm not finished yet."

"Sure you are." Mange's eyes began to glow.

"Let the him go!" a deep, raspy voice yelled.

Slymind and Mange turned around.

"Dark Viper!" Mange roared.

Dressed in all black, stood a six foot two inch being. His black cloak draped down to his feet. His black boots were scuffed and worn. His face was covered by his hood, but his sickly green slanted eyes were shining through.

"You!" Slymind stepped forward. "We were told to kill you if we ever saw you again!"

"Yes! I owe you for what you did to me," Mange said.

Taking advantage of the distraction, Eric swept Slymind's feet out from under him.

Tzzzzap! Mange shot his eye beams at Eric.

In an effortless motion, Eric leaped into the air and landed on the side where his illuminator lay.

Together, he and Dark Viper stood side-by-side.

"I need to know, whose side are you on?" Eric asked as they both prepared to attack Mange and Slymind.

"Not theirs That's all that matters."

"You're right"

"Watch out!"

Slymind threw a dozen white spheres at them

"What are they?" Eric asked Chasub as they landed on the floor and began to glow.

"I'm not sure, I'm reading a strange energy," Chasub warned.

"You've got your little friend, there. Well, now we've got ours. Twelve to be exact!" Slymind shouted at Eric. "Our holo-henchmen are more than capable of handling the both of you."

A moment later twelve men of the exact same size stood before them. They were dressed in black from head to toe. They wore black hats but the strangest part was that they had no faces. No eyes, ears nose or mouth.

"What in the world are holo-henchmen?" Eric braced himself for the battle.

"My scans are showing them to be holograms," Chasub replied.

"Really? What's so incredible about holographic bad guys? Holograms are supposed to be made of light, right? Light can't hurt me, can it?" Eric asked.

"All is not as it seems, boy," Dark Viper warned.

"Attack!" Slymind commanded.

The hologram in front hit Eric with a flying kick.

"Aah!" Eric slid across the floor, losing his illuminator once again.

"They have somehow found a way to make the holo-henchmen solid. They can hurt you," Chasub informed him.

"Thanks, but I already figured that out, Mr. Alien Genius. How do I beat them?" Eric asked as three came after him.

"Overload them," Chasub said. "If you hit them constantly and with enough force, their holo-emitters, the little spheres you saw, will overload and burn out."

Eric caught a punch thrown by one of the holograms. He hit it in the face (or what passed for a face) with a reverse punch, flipped it in the air and slammed it on the floor. As soon as the hologram made contact it disappeared; a blackened sphere was all that remained.

"Wow, that was so—" Eric was kicked in the face before he could complete his sentence.

Four of the holograms came charging at Dark Viper. He blocked several punches from one and gave it a hard kick in the chest, propelling it through the air. It disappeared before it hit the floor.

Two of the other holograms tried to double team him. One leaped over him and kicked him in the back. Another one attempted to punch him, but he ducked, causing the hologram to punch its fellow assailant.

From the corner of his eye, Eric saw Dark Viper, pull out a bo staff from his wrist. It extended itself out five feet. Dark Viper hit one of the holograms in the face with the staff. It landed on the floor and disappeared.

Two more holograms lunged toward Dark Viper. He caught the first one and threw it into the other hologram. Both of their holo-emitters overloaded, leaving two smoking spheres.

The remaining five approached Eric from all directions. He once again leaped into the air and landed in a roll, grabbing his illuminator in the process.

His shots took out two, but another one caught him with a kick from behind. The hit sent Eric sliding across the floor.

Eric stretched out his hand to reach for his illuminator. He felt the intense pressure as one hologram held his arm to the floor. Two more were coming. Eric tried to think.

Two throwing stars whistled through the air and struck a pair of holograms. Their black spheres fell to the floor. Dark Viper jumped in and punched the last one, turning it into a smoking black sphere as well.

Dark Viper reached for Eric's hand.

"Thanks. Who are you?" Eric asked once he was on his feet,

Before Dark Viper could respond, Eric caught sight of Mange and Slymind. They were making their way to the door with the emerald.

"We've got to stop them!" Eric shouted as he and Dark Viper ran towards them.

Tzzzzap! Mange's eye beams hit Eric in the chest, repelling him into a large column.

Eric's body was wracked with pain. He fought to get to his feet.

"You're an impressive fighter for a human," Slymind said. "But now you must see where the road to heroism leads."

Dark Viper stood in front of Eric.

"This is between you and me!" Dark Viper shouted at Mange. "Put down the emerald and I will let you leave."

"Try and stop me!" Mange yelled in reply.

"Shut up," ordered Slymind. "Listen."

They could hear the sirens in the distance.

"Get us out of here now!" Slymind shouted.

Mange threw the emerald to Slymind and wrapped an arm around his waist. Before Dark Viper could react, Mange spread his wings and flew through the skylight.

Dark Viper sighed in disappointment.

"Are you hurt?"

"I'm fine," Eric said as he painfully climbed to his feet. "I appreciate all of your help."

Dark Viper glared. "In the future you should be more careful, Eric."

"How do you know my name!?" Eric's eyes widened in shock.

"You're the same child from yesterday. I have an enhanced sense of smell. I recognize your scent. And you dropped this." Dark Viper pulled out Eric's school I.D. "I rescued you from the augments when you lost consciousness. I don't know how you are involved in all of this, but I warn you, this is not your fight."

Eric nodded appreciatively before reaching out and taking his I.D. "Look, thanks for the advice, but I think—"

"Freeze!" Twenty police officers ran into the room with guns drawn.

When Eric turned around, Dark Viper was gone.

Eric raised his hands as one of the officer's moved closer to him.

"Where is the emerald?" the cop asked.

"Oh no, they think I took it," Eric mumbled to Chasub.

"Hold on, I'll fling you out of there," Chasub ordered.

"I asked you a question! Where is the emerald?" the officer repeated.

"Excuse me, officers, but did it occur to you that if I had been trying to steal it, it would still be here with me?"

The officers paused to consider Eric's point.

A humming noise began and Eric was surrounded by a blue light.

"Grab him!" The officers ran towards Eric, but they were too late, the blue light was gone and so was Eric.

"Did you see that?" asked one officer.

"Nope. And neither did you. That's our report, and we're sticking to it!"

The lead officer scratched his head. "I need a vacation."

CHAPTER 6

"I hate Dark Viper." Mange landed outside the entrance to the villain's lair. He gently put Slymind down.

Slymind gave Mange a quick glance. "As do I. Just be glad we got the emerald."

"Did you see that guy in the uniform?"

"We were both there, remember?"

"What do you think his story is? I don't think that was normal tech."

"You think?" Slymind rolled his eyes.

"Stop always talking to me like I'm dumb." Mange got red in the face. "Command is going to ask us what happened."

"You *are* dumb, but so what if he asks. We have what he sent us for, don't we?" Slymind reasoned.

"Yeah, but you know he's going to ask. He told us to take care of anyone who gives us trouble."

"We'll have to explain that there were unforeseen circumstances," Slymind's tone betrayed that he wasn't sure that plan would work.

The two glanced at each other and took a deep breath as they walked into their headquarters

Command was waiting.

"Marvelous!" Command exclaimed, holding his hands out for the emerald.

Mange and Slymind followed Command over to the table with the tracking device on it. "With this, I can have our new scanner working in a few hours."

Mange and Slymind tried to smile. They each stood, arms at their sides, bodies braced for what was coming next.

"So, was there any trouble?" Command asked, watching each of them carefully.

Neither said a word.

"That was not a rhetorical question," Command's words were slow and deliberate.

"We got the emerald, sir," Slymind began.

"Yes, I can see the emerald, and I am holding the emerald, but that again was not my question!" Command raised his voice.

"We did encounter some trouble. Some guy in a fancy suit showed up," Mange said.

"Fancy suit?" Command turned to Slymind for clarification

Slymind sighed. "Some kind of uniform. It was like nothing I have ever seen. Some kind of advanced technology. He even had some sort of advanced technology that shot laser beams. Whoever built it had your level of intelligence."

"Probably smarter," Mange mumbled.

Command turned to Mange and narrowed his eyes. "What was that?"

"Dark Viper dropped in as well," Slymind quickly said.

"Him again? How is it that he is constantly aware of your whereabouts?" Command took his attention off Mange.

"We don't know, but you said yourself, sir, that he is an expert tracker," Slymind stated almost in a whisper.

Command caught his tone but chose to ignore it. "This is no coincidence. I think we may finally have got the attention of the one who created the technology that changed us."

Slymind took a step toward Command. "How could you know that? Maybe this guy is a government agent or something."

Command nodded. "No. Think about it. Just as we are closing in on these items, a man in a suit and some advanced technology appears. He was right where you were about to strike. How could he know? He must be working for the person or people responsible for all this and he's aligned himself with one of our enemies. They don't want us to succeed."

"What should we do about it, boss?" Mange asked.

"We can't let anyone stop our plan," Command walked over to the machine and affectionately rubbed his hand alongside it. "If you run into Dark Viper or this man again, bring them to me *alive*. We need to find out everything they know."

"I screwed up the mission," Eric lightly hit the wall in frustration.

"No, you fought well," Chasub said. "You have to remember that this was your first time in actual combat against augments. Your failure was disappointing, but you gained valuable experience."

"Yeah, well, intense or not, I almost got my head handed to me," Eric said.

Chasub stared at Eric. "It's not going to be easy, Eric. You will come very close to life-threatening situations often, I'm afraid. But you can do this. You proved that today."

"No, I proved that I can take a real beating by holograms that aren't real and augments that shouldn't be. If it hadn't been for this Dark Viper, I wouldn't be standing here now," Eric was pacing back and forth.

"His arrival was quite fortuitous," admitted Chasub.

"So, who's Dark Viper, and why was he there helping me?" Eric was ready to change the subject.

Chasub floated over to the ship's main computer terminal and displayed an image of Dark Viper. "I did some research, but I couldn't find much. It seems, though, based on old security footage, that he used to be allied with Mange and Slymind."

Eric nodded. "It sounded like they had some history."

"This Dark Viper character seems have quite a few abilities. I did a scan on him as he fought. From what I can gather, he has remarkable amount of strength and agility. His reptilian qualities give him enhanced senses. In addition to that, from the weapons that he used, gas bombs, throwing stars and a bo staff, he is a trained fighter. He is quite an amazing specimen. But, like I said, information on him is limited."

"So, I'm going to ask you the same thing that I asked him: Is he a friend or foe?" Eric asked.

"I'm not sure. Just because he assisted you in combat does not mean he is on our side. We need to get a better understanding of his motives."

"Ever hear the phrase, 'The enemy of my enemy is my friend'?" Eric asked.

"No, I don't think that I have. Is that some human proverb?"

"It means that if Dark Viper hates these guys it's good enough for me," Eric said confidently.

"Be careful. I know he helped you, but keep in mind that he also knows your identity. If someone appears to be an ally, that doesn't mean they are one," Chasub stated as he began pressing a few keys on his computer.

"How do I know you are one? An ally. I mean, how do I know that you aren't using me to find the Omnidisks so you can destroy the world? Didn't you help me as well?"

"I see your point, but if I wanted to destroy the world, Eric, I certainly wouldn't have given you weapons that could destroy me in the process."

"Good point. So, what you got?" Eric asked as he watched a figure appear on the screen in front of them."

Chasub was silent for a moment. "I might have some good news to share with you. Give me a few minutes to complete my diagnostic."

"Diagnostic?" Eric asked.

Chasub allowed a small smile to slide across his face. "Yes, I'm conducting a complete check of the ship's systems. I need to be sure that systems are working properly. It's a large vessel."

Eric watched as Chasub punched buttons here and there on his computer. Seconds later, the image of the ship appeared bigger. Eric could see it in detail.

"Wow, so that is *The Omega,* huh?"

"Indeed. You see those two flat triangular areas at the rear of the ship that are glowing?" Eric learned in closer as Chasub pointed. "Those are the ships engines. She's a simple ship, but she's also extremely fast and can maneuver around almost anything. She's even got a very powerful laser cannon, a ship sized version of your illuminator."

"She is beautiful, Chasub."

"Thanks. We had more, like this one, before… "

"You really miss home, don't you?" Eric attempted to comfort him. "I understand. I lost my mother."

Chasub tried to change the subject. "Well, it seems that our enemies grabbing the emerald may be both a blessing and a curse."

"I like the blessing part," said Eric. "What did you find?"

"If my calculations are correct and the emerald's molecular properties can be used as a tracking device, I can create something quite similar using the energy from the ship. Some minerals used in the ship are almost identical to properties found in the emerald.

"And that means…what?"

"It means, Eric, that I can generate enough energy from the ship that I can store into this device." Chasub flew over to a small box shaped machine.

"It looks like a car battery," Eric said skeptically.

"It's a super-charged scanner that is strong enough to accomplish exactly what we need it to do. I've synched your watch with this device. Once I've locked on an Omnidisk's location, it will send the information to your watch. We can find the Omnidisks so much faster than before."

Eric raised an eyebrow. "I'm sensing a downside."

"The bad part is that now that they have a tracker, it becomes a race to get to the Omnidisks before they do. The minute a scanner locates an Omnidisk, the Omnidisk ceases the measures that shield it. It will light up like a beacon, alerting anyone looking for it to its presence."

"So when they find one we'll know and when we find one they will know too," Eric said. "You're right, a blessing and a curse."

"Time to fling you home now."

"You know, one day," Eric stated, "I would like to hear you say that you've got good news and only good news."

"By the way, I know you were quite upset about what happened with your friend. I hope that you two are able to fix things. Friendship, was something to be cherished on my planet as well."

Eric nodded in agreement. "Thanks, Chasub. Archie has been my best friend forever."

"He will understand that you only had his well-being in mind, trust me," Chasub said.

"I hope you're right."

"Are you ready?"

"Fling away."

Chasub nodded as he activated the flinger and sent Eric home.

"Brynn, have you seen Archie?" Eric asked as she headed toward him.

"Yeah, about a half hour ago. He was by the front doors. I helped get rid of some football players who were pushing him around," Brynn said with pride, cracking her knuckles. "Did something happen between you two?"

"Why? Did he say something to you?" Eric hoped Archie hadn't blurted out his secret in anger.

"No, but I could tell something was wrong, especially when I asked where you were this morning. What's wrong?"

"It's a long story".

"What, you think I wouldn't understand?"

"It's not that. It's…personal. I need to find him before our next class starts."

"You had better hurry." Brynn watched as Eric darted off down the hallway. *I can't put my finger on it but there is something different about him.*

A solid thirty seconds of silence filled the hallway as Eric stood in front of Archie.

"Eric—"

"Archie—"

They both laughed and shook hands.

"I'm sorry, Archie; I shouldn't have gone off on you like that."

"No, you were right," Archie admitted. "I was totally out of my league. The hero job is your domain. I shouldn't have interfered."

"I'm hardly an expert. Besides, after you left, I had to go face-to- face against Mange and Slymind."

"Wow! I can't believe I missed that. What happened? Did you win?" Just that fast, Archie had forgotten about their quarrel.

Eric bowed his head. "Not really. In fact, if some guy named Dark Viper hadn't helped, I wouldn't be here now."

"Dark Viper?" Archie nodded. "Such a cool name."

"Yeah, we think he's another augment. A good augment as far as I can tell. Anyway, the whole experience helped me to realize that it pays to have someone watching your back." Eric glanced down the hallway and pulled Archie out of view from anyone else. He took out his illuminator and handled it to him.

"Are these brass knuckles?" Archie frowned. "I know I'm not the best fighter in the world but—"

"Put it on," Eric laughed.

Archie looked at Eric, shrugged and slipped it on. Half a second later, he had the illuminator on his hand. The color drained from his face.

"It's an alien scanner combined with a laser weapon. I'm not any good with this thing, but you were always the laser tag expert. Maybe you could use some of that skill to help me."

"I don't believe it. My own ray gun," Archie squeaked out.

Eric chuckled. "Ok, put that away before somebody sees it and let's get going."

Eric and Archie walked into the classroom right as the bell rang.

"Where's Ms. Pryce?" Eric asked. "She's never late."

"My own ray gun," Archie whispered.

Eric rolled his eyes.

"Excuse my tardiness, class," A tall man with brown hair and green eyes stepped into the room and stood behind the teacher's desk. "Ms. Pryce will be out for a while. My name is Jason Jeffries, and I will be teaching the class in her absence."

"Excellent," said Eric. "Any teacher has to be better than her."

"I don't know," replied Archie, finally coming out of his stupor. "He could be worse than her, you know. He could be a serial killer or something."

"What? A teacher as a serial killer?" Eric said sarcastically. "That will be the day. Archie, you have got to get a grip on that imagination of yours."

"Laugh if you want, but something is not quite right with him," Archie insisted.

"You could be right, but a serial killer, he is not." Eric rolled his eyes. "You let your imagination run away with you sometimes."

"Says the guy who spent yesterday on an alien spaceship and went to fight augments," Archie shot back with a forced chuckle.

"Do you two gentlemen have something you'd like to share with the class?" Jeffries asked.

Neither of them responded as the class stared in their direction...

"Good. I invite you both to join us on our wonderful journey to yesteryear." Jason smiled. "I have so many good things in store for you. You don't want to miss out."

CHAPTER 7

By the end of the class, Eric had become very impressed with Mr. Jeffries' teaching style.

"I enjoyed your class today, Mr. Jeffries."

"Why, thank you…Eric, is it? I enjoy teaching history. It helps us to learn some important lessons while looking at the common thread that ties our heroes of the past to the hero that is in each one of us today. Many people that we will study saw that something was wrong with the world, and they each set out to change it. They didn't let any obstacle stand in their way. A lesson all of us who strive to change the world should follow, don't you think?"

Eric nodded. "I couldn't agree more."

"In that case, I'm sure I'll see you tomorrow." Jeffries extended his hand. "And remember, I'm here to help, so if there is ever anything you need to talk about, don't hesitate to come to me."

Eric shook his hand, "I won't, thanks."

Eric found Archie waiting for him in the hallway.

"My own ray gun," Archie said.

"Don't start that again," Eric warned. "Come on, we have to hurry to second period."

Archie looked down the hallway. "Lifetime crush at twelve o'clock."

Eric followed his gaze. Christina Stephens was heading their way

Beautiful as always, Eric thought.

"I…don't…have…" Eric was too nervous to even deny it.

"Hi, guys," Chris said with a smile.

"Klatu, Chris," said Archie.

"H-Hi," Eric stammered, too nervous to tease Archie for his use of an alien language. "How are you?"

"I would be a lot better if I didn't have to take calculus," she replied. "So, I hear there is a new teacher here. How is he?"

"He's a cool guy," Eric finally managed to get out. "I like him. Archie, on the other hand, thinks he might be a serial killer or something."

"You wait and see, he's definitely evil," Archie insisted.

Chris laughed. "So, one says he's cool, and the other has him pegged as some kind of psycho. Nice. That gives me a much better character profile." She waved at both of them. "See you two later."

Eric continued to stare in her direction even after she turned the corner.

"You're right, you don't have a crush on her. My mistake." Archie chuckled.

Eric punched him in the arm. "At least I'm not in love with an illuminator."

Eric's watch began to beep.

"Man, it's him!" Archie could barely control his excitement. "Is he going to beam us up to his spaceship?"

Eric grabbed Archie and they both ducked into a nearby janitor's closet.

"Chasub, your timing is horrible. I'm at school. I was standing in the hallway. Anyone could have heard!

"That's why I beeped you instead of talking first."

"He got you on that one." Archie nodded in agreement.

Eric gave Archie a friendly shove.

"Anyway, this is a matter of urgency."

"Okay, I'm listening."

"I found an Omnidisk."

"Incredible!" Archie said. "Where is it?"

"Hey, I believe that I'm the hero here," Eric interrupted. "I'll handle this. So…where is it?"

"It is a considerable distance from your current position. Your watch can lead you to its exact location. My scans tell me that this is the Mind Omnidisk. It would give its user the power of telekinesis."

"What does that mean?" Eric asked.

Archie cut in. "The power to move objects with your mind. Come on, dude. The Jedi, Jean Grey, Eleven… it's a great skill, a lot of the greats have it."

"Archibald is right. The ability to move objects with one's mind can be useful during a fight," Chasub said. "I need you to go and retrieve it quickly."

"How am I supposed to do that? School is still in session," Eric objected. "If I leave, my dad will get a phone call!"

"And if you don't, the augments will be one step closer to accomplishing their goal."

Archie looked at Eric. "The little guy does have a point."

Eric sighed. "I am going to get in so much trouble for this."

"It is for the greater good," Chasub said. "The augments may be heading to that location at this very moment, so you don't have any time to waste."

"Ok, we're all over it."

"Be careful. But get there first."

"Got it," Eric stated as he tapped his watch to end the conversation.

"Dude, we're going to get an Omnidisk; so amazingly cool!"

"Archie, this could be very dangerous. Are you sure you can handle this?"

"I'm sure!" Archie exclaimed. "I'll be careful, I promise. I got your back and the illuminator, remember?"

Eric smiled. "Alright, let's get going."

The two walked out of the janitor's closet and out of the school without incident. Eric found a spot outside behind some bushes to change into his uniform.

"We're going to kick some augment butt!"

"We're going to get the Omnidisk," Eric corrected. "Hopefully, we can get there before they do."

"Eric are you there?"

"I'm here, Chasub. Man, it's going to take some time for me to get used to this instant communication thing we've got going on here.

"You will. Are you ready?"

Eric turned to Archie. "Do you have the location?"

Archie projected a holographic map with his illuminator. "I see it It's pretty far. We might not get there in time. Unless you have a super cool motorcycle to match your costume."

"Use your anti-gravity generator. It's built into your suit, remember?"

"You want me to fly?" The words felt so strange in Eric's mouth.

"In essence, yes," Chasub stated.

"Oh man, you can fly? That is so cool. Let's go!" Archie cut in.

Eric stood staring into his watch, not sure how to ask the question.

"The process is controlled by thought. All you have to do is focus on flying," Chasub said, sensing Eric's confusion.

"Are you sure this will work? What if it quits on me and I fall?" Eric swallowed nervously.

"It is highly unlikely. And even if that were to happen, the suit would protect you from sustaining much harm. Give it a quick try."

"Much harm?" Eric groaned.

"Come on, Eric we have to go! It's like Superman. All he does is lift his hands and bam! He's off with Lois Lane," Archie stuck out both of his hands to demonstrate.

"Ok, ok." Eric breathed in deep. *Think about flying. Nothing complicated. Lift your hands and—*

A second later, Eric felt his feet lifting off the ground.

"Dude, you're floating. You're getting ready to fly!" Archie shouted excitedly.

"I'm not getting much higher, Chasub."

"That's because you need to focus more. Focus, Eric. You can do it.."

Eric closed his eyes concentrated.

Think about flying. Concentrate. Focus. That's it. When Eric finally opened his eyes, he could no longer see Archie.

"You're doing it, Eric. Stay focused. Now try to come down. All you have to do is use your mind. Focus," Chasub said.

"Aaaaaahhh!!!" Eric came plummeting towards the ground.

"Eric, you have to stop!" Chasub shouted.

Eric abruptly halted in midair, his face a foot above the concrete.

"Good," said Chasub.

"I almost crashed landed," Eric replied shakily.

"Almost. Now try again. This time, try going in different directions and increasing your speed."

Over the next few minutes, Archie observed Eric as he learned to master the suit's ability to fly.

"This is pretty easy, once you get the hang of it," Eric said as he did a midair summersault.

"Great, now you need to get going. We don't have much time!" Chasub insisted.

"Okay, Archie, are you ready?"

"Dude, I was born to fly!"

"Nice view, eh?" Eric asked as they soared over the trees.

"Amazing! I love it. This must be how Superman feels all of the time!"

"Alright, Lois."

"Whatever. This is awesome!"

"Can't argue with you there," Eric looked at a strip mall they were approaching. "We need to land for minute."

"There is no time," Chasub insisted. "You must hurry to the Omnidisk."

"First, I need to find something to cover Archie's face. He doesn't have anything to disguise his appearance, both of us could be exposed."

"Good thinking," Archie said as they landed behind one of the stores. "Maybe you could find something to use as a cape and maybe some cool looking boots."

Eric deactivated his suit. "We're tight on time. I'll get you something more basic for now."

Two minutes later, Eric ran out of the store and threw Archie a ski mask.

"A purple ski mask?" Archie frowned and wrinkled his nose as if the mask smelled. "I look like a tacky criminal

"We will make you something cooler later. Right now we need to get this mission over with." Eric activated his suit, grabbed Archie and they headed towards the outskirts of town.

"Eric, please don't say anything out loud but I strongly believe your friend is a liability. After this mission I think we should discuss the pros and cons of working along with him in the future," Chasub said.

Eric sighed. *Maybe he's right. I want Archie's help but what if he gets hurt?*

"I just remembered something," Archie said as they approached their destination.

"You'd better not ask for another costume," Eric warned.

"No, it's not that. I was thinking that maybe we should come up with some cool super-hero names. I mean, I can't call you Eric in front of the bad guys."

"That… that's a good point," Eric admitted. "What do you think Chasub, can you choose some codenames for us?"

"No way!" Archie objected. "My idea, I should choose the names."

"Fine," Chasub said. "I do admit no codename was an oversight."

"He said go ahead," Eric said.

"Excellent!" Archie grinned. "I can be…Xenoshot!"

"Xeno…what?" Eric asked.

"Xenoshot. It's a character I created in a comic book I wrote years ago. He had a ray gun and was able to shoot it with deadly accuracy."

"Whatever. Not sure how I will remember it, but okay. What's mine?"

"Hmmm…since you can fly now…tell me, what's your favorite bird?"

"I'm not sure where you're heading with this, but I guess I like hawks and falcons."

"Excellent. You are now the Crimson Falcon!"

"Maybe I should assign you a number," Chasub suggested. "These names don't seem to carry the dignity of the assignment."

"The Crimson Falcon!" Eric smiled. "I like it. And it looks like we're here."

"Be careful, Eric" Chasub said.

"We will," Eric smiled at Archie. "And remember, during missions we're Crimson Falcon and Xenoshot."

CHAPTER 8

"*Drakeston Onstage,*" Archie read a worn-out sign that was hidden underneath a bush of dry leaves.

"I don't think I've ever been here before. What about you, Archie?"

"Xenoshot, remember? No more real names, Crimson Falcon."

"I am sensing a human life form inside," Chasub said.

"Here's to hoping they're in the mood to talk."

Inside, the air was thick with the odor of dust. Cobwebs and old folding chairs were everywhere. The curtains that draped the dirty windows were tattered and torn. The stage was in desperate need of repair.

Xenoshot walked over to a closet. "This place hasn't been used for quite some time. There's nothing in this closet except spiders."

"Good. Perfect place for you to stay."

"What? I thought we were a team! I can't help you from in there!"

"Yes, you can," Crimson Falcon put a hand on his shoulder. "You will be my element of surprise in case something happens."

Xenoshot smiled and nodded. "Alright, Crimson Falcon. I'll follow your lead."

Crimson Falcon watched as Xenoshot got into the closet.

"Be careful, Eric. I mean, Crimson Falcon. I'm detecting a life form headed your way."

"Thanks, Chasub." Before Crimson Falcon could end the conversation, he heard a voice.

"I'm sorry, young man, but there are no shows today. Try returning in a day or two. We will be accepting auditions at that time."

Crimson Falcon turned around to find a short, plump and partly bald man walking out from behind one of the stage curtains. He wore a hideous bright purple suit with a cape to match.

"Doesn't seem as if you've had in any business in quite some time."

The man chuckled. "You're quite wrong. I perform for the crowds every week."

"What crowds? Doesn't look as if this place has seen a crowd in centuries," Crimson Falcon stated.

"They come. I tell you that they come. They come for the greatest mastermind on earth! The show of all shows!" The man flipped his cape over his shoulder.

"Oh, I see." Crimson Falcon tried to sound sincere.

"You mock me!" The man's eyes flashed with anger

"No, I'm sure you're right," Crimson Falcon couldn't hide his grin

"NO! I will show you. I will show you my power, and you will be amazed." The man lifted his hands over his head.

Suddenly, the man began to lift an old sign over his head without touching it with his hands.

"Do you see? Do you see the power of the greatest mastermind on earth? Behold!"

"It's the Omnidisk. He must be using its power. You've got to get it from him before it alters his mind even more than it already has," Chasub stated.

"I know. I know. Let me handle this." Crimson Falcon took a step towards the stage "You're right, your powers are amazing. What's your name?"

"I am the great Maison. The greatest mastermind on earth!"

"Right." Crimson Falcon took another small step.

Maison watched him carefully. He began to grow nervous.

"Tell me something, Maison, how did you get your amazing power?"

"Well… I…I have always had these abilities."

Crimson Falcon took a few more steps until he was standing at the edge of the stage.

"Are you sure it didn't come from a small metal disk?"

Maison went pale. "How do you know about that?"

"Maison, have you been feeling weak lately? Tired, fatigued even?"

Maison took a step backwards. "I have been under a lot of stress lately. I…I put on a show every week. It's nothing that the great Maison can't handle."

"No, I'm sure it isn't." Crimson Falcon placed one foot on the stage. "Maison, that small disk is called an Omnidisk," the hero whispered, choosing his words carefully. "The Omnidisk requires specific DNA in order to use it. Your symptoms will only get worse. It will kill you. You have to give it to me, for your own protection." Crimson Falcon walked on the stage and held out his hand. "Please."

"I will never give away my power." Maison's voice was almost a whisper.

"Maison—" Crimson Falcon took a step towards him, still reaching out his hand.

"Never!

An unseen force hit Crimson Falcon, sending him sailing off the stage and into some chairs.

"You won't take it! I'll kill you first!" A crowbar floated alongside Maison. The end of it was pointed at Crimson Falcon. "I'm sorry, but I have to keep my power."

The crowbar flew straight at Crimson Falcon's head.

"Aaaah!" Crimson Falcon caught it right before it hit his head.

"Crimson Falcon, discard the rod and retrieve the Omnidisk!" Chasub commanded.

Crimson Falcon grunted as he held the crowbar above his head, struggling as it continued to press down on him. "I can't! He's still trying to kill me with it!"

Maison held out his hand, willing the crowbar towards Crimson Falcon's head.

"I can't hold it much longer!" Crimson Falcon's voice was strained.

Tseeew! A green energy beam grazed Maison's arm.

"Aaaaah!!" Maison screamed and grabbed his injured arm.

Crimson Falcon threw the crowbar away as Xenoshot ran over to him.

"Nice shot, buddy," Crimson Falcon complimented Xenoshot, getting to his feet.

"I've watched Han Solo enough to know how it's done," Xenoshot said with pride. "And that was on Level 1. Ooof!"

A chair hit Xenoshot in the back, knocking him off his feet. Crimson Falcon dodged another chair aimed at his head.

"I don't want to have to hurt you," Crimson Falcon warned.

"Makes my job a lot easier," Maison hurled two more chairs at Crimson Falcon.

"Have it your way!" Crimson Falcon avoided the last two chairs and flew at Maison, shoving him hard.

"Ack!" Maison fell to the floor.

"Please, give me the Omnidisk." Crimson Falcon walked towards him.

"You can't beat me." Maison waved his hand in the air, pushing Crimson Falcon off of the stage and onto the floor. He rose into the air, floating towards Crimson Falcon and Xenoshot.

"Arch— I mean, Xenoshot! Shoot him!"

Tseeew! Tseeew! Tseeew! Xenoshot fired three shots at Maison. The beams disappeared a foot in front of the would-be magician.

"He's protecting himself using some kind of force field!" Xenoshot said, firing two more shots at Maison. "He's using his powers to create a barrier. The illuminator isn't having any affect! That's so cool!!! Whoa!"

Maison mentally lifted Xenoshot off of the ground and threw him into the wall on the other side of the theatre.

Crimson Falcon gasped. "That is a powerful Omnidisk."

"So, you see why you need to retrieve it now!" Chasub said.

Crimson Falcon flew at Maison again.

"Stop!" Maison held up his hand.

Crimson Falcon stopped in midair, unable to move. Xenoshot pointed the illuminator at Maison.

"I warned you that you would not win." Maison waved his other hand, sending the illuminator out of Xenoshot's hands and across the room. The crowbar lifted off the floor and angled itself at Crimson Falcon again. "I will keep the device, and you will die."

"I'm afraid you are only half right, my good man," Slymind and Mange walked in the front door. "*We* will take the device, and he will die. As will you."

Tzzzzzap! Mange fired his eye beams at Maison.

"Aaaaah!" The beams hit Maison in his chest, making him fall to the floor and lose his hold on Crimson Falcon.

"Mange, grab the man in red. I will secure the device," Slymind ordered.

Mange grunted in agreement, flapped his wings and took to the air.

"Two can play that game," Crimson Falcon said as he flew at Mange.

Tzzzzzap! Crimson Falcon dodged Mange's eye beams and hit him in his midsection, throwing the monster off balance. Crimson Falcon rushed forward and punched him twice in the face. Mange blocked the third punch and spun around, hitting Crimson Falcon with his tail and sending him crashing into the floor.

"We can do this one of two ways," Slymind said, walking over to the still fallen Maison. "Painful or very painful. I would hand over that device if I were you."

"No, no, no!!! The disk is mine! None of you freaks will ever lay hands on it!" Maison leapt to his feet and waved his left hand, and instantly all of the chairs in the room flew at Slymind.

Slymind stretched his elastic neck and limbs and dodged all of the chairs flying at him.

"Your power may not be able to overcome any normal human foe, but mark my words, you will not defeat me!" Slymind punched Maison in the face. Maison fell to the ground, holding his jaw. He looked at Slymind.

"I don't care what powers you have; I can control the movements of anything I want!" He held out his hand, pointing it at Slymind. "Including you!"

"What's going on?!" Slymind floated off the ground.

"I told you. I will not let you take my disk." Maison floated Slymind to a column in the middle of the theater.

"What are you doing?! Stop!" Slymind's body was tied in knots around the column until he was completely immobile.

Maison smiled and walked towards the door. Xenoshot grabbed his illuminator off of the floor and ran after him. When he had almost reached him, Xenoshot raised the illuminator, leveled it at his back and fired.

Tseeew! Maison turned around and blocked the shot. He waved his hand at Xenoshot and snatched the illuminator from him. Xenoshot suddenly found himself unable to move. The illuminator floated in front of him and saw the setting on the side increase to ten.

Crimson Falcon kicked Mange in the face and knocked him backwards. He happened to look over and see the predicament Xenoshot had gotten into.

"Xenoshot!" Crimson Falcon tried to fly to him, but Mange grabbed his leg and slammed him into the ground.

"I am not sure how this weapon works," Maison said. "But I am confident that if fired on the highest setting, it will stop you from bothering me for a long time."

Xenoshot's diverted his eyes to the door as he saw Dark Viper silently walked in and slipped around Maison, being sure to stay out of his line of sight.

"Look behind you!" Xenoshot yelled.

Maison laughed. "Nice try."

Thud! Dark Viper hit him in the head and he fell to the floor. Xenoshot and the illuminator fell with him. Dark Viper glanced at Xenoshot and began rummaging through Maison's pockets. Xenoshot slowly reached for the illuminator.

Mange backhanded Crimson Falcon, the force of the blow throwing him off his feet. When he fell, he saw the crowbar lying on the floor next to him. He grabbed it, jumped to his feet and punched Mange in the stomach. When he doubled over, Crimson Falcon hit him in the head with the crowbar and made him fall to the floor.

"Grrrraahhhh!" Mange cried out as Crimson Falcon hit him in the head again, this time with all his strength behind the blow. Mange groaned but he didn't move.

Crimson Falcon flew over to Xenoshot right as he was aiming the illuminator at Dark Viper.

"Xenoshot, don't!" Crimson Falcon stopped Xenoshot before he could shoot. "He's on our side…I think."

Tseeew! Tseeew! Tseeew! Tseeew! Tseeew! Xenoshot redirected the aim of his illuminator and fired off an array of beams at Slymind, who had gotten free and was attempting to attack the group.

"Aaaah!" Slymind screamed out as one caught in his shoulder. Another hit his leg. He hit the floor and stayed there.

"He's got the Omnidisk!" Xenoshot shouted.

Crimson Falcon flew over to Dark Viper. "What are you doing?"

Dark Viper looked him in the eye. "Saving lives. Very evil beings are after this technology. I must keep it in my care."

"What are you going to do with it?"

"It made me who I am today. I need to examine its technology and find a way to turn myself into who I used to be. I want to be human again."

"I can't let you have the Omnidisk, Dark Viper."

"Do what you must. As will I," Dark Viper said as the two glared at each other.

Crimson Falcon stood his ground. He was ready.

Dark Viper moved into position. Each man looked the other in the eye. Each ready to make their move.

"You!" Mange shouted as he grabbed Dark Viper, knocking the Omnidisk out of his hands.

Falcon snatched the Omnidisk off of the floor and grabbed Xenoshot.

"Let's get out of here."

As he and Xenoshot made their way out the door, he saw Dark Viper heading toward Mange, his staff out and ready.

That's one fight I don't need to stick around to watch.

CHAPTER 9

"Man, what a fight!" Xenoshot shouted gleefully after the duo were a safe distance away.

"Yeah, and thanks again for saving me," Crimson Falcon said. "I may not have gotten out of there without your help."

"We saved each other. Xenoshot and Crimson Falcon, saving the world, one Omnidisk at a time! Talk about exciting. I can't wait to do it again. When do we go after another one?"

"Slow down there, buddy, I've had enough excitement today."

"What? We've got to find all of them before those two clowns do, or better yet, before Dark Viper does. And I guess you have your answer now."

"What answer?" Crimson Falcon raised an eyebrow.

"You wondered if Dark Viper was a good guy or bad guy," Xenoshot reminded him.

"Yeah well, the jury is still out on that one." Crimson Falcon nodded his head, unwilling to concede the point. "He doesn't know us any more than we know him. Maybe in time we can convince him to help."

"Dude, he was about to slaughter you."

"I could have taken him."

"Yeah, sure, you could have. Did you see that bo staff of his? That thing was amazing! And he knew how to use it. He was like… Robin or something. The Dick Grayson version, not Jason Todd."

"Okay, maybe I couldn't have taken him," Crimson Falcon sheepishly admitted.

"I know. See you tomorrow at school?"

"Yeah, I'll see you tomorrow at school, Xenoshot."

Eric watched as Archie walked down the street toward his house. "Ok Chasub, I'm ready."

"Well done." Chasub said as Eric handed him the Omnidisk. "Only six more to retrieve."

"*Only* six? Feels like we have a hundred to go."

Chasub watched Eric. He knew something was bothering him.

"You're concerned about Dark Viper, aren't you?"

"I guess. I'd hoped that he would help us instead of fighting for himself. I had hoped he was one of the good guys."

"At least now we know what his agenda is, and why," Chasub stated matter-of-factly.

"Maybe we can help him," Eric said, thinking out loud. "He wants to fix himself. Why don't we find a way to cure him?"

"I intend to cure everyone affected by my actions," Chasub said. "But there is still more to discover about him. Over time, we may learn the whole truth."

"So, now what?"

"Eric, now might be a good time to discuss your decision to bring Archibald along."

Eric frowned. "He saved my life. He's the reason we got the Omnidisk!"

"I disagree. I think there is a good chance you would have succeeded on your own," Chasub said. "He has no powers and no protection. He could have been hurt."

Eric nodded his head. "Chasub, I failed my first mission. I couldn't get to the emerald in time. The augments had those holograms and it took Dark Viper's help just to lose! I need someone I trust to watch my back and I don't trust anyone more than Archie. He is the reason we are closer to completing our mission. He's my best friend and I want him by my side. End of story."

Chasub wasn't sure how to respond to Eric's rather sore mood. He knew Eric wasn't going to change his mind, so he decided to leave the matter alone. "I'll listen to your judgment for now. Why don't we practice using the new Omnidisk.? Being able to move items and even people with your mind requires precision."

Eric smiled a little and nodded his head. "You're right. Watching Maison was cool, even though he wanted me dead. I could use that to my advantage. Did you see the way he lifted Slymind off the floor and flung him across the room? That was so great!"

Chasub handed Eric the Omnidisk and pressed a panel on the wall. A small black box slid out.

"What's in the box?" Eric asked.

"Training materials. Inside are ten metal spheres," Chasub explained. "I want you to focus on making them float by thinking about it. Just reach out and feel them with your mind."

"No problem." Eric held out his hand and focused. One by one the spheres floated out of the box and hovered in the air.

"Excellent," Chasub complimented him. "Now try to move them around in a pattern."

Eric waved his hand and caused the spheres to move in a spiral motion.

"Well done. It doesn't look like learning to use this Omnidisk will be a problem for you," Chasub said.

Eric grinned. "Yeah, I guess I'm good at using my head after all."

Without warning, the metal spheres hit the floor.

"Eric, what's wrong?" Chasub asked.

Two second later, Eric gasped and fell to the floor as well.

Chasub rushed to his side. "Eric!"

"I'm fine, Chasub," Eric assured him. "Just a little woozy, most likely from all of the action today. I'm sure I'll be ok."

"I am not taking any chances," Chasub said. He opened another wall panel, this time pulling out a device that looked like a two-pronged fork.

"Hold still," Chasub instructed.

He pressed a button on the device and the prongs extended vertically until they were on either side of Eric's head, scanning Eric's entire body.

"I'm sure it's nothing, Chasub," Eric insisted.

Chasub stared intently at the device as it continued to scan Eric. "This is strange."

"What is it?" asked Eric, beginning to get concerned himself.

"Eric, give me the Omnidisk!"

"What? Why?"

"Don't argue, give it to me!"

Eric reluctantly handed over the Omnidisk. "What is it, Chasub? What's going on?"

"I'm not sure," Chasub said, pressing a few more buttons on his device.

Beams of light shot out from both prongs and connected with Eric's head. After a slight tingle went through his whole body, he felt like himself once more.

"Okay, are you going to tell me what happened?"

Chasub hung his head. "It's amazing, but for some reason this Omnidisk didn't connect with your DNA. It's strange because the one that I gave you did. You were feeling ill because the minute you started using the Omnidisk, it began to poison you with the same harmful energy all of the other unauthorized users who might use the Omnidisk experience. Fortunately, my machine was able to cure you."

"How is that possible?" Eric asked. "You said that the Omnidisks had selected me. Didn't you?"

"I did, but for some strange reason, this one didn't. In fact, if I'm reading this right, it selected someone else. This is incredible!"

Eric stood to his feet. "All of this was one big mistake? I'm not the chosen one? And that felt awful, what's going to happen to Maison?"

"Yes, you are, but apparently, you're not the only one. Quite remarkable, isn't it? Maison will be fine. After some time of not using the Omnidisks his body will recover. I merely helped you along."

"You're telling me that there is someone else out there who can operate the Omnidisk?"

"Yes, it appears to be so. At least for this one. They must be close by; perhaps someone even close to you."

"You mean, it could be someone I know?" Eric felt as if he was starting to get a headache again. This situation got more and more complicated.

"It is a possibility; most of this is still speculation," Chasub admitted.

"Speculation?! I've been getting my butt handed to me all afternoon, and now you tell me that I could have had help! Please try to do more than speculate."

Chasub placed the Omnidisk on a computer panel. "Now that I have the Omnidisk with the DNA encoded within, it might be easier to find this person than it was to find you. I can download the information directly into my computer instead of scanning at length. It will only take a day or two at most."

Eric shook his head in disbelief. "In a day or two? The way this week is going, that seems like a lifetime."

"You should go home now; I will contact you as soon as I acquire any new information. I promise."

Eric looked at his watch. "Oh no, my dad is going to have a total meltdown."

"All the more reason to hurry home. Keep your watch on at all times. You will hear from me soon."

Seconds later, Eric found himself standing on his front porch.

CHAPTER 10

"What are we going to say?" Mange asked as he and Slymind stood outside the door to their lair.

"I don't know," Slymind said as he stood against the wall, scratching his head.

"We could tell him that it wasn't there."

Slymind walked over and gave Mange a hard shove.

"What, are you trying to get us killed?"

"Like going in there without that disk isn't?"

Slymind didn't respond. For once, Mange had a good point.

"You had better think of something, and fast."

"Why don't you come up with the plan, Mange?"

"I'm the dumb one, remember?"

"Whatever. Let's go inside. I'll think of something," Slymind promised, hoping he sounded convincing.

"You had better… For both our sakes."

Mange and Slymind found Command working on his machine as they cautiously walked in.

"There you two are. I was merely adding some features to my creation. I would have done it earlier, but I had matters to attend to outside this facility."

"What do you do when you're not out looking for supplies?" Slymind asked

Command gave Mange a nasty look. "If I wanted you to know how I spend my days, I would tell you wouldn't I?"

Slymind shot Mange a look that told him to keep his mouth shut.

Command smiled. "Okay, where is it? I can't wait to get my hands on our first device. You two don't understand the significance of it, but I assure you that soon you will." Command reached out his hand like a kid in a candy store for the first time.

Slymind spoke. "Dark Viper and the guy in the costume got there before us."

"What?!" Command rarely yelled but he was incensed at this disappointing news.

"You said it yourself that somehow Dark Viper continues to know our every move. Well, this time, he used it to his advantage. The other guy took off with it before we even had a chance to retrieve it.," Slymind explained. "When he realized the guy in the costume left with the disk, he ditched us as well."

"A disk?" Command rubbed his chin. "Interesting. At least now you know what the items look like. But I'm tired of Dark Viper's interference. And who is this unknown man?"

"Mange and I are searching for him, but without knowing his identity, it will be difficult. But there was another guy there in a ski mask. He called him Crimson Falcon. The man in the mask went by Xenoshot."

"That ski mask was ugly," Mange added unhelpfully.

"Our enemies grow in number and now they have a disk," Command clenched his fist. "By my calculations there are only six more energy readings out there. We have to get them first!"

"Yes boss," the augments said as they glanced at each other.

Command took a deep breath and began to pace the floor. "We'll have to be quicker in finding the others. We can't let this happen again, now, can we?"

"No, sir," they both said.

Slymind could tell from the look in Command's eye that a lot hung on how he answered this question. "Sir. I think Crimson Falcon is connected as you initially thought. He called the device an Omnidisk. He seems to have some knowledge of how it works."

"Omnidisk. Interesting." Command studied Slymind and Mange carefully. "It's more important than ever that we find these men and bring them here. But in the meantime, I have another job that I need you two to take care of. I'm almost done with the machine, but I'm missing some critical components." Command walked over to a computer desk and grabbed a piece of paper. "I need everything on this list and I need it now!"

Slymind looked over the list.

"We will take care of it, sir."

"You had better, because, gentlemen—"

"Yes, sir."

"If you fail to come return with my list, like you failed to retrieve my disk, you two will become my next meal!"

"We understand, sir."

"Good. Now leave."

Slymind and Mange hurried out into the corridor, each wiping their foreheads with relief.

"Man, that was good thinking in there," Mange stated as he stared at Slymind.

"All I did was buy us some time. Let's go. We had better find everything on this list and fast."

As Eric opened the back door of his house, he tried frantically to figure out what he would say to his dad.

He tiptoed into the kitchen and confirmed the coast was clear before heading toward the stairs.

With each squeaky step, he could hear his heart pounding. *This is one of those nights I hope he's working late.*

"Eric?" his sister asked from behind him.

"Rebecca," he said under his breath before turning around.

"Hi, Rebecca," he said in a whisper. "Can you do me a huge favor?"

She nodded her head eagerly.

"I need you to be very quiet and not tell Dad that you saw me come in. Can you do that?"

She nodded again.

"Thank you."

Eric smiled. *Maybe she's not so bad after all*, he thought to himself as he quietly made his way up the steps.

Right as he hit the top step, he heard her.

"Daaaadyyyy!"

On the other hand, she could be the very essence of evil sent here to torment me.

Eric's father stomped out of the room and stood in front of him. Arms crossed. Anger written all over his forehead.

"I thought I told you to come home right after school today?"

"You did. I'm sorry; I was working on a project."

"A project?! It's eight-thirty! Why didn't you call, Eric? I just got home myself. Your sister was here with nobody to watch her!"

"I got delayed, Dad. I'm sorry."

Eric's dad stared at him. "Why weren't you in some of your classes today? I got a call from the school. Where have you been?"

"Archie and I skipped a few classes, mostly it was gym and stuff, to work on an important project," Eric lied.

"What class was this 'important' project for?"

"Ummm...Pre-cal," Eric said.

"Pre-calculus? Really?"

"Yeah! We had to do a project on numbers and their history and so on—"

"Save it," his dad snapped. "I already called Archie's house, and he told *his* parents that you two were out working on a science project. So, which one was it, Pre-Cal or science?"

"Dad—" Eric started.

"I don't want to hear it! You are grounded!"

"Grounded?" Eric's eyes widened. "I have important things to do. I have responsibilities!"

"What responsibilities? Go ahead and tell me. This is your opportunity to explain yourself." Eric's father looked at him silently.

After a few seconds Eric's gaze finally drifted to the floor. "I can't tell you."

Russell nodded. "I figured as much. Your grounding starts immediately. I can't believe you, Eric. This is so unlike you. You know I have a lot on me, trying to raise you two kids without your… Anyway, you're grounded and that's that."

Eric watched as his father walked to his room and closed the door. He turned around and saw his sister grinning from ear to ear before she trotted off.

I swear, after we take out the augments, she's going to be the next biggest threat to the planet.

Archie was the first person Eric saw as he walked into school the next day.

"Eric! You were supposed to call me last night and tell me how everything went," Archie said before noticing the look on Eric's face. "You look terrible; what happened?"

"For starters, my dad doesn't trust me at all now," Eric said gloomily. "He asked me where I was yesterday, and I told him I was with you…doing a math project."

Archie's face turned red. "Oh no! I told my parents—"

"I know. That's how he knew we were lying. Doesn't matter now anyway; I'm grounded."

"You can't be grounded. We have the biggest fight of our lives going on here!" Archie yelled.

Eric looked around and was shocked to see several people looking over. He grabbed Archie's arm and pulled him to the side.

"Quiet!" Eric whispered, "You are about to blow our cover."

"Sorry, I'm just surprised. How are we supposed to fight the augments with you in the brig?" Archie asked.

"Archie, you are killing me with the *Star Trek* references. And unfortunately, we still have more problems. That Mind Omnidisk we caught didn't have my DNA encoded into it."

"I thought the Omnidisks selected you?"

"They did. Well, most of them."

"So, what does this mean?"

"It means that we have to find out whose DNA it selected."

Archie's eyes grew wide. "How are we supposed to do that?"

"Chasub believes that whoever the Mind Omnidisk scanned was standing near me at the time, so it could be someone I know."

"Hey, maybe it's me!" Archie said enthusiastically. "You saw my skills yesterday with the illuminator. I was firing that thing like Bullseye."

"Ok, Mr. Bullsye, before you start saving the world, we have to get to class on time."

"**Mr.** Eric Daniels, Mr. Archie Patterson, right on time," said Jasonas they walked into the classroom. "We thought we were going to have to begin the lesson without you."

"Wouldn't dream of missing it, sir," Eric said with a grin.

"Sure, just like we were working on a math project yesterday. Forgive me, I mean a science project," Archie muttered.

Eric gave Archie a quick glare.

"Today we will be talking about Alexander the Great," Jason announced. "A true visionary. He looked around and saw a planet ripe for the taking, and he rallied his troops and took it. He demolished all obstacles and crushed all those who opposed him. He created a remarkable empire, whether people served him or not. He was a true hero of his time."

"He looks like he admires Alexander a little too much," Archie whispered to Eric.

"Archie, you would see a conspiracy in a five-year-old's lemonade stand."

"What would a five-year-old need with all that money anyway?" Archie asked.

Beep! Beep! Beep! Eric's watch started to go off.

"Chasub is calling *now*?" Archie asked

"It must be important," Eric said.

"What is that noise?" Jason asked.

"It's...uh...the timer on my watch. I have to take my medication!" Eric ran out of the classroom.

"He gets really sick if he doesn't take it on time. I should go help him." Before Jason could object, Archie ran after Eric.

Archie caught up with Eric right outside of the back door of the school. "That was the best excuse you could think of?"

"I didn't have time to think of a good story," Eric pushed a button on the watch. "Chasub, perfect timing as always."

"I am truly sorry to interrupt your educational experience," Chasub said. "I have great news. I have found the user of the Mind Omnidisk."

"Excellent!" Archie put his face in front of the screen. "When do I start my training?"

"It is not you, I'm sorry to say, Archibald."

"Aw, man." Archie bowed his head and stepped away.

"Sorry, man," Eric looked at his watch. "Who is this guy?"

"It's not a guy. It's a girl. I'm sending you a photo of her now."

"Brynn?" Eric said in a shocked tone. "It can't be."

"It is. The Mind Omnidisk selected her."

"That is so unfair! She's never even seen *Star Wars*!" Archie fumed.

Eric paced the floor for a moment. *Brynn, I can't believe it. Our Brynn?* He stared at the photo again. "Okay," he finally said. "This may not be so bad. I mean, we already know that she can take care of herself." Looking at Archie, he asked, "Remember that time when she told us that she took on that mugger?"

"Yeah, I remember," Archie said, still getting used to the idea that Brynn had been selected and not him. "She's a fighter."

"And we know we can trust her," Eric said. "And we also know you have a thing for her, so I don't see the problem."

Archie's face turned red "That's the last thing on my mind. How are you going to tell her?"

"I don't know, but I'll find a way after school."

"Man, she's going to freak out. What if she doesn't believe you?"

"You believed me; why shouldn't she?"

"Dude, it's me."

Eric looked at Archie with his favorite *Star Trek* shirt on. "Yeah, you have a point there. I'll have to convince her, that's all. She'll believe me. I know she will."

"Good; glad that's settled," Chasub stated, "because I have more news. I found another Omnidisk."

"Which Omnidisk is it?" Eric asked.

"The Brawn Omnidisk."

"What does it do?"

"It gives you super strength, to put it simply. I know you will find use for it."

"That was quick," Eric said with a slight hesitation in his voice.

"That's because it appears to be close to where you are now." Chasub paused for a moment before adding, "And don't worry; I'm positive this one can be used by you."

Eric let out a sigh of relief.

"I'm working on getting the exact location. The minute I do, you should be on your way."

"Great. Archie and I need to get to class before we both get in trouble. I'm already grounded for getting home so late yesterday."

"I'll check in with you when I have the coordinates."

"So, how are you going to have time to get the new Omnidisk and tell Brynn about all of this after school? Don't forget, you're grounded." Archie asked on the way to the classroom.

"I guess I'm going to have to take after you and be…creative." Eric sighed.

CHAPTER 11

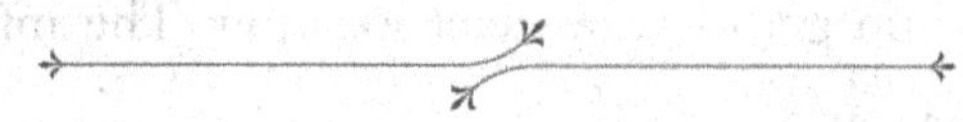

"Hi, Dad, it's me, Eric. I wanted to say that I'm sorry about yesterday. Archie and I were working on an important project. It wasn't school related, but it was important. I wish…I wish I could.…well, anyway, I know I'm grounded; I should have called. You were right… I'm sorry. But, Dad, here's the thing, please don't be angry at me, but I'm going to be home late once again. I'm sorry, Dad. I'm not trying to disappoint you. Trust me. Please," Having finished his voicemail, Eric hung up the phone.

"Do you think he'll still be mad?" Archie asked.

"Well, it's not like I'm lying… not exactly," Eric looked at the ground, unwilling to make eye contact. "And I am sorry for not calling."

"That wasn't the question."

"Does it matter?" Eric snapped. "What we have to do is more important than my grounding."

Archie put his hands in his pocket. "I surrender. Sorry."

"I'm not trying to take anything out on you," Eric explained. "I have a lot on my mind right now, and the Omnidisks are more important than my family issues. I need to focus."

"You're nervous about telling Brynn, aren't you?"

"Yeah, I guess I am."

"She's known you for years, so I know she will believe you."

"I hope so."

Three guys ran down the hall, flying toward Eric and Archie.

"Move out of the way, wuss!" One of the guy shoved Archie on to the floor as he passed.

Eric glared at the offender as he kept running.

"It's fine, Eric." Archie picked himself off. "I wonder what's going on?"

Eric shrugged his shoulders. "Let's go see."

As Eric and Archie got closer, they noticed that a huge group of kids were standing around in a circle. Someone was fighting in the center, but neither of them could make out who it was.

"Excuse me, sorry, pardon me." Eric pushed his way through the crowd with Archie right behind him.

"Oh no," said Eric when he saw what had everyone's attention.

Travis had pushed Will into some lockers with his fists in his face.

"So, you want to make fun of my hair? Let's see if your fists are as fast as your mouth." Travis yanked Will by the shirt and slammed him into the lockers. "I owe you extreme pain!"

"And usually I insist that all debts be paid promptly, but in your case an IOU will be fine," Will said with a nervous but painful chuckle.

"Nah, I'm the kinda guy who likes to pay what I owe." Travis made a fist and drew back his arm.

"Get off of him, Travis!"

Travis released Will and turned around to find Eric staring him in the face.

"I am so SICK OF YOU!!!" Travis swung and landed a fierce jab into Eric's chest, sending him sliding down the hallway.

"Leave him alone!" Archie screamed as he jumped on Travis' back.

In one quick motion, Travis threw Archie headfirst into the lockers across the hall.

"Now it's your turn." Travis laughed as he turned to Will.

"No, it's yours!" Will punched Travis in the stomach as hard as he could. "Ow!" He held his hand in pain, feeling as if he had punched a brick wall.

Travis grinned and cracked his knuckles.

"I don't suppose an apology would help at this point," Will said weakly.

Two school police officers ran toward them.

"This isn't worth the trouble. I'll take care of you later." Travis ran down the hallway and out the door.

"Are you alright?" Eric asked Will, who was still holding his hand in pain.

"I'll be fine. Check on Archie."

Eric turned around and gasped before running to Archie's side.

"Archie, are you okay?!" Eric asked, nudging him.

Archie groaned. "Huh? Ouch, my head."

"You'll be ok," Eric promised.

"Thanks, Super Geek." Will smiled. "You've got spine."

The two police officers walked over to where the boys were.

"I think he needs to see the school nurse," Eric told them.

"We'll get him to the nurse immediately," said one of the officers as they helped Archie to his feet.

"Do me a favor and keep an eye on him," Eric said to Will.

"You're not coming?" he asked.

"I wish I could, but I have something important to do."

Will nodded. "I'll call you if anything happens."

Eric walked out of the building and contacted Chasub.

"Yes, Eric?"

"I think I might have found the Omnidisk," Eric informed him.

"I know. I sent the coordinates to your watch."

"No, I mean, I think I know who has been using the Omnidisk."

"Who?"

"Yeah. There's a guy here in school with strength beyond what is normal. He used it to attack a friend of mine a few minutes ago."

"That explains why it was so close. Good work. You need—"

"I know. I need to get it from him as soon as possible. I got it."

"Time is of the essence, Eric. We don't know if the augments know about this one or not."

"I'm going, but I still have to tell Brynn. With all of the excitement I didn't get a chance to talk to her," Eric admitted.

"Well, according to my scans you will get an opportunity very soon. She is closing in on your position," Chasub said.

"Eric!" Brynn called, walking over. "I've been looking for you!"

Eric switched off his watch and turned to her. "Oh, really? Why?"

"I heard about the fight from one of my friends, and I wanted to check on you and see if you were ok. Please tell me that you at least put Travis in a full body cast because—"

"Brynn, hold on a sec," Eric cut her off. "We need to talk."

"Sure, but if it's going to take a long time, you're going to have to ride with me to the office. They said Archie is there and—"

"Brynn!"

"What?"

"This is serious."

"What's more important than checking on your best friend?

"How about saving the world?"

She gave Eric a frown.

"Really, Eric?"

Eric looked around to be sure no one was listening.

Brynn watched him. She began to get nervous. It wasn't like him to act like this.

Eric leaned over and began whispering in her ear. He told her everything, starting from the encounter in the convenience store to the recovery of the Mind Omnidisk. By the time he was done, Brynn was standing with her arms crossed and a slightly amused look on her face.

"Is that it?" she said with a small smile.

"Yeah, that's all of it," Eric responded. "Do you have any questions? Any comments? Any reaction at all?"

Brynn looked at Eric for a few seconds. Then, to his surprise, she started laughing.

"Brynn?" Eric was worried she was having a mental breakdown.

"Eric, you are a funny guy. I don't know whether to hit you or tell you to enter a storytelling contest," Brynn said with a chuckle. "The way you said all that, I almost thought you were serious."

"Brynn, I am serious!" Eric insisted.

"Ha, ha, ha! That's priceless! I think you have been spending too much time with Archie." She glanced at her watch. "Anyway, I need to get out of here. It's a good thing I have a sense of humor."

Eric stood still, completely stunned as she walked past him and towards the parking lot.

"Brynn, wait!"

She turned around, this time looking a little annoyed. "Eric, you had your fun, but now I'm going to the mall."

Eric opened his mouth to object again but stopped. "Aright, since you don't believe me; I can prove it."

He grabbed her by the arm and headed toward a large bush.

"Eric, what are you doing?"

Once they reached a secluded spot, he let go of her arm. "Stand back."

"Why?

"Just do it."

Brynn moved a few steps away from Eric.

Eric pushed a button on his watch. A few seconds later, he had his full suit on.

"What? Eric, what did you do?" Brynn's face turned pale. After a moment, it began to turn red. "Are you playing some kind of trick on me? This isn't funny; I want to know what's going on now!"

"Brynn, this is not a trick. This is the suit I told you about, the one Chasub gave me. I'm Crimson Falcon."

"No, that is not true. There are no such things as aliens, Eric, and nothing you say or do can— What in the world?!"

In the middle of Brynn's rant, Crimson Falcon picked her up.

"Eric Daniels, you are two seconds away from a black eye! You drop me right now before I— Aaaaaahhh!"

Before Brynn knew what was happening, she and Crimson Falcon were airborne.

"Believe me now?" he asked as he soared over the school.

"How?" was all Brynn was able to squeak out.

"I explained all of this to you. All of it is true; you have to believe me now."

"I…I don't know. There are a lot of explanations for this. Defying gravity is one thing, but aliens? That is one thing I will never believe until I…" A blue light surrounded them. A second later, they were standing in front of Chasub on his ship.

"….see it for myself," Brynn finished.

Crimson Falcon smiled. "Are you convinced now?"

"Brynn, it is a pleasure to make your acquaintance," Chasub said, floating over to her. "I trust that Crimson Falcon has filled you in on all of the pertinent details."

"You're an—" Brynn's eyes were glued to Chasub, wide and unbelieving.

"Yes, I am an extraterrestrial. I'm glad we have got that out of the way." Brynn was still staring at him in disbelief.

"I know it's hard to digest all of this so fast—but fast you must. I'm sure Crimson Falcon told you there is a very important matter that requires urgent attention. The Brawn Omnidisk must be recovered immediately, and with Archibald incapacitated we need your help more than ever."

"I don't know what to say. It all seems so unreal." Brynn's eyes were travelling all over the room.

"I am sorry that we must do all of this so quickly, but there is an important mission that you must handle. Will you help us?" Chasub asked.

"You'll get a good fight out of it," Crimson Falcon promised.

Brynn took a moment or two to stare at both of them. "Then I guess I'm in," she said with a very nervous smile.

Crimson Falcon nodded. "There's our answer. Chasub, let's get her some gear."

Chasub floated over to the wall and opened a sliding panel. Inside was a dark blue watch that looked exactly like Crimson Falcon's. He held it out to Brynn.

Brynn took the watch out of Chasub's hand, giving him a little pinch while doing so.

"Okay, so you're real," she finally admitted.

"Please put that on," Chasub requested, looking annoyed.

Brynn looked at Crimson Falcon.

"It's safe," he assured her.

Brynn put the watch on her wrist and turned to Chasub.

Chasub began to point out the function of each button.

"You mean I'll get a suit like Eric's?" Brynn asked.

"Similar," responded Chasub. "Your suit will look slightly different, but it will contain all of the functions that Crimson has, with the exception of the anti-gravity generator."

"So, I won't be able to fly?" Brynn frowned.

"Incorrect." Chasub retrieved the Mind Omnidisk from next to a computer console. "This Omnidisk will allow you to fly as well as control the movement of other objects with your mind."

Chasub handed Brynn the Mind Omnidisk. She closed her eyes and felt a wave of energy go through her. When she opened them, it dissipated as fast as it had come.

"Wow," she whispered.

"Yeah, it's pretty intense," Crimson Falcon said.

"I do not have time to give you a thorough training of how to use the Omnidisk, but I can help you to understand the basics before I send you off," Chasub said this as he retrieved the box with the metal balls in them. "I would like you to make these spheres float into the air and try to control their movement."

"How could I do that?" Brynn asked. "That is impossible."

"Not with the Mind Omnidisk." Crimson Falcon walked over and put his hand on her shoulder. "You have the power of telekinesis now; you can pull this off. Focus."

Brynn held out her arm and concentrated. The spheres floated into the air.

"Good," Chasub said. "Now try to move them around."

In fifteen minutes, Brynn was making shapes with the spheres and moving them in different direction.

"Very impressive indeed," Chasub complimented her.

"Thank you," she said and turned to Crimson Falcon. "I think I'm starting to like this. I could bash some heads with this kind of superpower."

Crimson Falcon looked at his watch. "Well, you are going to get your chance, because it's about time for us to go have a little talk with Travis."

"And I definitely don't want to miss out on that!" Brynn slammed her fist into her palm.

"Before you leave, there is one more action I would like you to attempt," Chasub said.

"Anything; I like a challenge."

"I want you to focus and try to make yourself float in the air."

"I can do that?" Brynn asked in a skeptical tone.

"Yes, you can," Chasub assured her.

"Ok. Let's do this." Brynn closed her eyes and put out both hands.

"It takes a lot of concentration, but I know you can do it," Crimson said with a nod.

Within seconds, Brynn's feet left the ground. "I'm doing it!" she laughed.

"Yes, now don't lose focus. Try to move yourself higher," Chasub instructed.

Brynn floated a few feet higher and flew a few circles around Crimson Falcon and Chasub.

"She is, as you would say, a natural," Chasub said with admiration as Brynn flew past again.

"So do you think she's ready now?" Crimson Falcon asked, looking at his watch again and shifting impatiently.

"I know I am," Brynn said as she took another pass.

"Good. I suggest you suit up," Crimson Falcon replied.

"So how does this work? I just press the button?"

"That is correct," said Chasub. "The suit will materialize instantly."

Brynn nodded and braced herself as a blue light surrounded her and her clothes began to shift.

"Look in the panel," Chasub told her.

"Wow!" Brynn stared at her navy blue suit. It covered her from her feet to her neck. She played with the belt that wrapped around her waist and loved the black stripe that went along the sides. As she touched her face, she could feel the material of her mask, which covered everything around the eyes and the ridge of the nose, leaving a black opening for her eyes. When she turned around, she noticed a small hole in the back of the mask.

"Boy, you sure thought of everything," she said as she pulled her hair through the hole and into a ponytail. I love it!" She looked at her costume once again. "It matches my eyes."

"The mask will alter other's perception of you, hiding your identity. The compartment on the front of the belt is made to hold your Omnidisk," Chasub stated as he went over to the computer console and began typing. "I have located Travis; I will fling you two near his coordinates."

"Are you sure you're ready for this?" Crimson Falcon asked Brynn.

Brynn flashed one of her famous smiles. "Are you kidding? I was born ready."

"Flinging now," Chasub announced. "Be careful but get the Omnidisk."

CHAPTER 12

"I love that teleporting machine! What a rush! Brynn cheered.

"Personally, I'm not a huge fan, but it's growing on me," Crimson Falcon responded as he immediately began scanning for the Omnidisk. "Travis isn't far from here."

"You should be arriving at his location in a few minutes. Be careful and—" Chasub said.

"Get the Omnidisk," Crimson Falcon said, completing Chasub's sentence. "We're moving."

Brynn looked around. "Where is he? I know I heard him."

"There is an audio and video link that connects us to him through our masks."

"Oh. I am going to have to get used to that. Any more surprises I should know about?"

"I'm sure there are for both of us." Crimson Falcon chuckled. "Chasub seems to operate on a need-to-know basis."

"You two can converse later. Travis is on the move. If you fly, you can make it to him much quicker," Chasub stated.

Crimson Falcon glanced at Brynn. "You ready to try this?"

"I think so; just have to focus, right?"

"Right, you can do it. Think about flying." He glanced her way again. "I'll see you there. Remember to focus."

She gave him a nervous wink.

Crimson Falcon took off into the air, but he stopped when he noticed that Brynn wasn't behind him.

"Having some trouble?" he asked.

"I can't seem to get more than two feet over the ground."

"It's a little harder out here in the open air. Here grab my hand."

"Are you sure it's safe?"

"Mostly. Come on, Archie did it."

"Archie is crazy."

"I'm going to guide you until you get the hang of it. I promise I won't let go until you tell me too."

"Okay, I trust you." It was one of the few times Crimson Falcon had ever heard nervousness in his friend's voice. She was always so brave.

"Don't worry; consider it another challenge!" Crimson Falcon filled his voice with confidence.

"Time is of the essence!" Chasub cut in.

Bryan grabbed Crimson Falcon's hand and they both soared into the coolness of the mid-evening air.

"Wow. This is amazing," she said.

"It is, isn't it. Don't tell Archie this, but now I know how Superman must have felt."

"You're right, never tell Archie." Brynn laughed. "He already thinks he lives in a comic book."

Crimson Falcon saw Brynn take a deep breath.

"You're doing great. Are you ready for me to let go?"

"Yeah, I think so."

"I'll be right here, just in case," he promised.

"That more like it!" Brynn shouted as she felt herself able to go faster

"Look at you!" Crimson Falcon laughed.

"This is awesome!"

Crimson Falcon watched her go faster and faster.

"Hey, wait up!"

"Come on, slow-poke."

"Who you calling slow?"

He increased his speed and flew next to her.

"I was thinking."

"Thinking what?" she shouted.

"I was thinking that we're going to have to think of a codename for you."

"A what?"

"A codename. Archie brought it to my attention before; we can't run around calling each other by our real names. If we do that, we'll get caught in no time. Any ideas?"

Brynn took a few moments to consider it. "What do you call it when someone is a lot smarter than most people? Like a braniac?" she asked.

"A prodigy?" Crimson Falcon guessed.

"Yes, that's it!" she said. "I want my name to be Prodigy. I think it fits since this Omnidisk is supposed to supercharge my mind."

"Okay, Prodigy it is. I like it."

"Thanks. You think Archie would be proud?"

"I think he'll be mad I gave you a name without him. Look, there's Travis!" Crimson Falcon said, pointing toward the ground.

Travis was lurking in an alleyway behind a movie theatre. He walked over to the back door. After making sure no one was watching, he pulled the door right off the hinges.

"Travis, drop it!" Crimson Falcon ordered as he and Prodigy landed a few feet away from him.

"Who the heck are you?" Travis was still holding the door in his hand.

"We're here to help you; we don't want any trouble," Crimson Falcon said, raising his hands as a sign of peace.

"Speak for yourself," said Prodigy. "I say we beat him up *and* down."

Crimson Falcon shook his head. "Let's try to avoid a fight with the guy with super strength."

"You two need to get out of here now!" Travis growled.

"Why don't you drop the door and let me talk to you for a minute!" Crimson Falcon suggested.

"I don't want to talk. You need to shut up before I crush you with this door!" Travis waved the door around threateningly.

"Now can we fight him?" Prodigy asked.

Crimson Falcon reached out his hand. "Travis, we know about the device you have, the one that makes you strong."

Travis froze. "Who told you about that!"

"That's not important, what is important is—"

Travis flung the door at Crimson Falcon. It slammed into his chest and sent him crashing into the far wall of the alley.

"Falcon!" Prodigy kneeled next to Crimson Falcon. "Are you alright?"

Crimson Falcon coughed and held his chest in pain. "*Now* you can get him."

"Thank you!" Prodigy floated a few feet in the air and flew towards Travis with a smile.

"You got a problem, little girl?" said Travis with a sneer.

Prodigy waved her right hand, mentally throwing Travis into a pile of trash.

"No problem here." Prodigy smiled. "Now, are you going to give me that Omnidisk?"

"No way!" Travis yelled, lifting his head.

"I was hoping you would say that."

Travis climbed to his feet and grabbed a pipe that was nearby. "Take this!" He hurled the pipe at her.

Prodigy raised her hands, stopping the pipe in midair before it could reach her, but Travis grabbed what was left of a tire and threw it at her full force. It slammed into her before she had enough time to react and she fell toward the ground.

"Gotcha!" Crimson Falcon said as he caught her right before she hit the pavement. "Stay here and catch your breath; I'll take it from here."

He turned his attention toward Travis. His nostrils flared with anger.

Travis laughed. "What? You're mad 'cause your little girlfriend got a tire handed to her? Come on, you want some too?"

Crimson Falcon clenched his fists.

"This is your last chance, Travis."

"Bring it!"

Crimson shot into the air and charged at Travis at full speed. His fist connected with Travis' face, powered by all of the anger for what he'd done to his friends.

The hit ricked Travis backward.. Crimson Falcon wasted no time. He came at Travis again, slamming into him with a series of intense punches into the chest.

Travis reached out and grabbed Crimson Falcon's body, holding him for a second before flinging him into the side of a dumpster.

Travis reached into his pocket and pulled out the small orange Omnidisk. "You want this, freak? Come and take it!"

As Crimson Falcon struggled to get to his feet, Travis rushed toward him and grabbed him by the throat with one hand.

His grip was tight, forcing Crimson Falcon against the dumpster. Crimson Falcon tried reaching out for the Omnidisk.

Travis taunted him. "Too strong for you."

Crimson Falcon could barely breathe. His body was getting weak.

"Crimson Falcon!" Chasub shouted with fear in his voice.

"Put him down, Travis!" Prodigy raised her hands over her head and several bricks rose with them.

"What are you going to do, little girl?"

"This!" She threw her hands forward and the bricks flew at Travis.

Travis released Crimson Falcon, dropping him to the ground like a rag doll.

"You're going to have to try something heavier than that." Travis used his arm to protect himself and the bricks bounced off him without leaving a scratch. He slid the Omnidisk into his pocket and walked toward her.

"Fine, have it your way." Prodigy focused all her thoughts on the dumpster. It began to move. "Can a little girl do this?" she asked as she flung the dumpster at him.

Travis caught the dumpster and threw it back at her.

"Lights out!" he yelled before it left his hands.

Prodigy used her powers to try and stop the dumpster, but it was coming at her too fast. The impact sent her reeling across the alleyway into a pile of trash.

"I hope you have a plan," Chasub said.

"I do," Crimson Falcon said confidently.

"Good, what is it?"

"I'm going to hit him as hard as I can."

"That plan seems to have a low chance of success, but as I cannot offer a better one, I hope it works." Chasub's calm tone seemed strange under the circumstances.

"You and me both. Travis!" Crimson Falcon shouted. "I'm not done with you yet."

Travis removed the Omnidisk from his pocket again.

"What? You still want this? Come and get it!"

Crimson Falcon lunged at Travis, hitting him with the full force of his body. Travis barely budged.

Crimson Falcon stumbled back, his whole body in pain. "Chasub, if you have a plan B, now would be a great time to use it. I don't know how much longer I can handle this guy."

Meanwhile, at the school, Archie and Will were leaving the nurses' office.

"Are you sure you can get home ok?" Will asked. "Because, if you need help...I'm sure somebody around here can give you a ride."

"Funny, Will, but no thanks, I'll be okay," Archie said with more confidence than he felt. He never felt that comfortable around Will and didn't want to be around him longer than necessary.

"Cool. I'm out." Will walked down the hall in the opposite direction.

Archie rubbed his head as he stepped outside. He cut across some bushes and was about to hit the sidewalk when a bright light encircled his entire body.

"What in the world is—?!"

"Welcome aboard, Archibald," Chasub said. "Crimson Falcon needs your assistance right away."

"You're Chasub!" Archie exclaimed. "And this is your ship! This is so amazing and—"

"Archibald! Please focus!" Chasub raised his voice. "Crimson Falcon and Prodigy are in grave danger, and you are the only one who can help them."

"I'm sorry?" Archie apologized. "It's just that...I've dreamed about this day my entire life and now—"

Chasub cut him off. "Archibald!"

"Sorry. Right, Crimson Falcon and who, need my help?"

"Crimson Falcon and Prodigy, or 'Brynn' as you know her, are fighting Travis. We discovered that he has the Brawn Omnidisk. He has been using it for its power of super strength," Chasub explained.

"I knew it! I knew that he was—"

"Archibald!"

"What? Oh, yeah, right. Crimson Falcon and Prodigy. Got it. What do you need me to do?"

"The illuminator, do you have it?" Chasub asked

"Of course, I've been sleeping with it next to me ever since Eric gave it to me."

"Good. Now, take this," Chasub pressed a button on the wall and a panel slid out. Inside it was a black watch that looked exactly like Eric and Brynn's.

"Wow," Archie gingerly picked up the watch as if it was made of glass. "I'm really part of the team now."

"Activate your uniform," Chasub ordered. "We need to get you there."

"This is so awesome!" Archie said as he pressed the transformation button.

He was surrounded by a silver light. When it faded, he was in his uniform. It was a lot different than the others. He was wearing black boots, black pants, and a black jacket. They all had a silver line going down the side. His mask was basically a high-tech pair of silver sunglasses. His jacket was open exposing a black shirt. It had a unique silver symbol in the middle. The symbol was a silver circle with a black teardrop type shape going through the center, the shallow end stopping the circle from closing. The upper left-hand corner and the lower right-hand corner had several small squares inside the circle. Finally, the top half of the symbol was a lighter shade of silver, while the bottom half was a significantly darker shade.

"This is great," Xenoshot looked at himself in the reflective surface of the ship's wall. "I love it!"

"Happy you approve. Now go help your friends. I will fling you to their location," Chasub instructed.

"I'm ready," Xenoshot said. "Send me down."

Xenoshot appeared at the end of the alleyway already aiming his illuminator. He saw Prodigy on the ground and ran over to her. "Prodigy, wake up!"

"Huh? What happened?" she asked as she rubbed her head. "My head is killing me."

"I'm not surprised, considering how strong Travis is. We need to figure out something and fast," a nervous chuckle escaped Xenoshot's lips. "I like your costume, by the way."

"Archie?" Prodigy asked, staring hard at his face.

"Yes, it's me."

"Wow!"

"What, you like it? Chasub—"

"We don't have time for idle conversation. Aim your illuminator at Travis," Chasub's voice cut in through Xenoshot's sentence.

Tseeew! Tseeew! Tseeew! Xenoshot leveled the illuminator and fired three shots at Travis, sending him reeling down the alleyway before he stumbled into the wall.

"Direct hit! The hero strikes again!" Xenoshot cheered.

Xenoshot helped Prodigy to her feet, and they ran toward Crimson Falcon.

"Are you ok?" Prodigy asked, examining the bruises on Crimson Falcon's face.

"That depends on your definition of 'ok'," Crimson Falcon said with a groan before looking at Xenoshot. "Nice costume, buddy."

Xenoshot reached over to examine Crimson Falcon's bruises as well. "Thanks. Man, you and Travis must've been—"

"Gaaaaahh!" With a roar, Travis threw Prodigy to one side and Xenoshot to another.

Crimson Falcon threw a punch, but Travis caught in in the palm of his hand.

"Ah!" he cried as Travis sent him flying into the alley wall.

"Game over." Travis chuckled as he looked at Crimson Falcon and threw one more super powerful punch.

In desperation, Crimson Falcon blocked the punch… and was shocked to realize he had barely felt the blow.

Travis was shocked as well. He frowned and threw another punch. This time, Crimson Falcon caught his fist and held on to it.

"Drop something?" Prodigy asked.

Both combatants turned to see that Prodigy had taken the Brawn Omnidisk and had it floating in midair.

"NO!" Travis screamed as Prodigy mentally threw the Omnidisk to Crimson Falcon. He caught it and slid it into his belt. The energy from the Omnidisk surged through his body, and a slight smile tugged at his lips as he realized how easy this fight was about to be.

"Are you ready for another round?"

Travis nervously shook his head.

"I didn't think so." Crimson Falcon looked at Prodigy and nodded his head toward the dumpster.

Prodigy smiled and used her powers to flip open the dumpster's top.

"Have a nice flight," Crimson Falcon said as he grabbed Travis by his shirt and effortlessly threw him into the dumpster. Prodigy closed the lid and used her power to lock it.

Xenoshot walked over and gave them both a high-five.

"We make a good team," Crimson Falcon saved as he looked at Prodigy.

"Hey, what about me!" Xenoshot said. "I was the one who saved both of you."

Crimson Falcon and Prodigy both laughed as they watched Xenoshot get flustered.

"I heard the fighting coming from back here!" someone from inside the theater yelled. "Hey! Where is the door?"

"Do you guys feel like getting blamed for this?" Crimson Falcon asked.

"They wouldn't dare. We're the heroes," Prodigy said.

"We are also standing next to a door with no hinges on it, an alleyway that looks like a tornado hit it, and our uniforms are still on," Crimson Falcon pointed out. "We need to go."

"I wonder what Spider-Man did on days like this," Xenoshot said thoughtfully.

"We can discuss it later. Chasub, we need to go."

"Initiating fling," Chasub said.

A few seconds later, a group of people from the theater walked out into an empty alley.

CHAPTER 13

"Mission accomplished, Chasub," Crimson Falcon said proudly. "Thanks for sending in Xenoshot."

"The gratitude goes to all of you," Chasub corrected him. "You are the ones who were injured during the battle, yet you succeeded."

"I'm glad to get out of this suit finally. It gets a little uncomfortable after too long," Crimson Falcon transformed into his regular clothes.

"I like it. It makes me feel powerful," Prodigy said as she also began to switch into her clothes.

"I didn't have time to ask you before, but what does this symbol represent?" Xenoshot touched the symbol on the chest of his uniform. "I've never seen anything like it."

"This is a symbol used on my world. We put it on various buildings, such as hospitals, children's care centers, and law enforcement buildings," Chasub explained.

"What does it mean?" Archie finally powered his suit down.

"There is no direct translation, but the best expression for the idea of the symbol is 'trust me'."

Eric smiled. "Archie's the most trustworthy guy on the team, so that works for me."

"If you all would be so kind as to give me your watches, there is an upgrade I would like to make," Chasub said.

"So, when do we get another mission?" Archie asked.

"Hopefully after we're all healed up from this one," Eric rubbed his arm and winced.

"There have been some interesting readings on the scanners," Chasub said. "I'm not sure what they all mean, but until I sort them out, I cannot give you a definitive location on the other Omnidisks."

"Why is it so hard to find the Omnidisks?" Brynn asked. "I thought Eric told me that you had designed some tracking device."

"I did," Chasub opened an image on his computer screen. "This is a map of Drakeston, and the bright blobs that you see here cover a lot of space. Plus, the energy from the Omnidisks continues to spread, making them hard to track.

"It will take several more scans before I can pinpoint the Omnidisks whereabouts. And there's an energy signature in the middle here that is not consistent with the Omnidisks, yet the computer is registering it because of its energy. It's very peculiar. I'm not sure what it is or where it is coming from."

"Maybe I can help you sort it all out," Archie suggested.

"This technology is far more complex than you could ever comprehend," Chasub said. "I doubt you could—"

"I'm guessing this controls thrust," Archie said, pointing to a few touchpads "And I don't know how you measure it, but it looks like you get a lot of speed out of this ship. These nozzles here control direction. And over these are the weapons, I'm pretty sure."

Everyone, including Chasub, stared at Archie in awe for a few seconds.

"I've memorized the schematics of enough alien ships," Archie smiled and crossed his arms. "They were fake, sure, but this proves they weren't very far off base after all."

"Maybe you should let him help," Eric suggested. "It must be difficult running this ship alone. Having some company would be good for you."

"Perhaps," Chasub stated. "Archie if you believe you could spare the time-."

"Yes, I can!" Archie exclaimed as he jumped a foot into the air with excitement. After he landed, he looked around and chuckled nervously. "I mean if you want me to."

"It is settled. You will spend a few hours here each day learning how to control the ship and how to decipher the scans. With your assistance, I might be able to locate the Omnidisks faster than planned. We might even find the augments we have been looking for."

"I can start right now! Anything you need, I'm your man," Archie said, giving Chasub a salute.

Chasub closed the back of the watches and handed them to the trio. "There. I have altered the watches so that now you will be able to communicate with each other as well as me."

Eric slipped on his watch. "Nice. So I guess this means we can talk all the time."

Brynn gave Eric a quick smile. "It's not that impressive. We all have cell phones."

"Oh no!" Eric cried as he glanced at his watch. "I need to get home, or my father will go crazy."

"Your father will issue an attack against you?" Chasub asked in a slightly alarmed tone. "I was unaware that human fathers used such aggressive parenting techniques."

"No, he means his dad is going to be mad," Brynn translated. "It's slang."

"I see." Chasub began typing some coordinates into his computer. "I will send you home. You will hear from me as soon as I find something new."

"I should go too." Brynn walked over to Eric's side. "I'm going to be late for my study group. Though, I can't believe I'm thinking about that after everything that's happened today."

"Well, I would tell you it gets easier but…well, that would be a lie." Eric patted Brynn on the back.

"I can stay for a while, Chasub," Archie said. "We can get to work on those scans."

"We're ready," Eric said.

Chasub nodded his head, activated the flinger and sent them to the Earth.

Slymind and Mange pulled into the alleyway behind the movie theater in an old beat-up black car.

"You would think we would have a better ride than this," Mange complained over the screech of the breaks.

"You're always complaining. It works; doesn't it?" Slymind said, cutting off the engine.

"I'm not complaining.; I'm just saying that since we're doing the leg work, we should have a better ride."

"What, so we can stand out and get caught by the police with a flashy car? Especially since it's the middle of the night!"

"Good point. I guess I didn't think about it that way."

"You didn't think as usual," Slymind stated as he tried to concentrate. "Now, according to this tracking device, the item should be here."

"I thought we were supposed to be finding the items on the list he gave us?" Mange scratched his head.

"Yeah, well, that changed once the boss got a hit that one of those disks was here. So, stop your questions and help me look for it."

"There's nothing here!" Mange threw a few pieces of trash aside.

"Looks like there was some sort of struggle here. Someone must have gotten here before us and grabbed it," Slymind said.

"We're dead!" Mange slammed his fist into the ground, making the concrete crack.

"Shut up. Did you hear that?" Slymind asked as he took a few steps toward the dumpster.

"Hey! Is somebody out there? Let me out!" a voice called out from inside the dumpster.

"Somebody is in there!" Mange said.

"Open it then!"

Mange tore the top of the dumpster off with one quick upward motion.

"I said, open it, not rip it off!"

Mange snarled. "Same difference."

Travis slowly poked his head out but ducked back inside when his eyes fell on Mange, who had pulled his hood off.

"Mange, what's wrong with you?! You trying to get us caught? Put your hood on before someone else sees you like that."

"I was hot."

"Put it on!"

"Alright already," Mange glared at his partner and shoved the hood back over his head.

"Get out here!" Slymind extended his arm and lifted Travis out of the dumpster.

"What are you…things?" Travis asked. He could almost hear his knees rattling as he continued to stare at Mange.

"Quit staring at me, kid, before I give you something to stare at," Mange said with a growl as he removed his glasses.

Travis turned to run, but Slymind stretched out an arm and held on to him.

"Where do you think you're going? And why were you in that dumpster?"

Before Travis could answer, Slymind's cell began to ring.

"You know it's him. I told you, we're dead," Mange said nervously.

"I'm warning you! Do me a favor and hold the kid while I answer this." Slymind answered the call.

"Do you have my disk?" Command asked.

"It wasn't here, sir, but we found a kid in the dumpster, and it looks like there was a fight before we got here. I think he might be able to tell us who took it."

"Good work, for once. Bring him to me. I'll question him myself. I want that disk."

"We're on our way," Slymind stated as he gave Travis a wink. "Looks like you're going with us, kid."

"Why don't we just kill him?" Mange growled.

"Do that, and the boss will kill *you*. Now, let's go!" Slymind yelled.

Slymind's phone began to ring again.

"Maybe the boss decided my idea is better," Mange said.

Slymind gave Mange a cold hard stare. "I'm getting sick of you."

"I've located another device," Command said excitedly.

"What do you want us to do with the kid?"

"Bring him to me first.."

"Sure thing."

"What did he say?"

"He found another disk, but we're to bring him the kid first," Slymind got in the driver's seat and slammed his door. The outside handle fell to the ground.

"I told you we needed a new—"

"Shut up!" Slymind hit the pedal and sped off toward their headquarters.

Eric reached over and slammed down on his alarm button, but to his surprise, the beeping noise that stirred him out of his sleep didn't stop.

He finally realized that it was his watch.

You've got to be kidding me, Eric said to himself as he fought to make out the time on his clock. *It's three-thirty in the morning. What in the world—* "Chasub, you really need to work on picking better times to call."

"Hey, buddy." Archie's smiling face appeared on the screen.

"Archie?" Eric rubbed his eyes. "What are you doing there this late?"

"I've been helping Chasub with the scans. This technology is amazing. I am learning a lot about the ship."

"Your parents are going to kill you!"

"No, they won't. They think I'm still in bed," Archie said proudly. "I went home long enough to eat dinner and make them think I went to sleep, but I came here instead."

"So, why are you calling me at three-thirty in the morning? All rational, sane people are asleep right now," Eric pointed out.

Archie rolled his eyes. "I had to call…. I found an Omnidisk. Well, Chasub and I found one. We have the location. I'm downloading it to your watch."

"And this couldn't wait till morning?" Eric asked.

"You know we aren't the only ones after those things. We need to get it immediately. Brynn is going to meet us there; I'll see you in a few. Archie out." The screen went blank.

Eric climbed out of bed and stared at his watch. *Why can't I sneak out to go to parties like everyone else my age?*

CHAPTER 14

It took hours, but finally, Common came out of the tiny room that held Travis.

"I believe he has told me all he knows," Command's announcement woke Mange and Slymind from their sleep.

"You tortured him?" Mange asked hopefully.

"No," Command stated in an annoyed tone. "What kind of person do you think I am?"

"What did you find out?" Slymind asked.

"He was so scared by you two; he was more than happy to tell me what I wanted to know. He seems to know quite a bit about the disks that we are looking for. In fact, he had the one I sent you to retrieve. However, Crimson Falcon took it."

"I knew it! How does he always get there before us?" Mange asked.

"That's not our only problem. It appears Crimson Falcon has friends. There was a woman who goes by the name of Prodigy. She can move things with her mind. She and this Crimson Falcon appear to be getting their ability to defeat the two of you from the disks. There was also another man, called Xenoshot. He didn't seem to have any powers, but apparently he has a beam weapon attached to his hand."

"He's probably the guy with the mask from last time," Slymind said.

"What are we going to do about the kid we brought here?" Mange asked. "He knows about us."

"That's why we're going to keep him here for now. I need him to be a test subject for my invention," Command said.

Each of them turned toward the gigantic machine that sat in the center of the room.

"Sir, the sun will rise in a few hours. Do you still want us to go after the disk?" Slymind asked

"I almost forgot about that. Yes, go get it." The intensity returned to Command's voice. "Hurry!"

"Where are we heading?" Mange asked.

"To a scrap yard nearby."

"Good, maybe they will have a handle for the car." Mange joked as he and Slymind started to walk out.

"Gentlemen," Command said, stopping them.

"Yes, sir."

"I *know* that you two will not return without my disk this time. Am I right?" Command's unspoken threat hung in the air.

"Right, sir," Slymind promised with a nod.

"And if Crimson Falcon and his team show up...don't hold back!"

"What took you so long?" Crimson Falcon asked as Prodigy flew in.

"I took a while for Archie to wake me up," Prodigy said. "I'm used to getting a full night's rest. Is this the place?" she asked as she glanced at the Marty's Scrap Yard sign.

"Yeah, this is it. Where in the heck is Xenoshot? He was supposed to meet us here."

"Yeehaw!" Xenoshot yelled from above.

"What is he riding on?" Crimson Falcon asked.

"You know Archie." Prodigy rolled her eyes.

"Yeah, that's what scares me. Come on; let's go see."

"Hey, guys, like the ride?" Xenoshot asked as he did a flip in midair.

"What is it? It looks like a large trash can lid that's been flattened out until it couldn't take anymore," Crimson Falcon laughed.

"It looks more like some a high tech skateboard to me," Prodigy pitched in.

"You are both incorrect. It's way cooler than some dingy skateboard. It's an early version of the anti-gravity unit Chasub uses to get around now," Xenoshot stated as he finally landed between Prodigy and Crimson Falcon. "Now I can fly like you two, and the best part is this…" Archie stepped off the metal circle and it instantly shrank to the size of a quarter. He slipped it into his jacket. "I call it the Hyperboard."

"Nice." Crimson Falcon walked over to the gate in front of the scrap yard and grabbed the padlock, yanking it off with one quick pull. "I think I'm in love with this super-strength," he said as he looked over at Prodigy.

"Of course," she agreed. "I'm a little jealous."

"Come on, guys, let's get in here and get this thing so we can all go back to bed." Crimson Falcon stopped and frowned. "I just realized something strange."

"What, how awesome all of this is?" Xenoshot asked.

Crimson Falcon shot Xenoshot a look. "No, I realized that we've been here a few minutes and we haven't heard from Chasub."

"Even he needs to sleep every few days," Xenoshot said. "I told him we could handle this one alone."

"I hope you're right," Prodigy said.

Crimson Falcon looked at the sensor on his watch. "The Omnidisk should be over there." He gestured to a pile of abandoned car parts.

"Rummaging through trash? I did NOT sign up for this," Prodigy complained.

Crimson Falcon threw a muffler aside. "All part of saving the world. See anything yet?"

"Nothing over here," Prodigy waved her hand and an old rusted engine floated out of her way.

"What you are looking for is not in there," a raspy voice said from behind.

The trio turned around and found themselves looking at a familiar scaly face.

"Who are you?" Prodigy asked.

"His name is Dark Viper," Xenoshot explained. "He wants the Omnidisks too. He's saved Crimson Falcon's life a few times, and we suspect that he has a history with Slymind and Mange, but that hasn't been confirmed yet."

"All I needed was a name Mr. Wikipedia," Prodigy rolled her eyes.

Xenoshot's face turned red. *I need to stop trying so hard to impress her.* "Where's the Omnidisk?" Crimson Falcon asked, taking a step towards Dark Viper.

"I have it," Dark Viper stated as he raised his hand, exposing a dark green Omnidisk.

"We need that," Crimson Falcon said. "You know as well as I do who else is looking for it."

"Yes, I do," he replied bluntly.

"We don't want to fight you, Dark Viper. We only want the Omnidisk," Crimson Falcon promised.

"I am not your enemy. This thing, this Omnidisk as you call it, turned me into this! I need to figure out how to turn myself into a human again."

The two stood face-to-face with each other. Prodigy stood behind Crimson Falcon, ready to provide any needed support.

"Maybe we can help each other!" Xenoshot offered as he tried to step in between them.

"How?" Dark Viper asked, still holding tightly to the Omnidisk.

"Yes, Xenoshot, how do you suppose we do that?" Crimson Falcon said through clenched teeth. He kept his eyes focused on Dark Viper.

"Our friend, the one who helped create the Omnidisk, knows everything about them," Xenoshot continued. "He may know a way to reverse the effects of the energy on you."

Dark Viper took a step back. "How do I know you aren't lying just to get the disk?"

"You can trust us. Chasub can help you, Dark Viper," Crimson Falcon insisted.

Dark Viper's face hardened. "Trust. I trust no one. There are no guarantees with trust. I will do this on my own!"

Crimson Falcon groaned as Dark Viper put the Omnidisk in his cloak and started to walk off again.

"That does it. Enough with the niceties. We came to get something, and I say we get it," Prodigy extended her hand, mentally calling the Omnidisk.

The Omnidisk flew out of Dark Viper's cloak but was barely a foot away before Dark Viper turned around and grabbed it out of the air.

"I am not easily robbed," he said.

"We're not thieves, we're heroes, and we aren't leaving without that Omnidisk!" Two pipes floated off of the ground and hovered over Prodigy's head. They began to spin around and around at a dizzying speed.

"Prodigy! What are you doing?" Crimson Falcon exclaimed; his eyes wide with shock.

"As he said, you can't trust anyone," Prodigy said as she began to fly and make the pipes follow her. "Those Omnidisks are as dangerous in his hands as they are in anyone else's as far as we know. We have to get them." She waved her hand, and the pipes sped towards Dark Viper.

Clang! Dark Viper whipped out his collapsible bo staff and knocked the first pipe to the ground. He leaped to the side, causing the second pipe to fly harmlessly into a scrap pile behind him.

"What should we do?" Xenoshot looked at Crimson Falcon.

Crimson Falcon sighed. "Fine, go for it. But try not to hurt him."

Xenoshot took out his Hyperboard and made it full sized. "Mission accepted, Captain." He hopped on his Hyperboard and took to the air.

Dark Viper dodged two more pieces of metal mentally hurled at him by Prodigy. "I have no desire to hurt you. Stop your attack."

"Give me the Omnidisk first." Prodigy pointed at a hubcap and levitated it at Dark Viper.

"You were warned." Dark Viper threw a strong kick at the hubcap, propelling it at Prodigy's head.

"Aaaah!" The hubcap hit her in the head, and she fell to the ground with a dull thud.

Tseeew! Tseeew! Two beams from Xenoshot's illuminator lanced at Dark Viper.

He jumped to the side and rolled when he hit the ground, stumbling as he got to his feet. Xenoshot saw the black mark on his pants where he had been hit.

"Give us the Omnidisk, and this will stop," Xenoshot said.

"I will not!" Dark Viper growled.

Tseeew! Dark Viper jumped on a pile of scrap and avoided the next shot.

Crimson Falcon managed to sneak up behind Dark Viper and prepared to strike.

Tseeew! Xenoshot fired, and Dark Viper ducked, causing the beam to miss him and hit Crimson Falcon in the shoulder.

"Ow!" He held his shoulder where the beam had hit him. "Watch your aim; I'm on your side!"

"Sorry! Oof!" Dark Viper hit Xenoshot with a flying kick. Xenoshot fell to the ground with the wind knocked out of him.

"My turn!" Crimson Falcon clenched his fist and flew at Dark Viper.

"I've got him!" Prodigy telepathically grabbed Dark Viper and pushed him into a pile of junk before Crimson Falcon could reach him.

"Careful! We're not trying to pulverize him!" Crimson Falcon reminded her.

"Sorry, didn't get the memo," she said, mentally throwing Dark Viper in the opposite direction.

In midair, Dark Viper reached onto his belt, pulled out his bolas and threw them at Prodigy.

"Hey!" The bolas wrapped themselves around Prodigy's arms and legs, rendering her entirely immobile.

Dark Viper reduced the size of his bo staff to half a foot long and in one motion turned around and threw it at Xenoshot, hitting his weapon out of his hand as he was preparing to fire.

"You *will* desist!" Dark Viper jumped at the disarmed Xenoshot with his arms outstretched.

"Hah!" Crimson Falcon flew into Dark Viper before he could connect with Xenoshot. Dark Viper slammed hard into the side of a nearby building, leaving cracks in the brick.

"You can't beat me; I'm stronger than when we last met. Please, stop fighting us!" Crimson Falcon pleaded.

Dark Viper responded by hitting him in the stomach with his bo staff, followed by a kick to his face knocking Crimson Falcon to the ground.

"That does it, now the gloves come off!" Crimson clenched his fists and launched himself at Dark Viper.

Dark Viper moved with grace, dodging and ducking every hit that was thrown at him, and occasionally hitting Crimson Falcon with blows of his own.

Xenoshot was freeing Prodigy from her bonds when he saw the trouble Crimson Falcon was in. "Prodigy, look!" He nodded in the direction of the fight.

Prodigy's hand shot out and caught Dark Viper's fist in a mental grip before it could connect with Crimson Falcon's face.

For the first time, surprise showed on Dark Vipers face when he realized he could not move his arm.

Crimson Falcon smiled and grabbed his arm and hit him with two short jabs in the stomach and one hard punch across the face, sending Dark Viper flying through the air and crashing into yet another pile of junk.

"I will not surrender the Omnidisk," Dark Viper insisted as he staggered to his feet.

"We can't let him have it," Prodigy said, walking with Xenoshot to Crimson Falcon. "You know what's at risk."

Crimson Falcon looked sympathetically at Dark Viper, doubled over from pain and breathing hard. "Please, don't make us do this."

Dark Viper stared back silently.

"We'll make it quick," Crimson Falcon said in a somber tone. "Xenoshot, stun him."

Tseeew! Xenoshot pointed and fired. But Dark Viper was no longer there.

Dark Viper jumped in the air and flipped forward, hitting Xenoshot in the chest with both feet. He landed next to Xenoshot's unconscious body and ran at Prodigy.

Prodigy thrust her hand out and threw an engine at Dark Viper. Dark Viper ducked, evaded the engine, and used the strength from his legs to execute a powerful uppercut, launching Prodigy off of her feet and on to the hood of a junked car several feet behind her.

Crimson Falcon flew at Dark Viper from behind, but Dark Viper spun around and hit him with a roundhouse kick. Crimson Falcon hit the ground and rolled, bringing himself to his knees.

Bam! Dark Viper hit him in the face with his bo staff as soon as he looked up. Crimson Falcon hit the ground, and Dark Viper placed a foot on his chest and held the bo staff an inch in front of his face.

"You weren't really hurt," Crimson Falcon looked at Dark Viper accusingly.

"I am injured. However, I have trained myself to be able to fight through the pain. Try to attack me, and I will kill him." Dark Viper's last statement was to Xenoshot, who was beginning to get on his feet. "I will leave now. Don't try to stop me." Dark Viper turned and silently walked away.

"Did we get him?" Prodigy asked as she too staggered to her feet.

"No, but he certainly got the Omnidisk and us," Crimson Falcon said grumpily, turning toward Xenoshot. "Are you okay?"

"I'll be okay," he stated, rubbing his head. "Man, that dude is good."

Crimson Falcon and Prodigy both gave Xenoshot a nasty look.

"What? He is."

"Crimson Falcon, Prodigy, what happened?" Chasub asked through Crimson Falcon's communicator.

"Dark Viper. That's what happened. He got the Omnidisk."

"How?" Chasub asked.

"We fought. He kicked and bo staffed us. In the end, he went off into the darkness with the Omnidisk," Crimson Falcon said irritably. He didn't like having to admit they had failed. He felt like the failure was his.

"Oh, I see. Is everyone alright?" Chasub asked.

"We'll all be okay, but that doesn't help the situation any," Crimson Falcon said.

"You did your best. Trust me. I know how sometimes even though you do your best, the enemy still defeats you," the tiniest hint of emotion entered Chasub's voice.

"Well, at least we know for sure why he wants the Omnidisk. He's using them to find a way to turn himself into a human again," Xenoshot said.

"Crimson Falcon, I need you to get out of there, right now!" Chasub shouted.

"What's the matter?" Xenoshot asked in a worried tone.

"Augments. They're close. Leave now!"

"Mange and Slymind," Xenoshot and Crimson Falcon said in unison.

"I was hoping I'd get to meet those two," Prodigy said gleefully.

"Not tonight. Let's go," Crimson Falcon said as he shot into the air.

"Darn," Prodigy followed.

Xenoshot whipped out his Hyperboard and rushed after them.

Dark Viper sat resting on a rock on the other side of the fence, watching the three leave. He was out of breath and in pain. He pulled out the Omnidisk and stared at it. He had no problem with the young heroes. Their motives seemed noble. But that didn't mean they could be trusted to look out for his best interests. And they didn't truly understand the enemy they were up against. Not the way he did.

I will learn your secrets, Dark Viper thought as he looked at the Omnidisk. *And then I will get my life back.*

Crimson Falcon looked at the junkyard as they flew away. He couldn't believe they didn't get the Omnidisk. He felt like he had let his team down. He felt like he had let the world down. That's when he spotted the car approaching Dark Viper. The augments were going after the Omnidisk. And that made Dark Viper a target.

"Guys… I don't think we should leave quite yet," Crimson Falcon said. "The party is just getting started."

"Hey, look over there," Slymind stated as he turned off the lights and parked a few feet from the gate.

"I don't see anything," Mange complained, squinting.

"That's because you aren't looking hard enough. Look, over there by that rock."

"Yeah, I see it now. Is that who I think it is?"

"Sure is. And look what he has in his hands."

"Let's get him!" Mange was snarling.

"Let's get the disk first," Slymind corrected."Right. Same difference."

"Get out of the car, but be quiet," Slymind stated as he eased out the driver's side door. "Don't make a—"

Tzzzap! Mange's eye beams sliced through the air and landed less than a foot away from Dark Viper. He calmly looked at the duo but didn't budge.

"Hello, old friend," Slymind said before shooting an annoyed look at Mange. "Looks like you're hurt. Too bad. Give us the disk, and we will let you live."

"Do you have a better deal?" Dark Viper asked in a disinterested tone.

"I got one!" Mange shouted as he rushed toward Dark Viper. Slymind reached out and grabbed his arm.

"Not so fast. I've got a better idea." Slymind reached into his pocket and pulled out twenty white spheres. "Remember these?"

Crimson Falcon and his companions stooped behind some bushes a few yards from the encounter. He placed his fingers to his lips.

"Are those the augments?" Prodigy whispered.

"Definitely, Mange and Slymind," Xenoshot replied.

Crimson Falcon narrowed his eyes. "Keep it down so I can hear what's going on."

"Let me give you a quick reminder," Slymind tossed the spheres toward the ground. "These are my holo-henchmen, with a few improvements, of course."

"I remember those," Crimson Falcon whispered grimly.

A few seconds later the holo-henchmen emerged in front of Dark Viper.

"Wow, check that out," Xenoshot said in amazement. "I've never seen a real hologram before."

"What's a hologram?" Prodigy asked.

Crimson Falcon put a finger to his lips and indicated to them to lower their voices.

"Figures made of light. But theoretically, with the right energy configuration, you can make them solid," Xenoshot whispered.

Dark Viper removed his bo staff and took a defensive stance. The first five holograms leapt forward. Dark Viper blocked a kick from one of them and kicked another in the chest, knocking it on the ground. Two more rushed forward, and he swung his bo staff in a wide arc, hitting them both with the full force. They disappeared and the smoking spheres hit the ground.

"I told you that guy was good," Xenoshot said in an impressed tone.

The remaining holograms held their hands out in front of them, and they slowly turned into razor-sharp spikes.

Dark Viper's eyes narrowed.

"Do you like my little upgrade?" Slymind asked, smiling.

"We've got to help him," Xenoshot said.

"What?" said Prodigy. "Did you forget that he handed us a beating a few minutes ago?"

The holograms attacked Dark Viper again. He swung his bo staff and blocked the attack of two of the holograms, but one slashed him in the arm. He withdrew, checked his arm and took a fighting stance.

"He never gives up, does he?" Prodigy asked.

"Chasub, what do you think?" Crimson Falcon asked. "They will kill him if we don't help."

"It is your decision as team leader," Chasub responded.

"Team what?" Crimson Falcon looked nervously at his friends. It felt like the weight of the mission just increased tenfold.

Xenoshot nodded. "Makes sense to me."

Prodigy smiled. "I trust you."

Crimson Falcon took a deep breath and shifted his eyes to the battle. "How did I know you were going to say that?"

Dark Viper swung his bo staff, but the hologram ducked, swinging out and knocking the bo staff out of Dark Viper's hand.

"If we're going to help him, now is the time Crimson Falcon," Xenoshot swallowed nervously.

"He's right. I'm scanning Dark Viper; he won't be able to last much longer," Chasub stated.

Crimson Falcon looked back again. A hologram's kick sent Dark Viper flying against the fence.

"Okay, let's go," Crimson Falcon stated, standing to his feet.

"Are you sure?" Prodigy asked.

"Come on," Crimson Falcon replied. He looked over at Prodigy. "It's the right thing to do."

Prodigy rolled her eyes. "Fine, but don't say I didn't warn you."

Dark Viper managed to lift himself to his knees right as the holograms began to move in.

"Finish it now!" Slymind ordered.

A hologram leaped into the air, pointing his spiky appendage downward toward Dark Viper.

Crimson Falcon flew forward and punched the hologram with all of his strength, the force sending it crashing into the fence. Its sphere hit the ground as smoke rose from it.

Tseeew! Tseeew! Xenoshot aimed his illuminator and took out two more while Prodigy lifted two other holograms off the ground and slammed them into each other. All of the attacked holograms disappeared.

Crimson Falcon grabbed Dark Viper's bo staff and held it out to him. "I think you dropped this."

Dark Viper glared as he grabbed it.

"You!" Mange raged.

Xenoshot and Prodigy took a defensive position beside Crimson Falcon and Dark Viper.

"Attack them all!" Slymind shouted to the remaining holograms.

Tseeew! Tseeew! Xenoshot took out another two.

"Come and get some!" Prodigy yelled as three holograms lifted off the ground and flew after her.

"You can fly too? More fun for me." Prodigy focused on a hubcap in a pile of trash. She hurled it straight through each of them, causing their spheres to crash to the ground, almost hitting Mange.

"That's right! You don't mess with—" Prodigy's gloating was interrupted when another hologram put her in a chokehold and drove her toward the ground. She tried to grab at it, but its grip was too firm. It cut off her air supply.

"Off you go!" Crimson Falcon shouted as he pulled the hologram off Prodigy and landed a punch into its head. It disappeared.

"I didn't need any help," Prodigy rubbed her neck.

Crimson Falcon smiled. "I know, I guess I can't help butting in."

Dark Viper slammed his bo staff into the head of an attacking hologram. There were only three left.

Xenoshot vaporized one of the remaining holograms

Prodigy lifted another into the air and slammed it on the ground.

Dark Viper swung his bo staff at a third, but it blocked the blow and slashed him. Crimson Falcon grabbed it from behind, held it over his head, brought it down on his knee. Its sphere hit the ground.

"That's it! We are done playing games!" Slymind screamed.

Tzzzap! Mange shot an eye beam at Prodigy and propelled her into a pile of junk cars.

Slymind extended his elastic arm and with one hit knocked Xenoshot out.

Tzzzap! Mange shot at Crimson Falcon, but Dark Viper threw him to the ground, just in time.

"Thanks," Crimson Falcon said as he jumped to his feet. "I've got dibs on the ugly one."

"Could you be a little more specific?" Dark Viper asked.

Crimson Falcon laughed and flew straight at Slymind. He slammed into Slymind's midsection and tackled him to the ground. "How about you and I take a little trip." He grabbed Slymind by the front of his coat and flew up into the air.

Mange came at Dark Viper. Dark Viper extended his bo staff and deflected Mange's eye beams.

"Stop hiding behind your fancy weapons and fight me!" Mange yelled.

Dark Viper swung his bo staff upwards at Mange's head, but Mange caught it, yanking it out of his hands before striking Dark Viper in the face. Mange reached for him again, but Dark Viper turned and executed a roundhouse kick to Mange's face. Mange cried out and fell backward, allowing Dark Viper to grab his weapon.

"Tell me who you're working for!" Crimson Falcon yelled into Slymind's face as they continued to climb higher.

"I'm sure you'd love to know. Why bother? Command is more powerful than you or your friends. You won't win!" Slymind said with a sneer.

Crimson Falcon shook him. "Command? So that's what you call him. Why do you need the Omnidisks? What kind of machine are you building and what is it for?"

"This course of action will not produce any results," Chasub said. "He will not tell you anything."

Slymind winced at his slip up. "I don't know how you found out about the machine, but all of this is pointless. I'm not going to talk!"

"So I hear." Crimson Falcon grabbed Slymind by the throat. "Which means there's no more need for finesse."

Dark Viper swung his staff and hit Mange in the stomach, and in the head, bringing him to his knees. He pulled his weapon back for another strike but before he could, Mange looked at him and flashed a bright yellow light from his eyes.

"Aaah!" Dark Viper stumbled and covered his eyes with his free hand. He opened his eyes in time to see the hazy image of Mange's head slamming into his. He was unconscious before he hit the ground.

"This is going to feel *very* good. For me." Mange looked at Dark Viper and fired his eye beams at full strength. After a few seconds, he stopped. His eyes grew wide as he saw Dark Viper still lying there, unscathed. "What?!"

"No big mystery there; that's a little force field provided by yours truly." Prodigy was hovering in the air a few feet away. "Now get away from him before something bad happens to you."

Tseeew! Tseeew! Tseeew! Xenoshot hit Mange with a barrage of laser beams. Mange stumbled back several feet and collapsed onto the ground.

"Too late," Prodigy smiled.

"We need to finish this and jet before they get the upper hand." Xenoshot set his illuminator to full power and started incinerating parts in the bottom of the scrap pile directly behind Mange.

"What are you doing?" Prodigy asked. Suddenly, pile started to collapse on top of Mange. "Oh. Good idea."

A large piece of metal plummeted at Dark Viper's head. Prodigy reached out with her mind and yanked him towards her and out of harm's way. When the heap of scrap finished collapsing, Mange was completely covered.

"Good job, nerd boy. As good as any solution I could've thought of." Prodigy smiled and elbowed Xenoshot playfully.

"Thanks," Xenoshot blushed. "Where'd C.F. go?"

Slymind hit the ground, face down, in front of Xenoshot and didn't move. Crimson Falcon landed next to his companions. "We've been here long enough; Chasub fling the four of us out of here!"

"*Four?*" Chasub replied. "I do not believe it would be wise to bring—
"

"Chasub, we can't leave him here. Please, bring us to the ship."

"Very well; stand by."

Slymind groaned and tried to lift his head. "No!" he cried. He slowly struggled to get up, but it was too late. They were gone.

Slymind turned around when he heard a loud crash. Mange shot out from under the heap of scrap. He growled. "Where are they?"

"Gone," Slymind said.

Mange clenched his fists with rage. "Gaaaaaaahhhhh!!!"

CHAPTER 15

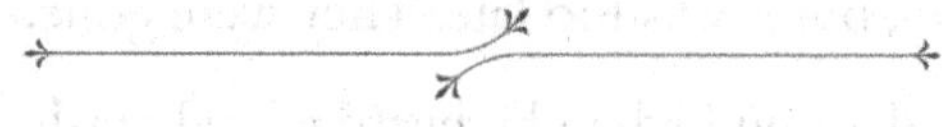

"Do you think he's going to be okay?" Xenoshot asked. The whole team stood around the bed that held Dark Viper.

"I have been able to heal his wounds. His pride is another matter," Chasub pressed several buttons on a display that showed Dark Viper's vital signs.

"I think we should take the Omnidisk off of him now and zap him home," Prodigy said.

"I disagree," Xenoshot objected. "He was trying to cure himself. He didn't ask for any of this to happen to him."

Prodigy nodded her head. "That's *his* problem, not ours. We have everyone else on this planet to worry about. We need to take the Omnidisk." She reached out to grab the Omnidisk.

"No!" Crimson Falcon grabbed her wrist. "This isn't just about the Omnidisk. We're all in this together, Prodigy. He knows the augments. He has tactical information that we can use. We need his help." Looking at Dark Viper, he added, "And whether he realizes it or not, he needs ours."

"He said he didn't want to help us," Prodigy said as she yanked her hand away. "Or did you miss the twenty punch memo he sent us?"

Crimson Falcon crossed his arms and began circling the table. "That was why I insisted we help him. He didn't believe he could trust us. I wanted to prove him wrong. Chasub, did you run the diagnostic like I asked?"

"Yes," Chasub pressed a few buttons on the panel on the side of the bed. A holographic image of DNA sequences and alien symbols appeared over Dark Viper's body. "This is the closest I have ever been to a human who's been affected by the Omnidisk's energy. My study of his DNA might help me determine a way to reverse the effects. I might even be able to return all those who have been mutated to their normal state."

Suddenly, without warning, Dark Viper jumped off the table and took a defensive stance. "Where am I?"

"Calm down," Crimson Falcon stated as he walked towards him slowly, keeping his hands visible. "You passed out. We brought you here so Chasub could help you heal. You were pretty badly injured."

Dark Viper examined himself and found that his wounds had indeed been healed. He relaxed, backing down from his defensive position. "Where is this place?"

"Well, this is the medical alcove, but I think the real answer to your question is…we're on Chasub's spaceship," Xenoshot said.

"I see," Dark Viper took a cautious look around. His gaze rested on Chasub but only for a few seconds. "Interesting. Very well, if you would show me the way out, I will leave you to your business."

"Don't leave yet, Dark Viper," Crimson Falcon said. "I need to ask you for a favor. We need the Omnidisk."

"I cannot give it to you," Dark Viper replied.

"I told you he wouldn't—"

"Prodigy!" Crimson Falcon raised his hand and cut her off.

Prodigy was about to object when Xenoshot put his hand on her shoulder.

"We all put our lives on the line to save you. We brought you here to give you medical assistance, and you still have the Omnidisk on you. We could have taken it then, but I was hoping you would give it to us willingly," Crimson Falcon stated, trying to reason with him.

"All that proves is that you will fight for the Omnidisk," Dark Viper countered.

"No, it proves that we can help you. We can work together. Chasub, show him what you found." Crimson Falcon gestured toward Chasub.

"I was able to obtain a great deal of information on the energy's effect on your original DNA." Chasub floated forward. "By studying those effects, I think I might be able to find a way to change you into a human again." Chasub turned toward Dark Viper. "It will take some time, but I believe I can do it."

"He's committed all of his medical technology to creating a cure," Xenoshot added.

"What are you?" Dark Viper took several steps toward Chasub.

"I come from another planet. And I am, in large part, responsible for what is happening here. However, I am using all that I have here to attempt to make things right."

"You can trust him, Dark Viper; he means what he says." Crimson Falcon moved toward Dark Viper again. "Give us the Omnidisk and let's work together. It would be better for everyone."

Dark Viper looked at Crimson Falcon suspiciously and walked over to Prodigy. "You don't approve of me, do you?"

She crossed her arms and looked him in the eye. "No, I don't."

"If that's true, why did you help me before?"

Prodigy sighed and put her hands on her hips. "I don't know. I guess…because Crimson Falcon believed it was the right thing to do."

"So, although you didn't agree with his plan, you trusted him to do the right thing?" Dark Viper asked.

Prodigy looked at Crimson Falcon, then at Dark Viper. "Yes, I do."

"Thank you." Dark Viper walked over to Crimson Falcon. "Your own team member didn't think helping me was a good idea. Obviously, she doesn't share all of your beliefs."

Crimson Falcon sighed and bowed his head in defeat, mentally accepting that Dark Viper would refuse him.

"However," Dark Viper continued, "she does *trust* you enough to put her own beliefs aside." Dark Viper put his hand inside his cloak and pulled out the Omnidisk. "Being the type of leader someone can trust to that level is very rare and very admirable."

Crimson Falcon smiled and took the Omnidisk from Dark Viper's hand. "Thank you. I promise we will fix you as soon as we can."

"I will give you a communication device before you leave so we can contact you with any updates," Chasub promised. As Eric handed him the Omnidisk. "Ah this is the Morph Omnidisk. Very nice."

"Interesting name. What does that one do?" Prodigy asked.

"It gives the user the ability to turn into any animal on Earth," Chasub explained.

"Like in the *Animorphs* books!" Xenoshot shouted.

Everyone stared at him in silence. Brynn glanced at Eric and raised an eyebrow. Eric shrugged.

"Oh, come on guys, I know you at least heard about them. A bunch of kids get the power to turn into animals to fight off an alien invasion. Written by K.A. Applegate and her husband Michael Grant. The coolest book series of our childhood!" Xenoshot looked around excitedly but only received blank stares in return.

Chasub stared for another moment and then turned back to Dark Viper. "I should escort you out and contact you with any updates."

Dark Viper nodded.

"Welcome to the team!" Xenoshot stepped up to Dark Viper and held out his hand enthusiastically.

"I am not part of the 'team'," Dark Viper said harshly. "I gave you the Omnidisk because you're the only ones I know with the resources to do the job. That doesn't mean I trust you. Now, show me how to get off this ship, immediately."

"Follow me; I will escort you to the main deck," Chasub stated as he gestured in that direction.

"I still can't believe neither one of you read *Animorphs*. Philistines." Xenoshot looked at his teammates one last time and nodded in disappointment before following Dark Viper out of the medical quarters.

Prodigy waited until she was sure they were alone, then she stepped in front of Crimson Falcon. "Go, team," she said sarcastically as she activated the watch to change into her regular clothes.

"Baby steps," he replied unenthusiastically. "At least we got the Omnidisk."

"Yeah, I guess you were right after all. I'm sorry for being so…abrasive."

Crimson Falcon laughed as he hit his watch to change into his normal clothes. "Don't be. You were sincere and honest about your convictions. That's why Dark Viper changed his mind. Jut do me a favor and try not to handle every situation that way."

"No promises." Brynn smiled. "So, what do you think the new Omnidisk does?"

"Beats me." Eric looked at his watch. "But we don't have time to figure it out now. We're going to be late for school."

"At least we got a full night's sleep," she said sarcastically.

"Eric, wake up." Archie shook Eric's shoulder.

"Huh? Where are we?" Eric rubbed his eyes and lifted his face from his desk.

"Jeffries's class," Archie said. "The bell is about to ring."

"Wonderful, at this rate, I'll sleep through every single class today." Eric groaned.

"At least we have a good reason."

"Right, I can tell my teachers that my grades are slipping because I've been fighting the forces of evil nonstop. That should get me some extra credit."

Finally, the bell rang.

"Don't forget to read Chapter 5!" Jason yelled as the students passed. "Eric, may I talk to you for a minute?"

Archie and Eric stopped next to Jason's desk.

"I would prefer to speak with Eric alone," Jason said, smiling at Archie.

Archie glared at Jason and walked out of the classroom.

"Yes, sir?" Eric asked.

"I noticed you were nodding off during class," Jason started.

"I'm very sorry about that, sir. I don't make it a habit to fall asleep in class."

"None of that "sir" stuff, please. Call me Jason. And I'm not trying to give you detention or anything. I want to know if something is wrong. I've heard good things about you, but lately, you seem so distracted."

Eric rubbed his eyes. "I had a long night. Well, a series of long nights, to be exact. My friends and I have been…working on a few projects lately. They've been giving us some trouble."

Jason frowned. "What happened?"

"I would rather not go into the details. I'll just say it wasn't a great situation to be in."

"I understand." Jason smiled at Eric. "I realize how hard it is for kids your age. A lot is going on in your life. Maybe I need to stop giving you homework."

"Really?" Eric said with an appreciative smile.

"I was joking, but seriously, I know how life can be for a guy your age." Jason put his hand on Eric's shoulder. "But still, no sleeping in my class. I'll let you slide this time if you promise not to tell anyone. I wouldn't want the other students to think I was soft."

"My lips are sealed, sir. I mean Jason!" Eric chuckled. "I should leave. I'm about to risk being late for my next class."

"Oh my goodness, I'm sorry." Jason grabbed a piece of paper and jotted something down before handing it to Eric. "Here's a hall pass."

"Wow. Thanks again. I'll see you tomorrow," Eric said as he walked out of the classroom.

"I don't trust that man. Why is he always so interested in you?" Archie was waiting for Eric in the hallway.

"He was making sure I was alright," Eric said. "Let's go."

Archie stopped and grabbed Eric's arm. "You didn't tell him anything, did you?"

"I told him everything. I was planning on showing him the spaceship after school."

Archie's eyes grew wide as dinner plates.

"Ha ha ha!" Eric doubled over with laughter at Archie's reaction. "Give me a little credit. I have *some* sense."

Archie frowned at Eric. "That was not funny at all. But you're right. You have a lot of sense. What you decided to do with Dark Viper was pretty great."

"It would've been even better if it had worked," Eric said. "He still barely trusts us."

"In time, I think he will. He's cautious, but there's something noble about him."

Eric crossed his arms. "So, you don't trust a respectable teacher, but you trust an augment who spends his time sulking in the shadows?"

Archie shrugged. "Of course it sounds strange when you say it like that."

"What sounds strange? Besides everything that comes out of Archie's mouth," Will walked around the corner.

"Nothing, just talking. You know how Eric is, always saying something crazy," Archie said quickly, glaring at Will.

"Says the guy who makes his Facebook status, 'May the force be with you'," Will joked, rolling his eyes.

"How would you know? You never accepted my friend request," Archie grumbled.

"Yeah, that's Archie alright." Eric shuffled his feet uncomfortably. "We should go; we're going to be late."

"Wait," Will stepped closer to Eric. "What has been going on with you lately?"

Eric pretended to be confused. "What do you mean?"

"I *mean*, you have been acting strange, and for the last couple of days, you both have disappeared almost immediately after school. We haven't been able to joke around much like we used to. What gives?" Will frowned.

Eric gave Archie a sidelong glance, the beginnings of guilt creeping in for the lies he was about to tell. "Will, I'm sorry that we've been a little…aloof lately."

"It isn't anything personal," Archie assured him.

"Good." Will crossed his arms and looked intently at both of them. "Tell me what's going on."

Eric and Archie looked at each other, before they turned to Will, unsure of what to say.

Will gave a sarcastic chuckle. "Thanks, I'm glad to see this is where our friendship has brought us."

Archie raised an eyebrow. "We're friends now?"

Eric glared at Archie before looking back at Will. "Will, it's not—"

He cut Eric off. "Forget it. I don't want to hear some lame excuse." Will walked off as hurt as Eric had ever seen him.

The late bell rang harshly in Eric and Archie's ears.

"At least you have a pass," Archie said, trying to get Eric to smile.

Eric walked past him, not acknowledging his comment at all.

"You didn't do anything wrong," Archie said.

"Then why do I feel like such a terrible person?" Eric whispered.

After school, Eric and Archie walked Brynn to her car.

"Any word from Chasub yet?" Brynn asked.

"He called me earlier. Neither you or Eric are a DNA match for the Omnidisk we detected the other night," Archie said.

"You're kidding me!" Eric was shocked.

"Nope. Chasub is as surprised as you are."

"So who is the user?" Brynn asked.

"I don't know. Chasub has been trying to crack the security protocol on this one and it's been difficult. He's been working all night and still nothing. He said he would give us a call when he has something. Are you okay, Eric?"

Eric stared off into the sky. "Yeah, I'm fine. It's just that Chasub had me believing that I was—"

"The only one?" Brynn said, finishing his sentence.

"Look at it this way, at least we get some more help, and you and I both know that we sure could use it. Plus, you're still the leader, right? I mean, you are the man. Our personal Captain America. Don't sweat it," Archie put his hand on Eric's shoulder.

"Wow, a pep talk from Archie. Nothing like it," Eric said, smiling. "And Iron Man was a better leader."

"How could you say that?" Archie sounded genuinely offended. "Did you even see *Civil War*?"

"Yes, and Iron Man was right!" Eric insisted.

"Well, now that the both of you feel better, I say we head to the mall, so I can feel better," Brynn unlocked her car.

"You're inviting us to the mall?" Archie's stomach suddenly felt like it was doing cartwheels.

"Yes, the mall. I think a new pair of shoes will hit the spot." Brynn looked at his *Star Trek: First Contact* t-shirt and grimaced. "And I don't think I'm the only one who could use some new clothes."

Archie smiled nervously. "I guess I could always stop at the comic book shop and see if anything good has come in."

Brynn sighed. "Comic books; why am I not surprised? Eric, are you coming?"

Eric's head shot up at the sound of his name. "I'm sorry, did you say something?"

"What's wrong with you? Does Archie need to give you another pep talk?" Brynn said in a joking tone.

"No, please don't," he said, looking at Archie. "I was just…thinking about something that happened earlier, that's all," Eric said softly.

"So, are you going to tell me what it is?" Brynn asked.

"It's nothing," Eric replied.

"I think I know what it is," Archie said. "Our friend Will is mad at us."

"The cute, short guy?" Brynn asked as she flashed one of her million-dollar smiles.

"Yeah, him." Archie felt a flash of jealousy. "But trust me, he's not very cute when he's mad. Eric here feels guilty about having to lie to him. I don't see why. Will isn't the nicest guy around."

"I didn't lie!" Eric yelled, making his friends jump. He rubbed his head and sighed. "I couldn't tell him the truth. And Archie, don't get mad because you two don't get along."

"So?" Brynn shrugged. "You did what you had to do. If he can't deal with it, that's his problem."

Eric shook his head in frustration. This was not what he needed to hear. "I forgot, I need to go talk to somebody." He turned around and started walking towards the school. "I'll talk to you guys later!"

Brynn looked at Archie. "Was it something I said?"

CHAPTER 16

"Mr. Jeffries, you got a minute?"

Jason was packing his things and about to leave for the day when Eric approached him with a serious look on his face. He placed his bag on his desk and took a seat.

"Sure; like I said, I'm always here to help. And it's Jason."

Eric sat down and explained how upset Will had gotten at him and Archie earlier. "…And he stormed off before I could even explain."

"It sounds like it wasn't something you could explain to him anyway," Jason said.

"You're right. But I didn't want him to take it so personally. I feel awful"

"I can tell. Is it because you feel as if you've lost the trust of a friend?"

"Yeah…that's it."

"I understand that it's a difficult situation, but I don't understand what it was that you couldn't tell him."

Eric glanced out the window. "It's just that I can't talk about it. Not with him or even…with you."

"I see. Must be something very weighty."

"It is…like saving the world weighty," Eric said in a whisper.

"What was that? I'm sorry, I didn't hear you."

"I was saying that you're right. It is a weighty kind of issue."

Jason smiled. "You don't have to feel pressured. But remember, you can trust me."

"Yeah, I know. There's a lot more involved in this than me," Eric stood up. "Anyway, I should leave. Thanks for taking some time to listen. I appreciate it."

Jason nodded. "Don't mention it. I'll see you tomorrow." He walked out of the room.

Eric smiled as he watched Jason rush out of the classroom. He followed a few minutes later.

"Eric!" Chris called from down the hallway. She ran to catch up with him. "How are you?"

Be cool. Eric took a deep breath. "A little better than I was earlier."

"Aw, I'm sorry. What happened?" she asked.

She shows such genuine concern. That's so great. "Me and a friend had a little bit of a falling out. It hasn't been resolved yet."

"Well, you're a nice guy. I'm sure things will be better in no time," she smiled and put her hand on his arm.

Eric's stomach did back a flip, and his heart started beating a thousand miles per hour. "I appreciate the compliment, but this is a tough one."

"A burger might make you feel better," she said cheerfully. "I was about to go to that diner around the corner. I wouldn't mind some company…if you're not too busy."

Too busy? Hmmm, well, I have to work every day and night, it seems, to save the world. "Sure, I'd love to."

"There you are!" Jeff Cook, the football team quarterback, walked up behind Chris and put his arm around her.

"Hey! I thought you had practice," she said before giving him a quick peck on the cheek. "Eric, have you met my boyfriend, Jeff?"

Wonderful. Eric faked a smile and held out his hand. "We've met. Good to see you, Jeff."

Eric had met Jeff but mainly knew him by reputation. He knew he was one of the jocks who pushed Archie around and he wasn't known for his humility. Most people who knew him said he was the most self-centered guy in school.

Jeff used his hand to brush back his short blonde hair and ignored Eric's hand. "Of course it is. Let's go, babe, I'm hungry." He took her hand and started walking.

Chris looked at Eric. "Rain check on that burger?"

"Definitely," Eric said, his heart sinking to his shoes. *Note to self: If it is too good to be true, it probably is.*

Just when he thought things couldn't get any worse, his watch went off.

"Yeah," Eric said in a sour mood.

"You're needed at the mall," Chasub said urgently.

Eric rolled his eyes. "Chasub, I thought you of all people would be too smart to let Brynn control you with her mall craziness."

"No, you misunderstand. There is an augment attacking civilians there. Prodigy and Xenoshot have engaged him, but he is very powerful."

"So, this isn't one that we've fought already? Not Mange or Slymind?"

"No," Chasub replied. "This one is new and seems to be far more dangerous."

"I'm on my way." Eric closed the communicator and ran toward the rear entrance of the school. In his rush, he wasn't watching where he was going and nearly ran into Will.

"Whoa!" Will stepped out of the way in time to avoid a collision.

"Will! I'm sorry I didn't see you," Eric said apologetically, not wanting to give his friend more of a reason to resent him.

"Nothing to be sorry for," Will said, crossing his arms. "My manly physique is more than a match for your scrawny body."

Eric laughed. *He's making jokes. This is a good sign.*

"I'm glad that you almost ran me over and knocked the life out of me," Will continued with a smile. "I want to apologize for earlier. I have a hard time understanding why you would want to keep something from me. But I am willing to talk about it."

"I would like that." Eric looked at his watch and winced. "But I can't; there's something I need to go do."

"Let me guess…you can't talk about it?" Will stated sarcastically.

Eric sighed. *Here we go again.* "All I can say is that it's something important."

Will rubbed his forehead in frustration. "Eric, you don't work for the FBI; nobody likes to feel like they're forcing a friendship." He started backing away. "Forget I ever said anything. I guess my apology was misplaced. I'm not the problem. *You* are." He turned around and angrily walked away from Eric for the second time that day.

"I can't get a break," Eric said under his breath. He looked at his watch again and ran out the back door of the school. *One problem at a time.*

A trashcan went flying through a clothing store display window, sending everyone running out of the mall in fear of their lives.

"Prodigy, are you alright?!" Xenoshot yelled.

"I'll be a lot better when we bash this augment's head in!" she responded. "I was going to buy that outfit in that window!"

"He is a big guy, isn't he? I can't tell if he's human or a wolf. Look at his legs. They are completely covered in some sort of grey coarse fur. And his muscles, they're the size of a bowling ball. I mean, this thing has got an upper torso that makes Batman look like a kid. He's incredible." Xenoshot stared in amazement.

"Incredible? No, he's a problem that we need to get rid of and fast!" Prodigy dove for the ground as the augment threw a table at her. "Xenoshot, shoot that thing now!"

"I'm on it." Xenoshot aimed his illuminator and fired off three beams. They both watched as the augment stumbled before shaking his head and charging at them.

"Man! Did you see that? No effect on him at all. Nothing!" Xenoshot yelled.

"Stop playing around, Xenoshot. Put that thing on a higher setting." Prodigy demanded.

"But it might kill him!"

The augment roared as he approached the duo. "Grraaaaaaahh!!"

"Do it, Xenoshot. Do it now!" Prodigy screamed.

Prodigy threw anything she could find at the augment. But he tore through them as quickly as she tossed them.

'Hurry, Xenoshot; I don't know how much longer I can hold him."

"Crimson Falcon is on his way!" Chasub shouted.

"Well, he'd better get here fast!" Prodigy shouted back.

"Here goes!" Xenoshot yelled as he fired.

Tseeew! Tseeew! The augment staggered, shook his head and came charging at them. He leaped in the air with his enormous paws. They hit Prodigy and sent her sliding across the mall floor into a wall.

Xenoshot increased the power setting on the illuminator again and shot at the augment. Tseeew! Tseeew!

He roared in pain, grabbed at the two burn marks the illuminator had left on his arm, and slammed his fist into the ground, grabbed a hunk of granite and hurled it at Xenoshot.

Xenoshot tried to duck, but a piece of the granite slammed into his shoulder, knocking the illuminator out of his hand and throwing him off balance so that he fell to the floor.

Crimson Falcon flew in and slammed into the augment, sending it flying across the mall.

He ran toward Prodigy and helped her to her feet. "Can you still fight?"

Prodigy laughed. "You're joking, right?"

He smiled. "Why did I even ask?" he asked as he turned toward Xenoshot.

Xenoshot picked his weapon off of the floor and winced in pain. "I think my arm is bruised, but I'll be ok."

Crimson Falcon looked to his left and saw the lights coming from the escalator. "The police are here. We have to go."

"What about the augment?" Prodigy asked in pain herself.

Falcon searched for a minute and spotted him running toward the other end the mall. A few seconds later, he was gone.

"We'll have to go after him, but right now, we gotta move."

Xenoshot tried to get up but couldn't. "I don't think I can, Crimson Falcon."

"Chasub!" Crimson Falcon shouted in his watch.

"I'll bring Xenoshot to the ship," Chasub said.

"Good; we're going after the augment."

"What are we going to do with him once we catch him?" Prodigy asked.

"One problem at a time. Let's go!"

"Archie, how bad is your injury?" Chasub asked, floating over to him.

"I think he broke my arm."

"Stand still, I'll return you to human-health in no time."

"I thought you said that aliens don't make jokes?" Archie smiled through the pain.

"I never said that. Humor is not common among my people, but it exists. And that was not a joke. I'm almost done." Chasub ran his prong device over Archie's shoulders. "How is that?"

Archie began to move his shoulders. "Wow. It's starting to feel better already."

"It has increased your healing rate, but you will still need a little time to recover completely. Come. I want to show you something."

"What, a new gadget?"

"Yes. I was thinking about Prodigy's question."

"What question?"

"The question about what to do with the augment once they find him."

Archie eyes filled with anticipation. "And what's your solution?"

"Come this way," Chasub floated down the ship's main corridor.

"Okay, what is it? A holding cell?" Archie asked as they stood in front of a small room.

"It's more than a holding cell." Chasub tapped a panel on the wall, and a computer display emerged. "I think I may have a way to repair some of the damage the radiation from the Omnidisks has done on the augments."

"How?"

"As you know, I've been working on a way to revert the augments to humans. Hence, this room. It contains a different type of energy. One that, once emitted, will counteract the Virocan energy and reverse the mutation in humans."

"Are you sure?"

"Mostly. We'll have to see. There is one small problem."

"What's that?"

"Flinging the augment to the ship. The energy in their bodies makes it hard to get a lock on them and even harder to get them to ship safely."

"Why is that a problem? You flung Dark Viper, and he is an augment. Right?"

"Yes, but Dark Viper was already very weak. And I have recorded his biometrics into the computer so I can compensate. The Virocan radiation in this new augment's body makes it impossible for the flinger to lock on to him. Nearly all augments have that issue. That is why I could never fling Slymind or Mange here," Chasub said as he displayed a picture of the augment's body on the screen. "But I have invented a device that can help me break through the energy interference." Chasub held up a silver cone-shaped object with tiny barbs on it. "I call it a Virocan inhibitor."

"So, if we stick this in him, you can fling him here and change him back into who he was?"

Chasub simply stared at him.

Xenoshot sighed. "I thought that sounded too easy."

"Before this device can be effective you have to weaken the augment. I've found that when augments are alert or active, they put off more of the radiation than if they are sluggish or inactive, such as being asleep, for instance," Chasub said.

"So, we have to put him to sleep somehow. I doubt a lullaby is going to work here," Xenoshot crossed his arms.

Chasub looked directly at him.

Xenoshot smiled. "I was joking, of course. So all we have to do is beat him up, slap this device on him, and *then* you fling him here."

"A crude explanation, especially coming from you, but yes, that will work. How is your arm?"

"It's great," Xenoshot moved it back and forth. "Send me down; I'll be sure to tell the others."

"I've locked on to Crimson Falcon and Prodigy; I'll send you to their location," Chasub and Archie headed toward the flinger console.

"Be careful this time."

"Why? What could possibly happen?"

Chasub gave him a blank stare.

"Another joke. I'm ready."

CHAPTER 17

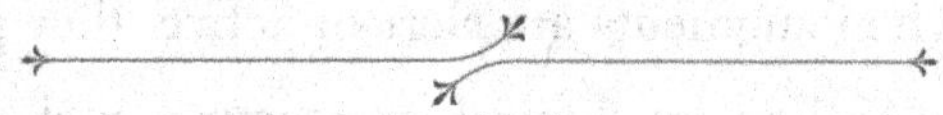

"Whoa!" Crimson Falcon veered to the right to avoid flying into Xenoshot. "Where'd you come from?"

"Chasub locked into your location and flung me here. I'll give you the details later. Why are we flying through a forest?" Xenoshot steered his Hyperboard around a tree.

"We followed the augment in here. He isn't far ahead. Prodigy is right on his tail. He's fast though; it makes him difficult to capture. How are you?"

"Chasub took care of me. I'm as good as new."

"Glad to hear it. Watch out!" Crimson Falcon and Xenoshot narrowly avoided hitting a tree.

"Crimson Falcon, I have given Xenoshot a device that needs to be placed on the augment. You and Prodigy must weaken him before it will be effective," Chasub said.

"I'll do my best," Crimson Falcon promised. "Now as soon as I catch—"

Roooooar!! The augment jumped in front of Crimson Falcon and hit him with the trunk of a tree. Crimson Falcon went crashing into another large tree.

"No!" Xenoshot shouted as the augment uprooted another tree and prepared to swing it at Crimson Falcon.

"Look out!" Prodigy tore the tree out of the augment's hands and tossed it into the forest. Next, she thrust out both of her hands and focused all her thoughts so that she could throw him. He landed several feet away.

"Nice save," said Xenoshot as he struggled to stay on his Hyperboard.

"Sorry it took me so long," Prodigy apologized. "I lost track of him in all of these trees."

"Here he comes again!" Crimson Falcon warned, finally getting to his feet. "Man, he's fast!" Crimson Falcon flew forward and landed a few punches into the augment's face.

ROOOOAAAR!!! The augment roared, slashed at Crimson Falcon with its paw, knocking him off of his feet.

Tseeew! Tseeew! Xenoshot pulled out his illuminator and shot at the augment twice. It barely left two scorch marks on him.

"We have to hit him harder!" Xenoshot yelled. "We have to make him weak enough for Chasub to fling him!"

"We'll have to work together!" Crimson Falcon shouted. "Prodigy, can you lift those two large rocks over there and hurl them at him?"

"Got it. Hurling!" she shouted.

The augment dodged the first rock. The second hit him in the head. Crimson Falcon ran over to the creature and kicked him in his diaphragm.

"Keep going, Crimson Falcon, you almost got him!" Xenoshot yelled.

Crimson Falcon delivered a stiff uppercut to the augment's face and another punch right after. The combination of blows was strong enough to make the augment stumble and fall on its back.

"Do it now!" Crimson Falcon yelled out to Xenoshot.

Xenoshot took out the inhibitor and slapped the device onto its neck.

The augment roared and slashed at Xenoshot, but he managed to fly off unharmed.

"Now, Chasub!" Crimson Falcon yelled.

The blue light began to surround the augment.

"Yes! It's working!" Xenoshot cheered

After a few seconds, the blue light disappeared. But the augment didn't.

"Chasub, what happened?" Crimson Falcon asked.

"The Molecular Flinger can't lock on him," Chasub replied. "There is still too much active energy in his system. You have to make him weaker!" Chasub shouted through their communicators.

The augment threw the inhibitor to the ground and roared triumphantly. Xenoshot looked nervously at Crimson Falcon. Prodigy smiled eagerly.

Crimson Falcon looked at the augment and sighed. "Let's try this again."

Across town, at the Drakeston Museum, a robbery was in progress. Two people dressed in dark clothing were slowly climbing down a rope that hung from the skylight.

"Are you positive the security system is offline?" a woman with a thick New York accent asked. Her name was Anira Franklin and she was a cat burglar. She was an expert at hand-to-hand combat and at avoiding detection by the authorities. She was five and a half feet tall with dark skin and short dark hair. "You remember what happened at the bank in Chicago," she said.

"Trust me, I did everything right this time," her accomplice responded. His name was Lance Brennan, Anira's right-hand man. He was sturdy looking, about six feet tall, and had a shaved head, tan skin and blue eyes. After Anira caught him trying to pick her pocket while in Detroit eight months earlier, she decided he had potential and had taken him under her wing.

"Good." Anira let go of the rope and dropped to the floor. "We can't let the security guards see us."

"What's the worry?" Lance asked. "We can take on some fake cops."

Anira cautiously scanned the area. "The point is not who we can fight. The point is to avoid a fight. Combat leaves physical evidence, which increases your chances of being caught."

"And being caught is a bad thing," Lance smiled.

Anira picked up a priceless Babylonian urn and examined the outside of it. "Unless you want to laugh yourself all of the way to prison, I suggest you get serious." She stuffed the urn into her backpack. "We got what we came for. Now, let's go. We can use the rear door."

They began walking down the sidewalk towards their van the street.

"I think that car is coming towards us," said Lance, noticing a black car driving in their direction.

"I heard it fifteen seconds ago," Anira said, her gentle reprimand clear. "Be ready for anything."

The car parked in front of their van. Slymind and Mange, dressed in trench coats and hats, stepped out.

"Excuse me," Slymind said. "Might we have a moment of your time?"

"Stay away," Lance warned.

"Sure, hand us the bag, and we'll be out of your hair," Slymind stated as he held out his hand.

"We aren't giving you anything," Anira said. "Now let us pass!"

"Give us the bag or I'll crush you myself!" Mange's eyes began to glow.

Anira nodded at Lance, and he whipped out a gun he had stuffed in his waistband.

"Get out of our way, or things will get very unpleasant," Anira warned.

Quick as lightning, Slymind's arm stretched out, grabbed the gun and punched Lance in the face. Lance hit the ground hard.

Anira pulled out a taser and lunged toward Slymind before he was able to do the same to her.

Anira jabbed the taser into Slymind's arm the elastic arm went limp. Slymind fell to his knees.

"Get up!" Anira shouted as she reached out her hand toward Lance. "Get back, crazy-eye, or I'll give you a taste of this taser!" she shouted, staring into Mange's eyes, which were still glowing.

Lance got to his feet, and the two of them took off toward an alleyway.

"Get them!" Slymind ordered.

Tzzzap! Tzzzap! Mange shot two beams into their direction, but they missed as Anira and Lance turned the corner into the alley.

"I don't see them," Mange said, running into the alley a few seconds after them.

"Right here." Lance dropped down from a fire escape, kicked Slymind with both feet and knocked him to the ground. "That's for hitting me."

"Come here!" Mange grabbed Lance by the neck.

"Unhand him!" Anira shouted as she stepped out from behind a dumpster.

Tzzzap! Tzzzap! Mange turned toward her direction and fired off two beams.

Anira did a sideways flip and evaded both of them.

Mange yelled in frustration, threw Lance to the ground and fired another round of beams toward Anira.

Anira was fast and agile. She continued to flip and dodge the beams.

"What are you, blind?" Slymind yelled, getting on his feet. He stretched his arms out toward Anira while Mange still tried to hit her with his eye beams.

Anira did a forward flip onto the wall of the alley and launched herself off of it just as Slymind's arms and Mange's eye beams converged.

Slymind screamed in pain and withdrew his arms.

Anira did another forward flip, kicking Mange in the chest. As he stumbled backward, she kicked his legs out from under him, whipped out her taser and jabbed it into his neck.

Slymind got ready to lunge at Anira again, but Lance grabbed his shoulder, turned him around and punched him in the face.

"Let's go!" Anira yelled at Lance as she pointed her taser at Slymind.

Anira ran out of the alley and toward the van. Lance was right behind her.

"Who are those guys?" Lance asked. "Why do they want the urn so bad?"

"I don't know or care. Keep moving. We're almost there!" Anira shouted.

Slymind's hand shot past Lance and caught Anira. Her backpack hit the ground.

"No!" she screamed as she heard the urn smash into pieces. "You've ruined it!"

"We don't want the urn," Slymind stated as he grabbed Lance's arm and threw him to Mange. "Get airborne."

Mange punched Lance in the face and knocked him out. The augment spread his wings and flew high into the air, holding Lance's unconscious body by his neck.

"Let him go!" Anira was back on her feet.

"If you don't give me what I want, he might," Slymind said.

"I don't know what you're talking about."

"It's in your bag."

Anira looked at Lance, sighing in defeat as she opened her bag. "There's nothing in here besides broken pieces of—" She stopped when she felt it. When she pulled her hand out, she was holding a transparent disk.

Slymind smiled. "Finally. Now, give me the disk, and I will tell Mange to bring your friend to us."

Anira looked at Lance once again and then at Slymind. Her expression turned cold. "This item must be valuable to you. I want my partner on the ground and safe before I hand it over. After that happens, we can negotiate!" She closed her hand around the Omnidisk.

"This is not a negotiation!" Slymind began walking toward Anira. "Give me the disk now!" He grabbed her wrist and attempted to pry her hand open.

Anira tried to hit him with the taser in her other hand, but he grabbed that wrist as well.

"Maybe you'd like to know how it feels." Slymind closed his hand around Anira's and activated the taser. She watched as the electricity sparked. She tried to fight as he kept pushing the taser closer and closer to her neck.

"You lose." With one final push, he jabbed the taser into her.

Anira screamed as the taser sent painful jolts of electricity traveling through her body.

"You are going to let go of the device," Slymind said with a smile. "One way or another."

Anira continued to scream in pain but tightened her grip on the Omnidisk, refusing to let go. Suddenly, the Omnidisk grew hot in her hand. It almost began to burn her skin.

"Give it to me now, and the pain will stop," Slymind offered.

Anira stopped screaming.

"Don't tell me you've passed out already," Slymind said with mock disappointment.

"Not yet." Anira glared at him, her eyes glowing a fiery blue. Electrical sparks began dancing all over her skin. "But you might."

Blue bolts of electricity flew off of Anira in every direction, engulfing Slymind and propelling him several feet away from her. He groaned and collapsed to the ground while smoke rose from his coat.

Anira looked at her hands, dazed and confused as the heat from the Omnidisk began to fade. *What is this?*

"I'll kill him!" Mange grabbed Lance around the neck and squeezed.

Anira frowned angrily. "No, you won't." She stretched out her hand and sent a bolt of electricity toward Mange.

Mange roared out in pain, dropping Lance as the bolt hit him in the chest.

Anira ran forward and caught Lance in her arms seconds before Mange hit the sidewalk in front of them. He didn't move. "Lance, come on." She lightly slapped him in the face a few times.

"Huh? What happened?" Lance jumped to his feet and looked around in confusion.

"Something wonderful," Anira responded with a smile. "Look." She held her hand open and allowed electrical sparks to move across her palm.

Lance widened his eyes in amazement. "How did that happen?"

"I don't know." Anira held up the transparent Omnidisk. "But it has something to do with this."

Lance took the Omnidisk from her hand and examined it. "Amazing. If you're right, this could be worth ten times as much as the urn! I wonder how you activate it."

"That's the mystery," Anira said, looking over Lance's shoulder. "I squeezed it in the palm of my hand while that stretchy man was shocking me with the taser, and I suddenly had the power."

Lance closed his hand tightly around the Omnidisk. "I don't feel anything."

Anira's eyes widened with shock. "Lance, look at your hands."

Lance raised his hands in front of his face, "I don't see them," he said breathlessly. He looked at the rest of his body. "I can't see myself at all."

"You are invisible!" Anira walked around Lance, expecting him to reappear any second. "How did you do that?"

Lance opened his hand and instantly reappeared. "This is awesome! Getting past security cameras will be easy as pie. I don't know what this is, but it has to be one of the most advanced things I have ever seen."

"That is why we are going to take it from you," Slymind said. He and Mange were standing on both sides of Anira and Lance.

Anira's hands started to glow bright blue with electricity. "Bring it on!" she shouted.

"Stand down!" Command stepped out of the car.

"Sir, we were about to take the device," Slymind said.

"The heck you were!" Lance said.

"I said stand down," Command repeated. "I don't want them harmed."

Slymind and Mange shared an angry glance before walking over to Command.

"These are your men?" Anira asked.

"Yes, and I apologize for any inconvenience you experienced," Command said with a slight nod.

"They tried to rob us!" Lance yelled in outrage.

"No offense meant, but haven't you robbed people on many occasions?" Command said with a smirk.

"What we do is none of your business," Anira said. "We were going to be paid very well for that urn."

"I'd say you have been paid well." Command gestured at Anira, "You can control electricity." He turned to Lance. "And you can become invisible at will. I'm sure those talents will help you make millions in your future heists."

Anira looked at Command suspiciously. "What do you know about our abilities?"

Command held out his hand. "Come with us, and I'll explain it all to you."

Lance grabbed Anira's arm. "We can't trust him! He sent those freaks after us."

"I can pay you much more than what you were looking to get for that urn," Command added.

"How do we know you won't try to kill us again?" Anira asked.

"The power is in your hands, isn't it?" Command said with a smirk.

Anira looked at her hands again.

Command gestured toward the car. Anira and Lance walked in front of them. Lance glanced back. The augment leader smiled.

Slymind's eyes widened. "You're really going to let them work for us?"

"Yes, I am." Command smiled as he allowed Lance and Anira to climb in the back of the car. He closed the door and looked over at Slymind. "And *then* I'll dispose of them and take the disk."

CHAPTER 18

"Let's do it!" Crimson Falcon yelled to his teammates.

Tseeew! Tseeew! Tseeew! Xenoshot fired his illuminator all around the augment to keep it distracted.

Crimson Falcon pulled a large tree out of the ground. "Prodigy, now!"

Prodigy held out her hand and pulled the augment toward Crimson Falcon.

"This one's going out of the park!" Crimson Falcon swung the tree trunk as hard as he could and connected with the augment. The force of the impact made the tree trunk shatter into splinters.

The augment sailed back into the woods, crashing into several trees before hitting the ground.

Crimson Falcon and his friends flew over to the augment. He growled at them one last time before he fell to the ground, unconscious.

Without delay, Xenoshot placed the inhibitor on the augment's neck.

"Ok, Chasub, give it another shot!" Crimson Falcon yelled.

Once again, the light surrounded the augment, but this time when the light disappeared, so did the augment.

"I have him," Chasub announced. "He is in one of my anti-radiation chambers now."

"Finally," Prodigy said.

Xenoshot collapsed on the ground. "I could sleep for a year. I feel like we've been fighting forever."

"Hours, actually," Crimson Falcon corrected. "And I agree. We need to rest."

"I could go another few rounds," Prodigy said.

"Only you, Prodigy," Crimson Falcon said with a smirk on his face. "I need some shuteye. We still have school tomorrow."

"You might have to hold off on that, Crimson Falcon," Chasub said in an urgent tone. "I'm bringing you to the ship."

"What now?" Crimson Falcon asked as they reappeared on the bridge. "We've been fighting nonstop!"

"According to my sensor readings, there was a lot of activity near the museum while the three of you were engaged in combat. I did not detect this before because I was focusing my attention on your battle. Mange and Slymind were there."

Prodigy's eyes widened. "Are they still there? We can go end this now!"

"No, the activity is no longer registering, but I have some more bad news."

Crimson Falcon groaned. "Go figure."

Chasub pressed a few buttons on the console in front of him. "The sensors also recorded an Omnidisk in the same area."

"They got it!" Xenoshot groaned.

"It appears so," Chasub agreed.

Crimson Falcon sighed with disappointment.

"I found something intriguing in these sensor records. It seems that a reaction took place sometime during the augment's presence."

"What kind of reaction?" Crimson Falcon asked.

"As far as I can make out, a human in the area got ahold of an Omnidisk and was shocked by a large amount of electricity. The radiation reacted with the electricity to turn the person into an augment," Chasub said.

"Awesome," Xenoshot said with a smile. He looked around and noticed the strange looks his friends were giving him. "What? It's like, instant superpower cocktail or something."

Prodigy rolled her eyes. "What kind of powers did this person receive?"

"I'm not sure. But since there was electricity involved, it would be safe to guess that their powers are based on that."

"You said they. It was more than one?" Crimson Falcon asked.

"Yes, but I don't think the other person gained any augment powers."

"So, there is an augment who can shock us to death and another party who is a complete mystery. Is it possible to get any good news?" Crimson Falcon asked.

"Actually, yes." Chasub pressed some additional buttons on the console. "I have found the user for the last Omnidisk you brought in. Since he was most likely someone who was physically close to you while the Omnidisks were doing their scanning, you might know him." He pressed one final button, and the face of the user appeared.

Xenoshot's eyes grew wide, and Prodigy gasped in surprise.

"I don't believe it," Crimson Falcon said breathlessly. "It's Will!"

Xenoshot groaned. "That is so unfair."

"This is great!" Crimson Falcon cheered.

"What's so great about it?" Prodigy asked. "The guy doesn't look like much of a fighter." She smiled. "No matter how cute he is."

"Chasub, see if you can get the Molecular Flinger locked on him." Crimson Falcon deactivated his suit, and his friends did the same. "We need to tell him what's going on."

"You want to do this now?" Archie asked. "Why don't we wait until tomorrow?"

"I can't; this whole mess with Will upset me, and now I can finally tell him the truth." Eric looked at Archie. "Didn't you feel better once I told you?"

"True. But we're a lot closer than you and Will. And he's always so skeptical of everything. He might not believe you," Archie pointed out.

"I'm sure I can make him believe me with us standing on an alien spacecraft with the alien a few feet away," Eric stated as he placed his hand on Archie's shoulder. "If you guys want to go home, I'll understand. But I'm going to do this tonight."

Brynn smiled. "I fought a mutated wolf creature with you. I can handle a little late-night conversation."

"That makes three of us, I guess," Archie said.

"It looks like he's at home." Chasub keyed in the command. "I can lock in on him and send him to you."

"Okay, let's do it," Eric responded.

A moment later, Will appeared on the floor in front of them, still sleeping.

"He sleeps with a teddy bear?" Brynn laughed, pointing to the stuffed animal under Will's arm.

"Mom?" Will's eyes fluttered open, and he lifted his head.

"Not exactly," Archie said with a smirk.

Will looked at Archie, "What are you doing in my—" He stopped and continued to look around. "Oh."

"I know this is probably a little unsettling," Eric said, stepping forward.

"Not really." Will stood up. "Looks to me like I'm in an alien spaceship in my pajamas; I'm obviously dreaming. But where's Scarlett Johansson?" Will looked around, noticed Brynn, and winked. "I guess you'll do."

"I'll *do?*" Brynn frowned and clenched her fists. "I'll show you what I'll do."

Eric put his hand on her arm. "Easy does it. He thinks he's dreaming."

Will's eyes landed on Chasub. "Wow, you are one funny looking little alien, aren't you?"

"I am a Zeph," Chasub said, sounding a little offended.

"This isn't a dream, Will," Eric said. "As hard as it might be to believe, this is all real."

"Of course," Will said with a laugh, "because everyone gets taken to an alien ship in the middle of the night."

Brynn walked over and punched Will in the arm.

"Ow!" Will stepped back and grabbed his arm. A second later, his eyes widened. "That actually hurt."

"Brynn!" Eric scowled at Archie, who was trying to stifle a snicker.

"What?" Brynn smiled mischievously. "I was helping."

"That hurt," Will's repeated himself and he tried to catch his breath. He looked at Eric. "What is this?"

"You wanted to know the truth," Eric said. "Well, now you're going to hear it."

CHAPTER 19

Will stood staring at the three of them—plus Chasub—as Eric finished telling him everything that had happened up to that point.

The air was thick with silence as everyone waited for his response.

"Will?" Eric said after a few minutes of silence.

"Yeah?" Will said quietly, looking at the floor.

"You haven't said much. I know it's a lot to comprehend."

"No, it's not." Will looked Eric in the eye. "You guys decided to dress up and play hero, and now you're dragging me into it."

"You know it's more complicated than that."

"Right." Will walked past Eric and looked around the deck of the ship.

"Is something wrong?" Eric asked.

"You mean besides the obvious?" Will walked over to Eric. "Have you considered that maybe…this is INSANE?!"

"Will, I know it all seems a little difficult but—"

"A little difficult? Did *you* listen to the little tale you told me?" Will put his hands on his hips and began to walk around, shaking his head in frustration. "According to you, these augment people are willing to kill to get what they want. And since you keep fighting them, I'd say you're at the top of their 'to-kill' list."

"We have help," Eric argued. "We have technology more advanced than anything the world has ever seen, and we have Chasub here."

"Right, you have him." Will dramatically waved his hand toward Chasub. "A member of a race of aliens who couldn't even defend their own planet!"

"Stop it, Will, that's not called for!" Eric shouted. "He's dedicating all of his time and resources to assisting us however he can."

"With what? A few tricks? Some funny costumes?" Will pointed at Archie and Brynn. "You think that's going to be enough for you, Mr. Spock, and Brittany Spears over there to do any good?"

A smile appeared on Archie's face. "Mr. Spock. Cool."

"He was insulting us, Archie." Brynn rolled her eyes.

"I said that's enough, Will! I won't have you disrespecting my team." Eric took a deep breath. "Look, think about what we're doing here," he continued. "Those Omnidisks can destroy the whole planet. We are trying to stop that. Even if the odds are against us, don't you think this is worth fighting for?"

"You don't get it." The anger was gone from Will's face. His eyes were now filled with sadness. "My dad left a few years after I was born. My mom recently recovered from it. What if something happens to me?"

"I understand exactly how you feel," Eric said sympathetically. "I lost my mother, remember? But that makes it even more important for us to do this. Chasub lost a whole planet. His family, friends. All gone. Our world could suffer that same type of pain if we don't do something." Eric walked over to the console where the Omnidisk lay, grabbed it and showed it to Will. "This is the Morph Disk. According to Chasub, this will give you the power to turn into any animal on the planet."

For the first time, Will showed a spark of intrigue. "How does it work? I'm sure it can't be that easy."

"It's similar to the *Animorphs.* You remember, the books about-."

"Not now!" Eric and Brynn cut Archie off.

"I can answer that question." Chasub hovered forward. "The Morph Omnidisk can store any number of DNA sequences inside it. I downloaded the genetic profiles of all known animal life from various scientific databases from your planet. Insect, amphibian, fish, reptile, bird, or mammal, the Morph Omnidisk will completely change your DNA until you are transformed into whatever animal you wish."

Will frowned. "What happens after my magical transformation? How do I change into a human again?"

"Your DNA will be saved in place of the animal you turned into. It is all thought activated, so you merely have to think of the animal or think of becoming human, and it will happen," Chasub said.

Will remained silent, but his face had softened.

Eric rested his hands on Will's shoulders. "Why don't we show you what we can do, so you can see how easy it is?"

Brynn got ready to activate her watch.

Will lifted his head and looked Eric in the eye. "Send me home."

Eric sighed with disappointment. "Will, please, think about it."

"I already have! And I won't have my mother crying her eyes out every night like she's done for almost all my life. I've been there. Call me selfish, I don't care, take me home, now."

"You're going to turn your back on so many lives?" Brynn yelled.

Eric turned to Chasub. "Do what he says."

Chasub walked over to the flinger console. "I will fling you to your home."

Will looked at Eric. "Don't try asking me again. My answer will be the same. I don't want any part of this. Oh, and by the way, when you say "fling", it sounds dumb."

After Will was gone, Eric looked at his friends. "I'm sorry for wasting your time. I expected that to go a lot better than it did."

Archie nodded his head. "It wasn't a waste. You tried your best. At least now he knows. I'm not sure he would have been a good fit for the team, anyway."

"Yeah, he was the one to turn his back on us and the planet." Brynn shrugged. "His loss. But now that we've been all supportive and all...can we finally go to bed?"

"Send us...I mean, fling us home, Chasub," Eric said with a small smile.

"Where the heck are we?" Lance asked as he and Anira walked into the augment's secret base of operations.

"This is where the world begins to change," Command said with pride. "I have a little project going on. And I need your help with it."

"Is someone gonna let me out of here?! Help!" Travis yelled from the room he was being held in.

Lance and Anira sent Command questioning looks.

"Don't mind him. Just an unhappy tenant," Command said with a smile.

"We don't care about whatever little experiments you're running here," Anira said. "We want to do our job so we can get paid."

"Very well. Lately, I have been attempting to collect a few pieces of technology. Unfortunately," he said, looking over at Slymind and Mange, "I have run into a little trouble so far."

"What type of technology are we talking about here? Military stuff?" Lance asked.

"No, nothing that drastic. Merely a few disks quite similar to the one you two had today," Command replied.

"You need us to find this special disk for you?" Anira asked. "How are we supposed to do that?"

"I have developed a device that can detect the energy from the disks. But recently, the device started sensing a person instead of a disk."

"The person must be carrying the disk," Anira concluded.

"I thought the same thing," Command said. "But after further investigation, I realized the energy was coming from the actual person. The scanner is giving me biometric readings not electronic ones."

"I don't understand," Lance replied.

"Nor do I. That's why I want this person brought to me." Command reached into his pocket and pulled out a small photograph.

"A simple snatch and grab," Anira took the picture from Command and looked at it. "Who is she, and how much are you paying?"

"She is a Drakeston High School student," Command said. "How much were you expecting from the urn?"

"One hundred thousand." Anira was quick to respond. Lance glanced at her with a raised eyebrow.

"Yeah, like she said…one hundred thousand," he chimed in.

"So be it. I'll give you a hundred thousand apiece. Bring her to me. Alive."

"How do we know you have that kind of money?"

"Look around you. Do you think this type of technology comes free?"

Anira nodded "Okay, but you had better have it or else!"

Command smiled. "Don't worry…you'll get exactly what I promised."

"One more thing. Does this student have a name?" Anira asked.

"Of course." Command nodded. "Her name is Christina. Christina Stephens."

"This is bad," Eric said as he walked to his first class.

"What, that we're no closer to finding the augments after two long weeks of looking for them?" Archie asked.

"No, but don't remind me. I forgot to do my Physics homework." Eric sighed. "Maybe Will is right. This is a lot for a group of teenagers to take on. Do we have a chance?"

"Don't let what he said get to you," Archie said. "You're our leader."

"Aw, come on." Eric rolled his eyes. "Don't call me that."

"It's true. You may not want to face it, but it is. You're the one who helped us to see how important what we're doing is."

"And what about Will?" Eric asked in almost a whisper. "I couldn't convince him. I didn't even convince you; this is something you've always wanted. And Brynn, well, she's always looking for a fight."

"Okay, that might be true. But you can tell that when you were talking to Will, you felt it in your gut, that saving the world is the right thing to do. I mean, look at me. Who would have thought I would be engaged in something so serious? I can't believe it myself. I am not just some nerd. I'm a nerd who is saving the world! And look at Brynn. She is an amazing person. She was living in a world that made it seem like she was too much. Now, that powerful personality and drive that she has is helping the entire planet because you recruited her. We need you, Eric. The world needs you. Like I said, you're our leader. I have a feeling you're going to be the one to get us all through this."

Eric smiled. "You're a good friend. I'm glad I didn't try to do this without you."

"You're the Batman to my Robin. I'll always be there for you."

"Hey, guys!" Chris and Brynn shouted as they caught up with them.

"Brynn, you look good," Archie complimented her.

"You know her, she could be dragged through the mud for an hour and not have a hair out of place," said Chris, giving Brynn a nudge.

Brynn laughed and shook her hair a little as if to show the truth of Chris' statement.

"It's like she has Kryptonian genes or something," Archie said.

Everyone stared at him for a minute.

"Yeah, I get that reaction a lot." Archie sighed.

"So Chris, what are you doing today?" Eric asked. For the first time, he realized that he was no longer nervous around her.

"That's what I wanted to talk to you about," she said. "I agreed to help the principal load some school supplies on Jeff's truck after school. I volunteered to send them to underprivileged children."

Man, she is perfect. Eric smiled. "It takes a special person to want to help kids that much."

"I think there are plenty of people who would help others if they found the right opportunity. But thank you." Chris gave Eric one of her biggest smiles.

Brynn sent Eric a look that said "nice move".

"Unfortunately, none of my friends want to help me move the stuff," Chris continued.

Brynn cleared her throat. "I told you I'd help."

"Sorry, I forgot. So now all I need now are a couple of strong gentlemen to assist," Chris grinned at Eric and Archie.

"Let us know if you see any," Brynn laughed.

Chris laughed. "Anyway, I was wondering if you and Archie could help us load the stuff into the truck. There's a lot of it, and we could use all of the help we can get."

"Count me in," Archie replied.

They all stared at Eric.

"There's nothing I'd rather do," Eric smiled.

"Oh, thank you!" Chris walked over and gave Eric a big hug. "You are awesome!"

I can officially die a happy man now, Eric thought to himself after Chris let him go.

"Hey, what about me?" Archie laughed.

The entire group broke into laughter.

"Daniels, you're not hitting on my girl, are you?" Jeff asked as he walked up and put his arm around Chris.

"I wouldn't dream of it," Eric chuckled.

"Eric and Archie agreed to help us move the boxes later," Chris said happily.

"She needed a couple of strong guys," Archie rubbed his arms.

Jeff looked at the two friends and laughed as if he had heard a funny joke. "Some of those boxes are pretty heavy. Are you sure you *boys* can handle it?"

Chris frowned at him. "Jeff!"

"That's ok, Chris, it's not the first time someone has underestimated me." Eric looked Jeff in the eye and smiled.

"Really?" Jeff said, not backing down.

Eric crossed his arms and took a step closer to Jeff. "Well, anytime you're ready for a demonstration just let me know."

Jeff scoffed. "Is that a challenge, Daniels?"

"I'm sure it isn't," Chris said with a smile. "You always take everything so personally. Come on, I'll walk you to class."

Eric looked at Jeff as he and Chris walked away. "See you after school."

Jeff looked turned and smiled. "Count on it."

Brynn walked over to Eric. "Where did that come from? I approve."

Eric shrugged. "I can't explain it. He irritated me for some reason."

"Think it might have anything to do with the fact that he's going out with the girl of your dreams?" Archie asked.

The second-period bell rang.

"It looks like we're about to be late. We'd better hurry," Eric walked off, thankful for the distraction.

Archie smiled and followed his friend.

By the time noon came Eric was getting very impatient.

"I have never been so ready for the day to end," Eric said as he and Archie walked toward the cafeteria for lunch.

"No worries; you will be in the arms of your love soon enough," Archie joked.

Eric shoved him into the wall. "Funny."

The communicator in Eric's watch went off. He ducked into the hallway and found a quiet corner. Archie followed.

"Chasub."

"Eric, sorry to disturb your noontime meal, but I need to talk to you and the others right away," Chasub said.

"Aw, come on! Its taco day!" Archie cried.

"Give us a minute to get Brynn before you fling us up," Eric said.

A few minutes later, they were all on the ship.

"What's so important?" Eric asked.

Chasub activated a computer display. "I have made an astounding discovery in relation to the Omnidisks. I explained to you before how the Omnidisks lock onto the genetic signature of a specific person."

"Right, and only that person can safely use the Omnidisk," Brynn started tapping her foot.

"Ignore her, she gets a little cranky when she's hungry," Eric said with a chuckle.

Chasub didn't seem to notice. "It seems that the scientists on my planet put one last safeguard in place. They programmed the Omnidisks to all tie into one life source. This person naturally would be called the Center. This was supposed to be used to protect the head scientist working on the project since he would be the only one who knew all the features of the Omnidisk."

"You mean, like if he were captured and tortured for all his information?" Archie asked.

"Exactly. Should that happen, the Omnidisk were supposed to stop working for a limited amount of time. In the event of his death, they were supposed to stop working permanently," Chasub responded.

"Wait, that doesn't make sense. Didn't you tell me that if the Omnidisks had no DNA they would stop working and that's why they locked in on me and the others?" Eric asked, rubbing his head in confusion. "So, which one is it?"

"Both, actually. Both safeguards were meant to provide layers of security. They were never able to test it to see if it worked."

"What does that have to do with us?" Eric asked.

"Somehow the Omnidisks scanned and found someone to lock onto for this function. Just as they scanned for you," Chasub said.

Archie frowned. "You're telling me that someone's vitals are connected to all of the Omnidisks?"

"Yes. If tragedy were to befall this person, the power the Omnidisks hold would be gone," Chasub said grimly.

"But wouldn't that be good for us too?" Brynn asked. "Whatever the augments were planning wouldn't work anymore if the Omnidisks were non-functional, right?"

"Unfortunately, that is not the case. The Omnidisk's ability to give you superhuman powers would be stopped. But the raw energy inside them would still exist and be a danger to the entire planet," Chasub explained. "If the augments were to find this out, they could use it to their advantage. They could simply kill the Center, and you would lose your powers."

"And a person would be dead," Archie added. "Which is also a bad thing."

"So basically, what you're saying is that not only are we trying to save the world, now we have to save the Omnidisks by saving the Center," Eric voice was full of irritation.

"Exactly," Chasub typed a series of commands into his console, and a holographic picture of Christina Stephens appeared. "This is the Center."

"Wow," Archie said. "What are the odds?"

"Eric, your mouth is hanging open," Brynn joked.

"Is something wrong?" Chasub asked.

"Nothing at all," Eric said, regaining his composure. "How do you want us to handle this? Should we bring her up and tell her what is going on?"

"In this case, I believe that would be a mistake," Chasub replied. "Unlike the rest of you, she is unable to defend herself from the danger she is in. The powers the Omnidisks contain do nothing for her. Informing her would only cause her to panic. It would be best to keep watch over her for now until we have eliminated the threat."

"Don't worry." Eric's voice was full of conviction. "No one will lay a finger on her."

"Yeah, he will be on her like stink on a bantha," Archie joked.

There was silence all around.

Archie sighed. "Okay, bad joke. I'm hungry. Can we go eat our tacos now?"

"I second that." Brynn rubbed her stomach.

CHAPTER 20

"I have to go talk to my Pre-Cal teacher for a few minutes," Brynn said to Eric and Archie as the last school bell rang. "Tell Chris I'll meet up with you guys as soon as I'm done."

"Sure thing," Eric said as he and Archie walked off.

"This must be a dream come true for you," Archie said. "You get to play secret service for Chris."

Eric groaned. "You're not going to let it go, are you?"

"Yeah, like I'd—" Archie stopped when Will shoved past them and continued down the hallway without a word.

"Will, hold on!" Eric ran after him. Archie followed.

"I don't want to talk to you," Will said, refusing to turn around.

"Will, just because you don't want to join us doesn't mean that we all still can't be friends," Archie said in an assuring tone.

Will spun around and pointed a finger at Archie. "Actually, it does! Because when these guys find out who you are, and they will, they're not just going to kill you. They will go after the ones you love."

Eric's eyes widened. He hadn't considered how dangerous this could be to those close to him.

The corner of Will's mouth turned up to form a bitter smile. "You didn't think about that, did you? Your family and friends will be the primary targets when they decide they want to hurt you. Which means that now I have to make sure they don't put me in either category."

"Will, hold on a minute," Eric said, trying to find some kind of flaw in Will's logic.

"No, Eric, you hold on! You know I'm right. Being friends with you is now officially an extreme sport that I have no interest in playing. I'm warning you. Stay away from me!" Will turned around to leave.

Eric was not willing to let their friendship die that easily. "Will, wait!" He grabbed Will's arm.

Will spun around and punched Eric in the face. The blow knocked Eric off balance and caused him to stumble into the lockers.

"Come near me again, and you'll get more of the same," Will warned. He turned and started to walk away once more. "This friendship is over."

Archie hurried to Eric's side. "Are you ok?"

Eric rubbed his jaw. "If you mean physically, then yes, but I never wanted to alienate Will like this."

"One problem at a time, remember?" Archie said. "We still have Chris to worry about."

"You're right. One problem at a time. At least she doesn't hate us," Eric said with mock enthusiasm as he and Archie stepped out of the back door of the school.

Chris, Jeff, and a large pile of boxes were waiting for them.

"Hey, guys!" Chris waved happily at her friends. "I was afraid you had forgotten about me."

"Yeah, we were worried you might've gotten lost or something," Jeff said with a chuckle.

Eric smiled and lifted a box. "We wouldn't miss this."

"The truck is over there." Jeff pointed to a white pickup a few feet away. "Try not to trip on the way over."

Eric stopped for a second, took a deep breath and resumed walking to the truck.

"Good decision." Archie set his box next to Eric's. "You don't have anything to prove to him."

"I hate how he tries to make me look bad in front of Chris," Eric said, enviously looking at Chris and Jeff kiss next to the school.

"Careful, buddy, the whole jealousy thing didn't work out too well for the Hulk. You don't want to go down that path," Archie said.

"Sometimes you might want to try using real people in these examples of yours." Eric laughed. "Maybe some of us normal folk can get something out of it."

Suddenly, a white van approached the group. It stopped several feet away from the truck. A man got out of the driver's side, and a woman got out of the passenger's side.

"Do you know them?" Archie whispered.

"No, but I'm sure you'll understand when I say my spider sense is going off," Eric answered in a whisper.

Anira and Lance walked past the truck without acknowledging either of the guys standing there.

"Christina Stephens?" Anira asked as she and Lance stopped a few feet away from where Chris and Jeff were standing.

"That's me. Are you here for the supplies?" Chris asked with a nervous smile. "I thought we were supposed to drop them off."

Anira nodded her head toward Lance as he began walking toward Chris.

"What's going on here?" Jeff stepped in front of Chris. "What do you want with my girlfriend?"

Lance punched Jeff in the face. The quarterback hit the ground and didn't move.

Chris began to scream as she stared at Jeff.

Eric looked over and gasped. "Christina! Archie, let's go!" They both ran toward Chris and her two assailants.

Anira turned around and stretched out her hands, and bolts of electricity shot out from them.

Both of the boys leaped to the side. Eric was able to avoid the blast completely, but Archie hit the ground after being grazed by the bolt.

Anira glared at Eric. "Take care of him, Lance. I'll grab the girl."

Anira reached out and aggressively grabbed Chris' wrist.

"No!" She lashed out at Anira.

Anira sent a shock through Chis' arm, knocking her out. "Kids."

"I won't let you take her!" Eric grabbed one of the boxes and threw it at Lance. Lance ducked, and the box hit Anira in the chest, knocking her to the ground.

"Chivalry is such a nuisance," Lance complained as he went to meet Eric head-on.

Eric grabbed Lance by the front of his shirt, spun him around and slammed him against the truck. Lance's eyes went wide, obviously surprised by Eric's strength. "Now, you're going to tell me who sent you and why you're trying to kidnap—"

Eric collapsed as Anira lowered her arm and stopped the flow of electricity she had used to incapacitate him. She walked over and stared hard at Eric for several seconds.

"What is it?" Lance asked. "Why are you staring at that kid?"

"I'm impressed at his strength and courage. Under different circumstances, I might have recruited him. Take her. I'll drive," Anira handed Chris' limp body over to Lance as they headed towards the van.

Eric's eyes fluttered open but he was too weak to move.

"What's going on here?" Jason stepped out of the school. "You two put that student down now.

"Jason, be careful. They're not what they seem," Eric managed to say before he passed out again.

Jason took out his cell phone. "Stay down, Eric. I'm calling the police, immediately."

Anira sighed extended a finger and hit Jason's phone with a bolt of electricity. "No, you won't. Let's get out of here."

Eric's eyes fluttered open right as the tail end of the van rounded the corner. "Archie," Eric said weakly. "We have to get up."

"What happened?" Archie grabbed his side and winced.

"They got her. They got Chris."

"They must have been the people that Chasub spoke about before. They're probably working for the augments now," Archie said as he dusted off his pants.

"Are you ok?" Jason ran over to Eric and Archie. "How did she do that?"

Eric looked at Archie nervously. "Well… you see…"

"She had one of those new age tasers," Archie cut in. "Military grade. Can shoot electricity over long distances."

"Of course," Jason nodded. "For a moment I thought the power came out of her very hands."

"It was probably just stress," Eric reassured him. "Shouldn't you grab the nurse and the school officer?"

"Right! There's been an abduction! And Jeff is hurt!" Jason ran back into the school.

Eric glanced around and activated his suit. "Chasub, we have a situation. That new augment with electric powers, and some other guy took Chris."

"I've got them on sensors. They aren't far; if you move now, you can still catch them," Chasub said.

"Tell Brynn what's going on and to meet us."

"What about him?" Archie asked, activating his suit and looking at Jeff as he still lay unconscious.

Crimson Falcon didn't even look at the fallen football player. "He will be fine. We have to save Chris!" Crimson Falcon took to the air.

Xenoshot jumped on his Hyperboard and followed him. "Don't worry. We'll stop them."

"We'd better. I don't know what I'd do if…there they are!" Crimson Falcon pointed to the speeding van.

"Ram it!" Xenoshot yelled.

"I can't; I might hurt Chris," Crimson Falcon objected. "Take out your illuminator and see if you can shoot out one of the tires."

Xenoshot aimed his illuminator at the van's tired and fired. Tseeew! Tseeew!

The first shot missed the van entirely. The van had to swerve to miss the second one.

"Be careful!" Crimson Falcon cried. "Chris is in there!"

"This is harder than it looks." Xenoshot fired again and missed.

"They are approaching a large structure. You must stop them before they reach it!" Chasub said.

"Talk about pressure." Xenoshot pointed downward and used both of his hands to steady the weapon.

Tseeew! The green beam of energy hit home. The rubber on the rear right tire of the van exploded.

The vehicle went into a spin. The driver fought to gain control as the vehicle approached the abandoned power plant that housed the augment's hideout.

"Pull into the parking lot. Hurry!" Anira shouted. "Get her inside!" Anira jumped out of the van.

Lance grabbed Chris and ran after Anira into the plant.

"Nice shot," Crimson Falcon complimented Xenoshot.

"I've been practicing," Xenoshot said proudly.

"Prodigy will be there in a few minutes," Chasub informed them.

"We're going in; they might get away!" Crimson Falcon replied. "We'll take the rear entrance."

"It's locked," Xenoshot said as he and Crimson Falcon stood at the back door. "Maybe I can burn through the lock with my illuminator."

"Maybe." Crimson Falcon grabbed the handle again and yanked it off its hinges. "But my way is faster. Why have super strength if I'm not going to use it?"

Inside, Xenoshot used his illuminator to scan the building, searching for Anira and Lance. "They must be around here somewhere," Xenoshot frowned at the readings.

"Wait a minute," Crimson Falcon said. "Chasub, why don't you fling Chris to the ship?"

"I cannot lock onto her. There is too much electrical interference from the augment."

"It's going to be impossible to find them in all of this. There are generators and old pieces of machinery everywhere," Xenoshot said.

"Can you at least tell us where they are?" Crimson Falcon asked.

"The augment and Christina are near the center of the building," Chasub informed them. "I don't know why."

"We have to find her before something happens. Where is Prodigy?"

"She got stopped by a teacher," Chasub said. "She will join you as soon as she can."

"Tell her to leave," Crimson Falcon snapped, trying not to shout. "There is too much at risk. Let's go, Xenoshot." Crimson Falcon briskly walked forward.

Xenoshot followed. "Right behind you, fearless lead—"

"Xenoshot?" Crimson Falcon turned around and saw Xenoshot fall to the floor. He ran over to his friend and tried to rouse him. "Chasub, someone is in here. Whoever it is knocked out Xenoshot."

"It must be the Veil Omnidisk," Chasub said.

"What does it—" A blow to Crimson Falcon's face sent him sliding across the floor. He jumped to his feet and put up his fists, ready for battle.

"You look confused," a male voice from nowhere said.

"I'm just catching my breath," Crimson Falcon looked around for the speaker. "Who are you? Show yourself!"

"My name is Lance," the voice replied. "We can't let you get the girl."

Another punch caught Crimson Falcon across the face, causing him to stumble back. He swung his right fist and followed with his left but hit nothing except air. "I know how you can stay invisible."

"Good, but that doesn't change anything." Lance kicked Crimson Falcon in the stomach.

"Who sent you?" Crimson Falcon held his midsection in pain.

"Like I'm going to tell." Lance kicked Crimson Falcon in the face. Crimson Falcon fell to the ground. "I was told you could fight."

Crimson Falcon jumped got to his feet. He kicked at the air in front of him, but his foot didn't connect with anything. "Show yourself, and I'll show how you sharp my fighting skills are!

"Maybe another time. Right now, my main goal is to keep you—"

"There you are!" Crimson Falcon's grabbed Lance by the arm. "You talk too much." The hero pulled Lance into a headlock. "Where's the girl?"

"Do you think I would tell you that easily?" Lance slammed his elbow into Crimson Falcon's stomach, breaking free.

"You shouldn't use that Omnidisk," Crimson Falcon warned. "The energy is going to make you sick."

"I appreciate your concern," Lance said with a laugh. "But I think I'll take my chances. By the way, you should check your belt. You may have dropped something."

Crimson Falcon looked down. The compartment with the strength Omnidisk in it was empty. "How did you do that?"

"I used to pick a pretty mean pocket in my day." Lance hit Crimson Falcon in the chest.

"Aaaaah!" Crimson Falcon flew through the air and into a wall.

"You must take those Omnidisks from him," Chasub ordered. "If he gets them to the other augments—"

"I know." Crimson Falcon rubbed his chest and got on his feet. "But if I could see him this would be a lot easier."

"Did you hit your head or something? It sounds like you're talking to yourself." Lance kicked Crimson Falcon in the back, and he soared into an old generator.

"Chasub, I have an idea. Don't scan for Lance's life sign. Instead, scan for the Omnidisk itself. He has it on him so that should tell us where he is. Aaaah!" Another kick sent Crimson Falcon flying into the air and crashing to the ground.

"Don't worry, this will be over as soon as my friend has the girl secured," Lance said.

"My scans are detecting the Omnidisk. He is right behind you!" Chasub warned.

Crimson Falcon leaped to his feet, turned around, and threw a punch at the seemingly empty space in front of him.

"Aaah!" The first punch knocked Lance off balance. The second punch sent him spinning.

"He is now standing to your left," Chasub said.

Crimson Falcon kicked his foot out to the left and felt it connect with Lance's body. There was a soft thud as Lance hit the ground.

"He is straight ahead of you. He is trying to move away," Chasub said.

Crimson Falcon picked a metal bar off of the floor and threw it directly in front of him.

"Aaaah!" Lance stumbled forward as the bar struck him in the side.

Crimson Falcon took two strides forward and threw another punch, but this time his fist stopped in midair.

"You had your fun. Now it's time to finish this," Lance said.

Crimson Falcon gritted his teeth in pain as Lance's hand began to crush his fist.

"I was told I could kill you if necessary." Lance grabbed Crimson Falcon by the neck and slammed him against the wall. "And since you've gotten on my nerves so much, that's exactly what I'm going to do!"

Crimson Falcon tried to break free, but with the Brawn Omnidisk aiding him, Lance was too strong. After a few seconds, his vision began to dim.

"Crimson Falcon!" Chasub yelled.

Crimson Falcon could feel unconsciousness begin to overtake him.

Tseeew! A green beam of light shot through the air and stopped a few inches in front of Crimson Falcon. He felt Lance release him. He fell to the ground and began coughing and gasping for air.

Xenoshot ran over to him. "Are you ok?"

Crimson Falcon gasped. "Forget about me; we have to find Lance."

Suddenly, the air in front of them shimmered, and the unconscious body of Lance appeared.

Crimson Falcon smiled. "Never mind."

Xenoshot reached into Lance's jacket pocket and pulled out the Brawn and Veil Omnidisks. He held them out to Crimson Falcon. "I guess these are yours."

"Well done, Xenoshot," Chasub commended them as Crimson Falcon took the Omnidisks.

"Where is Chris, Chasub?" Crimson Falcon put the Omnidisks in his belt.

"The augment is taking her to the lower level of the building." Chasub paused, and added, "That might be a good thing; there does not appear to be an exit on that level."

"If I've learned anything, it is that things are never as they appear. How do we get down there?"

"You'll have to take the stairs at the rear. They will lead you to the basement," Chasub said.

"Okay. Let's go." Crimson and Xenoshot began running toward the rear stairs.

"Once you get to the bottom of the stairs, turn left at the next corridor. They should be right in front of you," Chasub said. "Proceed with caution."

Crimson Falcon stopped at the corner and slowly peeked around. He could see Anira. Finally, he spotted Chris. Her mouth was taped shut and her hands were tied together. Anira had her by the arm and was dragging her down the corridor.

Crimson Falcon turned to Xenoshot. "As soon as I give the word, we'll go around the corner. I want you to fire off a warning shot to get her attention."

"Why can't I fire directly at Anira?" Xenoshot asked.

"You could hit Chris. They're too close, and the lighting is too dim. Getting her home safely is the priority."

Xenoshot nodded. "No problem."

Crimson Falcon waited a few seconds. "Now!"

Tseeew! Xenoshot jumped out and aimed his illuminator at the ceiling. Plaster landed in front of Anira.

"Get back!" Anira pulled Chris close to her and held up a hand that was glowing blue with electricity. "If you try to follow us, I will kill her."

Chris' eyes widened and she tried to scream through the duct tape.

"Let them go," Crimson Falcon said to Xenoshot.

Anira smiled and dragged Chris around another corner.

"We can't let her take Chris away!" Xenoshot said.

"I don't plan on it," Crimson Falcon replied. "I think it's time to try out my new toy. Hold onto me."

Xenoshot put his hand on Crimson Falcon's shoulder. A moment later, both of them disappeared.

"Don't let go of me or you'll be visible again," Crimson Falcon instructed him.

They turned the corner where Anira and Chris had disappeared and began to follow them at a distance.

"Do you have some kind of plan?" Xenoshot whispered.

"Give me a minute." Crimson Falcon looked around. After a moment he noticed Anira and Chris were about to walk under a series of pipes. "Xenoshot, when they walk under those pipes, I want you to shoot the one directly over Anira's head."

"Right," Xenoshot said.

Crimson Falcon observed them until Anira took the first step under a pipe. "Now!"

Xenoshot aimed his illuminator at the pipe and fired.

White steam billowed out from the pipe and engulfed Anira.

Anira dropped Chris and backed into the wall.

"Let's go!" Crimson Falcon deactivated the Veil Omnidisk and flew right into Anira, hitting her with his shoulder.

Anira sailed down the corridor and crashed into the wall at the end. Crimson Falcon ran toward Chris.

Chris cried as Crimson Falcon tore the duct tape from her mouth. She glanced at Crimson Falcon and Xenoshot and tried to move away, despite her restraints. "Who are you?"

"It's ok," Crimson Falcon reassured her. "We're the good guys. We are here to protect you."

Chris stopped retreating. "I don't know what I would've done if you hadn't …look out!"

Crimson Falcon and Xenoshot spun around as Anira stretched out her hands and prepared to fire.

They braced for impact. And were surprised when the bolts stopped right before they hit them.

"I can't believe you guys didn't wait for me," Prodigy said, dropping the force field she had put over them. "I should've let her zap you."

"You first!" Anira fired another bolt of electricity directly at Prodigy.

Prodigy threw up her hands and gritted her teeth from the stress of blocking the electric energy.

"I have one for you too!" Anira raised her other hand and fired at Chris.

"No!" Crimson Falcon jumped in front of Chris, and the bolt hit him in the chest, propelling him into a wall.

Tseeew! Xenoshot fired his illuminator.

The beam hit Anira in the arm. Anira grabbed the wound in pain and lunged at Xenoshot.

"Get away!" Prodigy pushed her hand forward and slammed Anira into a wall.

Crimson Falcon managed to scramble to his feet, rubbing his chest. "Chasub, are you there?"

"I'm here."

"Can we used one of those inhibitors on her so you can fling the augment to the ship?"

"Xenoshot, you should have another one in your jacket pocket."

Xenoshot reached into his pocket and pulled out an inhibitor. "Got it."

"Great," Crimson Falcon said. "Xenoshot, you stay here with Chris while Prodigy and I try to weaken her. When I give the word, move in." Crimson Falcon flew at Anira.

"Excellent plan," Chasub said. "I have the Molecular Flinger at the ready."

"You can't beat me!" Anira shot off another bolt.

"Everyone keeps saying that." Crimson Falcon dodged the bolt and kicked Anira, knocking her to the ground. "For some reason, I don't listen."

"Maybe you're picking up my bad habits." Prodigy flew forward and punched Anira in the face while she was still trying to stand.

"Xenoshot, now!" Crimson Falcon yelled.

Xenoshot ran over and tried to put the inhibitor on Anira's neck.

"Get away from me!" Anira released a surge of electrical energy from her body. Bolts flew in every direction.

One of the bolts hit Xenoshot in the chest and knocked him off his feet.

"Chris, get down!" Crimson Falcon flew over to her and used his body as a shield.

Prodigy used her powers to protect herself and Xenoshot from the electricity as well.

"Chasub, get us out of here!" Crimson Falcon yelled as a barrage of electrical energy assaulted his body.

"There is too much electric interference," Chasub said. "You must create some space between you and the augment before I can get a lock."

Crimson Falcon looked over at Prodigy. She was starting to weaken under the constant stress of blocking the electricity.

"Prodigy, I need you to try to give us some elbow room!" Crimson Falcon yelled to her.

"I'll do my best." Prodigy waved one of her hands toward Anira and lifted her off of the floor.

"Release me, now!" Anira screamed, continuing the onslaught of electrical shots into the air.

"No problem." Prodigy flicked her wrist and Anira flew down the hallway.

"Now, Chasub!" Crimson Falcon yelled.

In an instant, Crimson Falcon and his friends were materializing on Chasub's ship.

"Chris, are you alright?" Crimson Falcon asked, helping her to her feet.

Chris didn't answer him. Instead, she began to look around the ship, eyes wide with wonder. "What is this place?"

"*The Omega,* an interstellar spacecraft," Chasub responded.

"What are you?!" Chris gasped as she looked at Chasub. She turned to Crimson Falcon and his companions. "What's going on here?"

Crimson Falcon smiled. "No matter how many times I tell this story, it is never going to get old."

CHAPTER 21

"…And that's why we had to keep you safe," Crimson Falcon said as he finally finished the story.

Some of the color had drained from Chris' face. "So, I'm the Center? Why me; what makes me so special?"

"Actually, the scanning and choosing process was completely random as far as I can tell," Chasub said. "Anyone could have been chosen."

Chris seemed to be saddened by Chasub's response.

"I think you are special," Crimson Falcon said as he walked over and stood next to her. "You are the most important person on the planet now. Keeping you alive gives us a fair chance of stopping the augments."

"Crimson Falcon is right," Prodigy said. "Our Omnidisks work because you're here. That sounds pretty special to me."

They all turned toward Prodigy.

"What? I can be nice sometimes."

Chris took a deep breath and exhaled. "It's all so overwhelming. I never imagined I'd be in the middle of something like this. So, I can't even use the Omnidisks like you do? What if something happens and I need to defend myself?

Xenoshot spoke up. "That's our job. You're Queen Amidala and we're the Jedi Order."

Chris cracked a small smile at Xenoshot's comparison. "You remind me of someone. I can't put my finger on who…"

Crimson Falcon glared at Xenoshot, signaling him to stop talking.

Suddenly, Chris began to cry.

Crimson Falcon put his hand on Chris' arm. "I know you're scared, but you have to trust me. I will die before I let anything happen to you."

Chris rested her head against Crimson Falcon's chest. "I can't believe I was almost killed." She looked into Crimson Falcon's eyes. "I believe you. Somehow, I know I'm safe with you."

Crimson Falcon swallowed awkwardly.

Xenoshot nudged Prodigy and snickered.

"Here's a crazy question," Chris said. "Who are you guys? Crimson Falcon, Prodigy and Xenoshot can't be your real names."

"No, unfortunately, my parents aren't that creative," Xenoshot said bitterly.

Chasub hurriedly spoke before anyone else could reply. "Crimson Falcon. I would like a word with you and the others. Privately." Chasub glanced at Chris.

"Give me a minute." Crimson Falcon walked over to the Chasub. Prodigy and Xenoshot joined them.

"What's up?" Crimson Falcon asked.

"I do not believe it would be wise to tell her your secret identities."

"I wasn't going to," Crimson Falcon said, not entirely sure he was telling the truth.

"Why not?" Prodigy asked. "She's my best friend; I know we can trust her. She already knows everything else."

"Maybe so," Chasub replied. "But if the augments—"

"We won't let that happen," Crimson Falcon said firmly, finishing Chasub's sentence.

"I know, but we still have to consider the possibility. Something could go wrong, and if the augments do capture her, they might…make her tell them things."

Xenoshot shuddered.

"I told you, we won't let them touch her," Crimson Falcon repeated angrily.

"On second thought, Chasub is right," Prodigy said reluctantly. "If Chris knows who we are, she becomes a security risk."

Xenoshot agreed. "Yes, in the long run, it is a lot safer."

Crimson Falcon sighed and finally nodded. "Agreed, we won't tell her." He pulled the Veil Omnidisk out of his belt and held it out toward Chasub. "I think you should take this."

"Why?" Chasub asked. "You can use it to fight without being seen."

"Yeah, they won't even see how bad you're beating them down," Prodigy said.

"Lance used a lot of sneaky tactics while he was fighting me," Crimson Falcon said. "I'm not that kind of fighter. I wouldn't feel right if I used it."

"A lot of people could die," Prodigy reminded him. "We need every advantage we can get. We don't have time to worry about being proper."

"I admire how noble you are being," Chasub took the Omnidisk from Crimson Falcon. "But Prodigy's words are something to consider. Right now, we have to find a way to explain our decision to your friend."

"Why do I get the feeling you're talking about me?" Chris asked loudly.

Crimson Falcon walked over to her and sighed. "Because we were. And we decided…not to tell you who we are. We think the information may put you in danger."

Chris gave an understanding smile. "I thought you might say something like that."

"I'm very sorry," Crimson Falcon said.

"I'm not mad," Chris assured him. She looked around at the others. "I know all of you are trying to help me. I promise you have my cooperation and trust."

Crimson Falcon, Prodigy, and Xenoshot all smiled.

"This is good news," Chasub said with his usual lack of enthusiasm. "Now, I believe it is time for you to return home."

"What about those two kidnappers?" Chris asked. "What happened to them?"

"I gave the authorities an anonymous call. Hopefully, they will reach the power plant before the criminals can escape. There are outstanding warrants on both of them, so I am sure the police will do all they can to arrest them," Chasub said.

"Thank you all," Chris said gratefully. "I can't express enough appreciation for all you have done for me."

"From this point on, consider it our job," Chasub said. "Now we must have someone escort you home."

"I'll do it!" Crimson Falcon practically yelled. He looked around, embarrassed. "If nobody else minds."

"Not at all," Prodigy said with a smirk. "You two have fun."

Xenoshot stifled a snicker.

"I'll fling you a short distance from your home," Chasub said. "And don't worry. We will be watching."

"You didn't bbring the girl," Command said when Anira walked into the room. His back was turned to her, but he still made this statement with confidence.

"That team that you told me about arrived before we could complete our assignment," Anira simply said. There was no fear in her voice.

"I warned you about them," Command replied. "I told you they were skilled fighters."

"I thought I could handle them," Anira replied, an edge in her voice.

"And you were wrong." Command turned around. "Where is Lance?"

"The police got him. I was able to conceal myself."

"Where's the Omnidisk?!" Slymind asked as he and Mange walked into the room.

Command threw Slymind a look. "Don't ever interrupt me when I am talking."

"Sorry, sir." Slymind bowed his head.

Command turned to Anira. "Answer the question."

"The police have most likely confiscated it," Anira said. 'Lance still had it in his possession before they took him."

"Doubtful," Command said. "It is much more likely that Crimson Falcon and his friends took it."

"Whatever," Anira shrugged. "Do you want me to go after her again?"

"No. The girl is under their protection now. She must be very important."

"In that case, it seems our business is through," Anira said. "I'm going to find a way to free my partner."

"Wait!" Command shouted. "You may have failed in this mission, but you have great power. You can be helpful to us on a new mission."

"Sir, with all due respect, she lost the girl! She didn't successfully carry out her mission," Slymind objected.

"She is not the only one!" Command shouted, glaring at Slymind.

"How much are you going to pay me for this new mission?" Anira asked.

"Trust me." Command smiled. "The dollar amount will be... astronomical."

A small smile appeared on Anira's face. "I'm listening."

"First things first. You need a new name. One that represents the new power you possess." Command paced the floor for a moment, then stopped and stared at Anira. "You are Arcspark."

"Very well," Arcspark said respectfully. "Tell me more."

Crimson Falcon landed at Chris' back door, holding her in his arms.

"That was incredible," Chris said breathlessly. "I've flown in planes before, but I have never experienced anything like that."

Being a superhero has its perks, Crimson Falcon thought to himself as he set her feet on the ground. "Maybe we can do this again sometime."

"I would like that," Chris said with a smile.

Their eyes locked together for a few seconds. Crimson Falcon was the first to turn away. "I should go."

"Of course." Chris crossed her arms and shuddered, "I'm still a little nervous. I have to go to school tomorrow, and I don't even know if I'll be safe there."

Crimson Falcon looked at Chris and smiled. "We have eyes everywhere. Chasub is doing regular scans of your house and the area around it. I think you will be quite safe at school."

"Thank you, again. I feel so much better with you watching over me." Chris smiled. "I guess I'll see you around."

Crimson Falcon smiled and rose off of the ground. "Count on it."

Chris waved. "Take care! Hey, wait! What about Jeff?"

"Who?" Crimson Falcon asked, acting as if he had no idea whom she was referring to.

"He's my boyfriend. He was there when I got kidnapped. And there were two others, Eric and Archie. They were trying to help before I was knocked out."

"They were all knocked out by the time we got on the scene. They were okay, don't worry." Crimson Falcon allowed a small smile to form on his lips. "The other two looked like they put up quite a fight. Your boyfriend might want to get some boxing lessons."

Chris giggled. "I'm sure he did his best. I'm just happy you got there when you did."

Chris smiled as Crimson Falcon rose into the sky.

Crimson Falcon flew over the trees and did a backward flip in midair.

"I am sensing an elevated heart rate." Chasub sounded alarmed. "Are you ill?"

Crimson Falcon laughed. "Just the opposite, my friend. I feel great."

"Hello, my friends," Eric said to Brynn and Archie the next day, putting an arm over each of their shoulders as they walked down the hallway. "Isn't it a beautiful morning?"

"Are you feeling ok?" Archie asked.

"He's happy about Chris," Brynn said simply.

Eric sent her a surprised look. "I never said—"

"Tell me I'm wrong." Brynn got out from under Eric's arm and looked at him with a smug grin on her face.

Eric chuckled but didn't respond.

"Hey!" Chris waved as she walked over to them. "I've been looking all over for you two." She gestured toward Archie and Eric.

"Chris!" A huge smile appeared on Eric's face. "We were just talking about you."

Brynn cleared her throat and interrupted. "We were worried. They told me about the attack yesterday, right guys?" She looked pointedly at Eric.

"Exactly," Archie caught on.

"Right," Eric remembered hid duel identity. "We tried to stop them. I'm sorry we couldn't. We did call the cops."

"Don't feel bad," Chris said. "I'm sure you did all you could. My parents were freaking out when they heard, but in the end, they were glad I was home, safe and sound."

"How did you get away?" Archie asked.

"You would never believe me," Chris said with a laugh.

"Chris, I'm your best friend, and you can trust Eric and Archie," Brynn assured her.

"It's a long story." Chris leaned in close. "I had some *super-heroes* who came to my rescue."

"Super-heroes?" Brynn asked, pretending to be dubious.

"Yes!" Chris whispered urgently. "They pulled me away from the kidnappers just in time."

"It makes perfect sense to me," Archie said, holding in a laugh.

"Did you get the name of your 'super-heroes'?" Eric asked.

"Crimson Falcon, Prodigy and Xenoshot, and I can tell you that they were pretty amazing. Especially, Crimson Falcon. He was so cool," Chris said. Eric tried not to smile too big.

"Tell us more about him," Eric encouraged her.

"He is the leader, I think," Chris continued. "He is a great fighter. He's also caring, smart, and kind of cute," even with her brown skin it was evident that she was blushing.

"He does sound like a super-hero, alright." Brynn jabbed her elbow into Eric's side.

"Chris! There you are!" Jeff came walking up the hallway.

"Don't mention any of this to Jeff," Chris whispered. "I don't want him to get mad or anything. He got knocked out by the kidnappers."

"Really?" Brynn said, faking shock.

"Hey, babe." Jeff hugged Chris. "I heard the cops caught that goon. Good for them; I was about to lay him out. I would have totally won if he hadn't sucker punched me."

"Are you sure? He seemed a little much for you to handle." Eric repressed a grin.

"He caught me off guard, that's all," Jeff's face turned red, and he put his hands in his pockets. "I doubt you did any better."

"Actually—" Eric started to argue, but Archie put his hand on his shoulder. "You're right, his partner took us out," Eric finished.

Jeff laughed. "At least I got knocked out by a guy."

"Jeff!" Chris looked at him disapprovingly.

"Sorry," Jeff said, not sounding apologetic at all. "Anyway, you ready?"

Chris waved at her friends. "I'll see you later."

"Count on it." Jeff shoved Archie with his shoulder as he walked past.

"I'm cute," Eric said with pride.

"No, *Crimson Falcon* is cute," Archie corrected his friend as he glared at Jeff.

"And you need to remember that before you blow our covers," Brynn whispered harshly.

"Sorry," Eric said. "I guess I got caught up in the moment. I'll remember to do better next time."

"And don't forget that Chris only has a crush on one of you," Brynn said with a smile before throwing her long hair over her shoulder and walking away.

"I'll take whatever victories I can get," Eric muttered bitterly as Will walked past without even looking at him.

"Win some, lose some," Archie said. "But I'm with you. Will isn't one of the losses I wanted to take on either." He looked in the direction Brynn had gone. "Do you think a guy like me and Brynn could ever—"

"Nope," Eric looked at his watch. "Come on, class time. I don't want to add a tardy to my list of woes."

"Well, if you can't count on your best friend to be brutally honest, who can you trust?" Archie said in a bitter tone.

"I'm sorry," Eric said. "That was insensitive, but you and Brynn? You like reading about super soldiers and stuff like that. She wants to live it. I don't know if you two would be compatible.

"Still, there's something about her," Archie said.

Eric laughed. "You got that right. Now, let's go."

After school that day, Eric stopped by Jason's room before leaving.

"Please, come in," Jason said as Eric knocked. "How are you feeling after what happened yesterday?"

"I'm feeling a lot better, thanks. Nice lesson today on Julius Caesar. I liked it."

"It's not merely a story, you know," Jason put a few books in his bag. "There are a lot of things that we can learn from history. History gives us little pieces of information that each of us can glean from and use in our lives each day. For instance, take what we learned today from Caesar. He had to learn the hard way that sometimes even his best friends or his closet companions couldn't always be trusted."

"To me, he simply lacked faith in people in general," Eric replied. "But I agree that trust between friends is vital, though it can be difficult to maintain in certain circumstances."

"What do you mean?" Jason asked in a concerned tone.

"Well, I told you before about the huge fight my friend, Will, and I got into because I couldn't share a secret with him and how he felt as if somehow the trust between us had vanished."

"Yes, I recall that. How did you resolve the situation?"

Eric sighed. "Well, the circumstances changed slightly, and I was able to tell him everything."

"That's didn't help matters between you two?"

"Actually, it made matters worse," Eric said looked at the floor. "He didn't like what he heard, and now he's madder than ever at me."

"I don't mean to sound heartless here, but maybe you should find some new friends," Jason suggested.

"I can't walk away from Will like that. I value his friendship and would like to keep his trust," Eric said.

"Why? You told him about something significant, and he walked away from you," Jason said matter of factly.

"He considered the situation and found that it wasn't best for him to be involved; that's all."

Jason smiled. "You're a good friend, but perhaps I could better understand the situation if you told me what this big secret was in the first place. It's hard to give good advice when you only have half of the story."

"I wish I could tell you," Eric said. "I truly do."

Jason looked at his watch. "I have some spare time on my hands. I was planning to grab a bite across the street. Would you like to join me?"

"Actually, I'd like that," Eric said with a smile.

"Great, I'll buy," Jason volunteered. "And if you knew what a teacher's salary was, you'd realize that is a *real* sign of friendship."

Eric laughed and followed Jason out the door.

CHAPTER 22

"I love Fridays," Eric said as he ate lunch with Archie. "Actually, this whole week has been pretty quiet."

"Yeah, no augments bothering us. And I have learned a lot about the controls on *The Omega*," Archie said proudly. "I'm the only human who knows how to operate a Zeph ship!"

"How is that wolf guy we captured doing?" Eric asked.

"Oh yeah, I forgot to tell you. He's cured. He's one hundred percent human again. Chasub erased his memory before sending him home. That way, he won't remember us or the ship."

"That's great. I didn't even know Chasub could do that." Eric lowered his voice. "Are you any closer to finding a way to help Dark Viper?"

Archie's face fell. "The radiation has almost completely altered Dark Viper's DNA. It's going to take us a lot more time to find a way to counter it."

"I wonder where he's been lately," Eric said. "We haven't seen him in a while."

"That shouldn't surprise you," Brynn sat down with her friends. "I wouldn't go out in public if my skin was that dry and scaly either."

"Not all of us can look like we starred in a Noxzema commercial," Eric joked.

"Of course I can't expect him to look this good," Brynn said as she gave Eric and Archie a wide smile. "But that doesn't mean he can't use a little moisturizer; reptile or not, it's gross."

"Looks aren't the only thing that counts," objected Archie. "Look at Nightcrawler. He may be blue and furry, but he's one of the few beings who has teleportation powers."

Brynn rolled her eyes.

Archie saw her act of annoyance and looked at his food in embarrassment.

"Dark Viper has lots of good qualities. I'm sure he'll come through for us," Eric said.

"Hi, guys." Chris sat next to Brynn. "Who has good qualities?"

"We were just talking about a friend of ours," Eric said. "How are you?"

"I'm excited. Tonight, is the last game of the season. You guys are coming, right?"

"Game?" Archie asked.

"The football game," Eric said. "I know you've never been to one, but you had to know that we *had* them."

Archie blushed and remained silent.

Brynn sighed and looked at Chris. "You were saying?"

"I was hoping you guys would come out and support the team."

"Of course we'll be there, right guys?" Brynn looked at her friends.

"I don't think anyone could explain to me why guys slamming themselves into other guys for a ball is entertaining," Archie stated.

"Maybe we shouldn't, guys," Eric said. "I would like to, but our *friend* might have something for us to do. Now is a bad time. We need to have our priorities in order. I'm sorry, Chris, but—"

"Are you sure?" Chris gave Eric her most hopeful look. "I'd really appreciate it."

Archie and Brynn looked at Eric and smiled knowingly.

"You know I admire a man who sticks to his principles," Brynn said to Eric as they walked into the football stadium. "You haven't seen one around here, have you?"

"Oh, shut up," Eric said with a laugh.

"There she is." Brynn spotted Chris several rows down. The school's football stadium was very crowded, but she had delivered on her promise to save seats.

"I don't get this at all," Archie grumbled as he walked over to them. "An outdoor, crowded stadium full of people, all of them yelling at the top of their lungs and acting crazy. How is this fun?"

Chris waved to them and patted the seat next to her.

"I can think of a few reasons." Eric smiled as he walked to Chris' row.

"I am so glad you could make it!" Chris said happily. "The coach put Jeff back in."

"And it would have been such a shame to miss that," Eric muttered as he took his seat.

Chris looked at him for a few seconds. "You don't like Jeff, do you?"

Eric chuckled nervously. "I wouldn't say that; he is just a little rough around the edges that's all."

A group of guys walked past the group. One stopped and looked at Brynn. "Hey, baby. Why don't you and me head out to my car and—"

"Finish that sentence, and I will crush your windpipe," Brynn said, smiling sweetly.

The guy decided to pass on her offer.

"That's my girl," Chris smiled at Brynn. "Anyway, Eric, I know you try not to show your dislike for Jeff, and that's nice of you. But I was hoping the two of you could be friends. He is a good guy. Sometimes he cares too much about what other people think of him."

"It's kind of scary how you can see through me like that," Eric said.

"I can read people pretty well," Chris said. "But I'm sure you have a few deep dark secrets I don't know about."

"No comment. And I don't think Jeff has any interest in being friends with me either. We are…very different people."

"Do you think you could try?" Chris rested her hand on Eric's arm. "For me?"

Eric barely managed to keep from melting. "Sure."

"Eric, did you see that guy?" Archie yelled suddenly as he pointed to the field.

A barely audible growl escaped from Eric's throat. "Sorry, I missed it."

"Watch that guy, the one on the other team," Archie said.

Brynn looked at the field. "I don't notice anything special about him. Wait, that's not true. He does have a pretty nice—"

"Not that!" Archie cut her off. "Wait for the play to start."

A second later, the players began to move. Someone passed the ball to the guy Archie had pointed out. He grabbed the ball and began to run. Fast.

"So he can run. That's bad for our team, but it's not a crime," Eric said.

"Watch carefully." Archie didn't take his eyes off of the field.

Jeff moved to tackle the mystery guy. As soon as Jeff's hand touched him, he executed a spin that threw Jeff a few feet away.

"Oh no!" Chris covered her mouth with her hand. "Poor Jeff."

"Did you see what I saw?" Brynn asked.

"Yeah, that spin was pretty fast," Eric said. *Almost superhumanly fast.*

"I'll be back," Eric said to Chris. "I need to make a call."

Eric ducked into a bathroom and checked the stalls to make sure he was alone before pressing a button on his watch.

"Yes, Eric?" Chasub said.

"Chasub, I am in a bathroom at a football stadium," Eric informed him. "I need you to do a scan for any Omnidisks in the area. I have a hunch."

"I have found something," Chasub replied after a few seconds of silence. "Near the center of the stadium; a human has an Omnidisk in his possession and is using it."

"And I'd bet my grandmother's apple pie that the Omnidisk can give someone super speed," Eric said.

"Yes, that would accurately describe the abilities granted to someone by the Swift Omnidisk. Why would you wager a baked good?" Chasub asked.

"Never mind," Eric said. "I'll tell the others. As soon as the game is over, we're going after him."

When Eric arrived at the seats, he leaned over and whispered in Archie's ear. "You were right. When the game ends, we'll talk to him. Tell Brynn."

"Is something wrong?" Chris asked Eric.

"Nothing." Eric instantly felt guilty about the lie but continued. "We were admiring one of the players on the field. We want to have a talk with him after the game."

When the game was over, Eric and the gang followed Chris to the football field.

"You were wonderful!" Chris cheered as she walked over to Jeff and threw her arms around him.

"Yeah, you did do a good job tonight," Eric commended him.

"I know," Jeff replied without looking at Eric. "Too bad we lost."

"That one player was pretty fast," Archie said while looking around the field.

"Yeah, his name is Bernhardt," said Jeff angrily. "Some German kid. I think he's on steroids or something. There he is." Jeff glared at someone on the other side of the field. "I'm gonna go and find out how he ran so fast."

"Jeff, don't!" Chris grabbed his arm. "Not now."

"Yes, now," Jeff said as he pulled his arm away. "That guy and his cheating cost us the championship. I want to know what he's on."

"Bernhardt!" Jeff angrily walked up to the football player. "I need to talk to you!"

Bernhardt's teammates gathered around him, but he waved them off. "It is okay. There is nothing to worry about," he said with a German accent. He turned to Jeff as his teammates walked off. "May I help you?"

"You can *help me* by telling me how you're cheating!" Jeff grabbed the front of Bernhardt's uniform and pulled him closer. "No one can be as fast as you without some help."

Bernhardt smiled calmly and looked around. "Maybe we should talk privately. Give me some time, and I can explain everything."

Jeff let go of Bernhardt. "That's what I like to hear. Hurry and confess so we can tell everyone who actually won this game."

"Follow me." Bernhardt walked off the field.

"See, babe? I got everything handled," Jeff said confidently.

"This doesn't look good. Maybe we should help," Brynn said, clenching her fists.

"No," Eric whispered as he put his hand on her shoulder to stop her. "We can use the distraction."

"Hey, guys!" Eric shouted. "We're going to run, but we'll talk to you later, Chris."

She gave them a nervous wave as she watched them walk away.

"I have a bad feeling about this. Maybe we should let it go," Chris suggested to Jeff as they moved farther away from the stadium to a secluded area.

"Not a chance," Jeff said arrogantly. "I want my confession. Something is not right about that guy, and I want to find out what it is!"

"This should be far enough," Bernhardt said when they reached the trees.

Chris looked back at the stadium. They were out of everyone's visual range.

"Now, quit stalling and tell me how you did it," Jeff demanded.

Bernhardt smiled and crossed his arms. "No, I don't think I will."

"You cheater!" Jeff grabbed Bernhardt's arm. "Tell me now, or I'll—"

Before he could blink, Jeff had gone from standing upright to being face down on the ground with Bernhardt's foot on his shoulder. "You Americans are always so cocky and sure of yourself," Bernhardt said. "But with me, your brute strength means nothing."

"Get off of him!" Chris yelled, jumping on Bernhardt's back.

"Get your hands off me!" Bernhardt spun around and threw Chris to the ground a few feet away from them.

Jeff struggled to his feet right as Bernhardt kicked him in the face so fast, Jeff never saw his foot leave the ground. Jeff's eyes rolled into his head as he fell to the ground, unconscious.

Bernhardt grabbed a large stick from the ground and turned toward Chris. "Your turn."

"Hey! Over here!" Crimson Falcon grabbed Bernhardt by the arm and hurled him away.

Bernhardt slammed into one of the school trailers and hit the ground.

"Are you alright?" Crimson Falcon took Chris' hand and helped her to her feet.

"Thank you so much," Chris said. "I thought he was going to—"

"He's making a run for it!" Prodigy yelled as she and Xenoshot flew in.

"Chasub, lock onto the Swift Omnidisk and try to keep track of it," Crimson Falcon said.

"I'm trying," Chasub said. "But he's moving at an accelerated rate. My sensors are having a hard time."

Crimson Falcon turned back to Chris. "Sorry, I can't stick around," he said as he turned and looked at Jeff. "You should get him some medical attention."

Chris gasped as she ran over to Jeff. "I will. And be careful, that guy is fast." She looked Crimson Falcon in the eye. "I would hate to see something happen to you."

"I'll be okay. Don't worry, we'll get him," Crimson Falcon promised.

"Let's go, lover boy!" Prodigy yelled.

Chris watched as the three of them flew off.

"Ugh, what happened?" Jeff lifted his head off the ground and looked around. "Not again!"

"Chasub, where is he?" Crimson Falcon was flying full speed, looking for Bernhardt.

"He is three miles to the west," Chasub reported.

"A minute ago you said he was five miles to the north!" Prodigy said.

"He keeps going in different direction, so it is hard to get a good lock on him," Chasub said as he kept hitting buttons on his device. "He's stopped. He's about a mile from you—in an alley behind a McDonalds. Hurry, before he moves again."

"We don't see him, Chasub. Where is he?" Xenoshot asked, keeping his illuminator level.

"Right here!" Bernhardt yelled as he sped past, delivering three high-speed punches in the process.

Crimson Falcon, Prodigy, and Xenoshot were all knocked to the ground.

"I fled before, thinking you were a threat. I feel ashamed of myself," Bernhardt said with a laugh.

"Bernhardt, you have to stop using that Omnidisk," Crimson Falcon said, climbing to his feet. "It's going to make you sick. It'll mess with your head."

"We are *so* skipping that speech," Prodigy stretched out her hand, and Bernhardt slammed into the wall of the fast food restaurant.

"Prodigy!" Crimson Falcon yelled. "Calm down."

"He's dangerous!" Prodigy said as she launched him into the air and then to the ground. "You saw him before. He was going to kill Chris. We have to take him out and get that Omnidisk. I can do it faster than you."

Crimson Falcon groaned. "Fine. But don't hurt him! Immobilize only!"

"No problem." Prodigy threw him into a pile of trash.

Bernhardt's hand fell on a rock. He closed his hand around it.

"Wait a minute," Crimson Falcon ordered Prodigy. "I want to talk to him now." He walked closer to Bernhardt. "You see you are no match for us. Hand over the Omnidisk for your own good."

"I can't do that," Bernhardt said. "I need it."

Crimson Falcon sighed. "Prodigy, we have our answer."

Prodigy nodded and lifted the football player off of the ground again. "He doesn't look like he's going to put up much more of a fight anyway."

"Wrong!" Bernhardt hurled the rock at Prodigy.

"Aaaah!" she cried out in pain as the rock hit her arm.

Bernhardt dropped to the ground. He ran forward and punched Prodigy in the face.

Prodigy lost consciousness and fell to the ground.

Tseeew! Xenoshot fired at Bernhardt.

Bernhardt was gone before the beam reached him. A second later, he appeared in front of Xenoshot. In two swift moves, he took his illuminator and pointed it at him.

"Don't move," Bernhardt ordered Crimson Falcon. "I don't know what this weapon does, but if you come any closer, I'll shoot and find out."

Crimson Falcon clenched his teeth but didn't move. "Chasub," he whispered. "I want you to fling Xenoshot up as soon as possible."

"Aaah!" Suddenly, Bernhardt dropped the illuminator and clutched his hand.

Crimson Falcon's eyes dropped to the ground and saw a throwing star. He looked up, already knowing who he would see.

Dark Viper nodded at Crimson Falcon and drew his bolas from his belt.

"Dark Viper, no! He's too fast!" Crimson Falcon yelled.

The warning came too late. The bolas left his hand and flew right through where Bernhardt had been a moment earlier; they bound Xenoshot's arms and legs.

"Not again!" Xenoshot fell on the ground and hit his head on the concrete. He didn't move.

Crimson Falcon looked around. "Dark Viper, do you see him?"

"No," Dark Viper replied, continuing to scan the area.

"Behind you!" Bernhardt appeared on the roof.

Dark Viper spun around and threw a punch at Bernhardt.

Bernhard speedily ducked and slammed his shoulder into Dark Viper.

"No!" Crimson Falcon tried to reach Dark Viper, but he was not fast enough. Dark Viper fell from the building and hit the ground hard.

"Chasub, fling Dark Viper, Prodigy, and Xenoshot to the ship. They're all hurt badly," Crimson Falcon said.

"And you?" Chasub asked.

"I'm okay." Crimson Falcon looked around for Bernhardt. "I still have to get that Omnidisk away from him. That's what matters."

"Very well, but if you have too much trouble, I will fling you as well," Chasub said.

A moment later, all of Crimson Falcon's companions were on the ship.

"How did that happen?" Bernhardt appeared behind Crimson Falcon.

"If you hand over the Omnidisk, I will explain everything," Crimson Falcon offered.

"I don't want to know that badly." Bernhardt ran forward and hit Crimson Falcon in the face.

"Ooof!" Crimson Falcon stumbled. He regained his balance and punched at Bernhardt.

Bernhardt dodged the punch and rapidly punched Crimson Falcon in the gut ten times.

Crimson Falcon stepped back and held his stomach, his face wracked with pain.

"The way you threw me earlier tells me you must be strong." Bernhardt swiftly grabbed a pipe off of the ground and hit Crimson Falcon in the side with it. "But strength means nothing if you cannot touch me."

Crimson Falcon fell to the ground and tried to kick Bernhardt's feet out from under him, but he sped away before the kick could reach him.

"I must kill you now." Bernhardt stood Crimson Falcon up and hit him across the face before he could blink. "I cannot jeopardize my career."

Crimson Falcon coughed. "Chasub, I think I need to be flung out of here now."

Bernhardt slammed the pipe down on Crimson Falcon's stomach.

Crimson Falcon slowly rose to his feet, but before he could attack Bernhardt ran around hit him in his side and threw him into a wall. "Chasub!"

"I cannot." For the first time, Chasub sounded frustrated. "The speed at which he is moving prevents me from locking onto you."

Crimson Falcon tried to fly off, but Bernhardt grabbed him, spun him around and slammed him into the ground.

"You are very hard to defeat," Bernhardt said as he kicked Crimson Falcon in the chest three times.

"I'll take that as a compliment." Crimson Falcon lunged at Bernhardt.

Bernhardt sprinted around him and hit him in the back with the pipe.

"Chasub, I can't keep doing this. I need help," Crimson Falcon said weakly.

"The others are in the Medical Alcove's healing pods, but they are in no condition to come help you. The Eternity Omnidisk should stop you from being mortally injured in the meantime. Try to hold him off!" Chasub insisted.

"I guess it's time to improvise." Crimson Falcon jumped in the air and slammed his fist on the ground.

The gravel around them shifted and cracked. Bernhardt lost his footing, fell face first on the ground, and rolled into a wall.

Crimson Falcon flew over and grabbed the front of Bernhardt's jersey. "You're not going anywhere now. I'm getting the Swift Omnidisk off of you one way or—Aaaagh!"

Bernhardt rapidly spun around and stopped, propelling Crimson Falcon to the other side of the alley.

"It's no use, Chasub; I can't do this alone," Crimson Falcon said.

"I still cannot get a lock. I'm sorry," Chasub said sadly.

"What do we have here?" Bernhardt held out his hand, holding Crimson Falcon's Brawn and Eternity Omnidisks. "These look like the gadget I have. I bet they gave you powers too." Bernhardt threw them on the ground and in the blink of an eye he was directly in Crimson Falcon's face. "Not anymore."

Another blow from the pipe drove Crimson Falcon to the ground. "Chasub, you have to think of something," he said with a rasp. "He took my Omnidisks. If I don't get some help, we all lose."

CHAPTER 23

"Mom, I'm home!" Will yelled as he walked into his house. He noticed a note on the refrigerator. "Out at a play with friends. Dinner in the fridge."

"Great, she gets a night on the town, and I get leftover meatloaf."

Will began to walk towards his bathroom when suddenly a blue light surrounded him. A moment later he was standing on *The Omega* for the second time.

"Who do you think you are?" Will asked angrily. "You can't keep snatching people out of their homes! I told you I didn't want to join your little club!"

"It's your friend, Eric. He's in trouble!" Chasub said.

Will frowned. "Eric? What's wrong with him?"

"He is being attacked," Chasub said. "He has already been badly beaten. He needs help, or he may die."

Will breathed in deeply. "I told you this would happen. You have to get him here! Use the flinger gizmo."

"I cannot," Chasub replied. "He needs someone to help him. Prodigy, Xenoshot and, Dark Viper are injured. That leaves you."

Will shook his head. "No. No way. I told you I was not joining your suicide mission. I have my mother to take care of; she needs me."

"You spoke before of how your family suffered at the loss of your father," Chasub said.

Will gritted his teeth. "Yeah, what about it?"

"If you had the opportunity to stop him from leaving, would you?" Chasub asked.

"Of course I would!" Will answered angrily. "So what?"

"You have the chance to now save the life of one of your friends. How would you feel if you found that he had died when you could have saved him?" Chasub opened a panel on a computer console and revealed the Morph Omnidisk and a green watch.

"But…my mother." Will's eyes were full of conflict.

"Would she want another to die on her behalf?" Chasub asked.

Will looked about in frustration. He walked over to the console and picked up the watch and Omnidisk. "So are you going to show me how to use this stuff or what?"

Bernhardt reached grabbed Crimson Falcon by the neck. "Not so strong now, are you?" He began to squeeze.

"Chasub—" Crimson Falcon urged through clenched teeth. He had held off for as long as he could but he had no more ideas.

A hawk dropped out of the sky and clawed at Bernhardt's face with its talons, causing Bernhardt to loosen his grip and drop Crimson Falcon to the ground.

"Aaah!" Bernhardt blindly swung at the bird, but it flew off unharmed.

Crimson Falcon took advantage of the distraction and kicked Bernhardt in the chest.

Bernhardt stumbled back several feet before regaining his footing. "Do you really think you have a chance?" he asked with a laugh.

"Maybe not alone," Crimson Falcon said. "Fortunately, I have some help."

A wolf darted out of the shadows and clamped down on Bernhardt's calf.

"Aaaaaah, my leg!" Bernhardt screamed, dropping to one knee.

Crimson Falcon stepped forward and punched Bernhardt in the face. The football player lost consciousness and fell to the ground.

The wolf looked at Crimson Falcon. In an instant, all of the wolf's features had melted away, and Will was standing there instead. He was wearing a suit like Crimson Falcon's except his was green where Crimson Falcon's was red. He had one place on his belt for the Morph Omnidisk.

"Will, I'm glad you could make it," Crimson Falcon said weakly.

"Of course you are." Will reached into Bernhardt's jersey and pulled out a yellow Omnidisk. "Chasub knew this was a suicide mission without me. And my name is Bestial."

"Sorry. Bestial." Crimson Falcon limped over to where his Omnidisks lay and picked them up. "And thanks to you too, Chasub."

"Think nothing of it," the alien replied.

"So, does this mean you're part of the team now?" Crimson Falcon asked.

Bestial frowned. "Hard to say; there are a lot of factors involved. Do you guys have a dental plan? And what does this gig pay?"

Crimson Falcon laughed and grabbed his ribs in pain. "How about we save the jokes for later. I need a little TLC."

"Yeah." Bestial sent Crimson Falcon a concerned look. "You look like a Band-Aid or two would do you some good."

"Chasub, get ready to fling…" Crimson Falcon paused and stared past Bestial.

"What's wrong?" Bestial turned around. "Oh."

A white spot appeared in thin air. It grew larger until there was a glowing white circle. A moment later, three familiar figures stepped out of the circle of light.

"Bestial, watch out!" Crimson Falcon cried. "It's Slymind, Mange, and Anira!"

"I am Arcspark now." Arcspark stretched out her hands and fired two bolts of electricity.

At the same time, Mange fired his eye beams at Crimson Falcon.

"Aaaaah!" The bolts and beams converged on Crimson Falcon at the same time. They propelled him several yards away.

Slymind punched Bestial in the face. Bestial fell backward and dropped the Swift Omnidisk. Slymind's arm stretched out and grabbed the Omnidisk before it hit the ground.

"I have it!" Slymind shouted triumphantly.

"Finally," Mange said. His gaze fell on Crimson Falcon's unconscious form. "Now I get my payback."

"We got what we came for," Arcspark objected. "Anything else would be a waste of time."

"He's got this coming!" Mange's eye started to glow.

"No!" Bestial jumped to his feet and moved between Crimson Falcon and the augments.

Mange laughed. "I'll have you as my appetizer!"

"I'll give you indigestion." Bestial's form shifted, and in seconds he was a full-grown male lion.

"Not now." Slymind stopped Mange. "We finally have a disk. We need to get it to the base."

Mange growled at Bestial before turning around and walking into the white light. Arcspark and Slymind followed him. Seconds later, the hole disappeared without a trace.

Bestial changed to human form and crouched over Crimson Falcon. "Chasub, bring us up."

"Rise and shine," Will said as Eric slowly began to open his eyes.

"Where am I?"

"In the Medical Alcove," Chasub said. "You've been here all night."

"We all have," Brynn said, walking over to his bed. "It took that long for the pods to heal our wounds. Dark Viper, however, left as soon as he could walk."

"That guy is creepy, by the way," Will added with a little shiver. "I don't know how you can work with him."

"Baby," Brynn muttered, rolling her eyes at Will.

"What time is it?" Eric asked, climbing off of the medical bed.

"Almost noon," Archie said as he walked through the Medical Alcove doors. "Sorry, Chasub, I ran scans, but the augments are gone again."

"The Omnidisk!" Eric slammed his fist into the medical bed. "I lost it!"

"Be careful," Chasub warned. "You're still in recovery mode. We'll get the Swift Omnidisk another time."

"It wasn't your fault," Will said. "That stretchy guy took me out with one punch." He lowered his eyes. "I guess I wasn't the right guy for the job after all."

"On the contrary!" Chasub objected. "You saved Eric's life."

"Yeah, thanks a lot," Eric held out his hand. "We're glad to have you on the team. I wouldn't be here if it wasn't for you. We need you."

Will smiled and shook Eric's hand. "Glad to be part of the team," he said as he turned toward Brynn. "How about you? You happy to have me?" he asked with a smirk.

Brynn scoffed. "Dream on, munchkin."

Will laughed. "As long as you're in the dream."

Brynn laughed and walked over to shake Will's hand. "We are all happy to have you."

"Speak for yourself," Archie grumbled.

"So what do we call ourselves?" Will asked. "Does this little group have a name?"

"He's right!" Archie said, snapping his fingers, "We need a cool name. Every super-hero team has a cool name!"

"Why don't you work on that, Archie?" Eric suggested as he walked over to Chasub. "Chasub, we need to find out how they were able to open that rift in space. They came out of nowhere!"

Chasub moved to his computer. "I've been trying to examine the sensor readings—"

A loud beeping noise began to go off.

"What is it?" Brynn shouted.

"You need to get to Earth. There's a shootout taking place between an augment and the police! Get to the flinger console, now!" Chasub ordered.

"This is a great day for us," Command proudly held the Omnidisk.

"And thanks to that new spatial aperture generator," Slymind said, gesturing toward a large, circular machine, "we can go almost anywhere on the planet, at lightning speed."

"I thank you for putting it together for us," Command commended.

"Only after you secured the parts for us, sir," Slymind said.

"No more old, beat-up cars for us!" Mange laughed.

Slymind shot Mange a nasty look.

Arcspark watched them all. "Before we all celebrate, there is still the matter of my money. Where is it?!"

"Who needs money when you can rule the world?" Command asked.

"What do you mean?" she asked.

"I mean that, soon, money won't matter. We'll have the world at our fingertips and all the money we could ever imagine!" Command said as he pointed toward the huge machine that sat in the center of the room.

"What does it do?" Anira asked.

"As soon as it's finished," Command said, looking toward the room that held Travis, "I'm going to show you."

"There!" Crimson Falcon shouted as he pointed at the Drakeston City Bank. "The shots are coming from over there. Let's go."

Crimson Falcon and Prodigy took flight. Xenoshot jumped on his Hyperboard and Bestial transformed into a hawk.

"Come out with your hands up!" Four policemen stood outside with their guns drawn.

From a broken window, an augment with two large bat-like wings on his back, and a machine gun emerged. A sack of money was strapped to his side.

"It's one of those freaks!" an officer yelled. "Shoot it!"

The police officers opened fire. "They're bouncing off of him!" one police shouted. "He's wearing some kind of body armor!"

Ratatatatattta!!! The augment took a few steps back and fired his weapon. The police took cover behind their police cars as they watched him open his wings and take off into the sky.

"He's getting away!" another officer shouted.

"Hey, wing boy! Where do you think you're going?" Crimson Falcon flew towards him. Prodigy, Xenoshot, and Bestial were right behind him.

The augment stared at the group and took off into the opposite direction.

Tseeew! Tseeew! Tseeew! Xenoshot fired at him, but he dodged to the left and right. None of the shots hit him.

Ratatatattatata!!! The augment stopped, turned toward them and opened fire.

"Look out!" Crimson Falcon shouted.

"Don't worry, I got us covered!" Prodigy shouted as she protected the team behind a mental shield.

"This isn't working," Xenoshot said as the augment took off again.

"You're right," Crimson Falcon agreed. "Prodigy, Bestial, you two go to the right and try to cut him off. Xenoshot, we'll stay on his tail."

"Got it." Prodigy turned right and disappeared between two buildings. Bestial followed.

"Xenoshot, keep firing a few rounds at him. Force him to turn to the right."

Xenoshot fired off his illuminator. The augment dodged left, then right.

"That's it. Stay on him. Aim for his gun; don't stop."

Finally, a shot hit him in the shoulder. The gun fell to the ground. The augment landed on the roof of a building.

"Good shot!" Crimson Falcon shouted. "Prodigy, Bestial…he's on a lower roof to your right. We're on our—"

Without warning, Dark Viper dropped from the top of a nearby building and kicked the augment in the back with both feet. The augment fell from the building and hit the ground hard, while Dark Viper landed on his feet next to him.

"Dark Viper! Glad to see you," Crimson Falcon said. "I never thanked you for helping me yesterday."

"Get away, all of you!" The augment rose to his feet and flapped his wings at Crimson Falcon and the others. The wind began kicking up around all of them.

"Perhaps you would like to express your gratitude later," Dark Viper suggested, struggling against the increasing strength of the wind.

Crimson Falcon flew straight at the augment and hit him in the chest.

The augment extended his wings and regained his balance. "I cannot be thrown down that easily."

"I guess I'll have to try harder," Crimson Falcon said, throwing a punch.

The augment ducked under Crimson Falcon's punch and kicked him in the midsection.

Dark Viper and Xenoshot ran forward to help but with one strong flap of his wings, the augment had knocked them both off of their feet. He flapped his wing twice more and was airborne.

"Come on, he's getting away!" Crimson Falcon yelled.

"No, he's not." Prodigy dropped from the sky and used her telekinesis to yank the bag of money out of the augment's hand.

Roooaaar! A gorilla jumped off of the opposite roof and wrapped his arms around the augment, constricting his wings and arms. They dropped to the ground.

"Let go!" The augment struggled in vain to break free from Bestial's grip.

"Xenoshot, you know what to do," Crimson Falcon ordered.

Tseeew! With one shot to the chest the augment's head drooped and his eyes closed.

"Now for the finishing touch." Xenoshot took out an inhibitor and placed on the augment's neck.

Bestial released the augment and shifted to human form.

"Chasub," Xenoshot said, "we have him gift wrapped and ready to go."

"Beginning the flinging process," Chasub announced.

A minute later the augment disappeared.

"Add another victory for the good guys," Xenoshot said proudly.

"Thanks to your newest member," Bestial added. "I made a monkey out of myself and still managed to beat him."

"Crimson Falcon?" Prodigy was staring past the group with a surprised look on her face. "I think there is something you should see."

Crimson Falcon turned around and saw at least two-dozen observers standing on the other side of the road.

"Chasub, you should get ready to bring us to the ship," Crimson Falcon said.

One man in the front of the group began to applaud. Others followed until all of the onlookers were clapping and cheering.

"I could get used to this." Bestial smiled and stepped forward.

"I don't know about this." Prodigy said.

Xenoshot smiled and waved to the crowd.

"So much attention only causes problems," Dark Viper warned.

"I think you might be right," Crimson Falcon replied.

"Some positive attention for a change might not be too bad," Xenoshot said. "We do deserve some credit."

A news van screeched to a halt in front of the group. A cameraman and a newswoman jumped out of it and ran towards the heroes.

Crimson Falcon groaned. "Oh great."

"Excuse me!" the woman said. "Margaret Crup, Channel 4. Everyone in town has heard the rumors about you and your team. There has been constant talk about creatures, attacking all over the place and how you heroes have stepped in to stop them. The burning questions, our viewers want to know is… who are you?" Margaret Crup shoved her microphone in Crimson Falcon's face.

"No comment." Crimson Falcon attempted to wave the microphone away.

"My name is Xenoshot." Xenoshot stepped forward. "I use my illuminator and my Hyperboard to help my friends here fight evil." He pulled out his illuminator and fired a shot straight up into the sky.

"Fascinating," the reporter said.

"Excuse me for a minute." Crimson Falcon grabbed Xenoshot and pulled him to the side. "What are you doing?!"

"Some good press may help us later on," Xenoshot argued. "Besides, everyone loves a hero."

"Xenoshot might have a point," Chasub said. "Winning the confidence of the public may be beneficial. But be careful."

Crimson Falcon sighed. "Fine."

Xenoshot stepped to the microphone. "This is my friend Crimson Falcon. He is our leader. He has super strength and can fly."

Everybody looked at him expectantly so Crimson Falcon took his cue and flew high into the air before going in a circle and returning to the ground.

Their audience clapped in approval.

"Xenoshot is going to get us killed," Prodigy said angrily.

"It'll be okay," Bestial said. "I've always looked good in front of the camera."

"This is our friend Dark Viper!" Xenoshot gestured at his reptilian ally, who withdrew into the shadows, hesitated, and to their surprise, stepped out into the light.

There were gasps and whispers from the crowd in front of them.

"He is a good man!" Xenoshot said insistently. "He has superhuman strength and agility as well as enhanced senses. And an impressive arsenal of weapons that he uses to help us keep you safe."

Bestial snickered, and Crimson Falcon had to smile as Dark Viper made an awkward bow.

"This is Prodigy!" Xenoshot continued. "She has the power of telekinesis. She can move things with her mind."

Everyone's eyes shifted to Prodigy.

"Your turn," Bestial whispered to her. "Give them a show."

Prodigy grimaced at him, then put on a fake smile. "Fine." She grabbed Bestial and shot him into the sky. The crowd went crazy with astonishment.

"Is this enough of a show for you?" Prodigy shouted as she spun Bestial around.

"Put me down!" Bestial demanded.

"That is our newest member." Xenoshot pointed at Bestial. "Bestial has the power to turn into any animal on the planet."

Bestial transformed into an elephant. The form was too heavy for Prodigy to hold so she dropped him.

The audience gasped as Bestial plummeted toward the ground.

Right before impact Bestial changed into a dove and flew into the air.

Everyone cheered at the display.

"What do you call your team?" the newswoman asked, moving the microphone over to Crimson Falcon.

Crimson Falcon chuckled nervously. "Umm, well you see… we don't—"

"We are Omniforce!" Xenoshot announced.

"We are?" Crimson Falcon whispered.

"Thank goodness for nerd boy," Bestial said. "We'd look pretty stupid without a name."

"And what are you all here for exactly?" Margaret asked. "What do you do?"

"I am sure you all know about the outbreak of people with powers recently," Crimson Falcon answered. "The police have had some…difficulty handling the situation. We are here to help keep you safe. As you can see, we have the power to fight them."

"Why should we trust you?" a man asked from the crowd. "How do we know you're not as dangerous as all of the rest of the super-powered freaks out there?"

Some of the group grumbled in agreement.

Prodigy growled in frustration. "What kind of stupid question is that?"

"Prodigy, this is not the time," Crimson Falcon said before turning to the microphone. "We don't ask for anyone's trust. Only the opportunity to prove that all we want is to protect you from danger!"

"He's telling the truth!" Chris emerged from a cluster of bystanders and ran over to Crimson Falcon. "They have saved my life twice now!" She put her hand on Crimson Falcon's arm and smiled. "They're good people."

"Thank you," Crimson Falcon whispered.

"Of course," Chris said. "They deserve the respect of everyone here for what they're doing," she continued.

Three police cars came screeching to a halt. "Put your hands up now!" shouted a policeman as they each climbed out of their cars, guns drawn. "We have orders to take all of you into custody!"

"I don't think these guys share your opinion," Crimson Falcon said to Chris.

The crowd began to protest.

"Officer!" Margaret ran over to the officer. "How is that you aren't able to stop the augments, but these people are?"

"Out of the way, ma'am," the officer ordered. "Police business."

"I don't believe this," Prodigy said. "We catch a thief they couldn't catch, and now they want to arrest us!"

"Hands up, now!" the officer yelled again.

"We can finish this in five seconds," Prodigy extended her hand.

"No!" Crimson Falcon yelled. "We are not fighting the police. Chasub, get us out of here."

"Dark Viper is no longer there," Chasub responded.

Crimson Falcon scanned the area. "Fine. Bring the rest of us up." Crimson Falcon winked at Chris before the whole team was surrounded by light.

"Stop!" The officer ran forward, but in a few seconds, the whole team disappeared.

CHAPTER 24

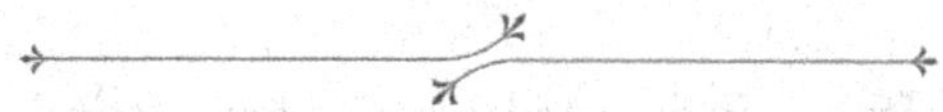

"Is the augment secure?" Eric asked as they all began to change into their regular clothes.

"I have the energy treatment flowing in the room as we speak," Chasub said, in an assuring tone. "He should be human again very soon."

"So bird boy gets his wings clipped, and we get hated by the police," Will grumbled. "I guess everyone had a good day."

"I can't believe those cops turned on us like that," Brynn said angrily. "After all we've done for this freaking town." She looked accusingly at Eric. "You should've let me take them down."

"It's the law that hates us; the civilians seemed to like us okay," Archie said optimistically. "Same thing Spider-Man went through."

"The good thing is that now that the public knows about us, we don't have to be so secretive," Eric said.

Brynn folded her arms. "Between last night and tonight, I need to spend a long day at the mall."

"Want some company?" Archie asked hopefully. "I never got a chance to show you around Game Stop last time we were there."

"Fine." Brynn shrugged. "But we're not stopping in one of your comic stores."

"Hey, I want to go waste my money on clothes too!" Will said with mock eagerness.

"Wouldn't hurt you to." Brynn glared disdainfully at Will's ensemble.

"The ladies happen to like what I wear," Will bragged, striking a pose.

Brynn laughed. "I'm sure that's what they tell you to protect your fragile male ego. Chasub, two for the mall please."

Chasub flew over to the flinger controls. "This is a starship, not a public transportation service, you know."

"After the day we've had," Brynn pointed out, "we're at least entitled to a free ride."

"I suppose." Chasub activated the Molecular Flinger, and moments later Brynn and Archie were gone.

"I should go too," Will said. "I've been gone for a long time. My mom is probably worried."

"My dad!" Eric suddenly cried out. "I was gone all night, and I didn't even call him. He is going to kill me!"

Chasub punched more commands in the flinger. "You should get home as well."

Will laughed. "You might've been safer fighting the augment."

Eric couldn't help thinking that there was some truth in his statement.

Eric slowly opened the door to his house and looked around. When the coast seemed clear, he closed the door behind him and tiptoed up the stairs.

"Dad, Eric just got home!" Rebecca screamed.

Eric clenched his teeth and gripped the banister tightly.

Eric's father walked out of his room and stood in front of Eric. "You didn't come home last night! Do you have any idea how worried I was!?"

Eric sighed. "I'm sorry, Dad. I was…with Archie."

Eric's father nodded his head. "You're always 'with Archie' these days. Or at least that's what you say. But I can't truly know, can I? You leave early, and you come in late. You're never home anymore. You may have joined a gang for all I know!"

"Dad…" Eric tried to speak but his father cut him off.

"I don't know what's got into you lately. You're not dependable anymore." Eric's father's voice was full of disappointment. "I've grounded you so many times, I can't remember when one stops, and another begins. You used to be such a help to me around here. But now all you do is worry me. You're just not trustworthy anymore. I need to go out and handle some business. Try to stick around for a few hour ant watch your sister!" Eric's father walked off without saying anything further.

Eric plopped down on the stairs and buried his head in his hands. He had been beaten, shot at, and electrocuted. But he had never felt as bad as he did at that moment.

"The machine is complete," Slymind reported. "The schematics you gave me worked out perfectly."

"Excellent," Command entered the lair. "I had to rush over here after watching the news. Apparently our friends are calling themselves Omniforce."

"How quaint," Slymind said sarcastically.

"Doesn't matter. Once my plan goes into action, they will all be wiped out. And this machine is the beginning of it all."

Arcspark stepped over to the machine. The machine looked like a large telescope with a small control panel on the side. On a pedestal next to the device was the Swift Omnidisk. The entire pedestal had a plastic covering over it, and there was a wire running from it to the machine. A chill ran through her.

"I have decided to go along with your plan," she said. "I don't care about power or ruling. But I want all of the riches I was promised. I want enough money to put this life behind me."

"Of course, I will deliver, in fact, I think it's time that I show you all what I am planning," Command said. "Mange, why don't you go get our guest."

"Yes, sir," Mange said as he walked toward Travis' holding room.

"Get your crummy hands off me!" Travis yelled as Mange dragged him out. "What do you want with me, anyway? You've been holding me here for weeks! I told you everything I know about those costumed freaks and that stupid Omnidisk thing!"

"Yes, we know," Command assured him. "And we are here to reward you for your assistance."

"I don't want any reward! Let me outta here!" Travis swung at Mange but missed.

"Strap him down!" Command ordered.

"Let me go, you freaks!" Travis yelled as Mange slammed him on a table and applied leather restraints to his arms and legs.

"What are you going to do to him?" Arcspark asked.

"I am about to demonstrate the basis of my entire plan!" Command announced. "This machine is going to take the energy from this Omnidisk and focus it into a single beam. This beam of energy will instantly turn any human it hits into an augment. I call it, the Biological Shifter."

Arcspark stared at Travis.

"Slymind, activate the machine." Command stated.

Slymind walked over to the panel and began pressing a few buttons. They all watched as the machine came to life.

"So what, we turn this guy into a augment?" Arcspark asked. "What difference does that make?"

"This is only a test," Command said. "A prototype. If it works, we will be able to use the same method on a larger scale. I plan to release this energy over the whole planet!"

"You're gonna make everyone on the planet like us?" Mange asked. "How?"

"Not everyone. But enough from every nation to make the world realize something is very wrong," Command replied with a smile. "The spatial aperture generator will open a hole. One end of the hole will be here. The other hole will be in outer space, not far above the planet. Then a much larger version of my Biological Shifter will fire a beam into the hole."

"Begging your pardon, sir," Slymind interrupted. "Even if the beam shoots down from orbit, it still will only affect a small fraction of people."

"You would think so," Command said. "But as you know, my absorption of other humans has made me the smartest man on the planet. My knowledge of this particular kind of radiation surpasses any scientist. When it hits the ozone layer, it will not pass through it. It will scatter along it until it covers the entire planet, turning a percentage of the human population into augments like us. As the changes occur, the governments of the world won't know what to do. That's where I come in. I'll be the only one with the power and intelligence to understand what's happening because, well, I started it. I'll win their hearts and minds over as I explain to them how to navigate through the crisis. Presidents and Kings will pay me handsomely and citizens will beg me to lead them. The one thing the entire planet will agree on is that I saved them. And with that kind of influence… there will be no limit to what I can do."

"The whole planet will be ours," Mange said happily.

Slymind nodded. "It's ingenious."

"You will control everything," Arcspark's voice gave away her skepticism. "So, you just want power for power's sake?"

"You're perceptive," Command nodded. "No. There's more. But you know all you need to know for more. If you want additional details, you'll have to earn it. In the meantime, let's proceed to the demonstration."

"No! No!!!" Travis screamed. "Let me out of here! Help!"

Mange laughed. "No escape for you, punk."

The small end of the telescope shaped machine was turned toward Travis.

"We are ready, sir," Slymind said.

"Good," Command said. "I need this to be a successful test. So, try not to die in the process."

"No!" Travis cried one last time but to no avail.

Slymind pressed a large red button. A violet light beamed into Travis' chest.

"I felt terrible," Eric said to Archie at school on Monday. "My dad looked at me with so much disappointment. It's like I totally let him down."

"He doesn't know what you're dealing with," Archie said. "He can't begin to understand the pressure you're under."

"Does it matter?" Eric asked. "I haven't been there for him."

"This has been tough on all of our family lives," Archie said. "My parents are on my case all of the time for not being around."

"That's not the same," Eric nodded his head. "Ever since my mom died, my dad has relied on me more than ever. Now he has this look in his eyes like he's alone again. Maybe that's why he's always out of the house."

"Why is that anyway?" Archie asked. "Did his work hours change?"

Eric shrugged. "I don't know. I haven't been around for him to share updated with me."

"Everything we have been doing is to protect them too," Archie assured. "It's the plight of all heroes, I guess. They slight the ones they love to protect them."

Eric groaned. "Comic books don't always contain the answers to life's problems."

"Are you kidding?" Will said, walking up. "Just the other day a *Daffy Duck* comic book taught me that girls dig sailor hats."

"It would be an improvement for you," Brynn said as she and Chris approached their friends.

"Hey, we heard about that German kid trying to hurt you guys," Eric stated. "Is Jeff okay?"

"Yes, he's fine." Chris smiled. "He's just mad that he got knocked out again."

"Too bad I wasn't there. I could have protected you," Brynn said. "Like that Crimson Falcon guy did. He seems nice."

"Yes, I did." Jason focused on putting papers in his briefcase. "He hasn't been to school in a long time."

"He was a real bully when he was here before," Eric said. "I'm worried he might start trouble again."

"Oh, I think Mr. Travis will have a different attitude going forward," Jason said, an almost invisible smile appearing on his face.

"Eric!" Archie appeared at the door. "We were supposed to meet with the others, remember?"

"Hello, Archibald," Jason said.

"Hi," Archie said shortly before he turned to Eric. "Are you coming?"

"Yeah." Eric walked out of the classroom. "See you tomorrow Jason."

"You too." Jason waved.

"Have a mentioned I don't like him?" Archie asked.

"A few times," Eric responded.

Archie followed his friend's gaze. "I guess your instincts were right."

Travis was standing outside the front of the school, harassing Chris.

"That does it," Eric said, taking a step toward Travis. Archie reached out and grabbed his arm.

"He's still strong, even without the Omnidisk," Archie reminded Eric.

Eric patted his pocket. "That Omnidisk has changed hands since I ran into him last. I'm not worried."

"I'll go get the gang, just in case," Archie said.

"Why the cold shoulder, sweetie?" Travis grabbed Chris' arm. "I only want a welcome home kiss."

"Travis, leave me alone," Chris said as she yanked her arm away.

"I'm not the kind of guy you want to turn refuse," Travis warned. "Especially now."

"And what is so special about you now?" Eric asked, stepping between Chris and Travis.

Chris gave Eric a grateful smile.

"You don't wanna know," Travis replied, staring him down.

"Back off, kid." Jeff shoved Eric aside. "She's my girl, so I'll handle this."

Eric wanted to point out how bad Jeff had been doing at that lately. Instead, he put his hands up and stepped away.

"Why don't you leave and save yourself a few bruises?" Jeff said.

"I heard you got a few of your own the other night," Travis said with a laugh.

Jeff clenched his fists and gritted his teeth. "Leave, now."

"Jeff, let's go," Chris said. "You don't need to prove anything to him."

For once, Jeff took her advice. He gave Travis one more look before turning around.

"You don't walk away from me!" Travis grabbed Jeff's arm and pulled him toward him.

"Bad idea!" Jeff swung and caught Travis in the left cheek.

"Jeff!" Chris cried.

Travis punched Jeff across the face. Jeff stumbled back. Travis moved in for another strike, but Jeff hit him in the stomach and then in the face. Travis stumbled backward and fell on the ground.

Eric nodded in approval.

"Now we can leave," Jeff said.

"You!" Travis shouted, getting on his feet. "Get over here!"

Jeff smirked. "Are you sure you want to do this again?"

Even Jeff can take this guy, Eric thought to himself as he began to walk off. But something told him to stick around, just in case.

"That was the first round." Travis laughed. "Now we're gonna try the best two outta three."

Jeff took off his letterman jacket and handed it to Chris.

"Jeff, no!" Chris protested. "Something is off. He's baiting you!"

She's right, Eric looked back at Uproar. *But why?*

"He disrespected you," Jeff said. "I'm not letting him get away with it."

"So, do something about it," Travis said with an evil smile. Suddenly, he began to change.

"What in the—" Jeff's eyes widened, and he took a step back.

Travis' clothes began to stretch and tear as his entire body turned deathly pale. His muscles began to bulge.

Eric slipped quietly away as Chris, and Jeff kept their eyes on what used to be Travis.

"Travis?" Chris asked.

"I am Uproar!" he screamed as he turned to Jeff. "Ready for that second round now?"

CHAPTER 25

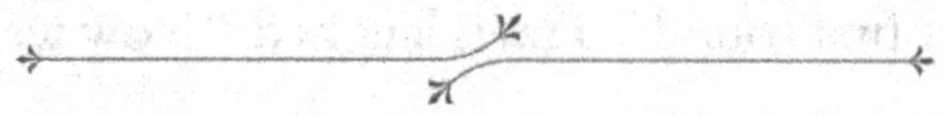

"Run!" Jeff shouted to Chris.

Chris turned around and took off.

"You're not going anywhere!" Uproar walked after Chris.

"If you want her, you'll have to get through—" Uproar slapped Jeff aside. The football player flew through the air and hit the side of the school, hard. His unconscious body fell to the ground.

"I still want my kiss." Uproar grabbed Chris' arm.

"Leave her alone!" Crimson Falcon yelled.

"I was hoping I'd see you again. You and I got a score to settle!" Uproar released Chris.

"Maybe you'll be smart and quit this time," Crimson Falcon said. "I have the Brawn Omnidisk now."

Uproar leaped into the air grabbed Crimson Falcon's leg and slammed him to the ground.

Crimson Falcon kicked Uproar in the leg with enough force to get him to let go. He rolled away and jumped to his feet.

"Be careful," Chasub's voice came through the earpiece. "I am sensing great levels of energy coming from Travis. He's quite powerful now."

"I noticed," Crimson Falcon said bitterly. "You might want to let the others know what's happening."

Uproar threw a punch at Crimson Falcon, but he dodged the blow and countered with a kick to Uproar's midsection.

Uproar slammed his foot on the concrete, and the ground around Crimson Falcon's feet cracked and shook. When Crimson Falcon lost his balance, Uproar charged and hit him in the chest.

Crimson Falcon punched Uproar in the face multiple times. Uproar shook his head a few times and smiled. "I always suspected you were thick-skulled. Want to tell me how you got these new abilities?"

"I helped out some friends lately, and they returned the favor." Uproar charged again.

"Glad you're becoming more social." Crimson Falcon dodged to the side.

"So am I!" Uproar slammed both fists on Crimson Falcon. "They have made me more powerful than ever!" He picked Crimson Falcon up and slammed him down on the ground. "I'm gonna pay you back for last time by leavin' you the way you left me. Beaten, broken and defeated." He punched Crimson Falcon in the chest.

Crimson Falcon flew through the air and landed on his back.

Uproar charged at him again.

Suddenly, anger flared within Crimson Falcon. *I took more than enough of this guy as Eric Daniels. There is no way I'm going to let him beat me as Crimson Falcon. This is* my *time to strike!* Crimson Falcon used his arms to leap onto his feet.

"Why are you even trying?" Uproar laughed. "You can't beat me!" The augment threw a punch at Crimson Falcon.

"Sure I can!" Crimson Falcon knocked the punch away and hit Uproar with a punch of his own. "I'm strong." Crimson Falcon delivered a second punch to Uproar's face. "I'm fast." Crimson Falcon dodged another punch and hit Uproar in the stomach. "I'm agile." he did a forward flip over Uproar's head and kicked him in the leg, bringing the augment to his knees. "Not to mention, I'm so much better looking than you." Crimson Falcon spun around and hit Uproar with a powerful roundhouse kick.

Uproar screamed in pain as he fell to the ground.

"Nice kick!" Prodigy commended him as she, Bestial and Xenoshot flew in.

"Wow!" Bestial transformed from bird to human. "And I thought Travis couldn't get any uglier."

Uproar climbed to his feet. "I can take you all!"

"I don't think so." Xenoshot leveled his illuminator at him. "We are really good."

Behind Uproar, a white hole began opening in midair.

"Not again!" Crimson Falcon said.

Mange and Slymind stepped out of the hole.

"Uproar, your time is up!" Slymind said. "We gave you your chance. Now you must return with us."

"But I almost—" Uproar began to object.

"We have more important things to do!" Slymind insisted.

Uproar frowned at the group one more time and walked toward the hole.

Xenoshot glanced at Prodigy. *Now is my chance!* "Stop!" Xenoshot ran forward.

"No! Don't!" Crimson Falcon warned him.

Tzzzzzap! Mange fired his eye beams at Xenoshot.

"Aaaaaah!" The beams hit Xenoshot in the chest, and he fell to the ground.

The three augments walked into the hole, and it closed behind them.

"Travis is working with them now?" Xenoshot rubbed his chest as he climbed to his feet.

"That doesn't surprise me," Prodigy said. "He was always slime. He's associating with his peers. Xenoshot, why didn't you stay behind and help Crimson Falcon?"

"What could he have done?" Bestial cut in before Xenoshot could reply. "He has no powers, and he wasn't much of a match for Travis when he was a normal bully."

Xenoshot looked away, too embarrassed to reply.

"Xenoshot did the right thing. And apparently, Travis goes by Uproar now," Crimson Falcon corrected. "He's very strong."

"Not strong enough," Bestial said. "I wonder how they were able to change him into that."

"I'd like to know the answer to that myself," Crimson Falcon replied.

"I'm studying his genetic profile as we speak," Chasub stated through Crimson's watch.

"Crimson Falcon!" Chris ran over and gave him a hug. "Thank you so much!"

"I gave you my word," Crimson Falcon replied with a smile. "I told you we'd be here if you needed us."

"Your boyfriend doesn't look so good," Prodigy smirked.

"Poor Jeff," Chris said sadly. "This keeps happening to him."

"Quarterback or not, he only *thinks* he has superpowers," Bestial joked.

"Eric!" Chris gasped. "My friend was here, but I think he got scared off. Did any of you see him?"

Bestial snickered.

Crimson Falcon shot him a dirty look. "Your friend Eric is the one who found us."

"Really?" Chris looked surprised.

"Maybe you should call an ambulance for Jeff," Crimson Falcon said, trying desperately to change the subject.

"Oh, what was I thinking?" Chris put her hand over her mouth. "I should go find a phone."

"I have already contacted the nearest hospital. They are on the way," Chasub informed them. "In the meantime, I need you all here now. I have tracked an Omnidisk, but unfortunately, that means the augments can detect it too. You need to get there as fast as possible."

"Right," Crimson Falcon looked at Chris. "Paramedics are on the way. We have to go now."

"Time is of the essence!" Chasub insisted.

"Bring us up!" Crimson Falcon nodded at Chris. "See you later."

"And try to stay out of trouble," Bestial said with a laugh.

The sound of the ambulance arriving made Chris turn her head. "They got here fast." Chris turned around, but Omniforce was gone.

"Which Omnidisk is it?" Crimson Falcon asked as Chasub floated in front of the computer.

"I have located the Cleanse Omnidisk," Chasub announced. "It can instantly heal any wound."

"I could use that." Crimson Falcon rubbed his ribs.

"Do you need to go to the Medical Alcove?" Chasub asked.

Crimson Falcon shook his head. "No time; tell us where we're going."

"And whose butt we have to kick next," Prodigy added.

"The Omnidisk is currently in possession of a doctor who lives across town from your school. His name is Santiago Menindez; there should not be much of a challenge involved in retrieving the Omnidisk. It seems that this doctor has been using it for good, and even if he was a bad individual, the Cleanse Omnidisk could only be used for medicinal purposes, a doctor's tool if you will."

"Got it. We'll get on our way," Crimson Falcon said.

"Allow me." Xenoshot ran over to the flinger control panel. After being embarrassed earlier that day, he was eager to impress Prodigy and redeem himself. "I think I found a way to make the targeting computer more accurate."

"You should not do that," Chasub warned. "That series of commands might—"

"Don't worry, Chasub. I spent hours studying how this works," Xenoshot assured him. "I will have us exactly where we want to be in a few seconds."

"Xenoshot, we don't have time for this," Crimson Falcon said.

"Trust me!" Xenoshot said. "Just one minor adjustment and—"

Sparks flew out of the control panel and smoke began to rise from it.

"No!" Crimson Falcon cried.

"I don't get it; I thought my calculations were flawless," Xenoshot said.

Chasub began to examine the panel. "The controls have been disabled. It will take me at least fifteen minutes to fix."

Crimson Falcon shot Xenoshot an angry look. "Help him. Every minute we're stuck here, the augments could be going after the Omnidisk."

"I will work as swiftly as possible," Chasub promised.

"I'll try to get a hold of Dark Viper," Crimson Falcon said. "Maybe he can buy us some time."

A white hole opened outside of the doctor's office. Slymind stepped out of the hole, followed by Mange, who was wearing a trench coat and a large hat. The two augments entered the building.

"May I help you?" the woman at the reception desk asked without looking up.

"Yes," Slymind said. "Is the doctor available? We need to have a word with him."

"He's not with any patients at the moment, so go right in," the receptionist replied, her eyes never left her magazine.

"Thank you." Slymind smiled as he and Mange walked down the hall toward the doctor's office.

Dr. Menindez walked into his office and found them sitting in the two chairs that were in front of his desk.

"What seems to be the problem?" he asked, sending a nervous smile in their direction.

"There is no problem," Slymind said. "Give us the Omnidisk, and we will be on our way."

"Omnidisk?" The doctor's eyes widened.

"We don't plan on asking again, Doc. Give us the shiny disk you have been using to heal people." Mange took off his hat and looked at the doctor.

The doctor gasped and leaned back in his chair.

"The Omnidisk," Slymind repeated.

Dr. Menindez put his hand in his pocket and shakily pulled out a purple Omnidisk. Mange snatched it out of his hand.

"Good." Slymind looked over at Dr. Menindez. "Now we have one more thing to take care of."

Before the doctor could move, Mange hit him in the chest with his eye beams. The doctor hit the wall and slumped to the floor, unconscious.

"He's still breathing," Slymind said disapprovingly.

"That can be changed." Mange cracked his knuckles.

"Surrender the Omnidisk!" a voice commanded from behind them.

Mange and Slymind spun around to find Dark Viper standing at the door with his bo staff.

"Do you actually think we're going to surrender?" Slymind laughed.

"No. I don't." Dark Viper leaped.

"Chasub!" Crimson Falcon said impatiently.

"Flinging now!" Chasub entered the command into the console.

A moment later, Omniforce was inside of the doctor's office.

"Dark Viper!" Xenoshot cried.

Dark Viper was lying on the floor facedown, severely beaten. Xenoshot turned him over.

Dark Viper gasped. "Outside."

Crimson Falcon punched his way through the wall and leaped outside.

"Too late, kid." Slymind laughed and stepped into the white hole.

"No!" Crimson Falcon shot toward the hole, but it closed an instant before he got there. Crimson Falcon cried out in rage and slammed his fist into the ground, punching a hole in the sidewalk.

"Where are they?" Bestial asked as he and the others ran out.

"They got away," Crimson Falcon whispered.

"Crap!" Prodigy said. "They have two of them now!"

"I know." Crimson Falcon stood up and glared at Xenoshot. "I know."

CHAPTER 26

"This is not good news," Chasub said when the group was on the ship.

"You think?" Brynn snorted.

"If only we had gotten there sooner," Eric said

"Well, we all know who's responsible for that little inconvenience," Will muttered.

"Where is Archie?" Eric asked.

"He is in the Medical Alcove observing Dark Viper's progress," Chasub responded. "The augments gave him quite a beating."

"They wouldn't have if we had been there earlier," Brynn said. "We have to be honest with ourselves, Archie messed up."

In the Medical Alcove, Archie saw that Dark Viper's health improving. He walked over to the communications console and opened a line to the main deck to update the rest of the team. Before he could say a word, he heard voices speaking.

"Messed up?" Will repeated. "Archie cost us the Omnidisk and could have cost Dark Viper his life!"

"He was trying to help, and let's not forget how many times he's saved us," Eric said.

"Eric, I know the kid is your friend and all, but we have to hold him responsible for his actions," Brynn said.

"His actions were part of an effort to assist us," Chasub pointed out.

"It doesn't matter," Will said. "Because of him, we got there too late. He was too busy trying to prove himself."

"He has no powers," Brynn added. "He's my friend but this isn't the first time that has been a problem, and it won't be the last."

Archie's face turned red as he continued to listen in.

"I'm starting to feel bad for dragging him into this," Eric said. "He was never meant to use any of the Omnidisks. This isn't his fight."

Archie bowed his head in shame. His friends had lost their faith in him. They didn't believe he should be part of the team.

"We have more important things to focus on," Chasub said. "We are no closer to finding the augments or the Omnidisks. And we still do not know their purpose for them."

"And now that they have a second Omnidisk, things are more dangerous than ever," Eric said.

"Wait a minute," Will said. "Remember when we saw Travis at the school?"

"You mean Uproar," Brynn corrected.

"How could I forget?" Eric said. "What's your point?"

"He reappears out of nowhere after all this time as an augment and disappears with Mange and Slymind? I don't buy it," Will shook his head. "And all of this happens right after they grab the Swift Omnidisk."

"I don't see the connection," Brynn said in a confused tone.

"Think about it!" Will insisted. "What if Command found a way to make humans into augments?"

"Like an army?" Eric asked.

"Exactly," Will said. "He knows augments are stronger than the average human. If he could build his own troops, he would be unstoppable."

Eric smiled. "Nice evaluation, Will. I knew you were what this team needed."

"Somebody has to be the brains of this outfit," Will joked.

"The augment's pursuit of the Omnidisks is in line with William's theory," Chasub said. "If he has a method of using the Omnidisks to change humans into augments, the more Omnidisks he has, the more humans he can transform."

"He would have to be quite smart to make a machine that can do that," Eric said. "Near genius level."

"If his calculations are off by the smallest margins, the Omnidisks could destabilize and—"

"Yeah, yeah the big bang all over again," Brynn cut off Chasub. "We got it. Now that we know what might be going on, how do we stop him?"

"We'll have to deal with that later. Right now, we need to focus. There is still one more Omnidisk out there." Eric turned to Chasub. "Anything on that one?"

"No," Chasub said, "and finding it may be more difficult than all of the others."

"Why?" Brynn asked.

"Because of the nature of this Omnidisk, we nicknamed it *Eel Feeensa.* In your language, it would be called—Wild Card."

"What's so special about it?" Eric asked.

"Since we were not able to stabilize it as completely as the others, it is more volatile. The user of the Wild Card Omnidisk is able to release destructive blasts of energy." Chasub explained. "And sometimes even the user of the Omnidisk may become unstable after extended use over time."

"I guess you had better keep those scanners running hot," Eric said. "And tell us the minute you find anything worth looking at."

"Dark Viper is awake," Archie said, stepping through the door.

Will and Brynn remained silent.

"Thanks," Eric said. "Is he well enough to be sent home?"

"Yes," Dark Viper said as he walked past Archie.

"We should go too," Eric said. "And remember, as soon as you find the Omnidisk, call me."

Three weeks later, Archie walked onto the main deck and saw Chasub observing an image on the computer. "Hey, Chasub. What's up?"

Chasub hastily removed the image and turned to Archie. "Nothing of interest, simply running scans over the area."

Archie nodded. "That's good. Need any help?"

"No assistance is necessary," Chasub promised. "I am progressing just fine."

Archie frowned. "Chasub, you haven't let me do anything important in a while. Ever since I caused that flinger accident three weeks ago, I promise you; it wouldn't happen again. I've been studying the systems lately, and I might be able to help you find the last Omnidisk."

"This has nothing to do with the accident," Chasub said stiffly. "I simply don't need help at this time."

"Okay, fine," Archie said, not believing him. "Where are the others?"

"They are all busy at the moment," Chasub said evasively.

Archie stared at the alien and considered digging, but he knew it would be futile. Lately, he had felt as if the rift between him and the rest of the team was getting bigger. They were constantly leaving him out of the loop.

"I think I'd like to go to the planet, Chasub," Archie said.

"Very well," Chasub began entering commands into the flinger. "If anything develops, you will hear from me."

"Right," Archie said, unconvinced. A minute later he was standing beside his house. He walked over and started to open his back door but changed his mind. In a few seconds, he was in uniform riding his Hyperboard over the houses in his neighborhood.

"Xenoshot, is there trouble?" Chasub asked.

"Not that I can see," Xenoshot replied. "I need to clear my head. Fighting some bad guys might help. That's what Peter Parker always does. Thanks for making my suit so warm by the way. It's wintertime, and I barely feel a thing."

A moment of silence from Chasub. "Contact me if you require assistance."

"Won't you be able to see it?" Xenoshot asked.

"I am currently…running another program," Chasub said hesitantly. "I will not be able to keep an eye on your progress."

"Whatever, I'll be ok. Xenoshot out," Xenoshot continued to scan the ground below and noticed a familiar figure standing on the snow-covered roof of the high school.

Xenoshot flew toward Dark Viper. "Hey, buddy. What are you doing?"

"I am not your *buddy*," Dark Viper replied without emotion. "And I am on patrol."

Xenoshot did not let Dark Viper's attitude discourage him. Despite the augment's standoffish attitude, he was the only one who wasn't treating Xenoshot differently.

"Cool, I'll come along," Xenoshot volunteered.

Dark Viper launched himself off the roof and landed on the ground. "I don't need help."

"Of course not." Xenoshot accelerated so he could fly next to Dark Viper. "But everyone could use some company."

Dark Viper sighed. "Fine, but don't get in my way."

Xenoshot did a mock salute. "Scout's honor."

Dark Viper ran did a forward flip onto the next roof.

"What have you been doing lately since Slymind and his friends seem to be missing in action?" Xenoshot asked. "Anything exciting?"

Dark Viper growled. "Stop… talking."

Xenoshot laughed. "Come across any bad augments?"

"Look out!" Dark Viper leaped to the side as a variant carrying a stolen purse ran past them.

"Get away!" The variant took a swing at Dark Viper but missed.

Dark Viper countered with a punch, knocking the attacker off balance.

"I got him!" Xenoshot pulled out his illuminator.

The variant kicked Xenoshot in the chest as he fell to the ground, and his weapon went off.

It shot a passing bird.

"Bestial!" Prodigy dived and grabbed the bird before it hit the ground.

"Oh no," Xenoshot moaned, realizing what had happened.

The variant tried to use the distraction to escape but was caught off guard by a punch from Crimson Falcon that knocked him out.

"Xenoshot, I need an inhibitor!" Crimson Falcon stretched out his hand.

Xenoshot fumbled the inhibitor and dropped it on the ground.

Dark Viper snatched the inhibitor off of the ground and tossed it to Crimson Falcon.

Crimson Falcon slapped it on the augment's neck. "Chasub, bring him up!"

The light surrounded the variant and he was gone.

"Are you insane?" Prodigy yelled at Xenoshot as she landed on the roof. "You shot Bestial!"

"What?" Crimson Falcon ran over to Prodigy. "Is he okay?"

"He won't answer me," Prodigy said. "And he won't revert to human."

The hawk in Prodigy's arms had a hole in the area where its wing met its torso.

"Chasub, Bestial needs to get to Medical Alcove!" Crimson Falcon shot a look at Xenoshot after Bestial had been flung. "What happened?"

"It was an accident!" Xenoshot said. "The augment kicked me, and my illuminator went off."

"If you knew how to use that thing—" Prodigy started.

"It was unintentional," Dark Viper said. "I saw it myself."

"You stay out of it!" Prodigy said, pointing her finger at him. "I remember you saying *you* weren't part of the team. This is team business."

"Perhaps." Dark Viper walked to the edge of the roof and looked back. "But if that is true, why were you fighting without your *teammate?*" Dark Viper gestured toward Xenoshot before leaving.

"That's none of your business!" Prodigy's face turned red.

"It *is* my business though!" Xenoshot shouted. "Why didn't anyone tell me you guys were on a mission?"

Crimson Falcon cleared his throat. "I didn't think you needed to be bothered. He wasn't that strong."

"So what? That never stopped you before!" Xenoshot yelled. "We're a team! Or at least we were supposed to be. You even have Chasub keeping stuff from me!"

"We wouldn't have to if you didn't keep holding us back!" Prodigy said.

"I pull my own weight!" Xenoshot objected.

"Bestial has a laser wound that says otherwise," Prodigy said. "Not to mention the little flinger fiasco."

"Prodigy, that's enough!" Crimson Falcon shouted at her.

"That was not my fault. My weapon misfired. It happens!" Xenoshot shouted at Prodigy before turning toward Crimson Falcon. "And besides, you're the one who asked me to join. You said you needed me to watch out for you."

"I know I did, and I meant it," Crimson Falcon said. "I just don't want you to get hurt. And with Prodigy and Bestial here—"

"I get it. You don't need me anymore," Xenoshot turned away.

"No!" Crimson Falcon stepped closer to Xenoshot. "Not true. I want to keep your exposure to danger at a minimum. Maybe you can help Chasub on the ship more. We need to find that last Omnidisk."

Xenoshot sighed. "Yeah sure. I understand. I'm not part of the *superpowers* only club. You know, I never thought you would change like this and become like the others."

Crimson Falcon's eyes widened. "What others?"

"Everyone who treats me like I'm different! It's just like school, I can't sit with the cool kids!" Xenoshot continued. "I could always count on you. But now you're as bad as them!"

"That's ridiculous," Crimson Falcon argued "I'm not like Travis or Jeff or those kids at school! I always helped and protected you. I never bullied you!"

"What about Will?" Xenoshot argued. "He takes shots at me all the time. Teasing me and making fun. But you like him, so it doesn't faze you. Sometimes you even laugh! Some part of you must believe what he says because everyone here makes mistakes, but I'm the only one who gets singled out for them. Now I'm treated differently, just like at school. You guys are part of the cool superpowers club. And I'm the nerd who doesn't belong. Maybe you're not as different as you think."

Without another word, Xenoshot jumped on his Hyperboard and took off.

"We were too hard on him," Crimson Falcon said to Prodigy after a few seconds of silence.

"I said what needed to be said." She folded her arms defiantly.

"You didn't need to say it that way!" Crimson Falcon insisted. "You forget, long before all of this started, Archie was our friend! The best one anyone could ask for. Despite his quirks, we can trust him with anything."

Prodigy's eyes fell to the ground.

"We aren't going to be doing this forever," Crimson Falcon continued. "And hopefully, when this ends, you, me, Archie, and Will will be right back where we began. But you can't let all this cause you to take a good friend for granted because when it ends, you might not have them anymore. You don't even know how he feels about you."

Prodigy's head shot up, and she raised her eyebrows. "You mean he—"

"I mean he thinks the world of you. And he would never do anything to intentionally hurt you. Think about that the next time you're considering going off on him. Chasub, bring us up," Crimson Falcon said.

In a flash, Crimson Falcon and Prodigy were standing on the main deck of the ship. They ran to the Medical Alcove.

"How is he?" Crimson Falcon asked.

"He was burned badly, but fortunately, the wound was only superficial," Chasub reported. "The beam missed the bone and muscle."

Crimson Falcon looked over and saw Bestial lying unconscious on the table. Despite him being in human form, they could still see the hole in his shoulder.

"After a few hours in the pod, he should be completely healed." Chasub hovered to a console and entered a command.

"Are you sure he'll won't have any long term damage??" Crimson Falcon watched a steel cocoon rise from the sides of the table and cover Bestial completely.

"I guarantee it," Chasub said. "Where is Xenoshot?"

"He felt bad about what happened." Crimson Falcon shot a look at Prodigy. "He's clearing his head."

Prodigy remained silent.

"Anything on the Omnidisk?" Crimson Falcon asked.

"Not yet." Chasub floated out of the door toward the main computer room with Crimson Falcon and Prodigy behind him.

Chasub displayed a map of the city on the view screen. "I have not been able to find any trace of the Omnidisk. I have tried every technique that I know."

"Maybe that's a good thing," Prodigy said. "If you can't find it, there is no way the augments can. That means it is safe."

"Maybe not," Crimson Falcon said. "Those augments have proven how resourceful they are. I'd be willing to bet they are working on some kind of plan to find the Omnidisk as we speak. I wish we could figure out who Slymind and Mange are working for. If we could identify Command, it would make all of this a lot easier."

"Still nothing?" Command marched over to Slymind as soon as he entered the lair.

"I am sorry, sir," Slymind apologized. "I have tried everything. I can't find it."

"We have two; isn't that enough?" Mange asked.

"No!" Command slammed his fist into his hand. "No. It is not enough. We need the radiation from all of the disks for my plan to work. With only two, we could barely turn the city!"

"That wasn't what you promised me!" Uproar was in his regular human form. "You told me we'd be runnin' this planet before long!"

"Your promises are starting to seem more unlikely with each passing day." Arcspark sneered. "The Omniforce have most of the disks in their possession. Without them, there is no chance of your plan working!"

"You're a fool if you think I hadn't considered that," Command replied.

"You newbies should trust the boss," Mange said. "He's the smartest guy there is!"

"His leadership has gotten us this far," Slymind added. "You should address him with some respect."

"*I* have my doubts," Uproar said. "This operation is starting to look bogus. Maybe I should take my new powers and go solo."

"That would be a mistake," Command insisted. "We're going to get the Omnidisks and defeat the Omniforce at the same time."

"How?" Mange asked.

Command smiled. "I have a plan."

CHAPTER 27

"Hey, Jason." Eric walked into Jason's classroom. A week and a half had passed since his argument with Archie, and Eric could still feel the tension between them. He was hoping Jason could help him.

"Good afternoon," Jason said with a smile. "How have you been?"

"Tired," Eric replied, plopping into a chair. "Studying for finals has been painful."

"Well, it's almost over," Jason promised. "Soon it will winter break, and you get to start all over with a new set of classes."

"I'm excited about that." Eric rolled his eyes and laughed.

Jason looked closely at Eric's face. "Is something else bothering you?"

"It's Archie," Eric admitted. "He's had trouble fitting in with my other friends lately. He's still my best friend, but he's a little different than they are."

Jason thought for a moment. "Why don't you try getting Archie and your other friends together and do something that doesn't make the differences so apparent, something fun?"

Eric's eyes lit up. "Of course, we never do anything fun anymore. I think that's a good idea. Thanks, Jason." Eric jumped out of his seat and ran to the door, pausing before leaving the room. "You know, Jason, I would have a lot more time to plan this if you gave me an "A" on the final."

Jason laughed. "I'm sorry, Eric I cannot do that. However, there is one grade I can give you if you decide not to take the final."

Eric grimaced. "No, thanks; I'll see you later."

Eric left the classroom and took out his cell phone. He dialed Archie's number and waited. After two rings Archie answered the phone.

"Hello?"

"Archie!" Eric responded. "Hey, man. How have you been? We haven't had much of a chance to talk lately."

"Probably because I've been too busy not getting in the way," Archie responded dryly. "I'm sure you understand."

Eric sighed. "Archie, listen, I'm sorry about the way things have been. We're friends, and I don't want that to change. I'm calling a meeting today at five o clock. I want the team to meet on the ship. The *whole* team."

"Really?" Archie's voice had lost its bitter edge. "Sure, I'll be there."

"Thanks; I'll see you on the ship." Eric hung up the phone. *This might actually work.*

"What's this all about?" Will asked irritably. "I have a hot date planned for tonight. I hate to keep my adoring fans waiting."

"So basically, your mom doesn't want you to be late for dinner," Brynn said with a laugh.

"Why do you insist on resisting me?" Will walked over to Brynn and put his arm around her.

Brynn rolled her eyes and shoved Will. "You're such a creep, Will."

Archie snickered.

"Don't worry, Will, this won't take long," Eric said with a laugh. "I had something I wanted to tell everyone."

"What happened?" Archie asked. "Did you find the last Omnidisk?"

"Or some augments for us to fight?" Brynn asked eagerly.

"There is something wrong with you," Will said to Brynn.

"No, it's not about any of that," Eric said. "It's about this Saturday."

Archie looked confused. "What happens this Saturday? The new episode of *Space Quest* isn't until next week."

"Oh, Lord." Will groaned.

"No, listen! I thought we should all go to the Winter Dance," Eric said.

"That lame thing?" Brynn asked. "Who would actually go to that?"

"As a matter of fact, *I* am. I have not one but two dates to it. Of course, there is always enough of me to go around." Will winked at Brynn.

"What's the point of this ritual?" Chasub asked. "I do not see how this will help us accomplish our goal."

"It gives us a break, that's how. I think we should all go," Eric said. "We've been doing too much lately, and it's starting to wear on us. I think we have earned a little normal time. It might be good for the team."

"I'm in," Will said.

Archie shuffled his feet uncomfortably. "I'm not really into dancing. I have the coordination of a drunk Tuskain Raider, not to mention the whole date situation…"

Brynn shrugged. "I could go with you."

Archie's eyes widened. "You mean that?" he asked breathlessly.

"Sure." Brynn smiled. "I think Eric's right; we deserve a little fun."

"So, a fearless leader that only leaves you," Will said. "You're going to need a date."

"Nah, I'll be alright, I'm going to go solo. Not Han Solo!" Eric said before Archie could speak up.

"So, it's settled," Brynn said in a satisfied tone.

"Now, all we have to do is survive the next two days," Will said grimly.

"From augment attacks?" Chasub asked.

"No," Will said. "Finals."

"Does everyone understand the plan?" Command asked.

"Yes, sir," Slymind replied.

"I have my doubts," Arcspark said. "If they find out what we're trying to do, we will never be able to finish the mission."

"The plan will work," Command insisted, "It's too simplistic not to. And simplicity makes the enemy complacent."

"So when do we strike?" Mange asked.

"We strike in two days," Command said. "It will be the turning point of our conflict with Omniforce."

"Finally!" Will cried as he appeared on the main deck of The Omega. "It's all over! Finals and the whole semester!"

"We should've known you'd be the last one to finish your exams," Brynn said.

"Those things were hard!" Will insisted.

"Your last exam was in P. E.!" Brynn laughed.

Will's face turned red. "It's not as easy as it looks, especially when you're not exactly the tallest person there. I'm sure Chasub knows all about that. Where is the little guy anyway?"

"Going through his sleep cycle," Archie said. "He won't be awake for another few hours at least."

"Is everyone ready for tomorrow?" Eric asked.

"I was born ready," Will said proudly.

"I'm taking Archie to the mall later," Brynn said. "He actually tried to get away with wearing a *Star Wars* shirt to the dance."

Eric and Will looked at Archie in shock.

"What?" Archie shrugged. "It seemed like a good idea at the time."

The ship's alarm started to blare.

"What's going on?" Eric asked.

Archie ran over to the controls and began examining the computer data. "There are a group of augments destroying cars in a supermarket parking lot." He turned to Eric. "It's *them*."

"All of them?" Will asked.

"Mange, Slymind, Arcspark, and Uproar," Archie confirmed.

Eric nodded. "We need to get down there."

"Finally!" Brynn cheered happily.

"Wait!" Will said. "Think about this. Those four are just wrecking things. That's not like them. It could be some a trap."

"You're right, but people are at that supermarket. Someone could get hurt. Everyone be on your toes and look out for a trap. Let's go!" Eric activated his watch and turned into Crimson Falcon.

Brynn and Will activated their watches.

"Archie, you stay here," Crimson Falcon ordered as Archie reached for his watch.

"But you're going to need me!" Archie protested. "There are four of them."

"That's why I need you here. Call Dark Viper," Crimson Falcon said. "He can be our fourth. With Chasub out of commission, we are going to need an eye in the sky looking out for us."

Archie glared at his friend.

"I promise; we are not throwing you aside. You will be of more assistance here," Crimson Falcon reasoned. "Now please, fling us down."

"If you can," Bestial muttered.

"Knock it off!" Prodigy said to him.

Archie smiled, surprised that Prodigy was defending him.

Crimson Flacon smiled. "Alright, Archie, we're ready to go."

Archie nodded and entered the coordinates, still not thoroughly convinced that his friends believed in him.

"It's Omniforce!" a shopper yelled when the team materialized in front of the store.

"Alright, guys, pick your man and take them out," Crimson Falcon ordered. "I'll cover Slymind and Mange."

Bestial transformed into a tiger and leaped at Uproar.

"Here, kitty!" Uproar snatched Bestial out of the air and slammed him into the ground.

Arcspark taunted Prodigy as she extended her hand and fired a bolt of electricity. "I'm going to have to mess up that hairdo of yours, girl."

"I'd say the same to you, but I doubt I could make you look any worse than you already do," Prodigy said with a grin as she deflected the bolt with a telekinetic shield.

Crimson Falcon threw his entire body into Mange's chest and knocked him on his back.

Slymind wrapped his elastic arm around Crimson Falcon's waist and flung him into a car.

"Where's your friend with the laser?" Mange asked, grabbing Crimson Falcon around the throat.

"Not your problem," Crimson Falcon slammed his fist on Mange's arm hard enough to break free and kicked Mange in the stomach. "You should be more worried about me."

"Why should we be worried? We have you outnumbered." Slymind hit Crimson Falcon in the jaw.

"Not anymore!" Dark Viper leaped off of the roof of the supermarket and landed on his feet.

"He's mine!" Mange extended his feathery wings and flew at Dark Viper.

Crimson Falcon dodged another punch from Slymind. "What are you doing here?"

"Augments can't have a little fun?" Slymind stretched his midsection and threw his upper torso at Crimson Falcon.

Crimson Falcon threw a hard punch at Slymind's face and sent him flying across the parking lot.

"It looks like Dark Viper could use some backup," Archie said.

"I'm on it," Crimson Falcon replied.

Dark Viper kicked at Mange's head, but Mange grabbed his foot before it could connect.

"I've got him!" Crimson Falcon punched Mange in his side and swept the augment's feet out from under him.

Mange released Dark Viper and landed on the ground.

"I was prepared to counter that move," Dark Viper said stiffly.

"You're just mad because you owe me one." Crimson Falcon grinned.

Suddenly, Dark Viper shoved Crimson Falcon to the side, right before Mange's eye beams could hit him.

Crimson Falcon chuckled nervously. "I guess we can call it even."

Bestial in wolf form howled in pain as Uproar slammed him into the ground.

"Turnin' into a bunch of hairballs ain't gonna do ya any good." Uproar wrapped his hand around Bestial's throat and pressed him into the pavement. "I'm going to put you to sleep, pooch." Bestial tried to transform into another animal, but he couldn't focus. He began to lose consciousness.

Prodigy raised her hands in front of her and put up a force field to block the oncoming blasts of energy from Arcspark.

"You can't hold me off forever," Arcspark said. "It's only a matter of time before my electricity dances all over you."

"Prodigy, Bestial needs your help!" Archie said.

"I'm a little busy," said Prodigy, her voice strained from blocking the constant barrage of electricity.

"Uproar is choking the life out of him; you have to do something!" Archie insisted.

Prodigy sighed and looked around. Using every bit of power she could, she lifted a car and hurled it at Uproar. The car slammed into him, sending him crashing through the wall of the supermarket.

Bestial changed to human form and stood on his feet.

"Bestial, I know you're worn out, but you need to help Prodigy deal with Arcspark," Archie said.

"I'm on it." Bestial rolled his eyes. "How did you guys ever get along without me?"

"Hurry, she can't hold on for much longer!" Archie warned.

Bestial changed into a kangaroo and leaped over to where Arcspark stood.

"What is this?" Arcspark looked at Bestial and laughed, still shooting electricity at Prodigy.

Bestial kicked Arcspark with both of his strong kangaroo legs. She flew backward, hitting the ground with a loud thud.

Prodigy lowered her force field and collapsed on her hands and knees.

"You're not the first girl to fall for me." Bestial chuckled after returning to human form.

"You will regret that move." Arcspark fired a bolt of electricity at Bestial.

Bestial fell to the ground and began writhing in pain.

Prodigy stretched out her hand, picked up Arcspark, and threw her at Mange. Both of them fell to the ground.

"Nice aim," Crimson Falcon complimented Prodigy.

Back on the ship, Archie furiously entered commands into the computer. *If I can find the last Omnidisk, they will believe in me again. Please work, Archie said to himself. Maybe if I tell the computer to scan for the specific composition of the metal...*

The computer scanned the area below, and after a few minutes, it began to beep. Archie looked at the map on the viewscreen and smiled. "Gotcha!"

Slymind took his phone out of his pocket and dialed Command's number.

"Status?" Command asked.

"We're getting beat pretty bad out here. We need a new plan." Slymind said.

"I think a situation has presented itself," Command said. "I am about to open an aperture for you. All of you must return to base immediately!"

"Yes, sir." Slymind ended the call before turning to the others. "We're leaving!"

"What?" Mange asked as he swiped at Dark Viper. "We can't go!"

"We have our orders. Let's go!" Slymind insisted as a large white hole appeared in front of him.

Uproar and Arcspark broke off their attacks and ran through the hole.

"Mange, now!" Slymind repeated.

"This isn't over!" Mange threatened as he flew through the hole.

After taking one final look at the area, Slymind stepped through the hole, and it immediately closed behind him.

"That was weird," Bestial said to Crimson Falcon, "The augments started trouble, fought us for a while, and simply left. I don't like it."

"Me either," Crimson Falcon agreed. "I think they have some other plan, a plan that has nothing to do with any of us. Slymind asked about Xenoshot."

"We better keep an eye on him," Bestial said.

"I agree," Crimson Falcon said as he looked around the parking lot. People ran out to try to assess the damage to their cars. "We'd better help clean this up."

Archie activated his watch and transformed into Xenoshot. He took another look at the map and entered the coordinates into the computer.

"Are you guys okay?" Xenoshot asked.

"We're fine," Crimson Falcon said. "Why?"

"No reason," Xenoshot said quickly. "I have to go offline for a while so I can do something."

"Fine, don't take too long," Crimson Falcon replied.

"Sure thing." Xenoshot closed the connection. "There shouldn't be a problem, just in and out."

Xenoshot walked over to the Molecular Flinger panel and entered in the coordinates. "Luke Skywalker did harder stuff than this before he became a Jedi; this should be a walk in the park for me."

Xenoshot materialized in a field a mile from the abandoned barn where he detected the Omnidisk.

"I need to work on being more accurate with the flinger." Xenoshot took out his Hyperboard and began to fly toward the barn.

A bolt of electricity struck Xenoshot's Hyperboard, throwing him to the ground.

"I'll get him!" Mange cried as he flew at Xenoshot.

Xenoshot rolled to the side, causing Mange to shoot right past him. When he jumped on his feet, he had his illuminator in his hand.

Xenoshot fired two shots at Mange's chest.

Mange roared and clutched his chest as the beams hit him. Two more shots sent him falling to the ground.

"My turn!" Uproar ran full speed at Xenoshot.

Xenoshot stood his ground, and at the last minute he dodged to the side and rapidly fired at Uproar's legs.

"My legs!" Uproar screamed. He fell to the ground, clutching one leg and then the other.

Without warning, a strong bolt of electricity hit Xenoshot in the back. He dropped his illuminator and fell to his knees, fighting to stay conscious. Seconds later he lost the battle and collapsed to the ground.

"Well done," Slymind complimented Arcspark before taking out his phone. "We have him."

"Grab the Omnidisk and bring him in, now!" Command ordered. "He's going to tell us everything we want to know."

They searched the barn for the Omnidisk, but couldn't find it.

"Sir, it's hidden pretty well. It may take some time to locate it," Slymind said.

"Get him here! His teammates will be on their way soon."

CHAPTER 28

Chasub awoke from his rest and took his position at the computer console. He looked at the latest readouts and noticed that the sensors had detected the last Omnidisk.

"Crimson Falcon," Chasub said, "I need you and the team on the ship immediately."

"Can it wait?" Crimson Falcon asked. "We're helping with the cleanup of the parking lot."

"The ship has found the last Omnidisk," Chasub said urgently. "Our time is short."

"Finally! Bring us up," Crimson Falcon said.

"Where is it?" Crimson Falcon asked.

"It is buried somehow underneath an abandoned barn on the outskirts of town." Chasub highlighted the area on the view screen's map.

"Where's Archie?" Crimson Falcon said.

Chasub frowned in confusion. "Archibald is not aboard the ship." Chasub looked at the flinger panel. "It would seem that Archibald has already gone after the Omnidisk. He flung himself to the same coordinates I am sending you to."

"Good, we'll bring him back with us," Crimson Falcon said. "And we'll discuss how dangerous solo missions can be."

"The Omnidisk is in an abandoned barn in the middle of nowhere," Prodigy shrugged. "What's the worst that could happen?"

"Wake up," Slymind said in a harsh tone. "Naptime is over."

Xenoshot slowly opened his eyes and looked around, his blurred vision slowly coming into focus. His eyes took in the machines that surrounded him, including the spatial aperture generator. When he spotted Arcspark and Uproar, he gasped.

"Look who finally joined us," Arcspark said.

Xenoshot jumped out of his chair, only to be slammed back into it by Mange.

"You're not going anywhere!" Mange roughly squeezed his shoulder.

"Let me go!" Xenoshot struggled against Mange's grip.

"Now why would we want to lose such a valuable guest?"

Xenoshot looked around. "Who are you?"

Command slowly stepped out from behind a machine. "Very well. I do not need to hide from you anymore."

Xenoshot's eyes widened. "You? What are you doing here? How could you do this?"

Command frowned. "You know who I am. Very interesting. Perhaps you would like to tell me yours and where we have met before."

"All I have to say to you is that I knew you were slime from the first time I saw you!" Xenoshot yelled.

Command sighed. "I see that you aren't going to make this easy for me. Remove his glasses."

"No!" Xenoshot struggled as Mange began pulling at his glasses.

"I can't get it off!" Mange cried.

"Take off that ridiculous mask," Command ordered.

Xenoshot stared defiantly at Command.

`Command's eyes dropped to Xenoshot's wrist. "Hold out his arm."

Mange grabbed Xenoshot's arm and extended it, despite Xenoshot's constant struggling.

"That's a fascinating watch you're wearing," Command said.

Xenoshot said nothing.

"Let's experiment with a few of these buttons." Command reached for the button used for an emergency fling to the ship.

Xenoshot's heart leaped. Command was about to send him to safety without even knowing it!

Command saw the excitement on his face.

"Hmm, no, let's try this one instead." Command pressed the button for communicating with the ship.

Everyone waited, but nothing happened.

Command reached for another button and smiled. "Let's give this one a try."

"No!" Xenoshot tried to jerk his hand away, but Mange had a firm grip on him.

Command pressed the button.

There was a quick flash of light, and the uniform disappeared. Archie's identity was exposed.

Uproar laughed. "Look! It's my favorite punching bag!"

Command smiled. "Archie? I'm surprised."

"Why, because I'm smarter than you?" Archie's eyes darted to his right and saw the edge of his illuminator sticking out of Slymind's pocket.

"Not smarter, Archie. Just clever."

Without warning, Archie's hand shot out and grabbed the illuminator out of Slymind's pocket.

Archie shot Slymind in the chest. He fell to the ground and didn't move. He swung his illuminator around and shot Mange in the midsection twice. Mange groaned and lost consciousness.

Archie pointed the illuminator at Command's chest. "I guess I'm full of surprises."

Arcspark and Uproar began to rush forward, but Command waved them off. "What do you think you're going to do with that?"

Archie used his thumb to adjust the setting on the illuminator. "Right now, this thing is on its most powerful setting. You're going to lead me to an exit right now, or I'm going to reduce you to a pile of ash. Your choice."

Command nodded. "Are you really prepared to take that kind of action? You and Eric are best friends. How would he feel about you if you killed me?"

Archie hesitated and his gaze wavered.

The augment's hand shot down, grabbed Archie's wrist and yanked it into the air.

Archie struggled and pulled the trigger, but the beams harmlessly hit the ceiling.

Command reached out with his other hand, grabbed Archie around the neck, and squeezed. "You have no idea who you're dealing with. Right now, I am the most powerful being on the planet. I have the power to absorb human's bioelectric energy. Their brain capacity and strength are added to my own! They give me abilities unparalleled by any human or augment. You are in our custody because you are the weakest member of your team. I knew if we could isolate you, you'd be as good as ours. Now, drop the weapon, or your life ends right here. Right now."

Archie grunted in pain as Command tightened his grip on his wrist and neck. The illuminator dropped to the floor.

"Now we're beginning to understand each other," Command said, letting go.

Archie fell on his knees and began coughing and gasping. *I can't believe I got captured! They were right. I should have never joined the team.*

Uproar grabbed him and yanked him to his feet.

"Let me put the same question to you," Archie said. "How would Eric feel if he knew what you were doing. Who you really were?"

"Believe it or not, I'm doing this for Eric. And I'm doing it for you too. You just don't see it yet. But that's going to change," Command snapped his fingers.

Arcspark stepped forward and pulled something out of her pocket that looked like a small gun with a long needle at the end.

"What are you going to do with that?" Archie asked nervously.

Instead of answering him, Command nodded his head at Arcspark.

She walked over to Archie and pointed the object at his ear.

"What are you doing? Let me go!" Archie tried to break free, but Uproar had a firm grip on him.

Arcspark forced the long needle into Archie's ear.

Archie screamed in pain.

Arcspark pulled out the needle.

"You can let him go now," Command ordered.

Archie fell on the floor and began shaking uncontrollably.

"No, this is not a torture method," Command said softly as he knelt next to Xenoshot. "It is a little something to help the process to go smoothly. Right now, a nanochip designed by me is making its way into your brain. When it gets there, it is going to alter the prefrontal cortex. That's the part of your brain that controls your ability to determine between right and wrong. It is going to get rid of your conscience. I know it sounds bad, but all a conscience does is confuse things anyway. Everything will be much clearer without it."

Archie moaned. "Noooo!"

Uproar laughed in the background.

Several seconds later, Archie stopped shaking. He slowly lifted his head off the floor.

"Take it easy," Command said, noticing Uproar tensing up. "How do you feel?"

"My head hurts. But I feel better." Archie looked Command in the eye and smiled. "Much better. Everything is so much clearer."

"Excellent!" Command said with a laugh. "I knew my little toy would do wonders for you."Archie looked around as if seeing the world for the first time. "Things seem so much simpler. No more bothering with right and wrong. Things I should and shouldn't do. All that matters is whether I want to or not."

"You're right. Now, tell me something. Why do you remain loyal to Omniforce?" Command asked.

"Because it's the right thing—" Archie paused. "No, that's not true, at least, not anymore. I don't know why I remain loyal to them. I shouldn't. They sure don't deserve it! I did so much for them, and they still treated me like a second-rate team member because I didn't have powers!"

Command nodded his head. "That doesn't sound very heroic."

"It's not!" Archie insisted. "But you aren't dealing with heroes anyway, just a bunch of kids in costumes."

Command rubbed his hands together. "Well, tell me who they are, and I'll make sure they get what they deserve."

Archie laughed. "Don't think it's going to be that easy. Just because I don't like them doesn't mean I'm going to hand them over to you."

The augments looked at each other with surprised expressions on their faces.

"At least not without getting something in return," Archie added.

Command smiled. "That is much better. So, what is it that you want? Money? Something else?"

"Nothing that simple." Archie walked right up to Command. "I want to join you. I want powers."

"I don't see him," Crimson Falcon said as he entered the barn.

"Xenoshot!" Prodigy yelled.

"Yelling isn't going to bring him out any faster," Bestial said. "He's probably less trouble to us out of the way."

"Shut up!" Prodigy snapped. "I am sick of you insulting him! Why do you have to be so cynical all of the time?!"

"I'm sorry," Bestial said sarcastically. "I get a little testy when somebody shoots me!"

"That's enough!" Crimson Falcon stepped between his teammates. "We need to find this Omnidisk, and to do it, I need you two to stop bickering. Chasub, where's the Omnidisk?"

"I am detecting it directly in front of you," Chasub said.

Crimson Falcon looked forward. "I don't see anything. All that's in front of me is a wooden support beam."

"Yes. It buried inside the beam, under the barn's floor," Chasub stated.

Bestial walked over to the beam and examined it. "How are we supposed to get it out?"

Crimson Falcon stepped forward, punched a hole in the floor and through the beam.

"I couldn't have said it better myself," Prodigy said in a satisfied tone.

Crimson Falcon rummaged through the wood for several seconds before triumphantly pulling out a dark red Omnidisk. "Chasub, I found it."

"Excellent," Chasub said.

"We still haven't found Xenoshot," Prodigy said.

"I haven't been able to find him on the scanners, which is unusual," Chasub said. "His watch communicated with the ship, but I can't track where the signal came from. Something is blocking me."

"Maybe he isn't Xenoshot right now," Bestial suggested. "Maybe Archie decided to go read comic books or whatever it is geeks do in their spare time."

"We can figure it out on the ship," Crimson Falcon decided. "We need to get the Omnidisk there now."

"Fine." Prodigy began nervously fidgeting with her hair. "But I can't shake the feeling that something is wrong."

"Join us?!" Uproar asked in outrage. "That's crazy!"

Mange groaned and climbed to his feet. "What the heck is going on here?"

"Archibald is trying to join our team," Arcspark stated bluntly.

"That is ludicrous." Everyone turned and saw Slymind had also regained consciousness.

"Why is it so difficult to believe?" Archie asked. "I saw what you did with Travis. He was a human like me. I want that for myself."

"Maybe he can be useful," Arcspark said.

"Maybe? I know *everything* about Omniforce. But I won't tell you a thing until I get my powers."

Mange stepped forward. "Listen to me, you little—"

"Deal," Command agreed.

"What?!" Mange and Uproar cried in unison.

"He has what we need." Command smiled. "And I like how he thinks. Let's get him prepped."

Omnidisk up and admired it.

"So do we get a demonstration of what this thing does?" Will asked.

"Not until I run an analysis to see who the user is," Chasub said. "I do not want any of you to suffer from energy poisoning."

"We found all of them now," Eric said happily. "That's the important thing."

"What about Archie?" Brynn asked. "We still have no idea where he is. We should suit up again and look for him. Maybe we can call Dark Viper; he could track him or something."

Will snickered. "Maybe we can call the FBI too. You'd better be careful, Brynn. Somebody might think you're sweet on the kid."

Eric spoke before Brynn could reply. "I agree with Brynn. We should look for Archie. But we'll look as ourselves. I'll go to his house. Brynn, you check the comic store at the mall. No one knows the mall better than you do. Will, I want you to look around the school."

"Why do I have to check the school?" Will complained. "I thought I was done with that place for a while."

"Stop complaining for once and do it, you big baby," Brynn snapped.

"I will fling you to your various locations," Chasub said. "I do hope that Archibald is in good health."

"Is the Bio Shifter ready?" Command asked.

"Both of the disks are in the machine, and it is ready to go," Slymind reported.

Command looked turned to the table to be sure Archie was strapped down. "I feel the need to warn you that the radiation we're using now is higher than the amount used on Uproar. I cannot guarantee you will survive the process."

Archie smiled. "Command, right now you are the smartest man around. If you can't make this work, no one can."

"You'd better not be yankin our chains, dweeb," Uproar warned.

"Let me worry about that," Command said. "Activate the machine."

The Biological Shifter fired, and the beam hit Archie in the chest.

Archie screamed in pain.

Command and the other augments watched in anticipation as Archie was bathed in the machine's violet light.

"I don't see any changes," Mange said doubtfully.

"Wait a little bit longer," Command said.

Nobody noticed the watch on Archie's right wrist, liquefy and sink into his skin.

"We should stop the process," Slymind insisted. "If we keep it going, it will kill him."

"Turn it off," Command said.

Slymind pressed a button on the machine, and it instantly shut down.

Mange unstrapped Archie from the table.

Archie was shaking and sweating.

"Take it easy," Command said as Archie tried to stand. "Gather your strength."

"I feel fine." Archie waved him off. "But I feel the same as before. No different."

"I don't notice any differences either," Slymind said. "Perhaps the machine malfunctioned."

"Perhaps." Command's gaze fell on Archie's bare wrist. "And perhaps…not. What happened to your watch, Archibald?"

Archie's eyes shot to his wrist. "I don't know. I didn't take it off or anything. I don't know what could have happened. My hand feels a little funny though."

Command grabbed a screwdriver from a nearby table and lunged at Archie.

"Hey!" Archie's hand shot up and grabbed Command's wrist.

"Looks like something happened after all," Command smiled and looked at Archie's arm.

"What in the world?" Archie stared at his arm in disbelief. His flesh had turned silver and metallic.

"Whatever alloy was in the watch is no doubt a part of you," Command said. "Pity, I expected more."

A section of Archie's wrist slid back like one of the panels on Chasub's ship. Several buttons and a screen appeared.

"It's like a part of my body is the computer that we use," Archie said. "I'm processing energy readings from all over this room."

A small nozzle appeared next to the buttons.

"What the heck is that supposed to be?" Mange asked.

Archie balled his hand into a fist and stretched out his arm toward Mange. A green beam shot out of the nozzle and hit Mange in the chest.

Mange flew backward and hit a wall.

Uproar snickered as Mange slowly climbed to his feet.

Command laughed and clapped his hands. "Bravo! That was the kind of response I was looking for."

"It's like my illuminator, except more powerful." Archie grinned evilly. "I guess the dark side is the true path to power after all."

Command put his arm around Archie. "Let's see what else that arm of yours can do."

"Nobody found him?" Eric asked when they met on the ship.

"For the third time, no," Will said. "I searched parts of the school I didn't know we had. Did you guys know we had a library? Because that is news to me."

"Observe the shock on my face," Brynn said without changing her expression. "I couldn't find Archie in the mall. I checked the comic book shop. I even looked in the clothing stores, thinking he may have tried to find a suit for the dance. Nothing."

Eric sighed. "I waited at his house for a long time. His parents are even worrying now. It's getting pretty late."

"This is so unlike him." Brynn began to fiddle with her hair.

"There isn't much more we can do tonight," Eric said. "We can meet here first thing in the morning. Chasub, run continuous scans all night."

Chasub nodded.

"If Chasub hasn't found Archie by nine o'clock in the morning, we meet back here," Eric concluded. "Then we can suit up and call in Dark Viper."

"Let's pray it doesn't come to that," Brynn said.

Eric slowly opened the door to his house and stepped in. He closed the door as quietly as he could and began to tiptoe up the stairs.

Maybe I can get away with this for once, Eric thought to himself.

Eric turned the corner and came face to face with Rebecca.

"Please don't," Eric pleaded.

Rebecca smiled. "Daaa…!"

Eric put his hand over her mouth and dragged her into his room before slamming the door.

"Now I'm going to tell him you were violent," Rebecca said, sticking her tongue out at Eric.

Eric sighed. "Rebecca, I need you to stop telling Dad when I come in late."

"Why should I?" she asked defiantly. "You're the one always sneaking around acting suspiciously."

Eric took a deep breath. "Can you keep a secret?"

Rebecca's eyes widened. She loved secrets. "Yes, I can. I promise."

"This is very important; you can't tell anyone," Eric insisted.

Rebecca nodded her head insistently.

"Have you heard about that superhero, the Crimson Falcon?"

"Yes, no one at school can stop talking about him." Rebecca stared at Eric. "Have you seen him?"

"Something like that." Eric pressed a button on his watch.

Rebecca gasped and put both hands over her mouth. "You're him?"

"Yes, I am," Crimson Falcon said. "That's why I've been coming home late. I have superhero stuff to do. I have to help people."

Rebecca bowed her head. "I'm sorry. I didn't know."

"Hey now, none of that crying stuff. You were doing what you thought was right."

"Why did you tell me?" Rebecca asked.

"Mostly because I don't want Dad to keep getting stressed out because of me not being here; I need someone to cover for me."

"I will," Rebecca said as she hugged Eric.

"And I was getting a little tired of you busting me all the time," Crimson Falcon said with a laugh.

"Nothing happens around here without me noticing," she said proudly.

Crimson Falcon nodded. "Don't I know it."

"Dad isn't here anyway, I was just messing with you," she admitted.

"That's odd," Crimson Falcon frowned. "Why would dad leave you here alone this late?"

"This is better than I imagined," Command said. "Your arm has so many abilities."

"You mean besides being strong and virtually indestructible?" Archie said happily. "It has a built-in laser and communicator. It can interface with any other piece of technology. And…" a long blade extended from a slot in Archie's wrist…"this thing, my personal favorite."

"I'm glad you are satisfied," Command said with a nod. "But a deal is a deal. I want Omniforce."

"Yes! Tell us what we want to know!" Mange demanded.

"So I am part of the team now?" Archie asked.

"Yes, you are," Command said.

"I want a chance to prove myself," Archie crossed his arms and raised his head proudly. "I have a plan."

Command rubbed his forehead. "You are testing my patience."

"Give me a chance, I'll beat it out of him," Uproar offered.

"Not so fast." Command looked at Archie. "What is this plan?"

"I know where they are going to be tomorrow," Archie said. "I can put them out in the open, and you can make your move."

"That is a plan I can sink my teeth into." Mange rubbed his hands together.

Command thought about it for a moment. "Keep going; tell us the details of your plan."

CHAPTER 29

The next morning Eric activated the communicator in his watch. "Chasub, did you find anything?"

"I am sorry, Eric," Chasub apologized. "I scanned the entire planet. There is no sign of him."

Eric took a deep breath. "Okay, let me make an appearance at the breakfast table, then you can bring me up."

"Eric, someone is at the door!" Eric's father yelled.

"I'll call you back." Eric closed the communication and walked to the front door. "Who is it?"

"I am Darth Vader from the planet Vulcan," a voice said from the other side in an obvious Darth Vader imitation.

Eric swung the door open. "Archie!"

"In the flesh!" Archie replied.

"Where have you been?" Eric asked. "We were looking for you!"

Archie shrugged. "I needed a little me time. Is that okay with you, boss?"

Eric frowned. "Yeah…it's fine. And don't call me boss. Try to keep in touch next time. We *are* your friends. We searched for you at the barn; I know you went there after the Omnidisk."

Archie shuffled his feet. "I did, but I didn't find it anywhere."

"Well, we—"

"Eric, I just stopped by for a quick minute. I was about to go meet Brynn so she could take me to get some clothes at the mall. You want to come?"

"I…guess so," Eric hesitantly agreed. "Are you sure you're okay? Nothing at all you want to talk about? Because you know Darth Vader isn't from Vulcan right?"

Archie shrugged. "I feel fine. And it was a quote from Back to the Future."

Eric nodded. "Right, I almost forgot that scene. I'll call Brynn and Will and tell them to meet us at the mall."

"Good idea," Archie said. "At the dance tonight, I want to be dressed to kill."

"So, Archie appeared at your door this morning?" Will asked Eric as Archie and Brynn walked into a clothing store.

"For the last time, yes," Eric replied in an exasperated tone. "What more do you want me to say?"

"I want you to say you grilled him until he told you where he was!" Will raised his voice.

"Keep it down." Eric glanced at Archie and Brynn.

"Look at him," Will gestured at Archie.

Eric looked over at Archie again. He watched Archie talking to Brynn. She giggled and looked at the floor, blushing.

"Did you see that?!" Will gasped, pointing.

"She laughed. So what?" Eric asked.

"She giggled like a little schoolgirl," Will corrected him. "Brynn is tougher than nails; no guy can do that to her."

Eric rubbed his forehead in frustration. "If you have a point, I would like to know what it is."

"Let me paint you a picture," Will said. "Yesterday our augment friends cause a commotion at the mall for no reason at all. In the middle of all of the chaos, one of them asks for Xenoshot by name. When he doesn't show, they take off."

"That doesn't mean that stuff had anything to do with Xenoshot not being there."

"I'm not done," Will continued. "The augments disappear, and we can't find Archie for the rest of the day. Even Chasub's sensors couldn't find him. And the only other people we can never find with the ship's sensors, are Slymind and the other augments."

Eric began to argue but thought about what Will was saying.

Will nodded as if he realized what Eric was thinking. "Look at Archie now. He is a completely different person."

"You think they grabbed Archie?" Eric asked." How could that happen? He's in perfect health."

"Don't forget the same thing happened to Travis. He was gone for a while, and we met Uproar," Will said.

Eric was silent for a moment. "You're saying that Archie is a traitor? That's crazy!"

"What's crazy?" Archie asked as he and Brynn walked over.

"Just Will…being Will," Eric said, looking at Will. "Let's see if we can find something for me to wear."

"Let Archie do it," Brynn said. "He's been picking out some great clothes. I don't know where all this enthusiasm is coming from."

"Maybe I had it in me all along," Archie said, walking toward another clothing store. "Are you coming, Will?"

"Sure," Will said, with a defeated sigh.

Eric observed Archie as they walked. Archie was his best friend. It was unthinkable that he would ever betray him. Wasn't it?

The school gym was packed. The music was blasting as students made their way inside.

"Excuse me," Will said. "My entourage awaits." He walked over to two cheerleaders and escorted them inside, one on each arm.

Brynn sighed in disgust. "Pig."

"Ah, forget him. My date rivals the Queen of Naboo herself." Archie held out his arm.

"And don't you forget it," Brynn said, talking Archie's arm.

Archie has gotten a little more charismatic. That doesn't mean anything is wrong with him. All of that other stuff is a coincidence, Eric reasoned. *Right?*

"How did you learn how to dance?" Brynn asked Archie on the dance floor.

"There's a lot about me you don't know." Archie smiled and spun her around.

Will walked over to Eric at the punch table. "You should get out there. I know you don't have a date, but you could borrow one of mine."

Eric declined. "No, thanks. And they're girls, not livestock."

"You don't have to tell me." Will waved to his dates. "Money can't buy that kind of beauty."

Eric laughed. "I cannot wait to see who you end up marrying."

"Hey, maybe you should ask her to dance." Will pointed to the other side of the gym.

`Eric looked over and saw Jeff talking to a bunch of his football buddies. Chris stood next to him, looking very bored.

"She has a boyfriend," Eric said.

Will smirked. "In my experience that doesn't mean much."

Brynn looked over at Eric and followed his gaze to Chris. "I'll be right back," she said to Archie.

"I'll be waiting." Archie waved. When Brynn walked away, he pulled out a cell phone. "Tell everyone to get ready. It's almost time."

Brynn walked over and stood next to Chris. "You look bored."

Chris laughed. "A little bit. So much has happened the last few months. Superheroes and kidnappers. Strange creatures."

Brynn nodded. "Nobody told us senior year was going to be quite like this."

"Exactly. And honestly, a dance seems so boring in comparison. Do you want to know a secret?"

Brynn smirked. "Do you even have to ask?"

"I miss the excitement. I miss the action. I don't love the danger, but I just feel like my life has started to change this year. I want to embrace that change and see what it means for me. I feel like I'm starting to become who I was meant to be," The whole time Chris was staring off into space.

"Believe it or not, I know exactly what you mean," Brynn said.

"I might leave early, I'm still deciding," Chris admitted.

"If you need a ride home let me know," Brynn walked toward Archie.

Chris looked indecisively at Jeff and. "Jeff, I'm going to go get some punch, okay?"

"Sure, babe. And get me one too." Jeff turned to his friends. "Like I was saying, I threw it into the end zone…"

Chris walked over to the punch table and tapped Eric on the shoulder.

"Hey." He grinned from ear to ear. "How are you?"

"Bored," Chris said. "Jeff and his football friends are at it again."

"Oh," was all Eric could say. "I'm sorry; hopefully, he'll be done soon."

Chris chuckled. "Yes, hopefully. He really gets into it. Just like your friend Archie when he talks about *Space Trek*."

"*Star Trek*," Eric corrected her. "You don't want him to hear you get that wrong, you'll never hear the end of it."

Chris smiled and nodded, "Of course, I'll have to remember that. He seems a lot different tonight. He's the last person I expected to see here."

Eric looked at Archie effortlessly dancing with Brynn and couldn't help feeling nervous all over again. "Yeah, it's like he's a completely different man."

Brynn, who was watching the whole thing out of the corner of her eye, groaned at Eric's response. "Ask her to dance," she mouthed at him.

Eric's eyes grew wide, and he swallowed nervously. "Um, Chris? I was wondering if…you know… that is, if you don't mind, I was hoping…"

Archie snickered at Eric's inability to form a sentence.

"Quit it, he's trying," Brynn said, surprised at Archie's reaction. She had never seen him make fun of Eric before.

"Yes?" Chris asked insistently.

You can do this. You have faced death multiple times in the past several months; you can do this. Eric took a deep breath. "Chris, would you like to dance?"

Chris brushed back her hair and smiled. "I'd love to."

Eric took her hand and led her onto the dance floor.

"Yes!" Brynn cheered quietly.

Archie scoffed. "Took long enough."

Will saw Eric dancing with Chris and sent him a thumbs up.

"You're a great dancer." Eric spun Chris around.

"So are you," she said. "I hate that I didn't realize it before."

"I guess it never came up." Eric chuckled. "We don't see that much of each other."

"I know," Chris replied sadly. "You're a nice guy; we should hang out more."

"That's what I was thinking," Eric said.

For the first time, Chris looked into Eric's eyes. "What is it?" Eric chuckled nervously.

"Something about you," Chris said. "You seem familiar somehow like I know you from somewhere else. You remind me of someone—"

"Eric!" Archie yelled. "Come here!"

Not now! Eric sighed. "I'll be back in a minute."

"I'll be here," Chris promised.

"This had better be good." Eric's voice had an edge to it.

"Yeah," Will said. "Me and the ladies were really dancing out there."

"Is that what you call that?" Brynn asked. "I thought you were having a seizure."

"Chasub contacted me," Archie cut in. "He said he detected augment trouble outside of the school."

"Chasub didn't tell me anything," Eric said. "Maybe I should check with him."

"What, you don't trust me?" Archie asked.

"Of course I do," Eric said. "Come on, guys, let's get this over with."

Will looked at his dates and groaned before following his friends out the doors.

Chris watched Eric and the others run out of the gym. "I wonder what's wrong with them?"

"Where's the disturbance?" Eric asked, "I don't see anything."

Archie smiled. "Not yet."

Eric gazed at Archie's wrist. "Archie, where is your watch?"

"I forgot it," Archie said nonchalantly.

"Wait…how did Chasub contact you?" Eric asked.

Archie remained silent.

"I knew it!" Will exclaimed, walking over to Archie and grabbing his arm. "You're up to something, and I want to know…what the heck is happening to your arm?"

Archie swung his arm and sent Will sailing into the side of the school.

"Oh my…" Brynn gasped.

"Are you nuts?!" Eric yelled at Archie. "Why did you do that? And *how* did you do that?"

"I recently had some work done," Archie said, proudly holding up his right arm.

"What in the world? We need to get you to the ship so Chasub can take a look at you." Eric took a step toward his friend.

Tseeew! Archie shot at the ground an inch in front of Eric.

"Don't take another step," Archie ordered.

"Did you shoot at me?!" Eric yelled in disbelief. "What the heck are you trying to do?"

"I'll tell you," Will said as Brynn helped him to his feet. "You made a deal with the devil, didn't you, Archie?"

"What do you mean?" Brynn asked.

"It's not hard to figure out!" Will cried. "There is only one person I know of that could give you augment powers."

"Archie, tell him he's nuts. Tell him you wouldn't do something like that!" Brynn yelled.

Archie remained silent.

"Archie," Eric said, keeping his voices steady. "What did you do?"

"Yeah, tell us, Archie," Will said angrily. "What was the price of your new powers?"

"Nothing big," Archie extended his arm. "This…for all of you."

A white hole appeared behind Archie.

CHAPTER 30

"No!" Eric gasped.

Mange, Slymind, Arcspark, and Uproar stepped out from the hole in space.

"Here they are," Archie said. "Like I promised."

"*This* is Omniforce?" Uproar asked with a laugh.

"Do you know them?" Slymind asked.

"Yes, I know them," Uproar said. "Eric Daniels, Brynn White, and Will Patel. These punks go to school here."

Arcspark narrowed her eyes. "That is the boy who interfered when I tried to take the girl. I should have known."

"He interfered with us before as well," Slymind said. "The first encounter at the corner store. It all makes sense now."

"This is bad," Brynn said under her breath.

"Why would you do something like this?!" Eric cried to Archie. "We're your friends!"

"That's a joke!" Archie shouted back. "You were as bad as those two. Treating me like an outsider, like I didn't belong because I wasn't one of the Omnidisk users."

"So you set us up to die?!" Brynn raged. "You disgust me."

"That's not what you said earlier, sweetie." Archie laughed. "These guys have given me a new lease on life. Now I am part of a team that truly appreciates me. And I've proven to you how hopeless you are without me."

"Enough talk!" yelled Mange. "I want to tear these brats limb from limb."

"That makes two of us." Uproar laughed, taking augment form.

"Alright, guys, I guess this means the cat's out of the bag," Eric said. "Time to go to work!"

Omniforce activated their watches, and their uniforms were instantly on them.

"Nice trick," Archie said. "I can do it too."

Archie closed his eyes, and a uniform appeared on his body as well. It was similar to his old one, but the jacket was missing a sleeve, exposing the entire metal arm. The symbol on his chest was backward now, a perverse mockery of what it once represented. A mask made entirely of metal materialized over his face with two black slits for his eyes.

"Meet the new and improved Xenoshot," he said. "I decided I needed a new uniform to match my new occupation."

"Eric, what is going on?" Chasub asked.

"Chasub, a lot is going on, and I can't explain it right now," Crimson Falcon said through clenched teeth. "I need you to contact Dark Viper and get him here."

"Who does he keep talking to?" Slymind asked.

"That's Chasub," Xenoshot explained. "He's on a ship in space. His people created the Omnidisks in the first place."

"Shut up!" Bestial turned into a lion and leaped at Xenoshot.

Uproar threw himself into Bestial, and the two began to roll on the ground, locked in battle.

Prodigy threw up a force field to block the bolt of electricity shot at her by Arcspark.

"I guess that leaves you and us," Xenoshot laughed as he gave Mange and Slymind a glance.

Without a moment's hesitation, Crimson Falcon launched himself at Mange. He punched him in the jaw with all of the power he could muster and sent him flying to the other side of the parking lot in pain.

Crimson Falcon spun around, caught Slymind and kicked him in the chest as Slymind went for his attack.

"Aaaah! Crimson Falcon was knocked to the ground by a punch from Xenoshot's metal fist.

"You're not dealing with weak little Archie anymore." Xenoshot laughed.

Crimson Falcon drew back his fist.

Xenoshot taunted him. "Go ahead; hit me."

Crimson Falcon sighed and put his fist down. "I can't do this. There has to be some part of you that still values our friendship enough to stop this."

Xenoshot said nothing.

"We've been friends since we were kids," Crimson Falcon continued. "We camped out in each other's yards and swapped comic books and trading cards. We never kept a secret from each other. You can't truly want to throw all of that away."

Xenoshot's gaze seemed to waver.

"Please stop all of this," Crimson Falcon said. "It's not too late to fix it."

Xenoshot's eyes filled with sadness and he bowed his head. "I'm sorry."

Crimson Falcon stepped forward. "It's okay. We can—"

Tseeew! A green beam hit Crimson Falcon in the chest and threw him several feet.

"I can't believe you fell for that!" Xenoshot laughed. "After all this, you still fall for the 'I'm sorry' routine. You aren't fit to lead these guys."

Crimson Falcon slowly climbed to his feet, his face full of anger and determination. "I didn't want to have to fight you. But now you've given me no other choice!"

"That's what I wanted to hear. Let me handle him," Xenoshot told Slymind and Mange as they approached. "He's mine."

Inside the gym, Chris looked nervously at the door. It had been awhile since Eric and the gang left.

"Jeff, I think something is wrong," she said to him. "Will you come outside with me?"

"Huh? Oh yeah, just a second. Let me finish telling the guys about this play." He waved his hand dismissively.

Chris sighed in frustration, still looking at the door.

Bestial changed into a grizzly bear and struck Uproar across the face with his large paw.

Mange tackled Bestial from behind and wrestled him to the ground.

Prodigy flew to the side, dodging a bolt of lightning.

"I'll get her!" Slymind yelled as he stretched his arms out toward Prodigy.

"I don't think so." Prodigy held up her hands and threw Slymind several yards away.

Prodigy crossed her arms. "You're not the first man to try to put his hands on me! Aaaaahhh!" A bolt of electricity hit her, and she fell to the ground, twitching.

Xenoshot ducked under a punch from Crimson Falcon and hit him with a strong uppercut. Crimson Falcon landed on the ground hard.

"You're holding back," Xenoshot said, kicking him in his side. "That's a bad idea."

"You're right." Crimson Falcon kicked Xenoshot in the stomach, propelling him several feet away. "You lost any right to mercy when you betrayed all of us."

"See? I knew you had it in you." Xenoshot extended the blade from his wrist. "Now let's do this the right way."

Chris ran out of the gym. "Oh my—"

"'It's the girl!" Arcspark yelled.

Without another word, Mange extended his wings, flew forward, and grabbed Chris.

"Help me!" Chris screamed as Mange carried her into the sky.

Crimson Falcon looked around. Bestial and Prodigy were both occupied by their own opponents.

"Crimson Falcon, please!" Chris cried as she was carried further away.

"I'm coming!" Crimson Falcon took off after Mange.

Tseeew! Crimson Falcon fell to the ground after Xenoshot's beam hit him in the shoulder.

"You're not going anywhere," Xenoshot said. He opened the communication panel on his arm. "Mange has Chris. The girl you have been looking for. Open an aperture for him."

"Why are you doing this?" Crimson Falcon tried to rise.

"Don't move." Xenoshot aimed his laser at Crimson Falcon. "You're staying right—" Xenoshot collapsed to the ground.

"Get her," Dark Viper said, looking down at Xenoshot.

Crimson Falcon nodded and flew after Mange.

"Let me go!" Chris struggled in Mange's grasp.

"Shut up!" Mange put his hand over Chris' mouth. "We're almost there; your squealing is pointless."

A white hole opened in the air in front of Mange.

"Mange, stop!" Crimson Falcon cried from behind.

Mange laughed. "You'll never beat me there!"

"He is right," Chasub warned. "You are not fast enough to reach the aperture before he does."

"Bring her to the ship!" Crimson Falcon cried.

"There is too much interference from Mange's energy output," Chasub responded.

Crimson Falcon thought for a moment. "Fling me to the ship!"

"I do not—" Chasub began to argue.

"Do it!" Crimson Falcon yelled. "Fling me up, then fling me in front of the hole. It's our only chance."

"No!" Chris screamed when she saw Crimson Falcon disappear.

"Almost there," Mange said.

Suddenly, Crimson Falcon appeared in front of the hole.

Mange roared in rage as Crimson Falcon punched him in the face.

Mange released his grip on Chris, and she fell toward the ground.

"I'm coming!" Crimson Falcon dived after Chris.

"Help me!" Chris screamed as the ground came rushing at her.

"Gotcha!"

"Give her back!!" Mange flew towards Crimson Falcon and Chris, eyes glowing yellow.

"Chasub, I have her!" Crimson Falcon yelled.

Tzzzap! Mange's eye beams shot out, but by the time they reached their target, Crimson Falcon and Chris were gone.

"Thanks, Chasub," Crimson Falcon said, grateful that they were safe on the ship's medical quarters.

"Yes, thank you so much," Chris said softly. "You've saved my life again."

"No gratitude is necessary," Chasub assured her.

"I can't believe they came after me again," Chris' voice was shaking. "I thought it was over."

"Yeah…" Crimson Falcon's eyes grew cloudy.

"Something's wrong." Chris looked closely at Crimson Falcon. "What happened that was so bad?"

Crimson Falcon bowed his head. "I was betrayed."

Chris frowned. "Betrayed? By who?"

Crimson Falcon blinked, and a single tear rolled down his face. "By my best friend."

"I'm sorry," Chris said, putting her hand on his cheek.

"I don't know how this could have happened," he said with a sob. "I can't help thinking I could have done something to stop this."

"Listen to me," Chris said firmly as she looked into Crimson Falcon's eyes. "You are a good person. You save people constantly. I owe you my life."

"I could never let anything happen to you," Crimson Falcon whispered.

"I know," Chris put her hand on his chest and face drew close to his. "You're always there for me."

Crimson Falcon took a deep breath. "Chris…I—"

"Crimson Falcon, you need to get down there!" Chasub shouted over the communicator.

"I'll be back." Crimson Falcon gave Chris a final nod before he left.

"I know…Eric," Chris said quietly to the empty room.

"There you are!" Prodigy exclaimed. "We were worried. I thought you were going to abandon us or something."

"Took you long enough," Bestial said bitterly.

"I'm sorry. I had to make sure Chris was safe," Crimson Falcon apologized.

"Yeah, I bet you did," Bestial said sarcastically.

"Are you two okay?" Crimson Falcon asked. "Where did the rest of the bad guys go?"

"The police arrived after you left," Prodigy said. "Dark Viper disappeared as usual, and the augments went through one of their little holes."

"And they took their new lapdog, better known as Xenoshot, with them," Bestial added.

"Don't you talk about him that way!" Crimson Falcon yelled.

"The truth hurts, doesn't it?" Bestial asked. "I tried to warn you about that traitor!'"

"You are an insensitive little punk!" Prodigy said. "How can you be so mean at a time like this?"

Bestial laughed bitterly. "I am *so* sorry for not being more sensitive, especially considering I was right the whole time."

"What are you talking about? You never said this would happen!" Crimson Falcon argued.

"Didn't I? I said from the start that the bad guys would find out who we are. And they did!" Bestial pointed to Crimson Falcon. "Your father and sister." He turned to Prodigy. "Your parents and brothers. And my mother. They are all at risk now!"

Crimson Falcon took a step back.

Bestial nodded. "Archie is going to tell them everything about us. And the few things he doesn't know, they are going to find out for themselves."

Prodigy's face grew pale.

"And when that happens…All of the superpowers in the world won't protect us."

"We had them!" Xenoshot shouted angrily, at Command. "We could have ended this, once and for all!"

"I'm with the geek," Uproar said in agreement.

Command chuckled. "Both of you are so short-sighted. Omniforce has constantly pushed us back, cutting us off at every turn."

"I don't see how that gives us a reason *not* to end them," Mange said.

"I don't just want to end this quickly!" Command shouted. "I want to humiliate them. I want them to feel the hopelessness of their actions. And when the entire planet is on its knees, and they know they have lost…then I will end it."

"Really?" Xenoshot smirked. "Even Eric?"

"Obviously, I have different plans for Eric," Command replied. "I didn't know he was Crimson Falcon. He has been misled by that alien. I'll think of a separate approach for him."

"Why should he get special treatment?" Slymind squinted at Command. "What aren't you telling us?"

Command walked over to Slymind until their faces were inches apert. "I tell you what I want, when I want. Let me know if that's a problem for you."

Slymind gulped. "No, sir."

"Nice plan, but I think you underestimate them," Xenoshot said. "They can cause you more problems than you think."

"Only while they're optimistic enough to think they still have a shot at winning," Command smiled. "They just suffered a body blow. They are not ready to experience a second. After my next move, they will be completely vulnerable."

Eric stood in front of Chasub. "I dropped Chris off at home. She's still a little shaken, but she'll be okay."

"I hope you have a game plan." Will looked intently at Eric. "Or else we are all in big trouble."

Eric looked at Chasub. "I want you to run constant sensor sweeps on our homes and the areas around them. If you even think you see augment life signs, let us know immediately."

"It will be done," Chasub promised.

"That's not going to be enough!" Will said in frustration, "We need to tell our families what's going on and get them out of town."

"No, you want us to run with our tails between our legs!" Brynn shouted. "I'm not a coward. I say we find them and fight!"

"Brynn! Calm down. Everyone, chill. Will is only being cautious."

"You're taking his side?" Brynn asked angrily.

"I'm not taking any sides," Eric insisted. "But I agree that it wouldn't hurt to do something with each of our families. We should think about telling them what's going on. No one has to decide now," Eric said before Brynn could object. "We'll sleep on it, and tomorrow we can vote."

Will chuckled to himself.

"Now what are you laughing about?" Eric asked irritably.

"Just the irony of it all," Will said. "All we wanted was to do something normal; now our situation is worse than ever. I knew there was a reason I hated school dances."

CHAPTER 31

Eric tossed and turned all night. *They have Archie. They know everything. Who we are and where we live. I could've prevented this. I drew him in, and I made him feel like an outcast. All of my friends' lives are at risk. My family too. And it's all my fault.*

He sat up in bed. "I tried to do the right thing," Eric whispered to himself as he glanced over at the clock. It was 4:46 in the morning. He knew he wasn't going to get any sleep with so much weighing on his mind.

He kicked off the covers and jumped out of bed. Yawning, he walked to the window and threw it open. He needed guidance. Somebody who could help him sort everything out. Eric activated his watch and became Crimson Falcon.

There was one man he knew he could trust. It was time to tell him everything.

Dark Viper stood on the roof of an office building, gazing the landscape. Rays of light were beginning to break over the horizon. Five more minutes and he would leave. He knew there wasn't much augment activity this time of night, and even he needed to rest.

Out of the corner of his eye, he noticed movement. Dark Viper turned and saw Crimson Falcon flying past him. A brief flash of sympathy went through him. *That boy is brave and resolute*, he thought to himself, *but there is no getting around the danger he and his team are in.* Omniforce had delayed the augment's plan, but he doubted they could stop it. Command would never allow that to happen. Dark Viper knew that better than most. He would kill half the planet if he had to. And now that their identities were known, he feared their defeat might come sooner than later.

Dark Viper followed Crimson Falcon, jumping across the rooftops as Crimson Falcon flew into the distance. When he saw Crimson Falcon slow down, he stopped and waited. A frown came over his face when he realized where Crimson Falcon might be heading. *It can't be*, he thought to himself.

Crimson Falcon deactivated his suit and rang the doorbell.

"Hello, Eric! Please come in."

Eric was surprised to see Jason fully dressed at this hour. And he didn't seem surprised to find him at the door. It was almost as if he was expected.

Eric shook his head and walked through the door. *You're being paranoid because of what happened last night. You can trust Jason.*

"Eric, are you okay?" Jason asked. "You look like you haven't had much sleep."

"I haven't," Eric said quietly. "I'm in some trouble, and I have always been able to turn to you for advice."

"Of course, you can tell me anything," Jason insisted. "I will help you in whatever way I can."

Eric nodded. "I know. That's why I came to you. Remember that big secret I had that I couldn't tell Will about?"

Jason almost seemed to be smiling. "Yes, I recall you talking about that."

"There's something I need you to see." Eric took a deep breath and activated his watch. A moment later, Crimson Falcon was standing in front of Jason.

Jason's face remained the same, not the slightest bit of surprise appeared on it.

"I am Crimson Falcon. I have been leading the force that has been fighting the augments."

"I see that," Jason's face was still devoid of emotion. "No wonder you have been having so much trouble with your schoolwork."

Crimson Falcon laughed, surprised at Jason's ability to joke at the situation. "Yeah, it hasn't been easy. And last night we ran into a problem."

"We?" Jason asked.

"My friends and I," Crimson Falcon clarified. He wouldn't tell Jason the other's identities. That was their choice.

"What kind of problem?" Jason asked.

"One of us joined the enemy," Crimson Falcon said bitterly. "He betrayed us and exposed all of our secrets. We're more vulnerable now than we have ever been."

A smile tugged on the corner of Jason's mouth. "And why do you think your friend made this choice?"

Crimson Falcon shrugged. "Does it matter? They're the enemy! They are dangerous. Countless lives are at risk because of what they have been trying to do!"

"Maybe he got their perspective on the matter," Jason said. "What if he took the time to find out what they are trying to do and realized their plans might have some merit?"

Crimson Falcon frowned. "No way; they're violent and ruthless. They can't have anything good planned for the planet. Anyway, you're getting off of the topic. I need some advice. How do you think I should handle this?"

Jason ignored Crimson Falcon's statement. "Maybe these augments explained their plan to Archibald, and he saw that some good might come of it."

"You're not hearing what I'm saying! Our families might be in danger…" Crimson Falcon's voice trailed off. *I never told him the traitor was Archie.*

"Perhaps he wasn't so short-sighted." Jason's gaze turned fierce. "He may have seen that the world needs a change. Think of all the crime and turmoil that is so prevalent today. The Omnidisks may be what are needed to make the planet better!"

Crimson Falcon's eyes widened as he watched Jason.

"The world could be better under augment rule," Jason emphasized. "A stronger, more powerful authority to make everyone fall in line! The Omnidisks can make that happen."

Crimson Falcon took a step back. "You almost sound like… like—"

"Like I'm one of *them?*" Jason finished, emphasizing the last word.

Crimson Falcon's eyes clouded over as flashbacks of previous conversations came to mind.

"Just because someone appears to be an ally does not make them one," Chasub had warned.

"I have a bad feeling about this guy," Archie had said.

"When there is an obstacle preventing you from changing the world for the better, one must eliminate it," Jason himself had advised.

Crimson Falcon finally gasped as he realized who he was dealing with.

"It was you," he said hoarsely. "You're the augment we've been looking for! You're Command!"

Jason nodded. "Yes, that would be me. But please allow me to explain."

Crimson Falcon curled his hands into fists and took a step toward Jason. "Why should I let you breathe another word? You sent those augments after us time after time! You almost killed my friends and me. You have hurt a countless number of people, feeding your desire for power and knowledge!"

"I did not know it was you before, I promise you that," Jason insisted. "I have always been kind and fair to you, Eric. You know it's true."

"It doesn't matter," Crimson Falcon said. "You are a monster! You hurt others with no remorse."

"I sacrificed lives for the greater good!" Jason held up his hands. "You haven't even heard me out."

"You don't have anything to tell me," Crimson Falcon replied through clenched teeth.

"Please! For the sake of our friendship just give me a few seconds to explain," The Augment begged.

Crimson Falcon glared but didn't say anything.

Jason took a deep breath. "I haven't told another soul what I'm about to tell you. I'm not just doing all of this for power. I'm doing it to save the planet. A threat is coming from outer space. An alien threat."

Crimson Falcon rolled his eyes.

"How could you of all people scoff at this?" Jason took something out of his wallet. "Think about what you know and what you've seen. Years ago, I wake up one day, and I find this note in my pocket."

Crimson Falcon read the note. *A large-scale alien attack is coming. It may take years. You have to protect the planet.*

"That was written in my handwriting," Jason continued. "But I have no memory of writing it. Someone or something erased my memory and I wrote that to give us a fighting chance."

Crimson Falcon almost laughed. Until he remembered Chasub mentioning that he erased the memories on an augment they caught.

Jason smiled. "I can see it in your eyes. My story isn't that crazy. I don't have all of the facts. Maybe this not is referring to your alien friend, maybe I was talking about a different species entirely. All I know is, my doubt melted away when I got wind of those Omnidisks. They were proof of alien life. And if I was right about that, I was right about the invasion. Everything I'm doing is to make humanity stronger and prepare us for what's to come."

"All because if a note?" Crimson Falcon asked. "You're a terrorist! Look at what you've done. You're not a hero. And a few scribbles on a piece of paper don't prove you right."

"You don't like my methods?" Jason asked. "Then work with me! I'm a reasonable man. Together we'll find a better way. We can protect humanity together. We can be heroes!"

Crimson Falcon shook his head. "Humanity need protection from you. You brainwashed Archie!"

"I didn't brainwash your friend," Jason corrected. "I told him a little about my grand plan and helped him appreciate what I'm going to do. I wouldn't have said anything if I wasn't sure it was the right thing to do.

He asked to join our team. He asked me to make him an augment. To give him power. I can do the same for you. You won't need that costume to fight for justice. You won't need the Omnidisks. The power to make a positive change in the world can always be inside you."

Chasub had been listening in. "Do not listen to him!" But Chasub's voice was little more than background noise to Crimson Falcon.

"You know I am your friend. Trust me. *Join* me. I can promise you a position of power in the new order and the safety of your father and sister. I can make sure no harm at all comes to them."

Crimson Falcon unclenched his fist. This whole time all he had been trying to do was protect his family. He was being promised this from the one man who might be able to guarantee it.

"That's right," Jason said, realizing that he had hit a soft spot. "I will keep them safe. And I will create a world where a child will never lose his mother because of a careless driver."

Crimson Falcon swallowed hard as his thoughts took him to when his mother was alive. He missed her.

Jason held out his hand. "So, what do you say? Do we have an agreement?"

Crimson Falcon raised his head and looked Jason in the eye. He knew what he had to do. He took Jason's hand.

Jason laughed and shook it. "You made the right choice."

Crimson Falcon yanked Jason toward him until their faces were inches away from each other. "I know I did. So, I'm giving you this one last chance to surrender."

The smile disappeared from Jason's face. It was replaced with a fierce glare. "I had hoped this could be avoided."

"I'm sure you did," Crimson Falcon replied with a bitter smile.

Jason thrust out his fist and hit Crimson Falcon in the chest.

Crimson Falcon flew through three different walls before crashing in Jason's backyard.

"Crimson Falcon are you okay?! Respond!" Chasub demanded.

Crimson Falcon rolled over and tried to rise to his feet. He collapsed on the ground. He could feel himself losing consciousness.

"I cannot fling you!" Chasub shouted. "Something is making it difficult to lock onto your life sign."

As his world grew dimmer, Crimson Falcon saw Jason getting closer and closer. Then everything went black.

Jason stood over Crimson Falcon's unconscious body. "Your extraterrestrial friend has no doubt discovered that we had arranged a few extra precautions. Just a little something your friend Archie helped us to put in place make sure you don't disappear. You're mine."

"Step away from the boy!" Dark Viper leaped off of the roof and landed next to Jason.

Jason laughed and lightly pushed against Dark Viper's chest, knocking him to the ground with ease.

"You of all peoples should know you're no match for me," Jason said. "Walk away."

Dark Viper jumped up and hit Jason with a roundhouse kick.

Jason caught Dark Viper's next punch before grabbing the front of his cloak and yanking him closer. He slammed his head into Dark Viper's and tossed his unconscious form to the side.

"Now where were we?" Jason turned around.

Crimson Falcon surprised him with a hard right hook.

"You have more fight in you than I thought." Jason laughed.

Without responding,Crimson Falcon hit him with a left punch and a kick to the chest.

Jason stumbled back a few feet and smiled. "You don't seem to grasp how hopeless this battle is."

Crimson Falcon lunged forward.

Jason shoved his shoulder with one hand, sending Crimson Falcon sailing across the yard.

"Even with your Omnidisk, I am far stronger than you," Jason walked towards Crimson Falcon. "But please, feel free to keep struggling."

Crimson Falcon looked at Jason and prepared to charge again. Suddenly, there was a flash of light, and everything changed.

Jason looked behind him. Dark Viper and Crimson Falcon were gone. He sighed as he reached into his pocket, took out his cell phone and dialed Archie's number. "He did not accept my offer."

"I told you he wouldn't," Archie said. "He's too far up on his high horse to see any point of view but his own."

"The alien flung him away," Jason said accusingly.

"He shouldn't have been able to do that," Archie said in a surprised tone. "The blockers I erected around your house—"

"Didn't work!" Jason interrupted. "Open an aperture. It is time to work on phase two of our plan. And tell Mange and Uproar to come clean up this mess"

"I was finally able to cut through whatever interference was preventing me from operating the Molecular Flinger. Dark Viper is in the Medical Alcove. I'm so sorry to hear about Archibald," Chasub said.

"I don't want to talk about him," Crimson Falcon said quietly. "Jason knew I was coming. I trusted him."

Chasub floated toward Crimson Falcon. "You did not know—"

"Jason betrayed me!" In his rage he punched a wall, leaving a large dent in the metal. "The same way Archie did last night! Two of the people I trusted most and both of them stabbed me in the back."

"Perhaps now you can see why I take the matter of trust very seriously," Dark Viper said as he walked into the room.

Crimson Falcon ignored his statement and turned to Chasub. "Get the others here; we need to talk."

"Jason Jeffries? The school teacher?" Brynn said after she and Will were onboard the ship. "He was there every single day! We could've beaten him down at any time!"

"I've said it all my life," Will said bitterly. "Teachers are evil."

"He has Archie; this keeps getting worse," Brynn replied.

"That's why we need to even the odds," Eric took a deep breath and walked over to his friends. "I don't know about you guys, but I'm tired of being one step behind. The augments know everything about us. I say we step up our game."

"And how do we do that?" Will asked skeptically.

"We pull a play out of their book," Eric said. "We grab one of the augments."

"Yes!" Brynn cheered.

"What?" Will screeched.

Dark Viper nodded in approval.

"Eric, the risks involved with bringing one of those augments here are many," Chasub pointed out.

"We've done it before with other augments," Brynn replied. "It's no different."

"It's *very* different," Will argued. "These augments are more powerful than the others. They know what we do here. You can't guarantee we can hold, whomever we get!"

"This isn't a debate. We are doing this!" Eric yelled.

Will walked over to him. "You have no right to—"

Eric growled. "I have every right! We're going through with my plan. If you don't like it, you can quit. Maybe you'll have a better chance of protecting your mom on your own."

Will glared at Eric but didn't say anything further.

Eric turned to Dark Viper. "Are you in?"

"I will assist," he simply replied.

Eric nodded. "Chasub, start scanning; the minute any of those augments appear, we'll be all over them."

"Answer me this, fearless leader," Will said snidely. "If we catch one of these guys, how are we supposed to make them talk?"

Eric looked at his friend. "By any means necessary."

"I have finally been able to lock onto one of the augments," Chasub reported an hour later.

"Who is it?" Eric rushed to the view screen.

"Uproar," Chasub said.

Eric nodded. "Alright, guys. Let's do this!"

One by one all of the members of Omniforce activated their uniforms.

"Are you sure you want to do this?" Bestial asked.

"Stop being such a baby!" Prodigy yelled. "Crimson Falcon is right; it's time to take off the gloves."

"Ready?" Crimson Falcon asked Dark Viper.

He nodded.

"Chasub, take us down."

Uproar was stepping out of a fast food restaurant when he felt his cell phone vibrating in his pocket.

"What is it?" he answered.

"We need you at the base," Slymind said, "We have a new plan."

"Yeah, Yeah, I'm on my—"

Three of Dark Viper's smoke bombs dropped around Uproar, thick black smoke rolling out of them.

"What's going on?" Uproar shouted.

Dark Viper swung in on a cable and hit Uproar with both feet.

Uproar sailed into the wall of the restaurant and hit the sidewalk.

Dark Viper landed next to Uproar, grabbed an inhibitor off of his belt and reached toward the augment's neck

"Get away from me!" Uproar shifted into augment form.

"Move in!" Crimson Falcon commanded from above.

With a mighty bellow, Bestial in rhinoceros form rammed Uproar in the back.

Uproar screamed as he flew forward.

"I've got him." Crimson Falcon hit Uproar with an uppercut, sending the augment flying upward.

"My turn!" Prodigy telekinetically grabbed Uproar in midair and held him there.

"Let me go!" he demanded.

"That's exactly what I was thinking." Prodigy smiled and with one downward sweep of her hand, sent Uproar plummeting to the ground.

Uproar crashed into the street, cracking the asphalt all around him. With a groan, he closed his eyes, his body changing back as he slowly lost consciousness.

Dark Viper landed next to him and stuck the inhibitor on his neck.

"Stop!" Slymind shouted, stepping out of an aperture a few yards away, Mange and Arcspark were behind him.

This time, *you're* too late!" Crimson Falcon crowed. "Chasub, we're ready to go."

The augments rushed forward, but before they could reach their fallen comrade, he disappeared. And Omniforce disappeared with him.

CHAPTER 32

"Lower the energy field. Quickly!" Crimson Falcon urged as he carried Uproar into the holding cell.

"Energy field offline," Chasub reported.

Crimson Falcon tossed Uproar's unconscious body into the cell.

"Now what?" Bestial asked, "Do we wait for sleeping ugly in there to wake up?"

Crimson Falcon folded his arms. "No, we don't have the time. We do this now."

"You know I'm with you," Prodigy said. "But he's not going to say much while he's sleeping."

"So we wake him up." Crimson Falcon turned to Chasub. "Do we have anything that might help do that?"

"I think I may have—" Chasub began.

"Here." Dark Viper opened a small pouch hanging on his belt and pulled out a syringe. "I made it myself; it will wake up the augment and alter his brain chemistry, allowing him to be more susceptible to questioning."

"I didn't know you were a chemist. How do you know it won't kill him?" Bestial asked.

"There is much you don't know about me. And I don't," Dark Viper replied.

"We cannot use it. It is highly unethical," Chasub insisted.

"Who cares about ethics!" Prodigy yelled. "Our families are at risk!"

"That justifies murder?" Bestial asked. "No way, I can't go along with this."

"He who hesitates—" Dark Viper simply said.

"Everyone stop!" Crimson Falcon said.

They all turned toward him.

"We may have to do some questionable things during all this, but murder will not be one of them," he said.

"But he said he didn't *know* for sure—" Prodigy started.

"It doesn't matter!" Crimson Falcon insisted. "We won't risk it."

"Finally, you make some sense," Bestial said in an approving tone.

"Chasub, can you do something to make sure he can't power up?" Crimson Flacon asked.

Chasub pressed several buttons on the cell's control panel "According to these scans, the process Jason used to turn this boy into an augment may well be irreversible. I can, however, provide a constant flow of radiation that will prevent him from taking augment form and using his powers."

Uproar groaned from inside the cell.

"Well, I guess it's time to get this party started," Crimson Falcon rubbed his hands together.

"Where am I?" Uproar asked.

"I'll be asking the questions here." Crimson Falcon stationed himself outside of the cell with his friends around him.

Uproar looked around and laughed. "You think you and your punk friends can keep me here?"

"Yes, I do," Crimson Falcon said confidently. "Especially since you can't use your powers."

Uproar's eyes widened.

"Now," Crimson Falcon started, "you're going to tell me everything you know about Jason's plan."

"How could you let this happen?!" Jason yelled.

"It happened so fast, sir," Slymind explained. "We weren't able to stop them."

"'I should have known they would pull a stunt like this," Xenoshot said. "We've backed them into a corner, and now they are lashing out. Just like the episode of *Enterprise* where the Sulibaan take Archer. Well, I guess we'd be more like—"

"Do you have any useful advice?" Jason asked Xenoshot in a bitter tone.

"I have an idea," Mange said. "Why don't we tear through all of their homes until we find Uproar!"

"He wouldn't be in any of their homes, you fool," Arcspark replied as she rolled her eyes. "They took him to their spaceship."

"She's right," Xenoshot agreed.

"Let's go there!" Mange cried.

"And how do you suggest we get there?" Slymind asked. "We don't have any spacecraft."

Xenoshot stared thoughtfully at the Spatial Aperture Generator. "We might not need any."

"What are you suggesting?" Jason asked.

Xenoshot walked over to the machine and made his arm become robotic. "I might be able to modify this machine to give it more range."

Jason crossed his arms, "How much range will it give us?"

"I can get you to the ship." A long tube shot out of Xenoshot's robotic arm and connected with the machine's controls pad. "I'm inputting the coordinates of the ship and boosting the range of the machine. We should be able to walk right in."

A smile finally appeared on Jason's face. "Well done. But you will not be coming with us."

"I won't?" Xenoshot frowned. "Why not? I know that ship better than anyone!"

"True, but I need you for my new plan," Jason insisted. "This bold step your friend Eric has taken shows me I need to try a little harder to get rid of him. I need to think a few steps ahead. Like I did when I told Arcspark to attack me during their abduction of Christina just to be sure no one connected us. I need a preemptive strike and you are the only one who can carry out the task. When we're done, Omniforce will have no leader. And without a leader—"

"They don't stand a chance." Xenoshot smiled.

"I told you, I ain't sayin nothin!" Travis yelled defiantly. "Now let me out of here!"

Crimson Falcon groaned in frustration and walked to the main deck.

"Anything?" Prodigy asked.

"No," Crimson Flacon responded.

"We have to change tactics," Bestial said. "Hammering him with questions isn't going to work. It's been over an hour, and he hasn't said anything useful."

"I thought you didn't even like this plan," Prodigy said, raising an eyebrow.

"I don't. But I don't have a better one either, and we need the information he has."

"Give me a few moments alone with him. I'll bet I can loosen his lips." Prodigy cracked her knuckles.

Will cringed. "Just when I think you can't scare me anymore—"

"A thought has occurred to me," Chasub said.

Everyone looked his way.

"The augments know you have captured Uproar. It would not be above them to take another hostage in exchange. And now that they know who you are—"

Prodigy gasped. "They could go after our families!"

Crimson Falcon was quiet for a moment. "Chasub's right. Our families need to protection. Prodigy and Bestial, you should go home and watch over your families."

"What about you?" Prodigy asked.

Crimson Falcon sighed. "I should stay here. I have to try to get him to talk."

"But your family—" Prodigy said.

"I can watch over the Daniels' household from afar," Dark Viper volunteered.

"Wait a minute." Bestial narrowed his eyes at Crimson Falcon. "*He* knows who you are?"

"Yes. He's known for a while, and we don't have time to go into that right now," Crimson Falcon replied.

"Point of fact, I know who all of you are," Dark Viper said. "I like to know who I am working with?"

"You spied on us?" Bestial glared ad Dark Viper. "Who do you think you are?"

"It doesn't matter! What's he going to do, tell the bad guys? Too late!" Prodigy said sarcastically.

Bestial rolled his eyes. "Fine, why not? Everyone else knows who we are. I have a nice reporter friend I was going to call with the information."

Crimson Falcon looked at Dark Viper. He trusted him, but lately, his trust in people had not been serving him well. On the other hand, he didn't have many options.

"Thank you," Crimson Falcon said. "Chasub, keep scanning our homes. Especially Chris; she's a target too."

Chasub entered the command into the Molecular Flinger console.

"Be careful," Prodigy said before everyone disappeared.

Crimson Falcon deactivated his uniform.

"What are you planning to do?" Chasub asked.

"Something I have to do," Eric said. He walked over to the main console and sat all of his Omnidisks next to the Omnidisk they had acquired two days earlier. "I'm not going to need these."

Eric walked out of the main deck and stopped in front of Travis' cell.

"Open it," he said into the communicator next to the cell.

There was a flash of light as the energy field was deactivated. Eric stepped into the cell.

"You just made a big mistake!" Travis lunged at Eric and threw a punch at him.

Eric ducked and swept Uproar's feet out from under him.

Travis jumped up and rushed at Eric again.

Eric kicked him in the chest, knocking the augment against the wall. He twisted Travis' arm behind his back and pressed him into the wall.

"Get your hands off me!" Travis screamed.

"I don't think I will. You have information that I need, and I am going to get it from you," Eric's voice was low and intense.

Travis laughed. "You don't have what it takes to get me to talk! I'm not like those other augments, I've known you for years. You spend your time protecting people from bullies. You don't know how to be one. You won't do anything to hurt me."

For a moment Eric thought he was at an impasse. Suddenly he had an idea.

"You remember my friend Dark Viper," Eric kept a firm grip on Travis' arm.

"Yeah, lizard face, what about him?"

"He's right outside," Eric lied. "He has a very dark past. And he is very eager to get in this room and talk to you himself. You might think I won't do what's necessary to talk, but I promise he will."

"You're lying! You'd never let him in here!" Travis said in a rage, struggling to get free.

"I've changed a lot in the last few months," Eric released Travis' arm. "But I'm done trying to convince you. I'm doing to let Dark Viper in here now. You'll wish you had talked when you had the chance?"

"Okay, okay!" Travis screamed. "I'll tell you everything! Just keep that guy away from me! They're—"

The ship's alarms began to blare.

"Eric, I need you here now!" Chasub cried.

Eric threw Travis to the floor before rushing out of the cell.

"Chasub, this had better be—" Eric started, running onto the main deck.

A white hole appeared in the middle of the room.

"It appeared before I could prepare any countermeasures," Chasub pointed at the aperture.

One by one, Slymind, Mange, Arcspark, and Jason each stepped out of the hole.

"Knock, Knock," Jason looked Eric in the eye and smiled before his gaze shifted over to Chasub. "Hello. A pleasure to meet the brain behind these thorns in my side."

"Chasub, get out of here!" Eric shouted.

Chasub hesitated.

"Go!" Eric hissed.

Chasub hovered out of the room.

"The alien doesn't concern us," Jason said. "We have come to…collect a few things."

"You'll have to go through me first," Eric said. His eyes drifted over to the console, and he gasped. He didn't have his Omnidisks!

After following Eric's gaze, Jason also saw the Omnidisks. "Well, now."

Eric dashed toward the console. He stretched out his hand to grab the Omnidisks.

"Not today!" Slymind's elastic hand shot out, grabbed Eric and threw him into a wall on the other side of the room. His let out a sigh before he passed out.

"I'm taking these to the base." Jason grabbed all of the Omnidisks and put them in his pocket. "Slymind, find Uproar. The rest of you, tear this place apart."

"I'll handle the boy myself." Mange took a step toward Eric.

"No!" Jason ordered firmly. "I want him alive to see what happens next. Don't touch him."

Russell Daniels and his daughter carried groceries out of the supermarket.

"I told your brother I would need his help with this today!" Russell said angrily. "He has become so unreliable!"

"I think he has a …important project to take care of. A community service thing!" Rebecca said quickly.

Russell raised an eyebrow at her. "When did he start telling you so much about what he does?"

Rebecca laughed nervously. "He tells me things sometimes."

"Well, he doesn't tell *me* anything anymore." Eric's father started to lose his grip on one of his bags. "I'm going to drop the cans!"

A can of soup dropped out of one of the bags and fell toward the ground.

"Gotcha!" A hand shot out and grabbed the can right before it hit the concrete.

"Thank you so much," Russell said with a smile. "It would have been a shame to lose perfectly good can of tomato soup."

"No problem," Archie responded. "Always happy to lend a hand. I'll help you put these into the car."

Minutes later, the groceries were loaded, and Russell drove away.

Archie looked at the communicator on his arm and smiled. "It's done."

Eric woke up to the smell of smoke. He slowly opened his eyes and scsc anned the room to assess the damage.

All of the consoles had either been smashed or electrocuted, and some of the machinery lay on the floor in pieces. Others had sparks flying from them.

"Chasub!" Eric yelled. "Chasub, where are you?"

The door opened, and Chasub hovered into the room. "Eric! It pleases me to see that you are still well."

"It pleases me too," Eric joked as he rose to his feet. "I'm glad they didn't find you."

"I sealed myself inside the Medical Alcove," Chasub explained. "They tried to enter but were unable to. However, they did succeed in destroying most of the machinery in this room, my personal quarters, and several other systems on the ship. I was able to lock some important rooms from where I was, but the damage to the ship is still considerable."

"Uproar?" Eric asked, already knowing the answer.

"He's gone," Chasub said. "The power line that controlled the energy field to his cell was destroyed."

Eric looked at the destruction around him and felt like crying. "How long do you think this will take to fix?"

"Days. Possibly weeks," Chasub said. "If only Archibald were here, I could get the task done much faster."

"Don't mention him," Eric balled his hand into a fist. "He is the only one who could have told them how to get here. Because of him, they have all of the Omnidisks that were on the ship, including mine."

Chasub's color seemed to fade, and he muttered a string of words Eric could not understand.

"What did you say?" Eric asked.

"I apologize," Chasub's voice was slightly deeper, a sign of frustration. "Those words are…not polite on my planet."

"I feel the same way," Eric looked around the room again "All that work and planning, and they still pushed us back! Travis was going to tell us everything! And after everything we went through, they still got the Omnidisks! What else could go wrong?"

Eric's cell phone began to ring.

"I can get reception here?" Eric asked as he pulled it out of his pocket.

"After you told me about the troubles you were having with your father, I thought it would be easier for you if I programmed the ship's communications array so you would be able to receive phone calls."

"And any other time I would love that." Eric pulled his phone out of his pocket. "Yes, Dad?"

"You didn't meet us at the supermarket like I asked," his father replied.

"I'm sorry," Eric said hurriedly. "I had a project I was—"

"Yes, your sister told me all about it," said Russell. "Next time you need to be the one to tell me."

"Yes, sir; I'm sorry I didn't tell you. Now, if you don't mind, I have to get to my…project."

"Okay, just make sure you're home *on time* tonight," Russell stressed. "Oh, and I almost forgot to tell you, I ran into your friend Archie at the store."

Eric's blood froze in his veins. "You did?"

"Yes, and he asked me to give you a message. He wanted me to say, 'I took care of your family.'"

"He said that?" The words nearly got stuck in Eric's throat.

"Yeah, and he did help us out a lot. He helped load all of the groceries into the car and saved us a can of soup." Russell laughed. "You had better be careful, or I might adopt him."

"That would be a big mistake," Eric said. "Listen, Dad, I'm going to meet you at home. I have to tell you something."

"Is something wrong?" Russell asked.

"Just meet me at home, and I promise I'll tell you everything," Eric said. "*Everything.*"

Russell was silent for a moment. "Okay. I'll see you at the house, and we can talk."

"I'll be there," Eric promised before hanging up the phone.

"Do you believe telling your father is the best course of action?" Chasub asked.

"Archie is targeting my family now," Eric spoke through clenched teeth. "My dad needs to know what he's dealing with. Can you fling me down?"

"The flinger is badly damaged. I could not assure you safe pass—"

"I don't care, do it!" Eric yelled. "I have to get back there and protect them."

Chasub hovered to the flinger console as smoke continued to rise from it.

Eric looked at the wires that hung from it. "Do it," Eric repeated.

Chasub entered the command into the console. "Be careful," he said as he watched Eric disappear.

Eric looked around. He was in the forest. "Chasub couldn't have gotten me any closer than this?" he grumbled to himself as he activated his uniform. "I'm going to have to fly to the house from here."

A few minutes later, Crimson Falcon's house was in view. He saw his father pull the car into the driveway.

"Here goes nothing." Crimson Falcon landed behind his house and walked around.

Rebecca gasped when she saw Crimson Falcon walking toward them.

"What in the world—" Russell said.

"Dad, we need to talk," Crimson Falcon said.

Rebecca opened her door, climbed out of the car and started walking toward Crimson Falcon. "What are you doing?"

"Eric?" Russell's eyes opened wide.

"Yes, Dad, it's me," Crimson Falcon said. "Let's go into the house, and I promise I'll explain everything. You too, Rebecca."

Russell nodded slowly. "I can't wait to hear it." He turned the key and shut off the engine.

BOOOOOM!!! Crimson Falcon was knocked back on the ground as the car erupted in flame. Then everything went dark.

CHAPTER 33

When Eric woke up, his eyes darted back and forth before he realized he was in a hospital bed. He gasped and jumped out of bed, noticing he was wearing a hospital gown.

Brynn walked into the room. "Thank God! We didn't think you would make it!"

"What happened?" Eric grabbed his clothes off of a nearby chair and rushed into the bathroom.

"Dark Viper found you unconscious outside of your house after the explosion. He deactivated your uniform so when the paramedics got there—"

"Explosion?" Eric asked from inside the bathroom. "What are you talking about?"

"I can't even find a decent soda machine in this dump," Will said as he walked into the room.

Eric walked out of the bathroom with his clothes on.

"Oh, you're awake," Will looked at the floor and shuffled his feet

"He doesn't remember the explosion," Brynn spoke softer than usual as if she were afraid her voice would bruise Eric.

"*What* explosion!" Eric yelled.

"Your father's car," Will explained. "That's why you lost consciousness. The car exploded, and you hit your head on the ground."

"No—" Eric felt as if the room were spinning. He stumbled back and almost fell into a chair. "My dad? Rebecca? How are they?"

Brynn swallowed. "Your sister is alive. She's in intensive care right now. She was burned pretty bad. The doctor said your grandparents are on the way."

"And my dad?" Tears welled up in Eric's eyes.

Brynn and Will remained silent.

"What happened to my dad?" Eric demanded, his voice full of pain.

"I'm so sorry, Eric." Brynn walked over and put her arms around him. "He didn't make it."

"No!" Eric now had tears streaming down his face. "Not my dad! Where is she?" he choked out.

"Down the hall," Brynn whispered.

Eric ran out of the room and stopped at his sister's room. She was lying on the bed, and her arms and torso were wrapped in bandages.

"Rebecca." Eric's voice quivered as he looked at his little sister. He walked over to her bed got on his knees, and sobbed. "Please forgive me. I'm so sorry. Oh God, I'm so sorry!"

"You can't be in here." A nurse suddenly walked into the room.

"He's her brother," Chris explained, also appearing at the door.

The nurse looked from Chris to Eric and nodded in approval.

"I heard what happened on the news," Chris said quietly. "I thought you might need—"

"You shouldn't get too close to me," Eric said through sobs. "You might get hurt."

"Eric, you can't blame yourself for this." Chris put her hand on his back. "You had nothing to do with it."

"It is my fault," Eric insisted.

"It can't be," Chris argued. "Not unless you're the one who put the bomb in the car."

Eric suddenly stopped sobbing. He stood up, and Chris saw that the sorrow in his eyes had been replaced by something else. *Rage.*

"Eric?" Chris asked in a concerned tone.

Without a word, Eric ran out of the hospital room. Will and Brynn walked in a moment later.

"Where's he going?" Brynn asked.

"I don't know," Chris answered. "All I did was try to comfort him by reminding him that he is not the one who put the bomb in the car. Then he stormed off."

Will's eyes widened. "Oh no."

"What is it?" Brynn asked. "Where did he go?"

Will pulled Brynn into the hallway and closed the door. "If you knew who had killed your father, where would you be heading?"

Brynn thought for a moment and went pale. "Oh, no!"

Chris opened the door and walked out. "Do you know where he's going?"

Will began to speak, but Brynn cut him off. "Yeah, we do."

"What are you doing?" Will hissed.

"There's no point in keeping the secret now," Brynn said. "We should tell her."

"Tell me what?" Chris asked.

Brynn pointed to herself. "Prodigy." She pointed to Will. "Bestial. We're Omniforce."

Chris smiled. "I know. Followed you outside after the dance. I put most of it together that night. Brynn, you're my best friend. Why didn't you tell me?"

"We kept the secret for your protection," Brynn said. "You know what we're up against. We didn't want them using you to get to us. You never lost my trust."

Chris looked thoughtful for a moment. "I guess you're right. So what was all of the drama about that night at the dance? How is it connected to what Eric is doing now?"

"Archie turned on us," Brynn's face turned red with anger. "He told the augments everything."

Chris gasped. "Archie? But why?"

"We don't know," Will said. "And personally, I don't care. What I do know is that now we are all targets because of him. He's the one who put the bomb in the car."

"We *do* know," Brynn looked Will in the eye and corrected him. "We made Archie feel like an outcast because he doesn't have powers. Somehow the augments used that against us."

"Whatever," Will rolled his eyes. "Eventually that excuse stops working. He's a murderer now. We have to handle this."

Chris bit her lip and stared out into space as if she were in deep thought. "When you find him, are you going to stop him? Or help him?"

Will and Brynn looked at each other. Neither had an answer.

Sparks flew from the Molecular Flinger console as Eric appeared on the ship.

"Eric, this was a terrible time for an emergency fling," Chasub said. "The sudden power surge damages more circuits."

"When we first met, you told me your people made weapons to fight the Thyders. Did you bring any?" Eric asked in a demanding tone.

"Why would you want those?" Chasub asked. Then he saw the rage on Eric's face. "Did something happen?"

"They killed my dad," Eric's voice was emotionless when he said the words. "And hurt my sister. Where are the weapons?"

"Even if you had them, how would you find the augments?" Chasub asked.

"I can handle that," Eric said. "Just tell me where the weapons are!"

Chasub began to argue before stopping himself. "They are in the main cargo hold, the large metallic box."

"I'm going to need your help with them."

"I can't get in touch with Chasub," Will said as they stood outside of the hospital. "I keep trying to contact him, but for some reason, it's not working."

"Did you try to fling yourself to the ship?" Brynn asked.

"That doesn't work either." Will rubbed his hands together. "Something happened, I can feel it."

"You don't think they got to the ship, do you?" Chris asked.

"No way," Brynn said, shaking her head. "They could never get to the ship, not in a million years."

"Why not?" Will argued. "With Jason's intelligence and Archie's knowledge, nothing is impossible anymore."

"I sure hope Eric's okay," Chris said quietly.

"Me too," Will agreed. "Me too."

"Use caution when wielding those armaments," Chasub warned. "They are prototypes. They could stop working at any time."

Eric began strapping on the weapons. His arsenal was made up of three small square grenades that Chasub called "bright bombs." They produced an intense flash of light that could disorient enemies. In his pocket was a metal rod Chasub referred to as an EMP generator. It released a pulse of energy that deactivated all non-Zeph technology. On his back was a short gun with a dozen small barrels sticking out of the handle in a circular pattern. Chasub called this a "light rifle"; it shot quick bursts of energy strong enough to render foes unconscious. The last weapon consisted of five elastic silver bands that Eric wrapped around his waist, wrists, and ankles. They were called "battle bands." When activated, they produced an energy field that covered a person's whole body, making them indestructible and giving them enormous amounts of strength.

"I'll take my chances." Eric tested the stability of the weapons. "Is the flinger ready?"

"Proper repairs would take hours," Chasub replied.

"All I need you to do is hotwire the thing so I can get from point A to point B as quick as possible," Eric said. "And don't start lecturing me about how it could malfunction."

"What you are about to try is suicide," Chasub said as he continued repairing the console. "You were barely a match for Jason with your Omnidisks. He will slaughter you without them."

"Maybe." Eric's voice was emotionless. "But this time I won't hold back. One of us won't make it out of there alive."

"What are you doing now?" Chasub asked, noticing Eric typing commands into the scanner. "The scanners are damaged, like everything else."

"I'm scanning for the communicator we gave Dark Viper," Eric said. "The ship's communications array isn't working, so I need to know exactly where he is. My plan involves him."

Chasub moved away from the machine. "I did what you asked, but I still don't think—"

"Hit it," Eric ordered.

Chasub sighed and entered the commands into the console. "Do try to be careful."

"Goodbye, Chasub," was all Eric had time to say before the light surrounded him.

Dark Viper lived in a dilapidated storeroom that was part of an abandoned building. Most of the building had already crumbled to the ground.

He had only been home five minutes when he heard a banging on the door. He immediately took out his bo staff and extended it to its full length.

"Open up!" Eric demanded from outside the door.

Dark Viper sighed and put away his weapon before opening the door.

"Where are the augments?" Eric asked, storming in.

"It has been a long time since I have been allowed in polite society," Dark Viper said. "But I believe it is customary to ask before entering another's home."

"I know you used to work with them, so I know you know where they are," Eric said forcefully. "Jason knew exactly who you were when you tried to protect me the other day. That means you, and him must go way back. You knew what they were doing this whole time! Why didn't you tell us?"

"'Because I knew you would never stand a chance against Jason and his augments in a confrontation. No one knows how skilled they are as well as I do," Dark Viper pointed out. "Your guerilla tactics had a much better chance of success than a head-on attack."

Eric walked over to Dark Viper and stopped with his face inches away from the augment. "They killed my father and wounded my sister. I don't care how skilled they are, I *will* take them down. Tell me!"

Dark Viper remained silent.

Eric pulled out the light rifle and pointed it at Dark Viper. "I'm not going to ask again."

Dark Viper nodded. "Very well, but I am not giving you the location because you threatened me. I am giving it to you because I believe every man has the right to avenge the death of a family member."

"I'll take it any way I can get it," Eric said. "Now, tell me."

"Status report," Jason ordered at the augment's base.

"The bomb had the expected effect," Archie said. "The father is dead. The sister is in intensive care."

"Excellent." Jason nodded in approval. "Slymind?"

"We destroyed most of the machinery on the ship," Slymind reported. "There were a few rooms we couldn't access. The alien was probably in one of them. Oh, and we did manage to bring Uproar back."

"I could've made it out of there," Uproar grumbled.

"Have you successfully integrated the Omnidisks into the machine?" Jason asked.

"Unfortunately, the radiation levels are too high. The machine can't handle the stress. We will have to build the full-scale model before we can run a test. We have located most of the suppliers that have the materials we will need."

"That will be the next matter of business," Jason decided. "Oh, and while you were on the spacecraft…did you leave the package?"

Slymind laughed. "Oh yes, I believe it will be quite some time before it is discovered."

"And there hasn't been any trouble out of Omniforce since," Arcspark added.

Bang! The door to the base was knocked off its hinges, and it fell to the floor. All of the augments turned toward the noise, alert and ready for a fight.

Eric stood in the threshold for a moment before stepping in. "Who's first?"

"I am really worried now," Will said outside of the hospital. "If they can get to Chasub, they can get to anyone."

"What do we do?" Brynn kicked a trash can. "We can't get to Chasub, Eric is MIA, and we don't know where the augment base is!"

Dark Viper dropped down from the roof. "I can assist you."

"How?" Brynn frowned and crossed her arms.

"I can tell you where your friend is, and I think he is in trouble."

Will turned to Brynn. "Go tell Chris we're leaving." He looked back at Dark Viper. "Okay, where is he?"

Slymind put his hand in both of his pockets and pulled out fifty small spheres. He threw them in the air.

Fifty holograms instantly appeared in their place, landing in front of Eric.

"You may want to think before doing anything you'll regret," Jason advised with a friendly smile.

Eric took out the EMP generator and pressed the button.

There was a large humming noise, and the holograms suddenly disappeared.

"How did you do that?" Slymind looked around the room, the shock on his face was obvious.

Eric pulled one of the grenades off of his belt and threw it on the floor in front of the augments.

Nothing happened.

"Get him!" Jason ordered.

The augments began to walk toward Eric.

He quickly stripped another grenade and threw it before closing his eyes.

Flash! A blinding white light shot out from the grenade.

The augments screamed as they tried to shield their eyes.

Eric pulled the light rifle off of his back and aimed.

The barrels began to spin around the center of the gun as small blue energy beams shot out of them.

Eric swept the gun right to left, hitting Arcspark first, then Mange and Slymind. One by one they lost consciousness and fell to the floor.

Uproar screamed in rage and took augment form.

Eric pointed the gun at him and fired, hitting him with dozens of tiny energy beams.

Uproar began to stumble as Eric continued to fire the weapon at him.

With one final groan, Uproar fell, face first on the floor, knocked out like the rest.

A green beam of energy knocked the weapon out of Eric's hand.

"Hey, buddy!" Xenoshot raised his wrist and pointed the nozzle at Eric. "How're you doing?"

"You killed him," Eric whispered. His eyes grew wide with rage, and his nostrils flared. "YOU KILLED HIM!!!"

"It wasn't anything personal," Xenoshot said with a smile. "Just part of my new job."

"You betrayed me," Eric said breathlessly, walking towards him with clenched fists. "I treated you like my brother, and you did this to me."

"I put something in his head, you know," Jason said in a conversational tone. "It took away his conscience."

Eric stopped, startled by this revelation.

"It looks like you were right all along," Xenoshot said with a laugh. "I could never do this to you with all of that right and wrong stuff in my head," He lowered his arm and walked closer to Eric. "Do you think you can still hurt me, knowing my brain has been altered in some way?"

Eric's eyes darted back and forth, indecisive and full of confusion.

Xenoshot walked up to him. "I didn't think so. You're too full of honor and—"

Eric slammed his head into Xenoshot's skull. He watched with satisfaction as his former friend fell on the floor, unconscious.

"I guess I'm not so full of that honor stuff after all." Eric glared at Jason. "Your turn."

"Are you sure you want to do this?" Jason asked, addressing Eric like a child. "You remember what happened last time you faced me, don't you?"

Eric pressed the button on the strap around his waist and activated the battle bands. A bolt of light shot from his waist to his hands and feet, and all of the bands began to glow.

"Have it your way," he said as Eric walked over.

Eric smiled and threw his punch.

"Aaaaah!" Jason flew through the air and landed in the middle of the floor.

"I am going to make you suffer for what you did!" Eric walked over to where Jason had fallen and hit him again, sending him sailing into a pile of machinery.

Jason got on his feet and tried to punch Eric, but his hand met with an invisible barrier that threw him back on the ground.

"Wait, we can work something out," Jason said, trying to move away.

"Like you did for my dad?!" Eric kicked Jason in the stomach.

Jason gasped. "That wasn't me!"

Eric grabbed the front of Jason's shirt and yanked him off the floor. "But you ordered it! You are responsible for making my life miserable for months!" He hit Jason in the face and pulled him up again. "My dad stopped trusting me! He said I was unreliable! I never even got the chance to explain before you had him killed!!!" Eric ended every sentence with another punch.

"You have to look at the bigger picture," Jason said, his voice starting to weaken.

"Get this picture!" Eric hurled Jason at a wall. "I am going to make you feel all of the pain you've put me through!"

Eric grabbed Jason by the collar and yanked him up once more.

Pop! A spark flew from Eric's waistband, and all of the bands stopped glowing.

Jason kicked Eric in the chest, sending the teenager soaring across the room. "That was interesting. Now playtime is over."

Across the room, everyone except Archie began to stir and rise to their feet.

"Nobody touches him," Jason ordered. "I owe him."

Eric struggled to stand.

"Please, don't get up." Jason slid Eric across the floor into a pile of boxes. "I want you to feel at home."

"I'm going to kill you," Eric said through gritted teeth.

"I don't think so." Jason grabbed Eric by the throat and lifted him into the air. "I told my team here to keep your little friends alive, but you have irritated me so much, I think I'm going to make an exception for you."

"Sir! Maybe we should let him live," Arcspark suggested, the slightest hint of concern in her voice. "He might have useful information."

"No!" Jason glared at Eric. "After what he did to me…he dies. End of story. Be careful, Arcspark. Someone might think you're not as committed to the cause as you led us to believe."

Eric felt the energy drain from his body as Jason's hand began to glow.

"I'm going to do this nice and slow," Jason said with a laugh. "This might be the best meal I ever had."

CHAPTER 34

"Let him go!" Prodigy flew into the base, followed by Bestial in wolf form and Dark Viper.

"Stop them!" Jason ordered, still focused on Eric.

Prodigy fired a telekinetic blast at Arcspark and Slymind, repelling them several feet away.

Bestial leaped, turned into a gorilla in midair, and brought a fist down on Mange and Uproar's head.

"Save Eric!" Prodigy yelled to Dark Viper.

Dark Viper used his bo staff to vault off of the ground, flying toward Jason.

Jason dropped Eric and stumbled backward as Dark Viper hit him in the face with both feet. As soon as he hit the ground, Dark Viper used all of his strength to swing his staff at Jason's legs, knocking the augment off his feet.

Eric lay on the floor, coughing and holding his throat.

"Let's move!" Dark Viper held his hand out to Eric.

"Can't move," Eric said in a shaky tone, feeling as if his limbs were half frozen.

Dark Viper reached down and threw Eric's arm over his shoulders. "Lean on me."

"No!" Jason jumped up and leaped at Dark Viper.

"Prodigy!" Dark Viper snapped.

She threw up her hand and held Jason in the air.

"Let me go!" he screamed.

"Sure!" Prodigy threw him into a room on the other side of the base and used her mental powers to close and lock the door.

Bestial shifted back to human form. "Everybody gather around Prodigy! She can surround us with a telekinetic bubble and get us out of here!"

"Kill them!" Slymind ordered.

Mange fired his eye beams, and Arcspark shot her electricity at Omniforce.

"We have to leave!" Prodigy grunted as she shielded the group. "I can't hold this for long!"

"We're all here," Dark Viper said. "Let's go."

Prodigy began backing toward the door with all of her friends behind her. She saw the case next to the machine with all of the Omnidisks inside of it. "The Omnidisks!"

"Can you get them?" Dark Viper asked.

"I have to try!" She focused on the case.

The container rose off the pedestal and flew toward Prodigy.

"No you don't!" Jason had kicked down the door and was running after the Omnidisks.

"Hurry!" Dark Viper hissed.

Sweat began to drip down Prodigy's brow from the stress of protecting her friends and holding on to the Omnidisks. Nevertheless, she was still able to speed up the case.

Suddenly, Slymind's elastic hand shot out and grabbed the Omnidisks.

"No!" Prodigy screamed.

"We can't fight them here; we have to leave," Dark Viper insisted. "We will perish if we try to battle them all."

"No choice." Prodigy gasped. "Can't keep holding them off."

The group continued to head toward the door when Prodigy's gaze fell upon Xenoshot. She stretched out her hand.

"What are you doing?" Bestial asked.

"We can't leave him behind," Prodigy said, her voice full of exhaustion.

Eric lifted his head. "Leave him."

Uproar walked over to Prodigy's telekinetic bubble and started pounding on it.

"We are not risking our lives just so this guy can stab us in the back again!" Bestial argued.

Unexpectedly, Mange, Arcspark, and Uproar stopped their assault. Jason walked up to the telekinetic bubble.

"It's too late," Eric's voice was almost a whisper.

Jason drew back his fist and delivered a powerful punch to Prodigy's bubble.

Prodigy screamed and collapsed.

"Kill them all, now!" Jason ordered.

A bright light surrounded them, and seconds later they were on *The Omega*.

Bestial sighed with relief. "Chasub, I take back every short joke I ever made about you."

"I don't recall any jokes about my stature," Chasub said.

"Oh…never mind," Bestial said with a nervous laugh.

Prodigy's eyes fluttered open. "Did we make it out?"

"Yes," Dark Viper said.

"Were you able to retrieve the Omnidisks?" asked Chasub.

"We were barely able to retrieve our lives, thanks to the Lone Ranger over there." Bestial scowled at Eric.

Eric was finally regaining feeling in his body. He climbed to his feet.

"I don't remember asking you to come," he said in a low, angry tone.

"We're your friends; we couldn't just let you die," Prodigy said, deactivating her uniform.

"No matter how boneheaded you act," Will added after doing the same.

Eric looked at Dark Viper and frowned. "I didn't expect you to be the snitching type."

"You're the last one who needs to be getting mad at people," Will said. "He risked his neck, along with the rest of us. We almost died because we ran to help you."

"My dad died because of me," Eric's voice picked up strength. "My sister got hurt, and my best friend got captured by the bad guys! Why should any of you get special treatment?"

Everyone stood around silently, unable to think of anything to say.

"I can't do this anymore." Eric's voice suddenly became soft.

"That's the best thing I've heard all day," Will said. "Because I'm not flying into an enemy stronghold to save you again."

"No," Eric corrected. "I mean I can't do *this* anymore!"

Brynn looked at him in confusion. "You don't mean—"

"Yes, I do. I quit!" Eric looked each person in the eye.

Will scoffed. "I don't believe this! After all the crap you gave me about how important this is—"

"I'm not interested in hearing your arguments," Eric waved his hand. "My father is dead!"

"Eric, I know how you feel—" Brynn started.

"No," Eric cut her off. "There is no way you can know how I'm feeling right now."

"I can." Chasub hovered forward. "I lost all of my family in the war on my planet. Yet I still saw the need to do the right thing. There are so many people who rely on your protection. This team needs you."

Eric looked at Dark Viper. "Do you have anything to add?"

"Only this," he replied. "When there is a great battle to be waged, one must decide for himself whether he desires to fight. Without desire, the warrior begins every battle at a disadvantage."

"Well put." Eric tore the watch off his wrist and threw it to the floor. "I'm done."

Bryn stepped forward. "At least take some time to think before—"

"Chasub, send me home," Eric snapped.

Chasub hesitated.

"Now!" Eric yelled.

Chasub hovered to the flinger and began entering coordinates.

Eric took one last look around at his friends and teammates. "You're better off without me."

As he walked toward his house, Eric's mind drifted to conversations he'd had with his friends in recent months.

Archie, if I can trust anyone to watch my back, it's you.

Brynn, this is going to totally rock your world.

Will, you have the brains that this team really needs to succeed.

Eric swallowed hard as he walked up the stairs to the front door. *This house is like me now*, Eric thought as he opened his front door. *It's empty. Everyone attached to it is gone.*

Eric went to his room and began to change out of his clothes. He stared at himself in the mirror.

No, I can't go back, he said to himself. They're after me. And as long as I'm near Rebecca, they'll be after her too. And they'll go after my friends next. As long as I'm around, everyone I've ever loved is a target.

Eric looked around his room and sighed sadly he realized what he had to do. *I have to leave Drakeston.*

"Now what do we do?" Will asked out loud. "I hate to admit it, but we need him."

"This team is at a great disadvantage without its leader," Chasub agreed.

"We just need to give him time," Brynn insisted. "His father is dead, and his sister is in ICU. We can't expect him to think rationally right now."

"Well, in the meantime we should still be on high alert," Will said. "Brynn, maybe you should head to Chris' house and watch out for signs of augment activity."

"Wait, who died and made you boss?" Brynn asked angrily.

"Somebody has to be in charge," Will argued. "Why not me?"

"Why you? I've been at this a lot longer than you have."

"Yeah, and you've been a loose cannon the whole time!"

Dark Viper cut in. "Arguments will solve nothing."

Will looked at him. "You have no part in this! You used to be one of *them*. Why should we listen to anything you have to say?"

"Enough!" Chasub yelled.

Everyone turned toward him, amazed to hear him raise his voice that way.

"Our situation is dire!" Chasub hovered a little higher than usual and began to float around the room. "All of our secrets are exposed, and all but two Omnidisks have been taken. Cooperation is the only ally we have. We must work together. *All* of us. During the war on my planet, many of my people panicked and fought each other; they were the first to die. And although we ultimately lost, we were still able to put up a good fight before it all ended because we worked together. Right now, we are all each other have. If we don't cooperate, we will lose."

Everyone looked silently at him.

Will smirked. "When you're right you're right. Although with that voice, I would have never thought you would be able to give a decent speech."

Chasub nodded.

Will turned to Dark Viper. "I'm sure you can understand why I might have some trust issues right now."

"Better than you might think," Dark Viper replied.

"Still, we're short on manpower so if you could watch over Chris—"

"I will," he agreed.

Chasub hovered to the flinger and entered the proper sequence.

"Call us if anything happens," Brynn said before Dark Viper disappeared.

"Brynn, I'm sorry for what I said before," Will apologized. "You know I'm not the type to think before I say stuff. It's part of my charm."

Brynn laughed. "I'm no Mother Teresa myself. We can call it even."

Will held out his hand. "Friends?"

"Friends." Brynn shook it.

Will took a step closer. "How about a kiss to seal the deal?"

Brynn punched him on the arm and scoffed. "Unbelievable."

"Chasub, why don't you stop playing with your instruments and come bond with us?" Will asked, rubbing his arm.

"Something is wrong." Chasub stared at the panel, and his fingers flew over the controls. "There is a strange energy signature onboard."

"Where is it coming from?" Brynn asked.

"Follow me." Chasub hovered out the door.

Brynn and Will shared a worried glance before running after him.

Chasub flew to the rear of the ship. He placed his hand on a glowing square near the floor, and a small hatch opened up in the wall. He flew inside.

"What is this?" Brynn asked as she climbed inside.

In the center of the room was a large pillar. It was glowing with golden energy and had a small door on its side. There was another control panel on the wall of the room.

"This is the ship's energy matrix," Chasub explained as he opened the door on the side. "My people made a technology that can alter almost anything on a molecular level and turn it into energy. If I put something in this compartment, it turns into a power source. In theory, this ship could fly forever."

"Seem like a good design," Will said. "So what's the problem?"

"That." Chasub pointed to a small box attached to the inside of the pillar.

"What is it?" Brynn asked.

Chasub looked grim. "An explosive."

Eric grabbed a suitcase and carried it out to the taxi he had waiting in the driveway.

"Is that it?" the driver asked.

"I have one more." Eric turned around to walk inside.

"Where are you going?"

Eric looked for the source of the voice. It was Chris.

"I need to leave," he said. "After everything that's happened—"

"What about your sister?" Chris asked. "She needs you."

"My grandparents are coming in from New Jersey." Eric grabbed his bag from the doorstep. "They'll take care of her. Trust me, she's better off without me around."

"Your friends told me everything," she admitted. "I know who you are."

Eric rolled his eyes and chuckled. "No. You don't."

"You have saved so many lives—"

Eric held up his hand and cut her off. "Don't. Don't start listing all my 'good deeds' and trying to use that to tell me I'm a good hero. I got my father killed and my sister hurt. My best friend was taken by the enemy and turned against us. I can't even protect the people closest to me."

Chris softly put her hand on his face. "What about me? You rescued me so many times."

Eric hesitated before shaking his head and pulling away. "None of that means anything."

"And last night? Does that mean anything?" Chris asked.

Eric closed his eyes and bowed his head. "You misinterpreted last night."

Chris' eyes filled with pain. "You don't mean that."

"You don't get it, do you?" Eric said angrily "Everyone around me gets hurt. You're already on their list, and if they find out, I—"

"You what?" she pried.

"If they find out we're friends; they will never stop coming after you. And you don't have powers like the others."

"I can take care of myself," she said.

"No, You can't." Eric turned away and walked toward the taxi. "Not from them."

"I have feelings for you!" she blurted out.

Eric stopped.

"I've felt like this for months. Ever since the first time you held me I knew there was something there." She took a step closer. "Tell me you don't feel the same way."

Eric's heart leaped to his throat. *This is the moment I've been waiting on for so long. I want to say yes, to stay with her. I want…*

"No, I don't." Eric opened the taxi door and climbed in.

"Are you sure you want to do this, kid?" the driver asked. "It's not too late to change your mind."

Eric looked out the window and saw Chris' eyes. They were full of tears.

Eric looked forward. "Drive."

"A bomb?" Brynn asked. "How did it get here?"

"How do you think?" Will slammed his fist against the wall. "The augments left a present when they were here. Can we get rid of it?"

Chasub examined the bomb closely. "If I move it, it will most likely detonate."

"How powerful is it?" Will asked.

"The sensors detected traces of plutonium," Chasub said.

Brynn breathed in sharply. "This thing is going to go nuclear."

"Absorb it! Turn it into energy!" Will said.

"If you recall, I said "almost" anything," Chasub reminded him. "This bomb is lined with lead. Lead cannot be converted. If I attempt a conversion, the entire system will be torn apart. And I don't have enough knowledge to dismantle it without triggering an explosion."

Will looked thoughtful. "Fling it off of the ship. Set the flingers to maximum range."

"Excellent idea!" Chasub flew to the panel on the wall. "I can access the flinger controls from here."

White light began to surround the bomb.

"It's working!" Brynn cheered.

Snap! Hssssss! Sparks flew from the panel and smoke began to rise.

"Oh my!" Chasub examined the panel. "Somebody enabled the bomb to send a feedback pulse in case a fling is attempted. The flinger is offline."

"We can't even get off of the ship now," Will said. "We have to do something before this thing goes off!"

"How long before the bomb is programmed to go off?" Jason asked back at the augment base.

Archie checked the timer on his watch. "Two minutes."

Jason laughed. "Without that ship and that alien they will be crippled. We will have completely removed them as a threat."

"Oh my…Chasub!" Brynn cried. "A timer activated on the bomb!"

Will and Chasub rushed over to look at the timer.

"We have less than a minute," Chasub reported. "This is quite unfortunate."

"You have another plan, right?" Will asked.

Chasub remained silent.

"Chasub!" Will demanded.

"My apologies," Chasub said. "I do not."

Tears welled up in Brynn's eyes as she watched the seconds tick away. "Maybe Eric was right after all."

15…14…13

"This can't be it." Will's voice was hoarse. "Not after everything we've been through."

Suddenly, Chasub rushed out of the room and headed to the front of the ship.

"Can you blame him?" Will joked as he tried to muster up a smile.

8...7...6...

Brynn looked at Will. "I'm glad you came along for the ride."

4...3...

Will nodded. "Me too."

1

"Did you see that?" the cab driver asked Eric excitedly.

"I'm sorry?" Eric asked, having been snatched out of his thoughts.

"It was like…an explosion or something!" he said. "I would say it was fireworks, but it was too high. Almost like it was in outer space."

"Ah," Eric replied, not focusing at all on the conversation. He looked out of the window and stared blankly into space.

No more Xenoshot. No more Omnidisks. No more Dark Viper. No more Chasub, Prodigy, or Bestial.

No more Crimson Falcon. No more Omniforce.

A tear appeared in his eye. *No more Christina. It's over.*

It's all over.

EPILOGUE

A few months later….

Eric ran straight at the cloaked figure, his sword at the ready. He immediately lashed out, but his opponent was fast. There was a *clang* as their weapons connected. Eric attempted to strike his foe repeatedly, but every time the attacks were blocked.

I can barely see in this alley, Eric thought to himself. *This darkness is working against me.*

Seconds later Eric had switched from offense to defense. His opponent was coming at him hard and fast. Eric was surprised. Their fighting style had been entirely different last time Eric had fought them. As Eric deflected some of the blows, he realized that the fighting style was familiar, but not from a recent battle. Almost as if they had fought long ago.

His opponent got the upper hand, and Eric immediately moved his sword to stop the blow he knew would be coming in high. Eric was starting to suspect that this wasn't who he thought it was. It was someone he had fought before. After blocking and deflecting the last strike, Eric threw his body forward, slamming into his opponent and forcing them into a wall of the alley. There was a small blinking light bulb above their heads, and it provided just enough visibility for Eric to see who he had been sparring with all of this time.

"Dark Viper!" Eric cried out in shock, lowering his weapon and backing away. "How did you find me? And why were you attacking me?"

Dark Viper, never one for conversation, silently adjusted himself before putting away his bo staff and replying. "I was not looking for you. My being here is pure coincidence. And as for my fighting you, I thought you were assaulting me to protect this new location you had chosen for yourself. I have not seen you in some time. I had no way of evaluating your mental state."

Eric was speechless for a moment. Dark Viper and Eric were never especially close. However, he was an ally, and the first sign of home Eric had seen in a long time. For a moment it was almost as if Eric was transported back to Drakeston. In less then a second, it seemed like Eric that he had cycled through a million good memories. Unfortunately, a million bad memories followed immediately after.

"You have to leave," Eric said decisively. "I don't know what you're doing here but get it taken care of and go. Now."

"Drakeston needs you, Eric," Dark Viper started.

"Don't!" Eric interrupted. " Don't do that! Don't tell who needs me! They need me as far away as possible. Whatever is going on now can't be any worse than when I was there!"

"You're wrong," Dark Viper took a step forward, and Eric could see the emotion on his face as he spoke the next words. "Things are so much worse."

Eric knew he would regret the question, but he couldn't stop himself from asking. "What happened?"

ACKNOWLEDGEMENTS

To my wife Ellesse: This would not have been possible without you. I wanted to quit writing and you refused to let me. I can truly say you believed in me when I didn't believe in myself. From hours of proofreading to building the website, even as an author I don't have the words to describe how much I appreciate all you do.

Mom and Dad: I have the most supportive parents in the world. From day one you believed in me, and you did everything in your power to help me succeed. Thank you for always encouraging me to develop my creativity and work hard to achieve my goals. Thank you for always telling me I have greatness within me.

To my sister: Your enthusiasm and support has been such a motivator. I really appreciate your continued interest in my success. There have been so many times during this process where you have encouraged me to keep going despite challenged. Thank you.

Nana and Papa: You don't know how much I appreciate your support and encouraging words. You constantly give me the gift of advice and love. Your friendship will always be priceless.

To all of my extended family who has encouraged me throughout this process: Thank you for pushing me forward. I've been able to lean on you and depend on you, and it's meant so much to know that I've always had support.

Mrs. Farrar-: As my 4th grade teacher, you always encouraged me to reach my full potential. I have never forgotten your kind words. You are a wonderful educator.

To Mrs. Winfree and Mrs. Berenger: High School was a rough time, yet you both took a personal interest in me. Thank you for encouraging me to become an author. You are both great teachers!

Professor Laurah Norton: I took three of your courses and they were worth every second. The advice and guidance you gave me enhanced my writing skills. I appreciate the personal interest you showed as well. Thanks!

To all of my friends: I would love to thank you my name but I have so many good one who've supported me, I know I'd end up forgetting someone. Thank you all for constantly encouraging me, asking about the progress of the book, and telling me not to quit. Thank you for believing in me.

David Pielech and Colin Harker: You are two amazing artists. You took characters that only existed in my head and made them look beautiful on the page. You put in a lot of late nights and handled so many revisions. You helped bring this project to life and I'm so grateful for your hard work.

And to Goldie… the best dog a guy could ask for. Thanks for laying at my feet during all of those late nights. I miss you, girl.

MEET THE AUTHOR

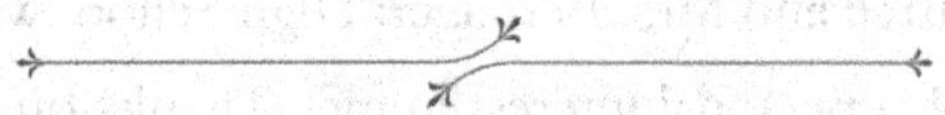

Aaron Robert Bingham was born in Poughkeepsie, New York, but he and his wife currently reside in the Metro Atlanta Georgia area. He enjoys reading Sci-fi Novels, comic books and watching superhero movies. He plans to continue writing books about young people who save the world.

Printed in the USA
CPSIA information can be obtained
at www.ICGtesting.com
LVHW030736171023
761014LV00093B/1669